THE
DEVOURERS

Alexander Fisher

ISBN: 1481059157
ISBN-13:9781481059152

DEDICATED TO

My Mother, who taught me to fight through life with an open mind.

And

My Father, who taught me to laugh in the face of danger.

PROLOGUE

Deep within the thick and towering trees, a swirling haze rushes in the silent wind. Beams of light from the crisp morning sky floods the forest, casting shifting shadows on every surface. The forest is agitated. Birds randomly launch themselves into the air rattling branches in their panic. Other animals, even insects scurry together down trees and strangely against the flow of the moving haze.

Through the veils of smoke and falling orange leaves a dark silhouette appears. Silently it moves in the opposite direction of the animals, with the flow of the mysterious fog. The figure passes in and out of light and shadow. The unmistakable dome shape of a helmet looks from left to right and up into the trees. The shadow briefly steps through another beam of light revealing he is a soldier wearing fatigues and completely coated in a dark red substance. With his rifle aimed, his bayonet follows his every stare. He carries no other equipment on him other than a canteen and a knife that hangs from his belt. The vapor from his mouth thickens in the cold air and lights up bright in the moody yellow streams of sunlight.

In the distance, a continuous howling sounds. The soldier looks upwards and continues towards it, periodically stopping to look over his shoulder. He catches a glimpse through a break in the swaying trees below, of black smoke and a burning town in the distance. The sounds of the restless woods blur together and for a moment, he starts to wonder if the chatter of the enemy he hears is real or the fresh memories from a few weeks ago. From the jungle and the war, he had just left behind. He presses on.

A heavy thumping sound alerts him. He crouches down next to a tree in the underbrush. His hands are slippery from the syrupy fluid but he grips his rifle tight. His dark eyes narrow as he strains to see more than a few feet ahead. The sound rushes closer. He takes a deep breath to retain his calm. The underbrush tears away and another silhouette bursts through the smoke. Flailing its legs backwards, a large cougar skids to a stop barely a foot away from the soldier. Both of them startled it drops to a low crouch, ready to pounce. A growl escapes its snarled mouth. It smells at the air and turns to look behind itself then returns its yellow eyes to the soldier and snorts the air again. The man holds his ground but the cougar, still crouching slowly paws its way towards him, eyes locked. He follows it with his gun. It passes around him and looks back to the direction it ran from, then back at the man again, as if to warn him. It turns and bounds away, vanishing from sight. The man looks forward again and continues marching into the thickening veil, to where the animal came from.

Closer to the source of the howling as wind whistles and blows, he crouches on a few boulders over a small creek. The water looks more like oil and a black moss grows along the rocks. The soldier pokes at it with his bayonet, showing an emotion on his rigid face, disgust. Silently he steps into the creek. The black sludge sizzles and quietly screams as it reacts to the red fluid that he has used to coat his body. He is more disturbed than in pain as he trudges on through the strange knee high waste.

Flanked by more rocks, the creek opens up to a shallow pond, it is the source of the black substance. At the ponds far edge, hacked into the side of a rock out cropping is a hole leading into the earth. It is a twisted gash no wider than a car, and the source of the noise. The smoke whips and thrashes as it is sucked in. Shaken, he carefully keeps moving towards it. He passes a large wood cylinder snapped at its base that is lying in the oily pond. Half sunk next to it is a barely recognizable and almost completely corroded construction vehicle. More of the black moss covers it.

The noise is deafening near the mouth of the cave. Sorrow shows on the man's face when he sees shreds of bloodied clothes and shoes scattered around the opening. His body weakens. Like a filthy wound, the gash of an entrance is not only sucking in the smoke and air, it is draining away the warmth and infecting everything around it with its emptiness. He raises his canteen over his head and more of the thick red fluid spills down his face and into his mouth. He swallows it, takes a deep breath and steps towards the cave.

A hand reaches out from the filth piled up in front of it and grabs his leg. He jumps and readies to stab it with his bayonet. The hand belongs to another man lying on his back almost upside down, his head points away from the entrance. It is as if the sucking wound had vomited him out. Rejecting and leaving him there to die. The soldier recognizes the broken being at his feet. He drops down and holds the man's head up.

Confused the dying man looks up and tightly grabs the soldier's collar pulling him close to his chalk white face. "They, they took her," he struggles to speak.

"I know." The soldier says in sad deep voice.

"They took my baby!" His quivering blue pupils glow against the ruptured red blood vessels of his eyes.

The soldier tries to make him drink from his canteen, but the man pushes it away and motions with his eyes to his chest. His insides are pushing their way out of the large jagged wound running up his stomach.

"I'll kill them."

"No," the dying man pathetically shakes his head and stutters, "you can't." He breaks his other half-buried hand free from beneath the filth revealing his clenched fist. "Take it!" He presses an object into the soldier's hand.

"But this?" the stunned soldier stares at it.

"I know. . . I know," he repeats as tears well up in his eyes. "We tried."

The soldier grips it tightly, "But now I can—"

"No! Was more than what we. . . ." He drifts back into unconsciousness.

"I can stop them!" he shakes the man awake.

Once again, the dying man shakes his head, "Keep them here. Keep them," he pleads. "There was a man who could. Help *him*."

"What man?"

"The man from the—"

The dying man jerks and blood sputters from his nose and mouth. The soldier hugs him tightly as his body goes limp. Gently he lays his head back down into the filth and looks at the metal spike in his hand. He rises into the screaming gales and stares at the void as a gurgling roar bursts from the hole and shakes ground. The soldier responds to the challenge, walks forward and is swallowed by the darkness.

CHAPTER 1

The summer's slow dusk gently spills its orange light across the rural American town. Single story homes of white, yellow and creamy blue sparsely line the old paved roads. Some separated by vacant lots, others by small town shops that have closed for the day. While most of the lots are lush with trim grass, some had grown wild and appropriately caged within their rusty fences. Of these wild lots, one is filled with dead and rotting cars. Their makes and models are various and span decades into the past. Next to the automotive cemetery, at the corner of one of the town's few large intersections stands a worn but sturdy structure. Its original color long forgotten, its skin is a patchwork of wood planks and corrugated metal sheets. A faded marquee above the middle of its three garage doors says nothing. However, the stacks of tires, tables laden with tools and various mechanical parts reveal this place to be a garage. Although the slumbering town has given way to the songs of crickets, the lights and noise coming from within tells otherwise.

Inside the garage, in a small dusty and dimly lit office, a young man sits on a wooden bench. He stares up at another man a few feet away who is sitting at a high desk. The man at the desk is oblivious to the grease on his person. His hands spread it around his face and the various papers that he squints to read. He is just as oblivious to the sitting man who stares up at him. Bored and irritated, the man on the bench looks away and out the dirty window. The receding sun highlights the hazel centers of his bright eyes as its rays pass through the fenced window. He leans closer to see his illuminated reflection better. Despite the fence's shadow casting across his face he reaches up to try and fix his brown scraggly hair, which is a few weeks past due on a cutting. He leans his stubbled chin in his hand when a loud machine sound whinnies its way from the office's door to the garage. Accompanied by the sound is the flickering of a dim old ceiling light, as it had done for most of that day. The man cringes as he thinks of what they might be doing to his car, if they were working on his car at all.

He leans back to relax as best as he can in the creaking bench and sighs. The man wears old jeans, brown hiking boots and a thick black hooded sweatshirt. He is dressed plain enough, but it had still been obvious to the people in town that he was not a local. As he walked through the town earlier, he thought it was most likely because everyone there knew each other. They were still kind though and no one had bothered him. That is the way he likes things.

The noise from the garage stops and the door opens. A short, balding mechanic steps through and rigidly turns to the man on the bench. It could have been his out of place smile or his soda bottle glasses or both that makes him look so energized, but he seems very excited.

"Jason?" the mechanic asks.

"Its, Jake," the man on the bench replies.

"Oh, Jacob," the mechanic stammers. "Sorry, I know you told me a few times before."

"Well," the mechanic announces, "figured it out! It was the alternator."

"Is it fixed?" Jake asks, his shoulders in a shrug, trying to draw the information out of the quirky man.

"Uh, yeah. Um, just five more minutes. We have to finish charging your battery."

"How much then?" he replies. Exhausted from his day spent

waiting for his car.

"Ask Gus, he'll tell ya'," he motions towards the man at the desk.

"Six hundred dollars," Gus casually states. "Cash or one of these?" his oily hand slides a scuffed old card imprinter towards Jake.

Too tired to fight or haggle Jake reaches towards his back pocket when the mechanic interrupts them.

"No Gus, we had to pop in a used alternator."

"Four hundred," Gus restates.

Jake gives the mechanic a look that is both surprise and subdued anger.

"Don't worry," the mechanic teases, "it'll get you back to civilization."

Gus chuckles as well.

Jake does not want to play along, but it seems like a game these two like playing with outsiders. He only has a little over sixty bucks in cash, so he hands Gus a card, which is one of the only other things in his wallet, besides a few twenties, old receipts and a condom.

As the transaction proceeds the mechanic continues excitedly talking, not having moved from his rigid stance. "Sorry about the long wait Jason. Our alternator guy has been out doing tows all day. Mike is the man when it comes to alternators." On that, the mechanic spins around and walks back through the door to the garage.

"It's Jake!" Gus shouts at his coworker, but the door is already closed.

Jake sits back on the bench relieved he can finally get back on the road. He looks up at Gus again who has returned to squinting at his papers.

"Hey Gus, what's the fastest way to get back to the interstate—"

Wham!

A chain bound scraggly man's body bursts the front door open. He staggers and falls to his knees briefly, before the large man who is wielding him yanks the prisoner back up to his feet and slams him into the bench right next to Jake.

"Get the chains on his legs deputy!" the big man wearing a sweaty white collared shirt barks as spittle and sweat flies from his wet face.

Between the sound of the door nearly shattering and the wild clinking of the prisoner's heavy chains, no one had noticed the nervous deputy come in behind the two. The sweaty giant literally drops his heavy rounded frame onto the prisoner and jams his meaty elbow into his neck, immobilizing him. The deputy hastily but cautiously stoops down and begins attaching the chains around the prisoner's ankles to the bench.

He heaves himself off the prisoner. Breathing heavily his short wiry mustache curls into a sneer. "I want no more shit from out of you!" he says, pointing down at the prisoner.

He directs his fury to the tall desk and Jake notices a gun holster cutting into his girth.

The force of his mitts slamming onto Gus' high desk blows the greasy paperwork away. "I called you people over five damn hours ago!" he roars, and wipes the running beads of sweat from his bald sunburned head.

"Hey now!" Gus forces out the words while attempting to posture himself against the energized angry giant. "First of all, I said we would get to you when we can! And second, you're gonna pay for that door!"

"Door? I don't give a damn about your door! If I would have known it was going to take you damned—"

"Us damned what?" Gus snaps.

"Hold on Gus, you have to understand the situation," the deputy enters the conversation his hand raised calmingly. "This convict here is a genuine maniac and FBI guy's partner has already been hospitalized because of him."

The men continue arguing and it is at that moment Jake notices the horrible smell wafting over from the man next to him. It is not the average funk a person develops from being in the heat. It is something Jake had never smelled before and it is offensive. Jake looks over at the prisoner, whose face is covered by his long jaggy grey hair. His filthy orange coveralls are soaked with sweat as well.

The prisoner sits leaning forward with his chained hands cupped together, as if he were in church and with an interest in what the pastor had to say. In this case, he is interested in the argument that is taking place.

Jake notices prison style tattoos all over his hands. Some are more faded than others are but they have very clean borders, not the sloppy fuzzy ones he has seen before. They all look intentional and not random, but he is sure they are not in English. Curious, Jake looks up to see if there are more of the strange tattoos and he raises his eyes right into the prisoner gaze. Startled Jake leans back but tries to keep his cool. The man is smiling. Although his small pupils are a cold deep black, his eyes are wide open with excitement. He is old, at least in his late sixties. His face, wracked with heavily wrinkled folds and cuts. Sure enough, more of the same tattoos cover his face. They are all equally spaced from one another, with the same intentional layout on the man's hands. To Jake's great discomfort, they seem to accentuate some of the deep scars across his body.

Did this guy cut himself up on purpose? Jake thinks to himself.

He looks away, trying not to engage the so-called maniac in any conversation. Jake cannot quite tell where he is from. He has a tan complexion, but there is a strange gray tint to his skin. He looks over at greasy Gus to compare.

No, its not oil, he thinks. Not dust or ash either, doesn't really matter.

"What the heck is going out here?" the mechanic pops his head through door leading to the garage.

"Nothing unexpected for a Friday," a new voice joins the chaos.

A tall, black haired man walks in through the front door carrying a clipboard. He locks eyes with the large FBI agent in a stare down, and the agent's anger visibly grows. He walks past everyone smiling with a toothpick in his mouth, and tips his dingy red ball cap to him.

"Hey Mike, what's going on? Who is that?" the curious mechanic hops around as Mike ushers him back into the garage.

"Oh, by the way Jason," the mechanic yells past Mike, "your car will be ready in uh, just give me another three minutes!"

Jake does not look up, but instead begins rubbing his temples. He decides he cannot take the shackled man's stench anymore or the shouting match that the deputy is trying to referee. He stretches his back getting ready to stand.

"So where are you headed?" a new voice quietly enters, but still somehow manages to take a precedence over the noise in the small room.

"Where are you headed, Jason?" the prisoner's voice raises a bit and sounds like a shovel being drug across a sidewalk. It has a dangerously inquisitive undertone to it.

"It's Jake." Without looking over, Jake corrects him out of a recent habit more than anything else.

"Ok, *Jackie*," the prisoner annoyingly corrects himself.

Jake turns to look at the prisoner and correct him one more time, when he sees the prisoner's freaky smile again. The old man's eyes are just as piercing as before, this time he is smiling with his mouth open. His teeth are wickedly packed, crooked and nasty shades of brown and black. The visible areas of his gums are darkened and inflamed as well, possibly the origin of the horrible stench.

"West," Jake replies. His expression crumples at the site of his ruined mouth.

The old man's demeanor changes, he becomes more civil and seems to drift off in his memories. "Going west huh? Would you happen to be traveling through a town named Prudence? It's a little isolated, just a couple hours west of here."

Jake shrugs, as if he would have any business in some small town. "No, just sticking to the main roads."

"Aw, Jake," The old man has a smug but cheerful look. He appears to act normal, except when he clicks with his mouth and winks his left eye at Jake.

"Jake," he coos. "Don't let the name fool ya dude, if I were a young man, I would get myself right to Prudence. It wouldn't be that far out of your way."

"If you were a young, free man," Jake adds, sarcastically matching the prisoner's newfound candor.

"True," the prisoner gleefully says as he pulls the chains

between his wrists and ankles taught. "Crazy 'ole place is the reason I got into this mess," he tilts his head back in reminiscence. "That town always had the best women, and there were so many." He looks down seriously thinking. "Yeah, there were at least four women living there for every one man, all beautiful women too. At least back in my day. I've been away for, what do they say now, a minute?" he chuckles. "But I don't see that ratio changing in just a few—"

A large meaty fist cracks into the prisoner's nose sending the back of his head into the wall and shaking the entire bench.

"I told you not to start any of your shit!" the agent yells.

The prisoner leans forward and pulls his hands up to catch the blood gushing from his nose.

"One more damned word!" the agent pulls his gun out and jabs the muzzle into the top of prisoner's head. Oblivious, the prisoner snorts back his blood while probing his face with his dirty fingers.

"Whoa!" the deputy steps in. "You do what you want in your house, not in my mine!"

The agent glares at the deputy, "This whole country is my house."

Jake remains leaned back. Still surprised from the hit the agent gave the prisoner. He definitely is not going to move now. Jake cannot help but stare at the agent's ornate silver and pearl handled gun. Tension presses against every surface in the room, and the only person not affected by it is the man with the gun to his head.

Slowly he lowers his gun, holsters it and turns back to Gus, to continue with the vehicle and shop door repair dispute.

The deputy steps over to Jake, "Jake, right?"

He simply nods.

"I have to apologize for all this, and the long wait. I'm sure that Mike is back there fixing your car right now, and that you will be on your way in no time."

A confused look spreads across Jake's face, "The tow truck driver? The other guy said my car was fixed?"

"Oh? Then I'm sure it will be ok if Bobby fixed it." Aware of Jake's expression he tries to change the subject. "Hey. As soon as you get back to the interstate or right before you get on actually,

11

there's a diner. Go on in and tell them that Deputy Scott sent you, and they'll give you a free dinner."

Jake relaxes. "Thank you, Deputy Scott."

"Hey, no problem Jake. Your ah, brother is an officer right, that where you're heading?"

"He was an officer, he just made detective. I'm heading out to congratulate him." Jake proudly admits.

The prisoner sits upright, his head still down he begins to chuckle.

"A detective in the big city," the deputy smiles. "That's not bad at all. And what is it you do?"

Jake hesitates, "I, ah, do this and that right now."

"Oh, I see," the deputy jokes. "There's nothing wrong with not having found your path just yet. So he's your older brother?"

Jake uncomfortably answers, "Ugh, no. We are actually the same age. We're twins."

The prisoner's chuckling becomes louder and he turns his head again looking Jake directly in his eyes. The prisoner looks even more insane. The blood from his nose is running freely down his face over his rotten teeth and drips away from his grizzled chin. He is ecstatic, giddy, and he begins muttering some indiscernible words between his chuckles.

Not wanting to have an unarmed, chained up prisoner shot in his town by a crazed federal agent, Deputy Scott looks over his shoulder to see if he has noticed. He has not and the deputy thankfully looks back to the prisoner, points at him and silently mouths, "Shut the hell up."

The convict gets louder, smiling wildly his garbled words become a rhythmic humming.

Confused, Jake scoots away. "Hey man, what the hell is your problem?"

The prisoner reaches his shaky hand up to his mouth and rubs his quivering fingers in his own blood as he continues to hum. Jake stands then backs up behind the deputy.

In turn, the deputy puts his hand on the hilt of his gun, "Convict! Stop whatever the hell you're doing, and calm down!"

The argument at the desk stops. The agent slams his fists on it again and begins turning around, "I warned you mother—"

The prisoner's murmurs become growls and he lunges hands first like an animal. The force of his jump drags the end of the bench he is chained to with him. His bloody hands aimed at Jake. With his uncannily fast leap, the prisoner lands a single swipe with his fingers, drawing a thick line with his blood across Jake's forehead. Jake falls backwards into the front door and crumples to the ground. The deputy and the agent grab the prisoner and shove him back into the bench so hard it shatters. They then proceed to stomp and kick the convict repeatedly.

Jake sits up against the tall desk and frantically uses the sleeve of his hooded sweater to remove the blood from his forehead. He even spits on his sleeve hoping to rub more of the blood off. He reaches to inspect the back of his head to see if there was any damage from colliding with the door. Gus makes his way out from around his desk and is joined by Mike, who helps restrain the crazed prisoner. The chaotic noise of the rattling chains, broken wood flying around and the men cursing and screaming fills the small office that was almost serene not even ten minutes earlier.

In a few minutes, the four men gain control of the situation. They have the prisoner on his stomach, with the agent laying mostly on top of him and breathing heavier than before. Gus and Deputy Scott are holding his legs and Mike is sitting back, exhausted, and fanning himself with his dirty red hat. Jake and the four men all look at each other with the dust still floating through the air, as if to confirm that what just happened, really happened.

The front door creaks open but is stopped by Jake's leg. The mechanic leans his head through the opening in the doorway, his magnified eyes dart around assessing the bizarre scene.

Standing over Jake as he is, he looks down and says, "Jason. Uh, your car is ready. It's out front."

Jake just laughs to himself, a tired laugh. He slowly stands up and appraises his body for any other injuries. He wipes his forehead some more with a clean part of his sleeve. He looks to the men on the floor and leaves saying, "It's been real guys."

Outside again in the fresh clean smelling air, Jake realizes it is almost dark. More upbeat, he approaches his blue sedan, and hears it is running fine. He quickly assesses the area, to make sure he gets back to the highway correctly and sees what must be the agent's car. It is a heavily armored transport vehicle and looks like it had skid for a while on its side. The windshield is shattered and blood is caked inside the broken glass's grainy cracks.

Jake wonders if that crazy old bastard had caused something to lead to the accident or if it was just an unfortunate situation he tried taking advantage of when he hospitalized the agent's partner.

That is some serious transportation to move an old man, he thinks, although he did seem strong as hell.

"Maniac." Jake says aloud and looks at the half-broken door to the garage office one last time. The exterior lights to the garage pop on, casting their green hue across the gravel parking lot. Jake gets in his car and checks his reflection in the mirror. Some of the smeared dried blood remains.

"Damn." He wipes it off, then turns the car around and drives away.

* * *

Back inside the office, the men have draped the limp prisoner, to Gus' dissatisfaction, over his desk.

"Is he alive?" Mike asks.

"Yeah, he's an extra tough old son of a bitch," the agent replies.

"What did he do?" Mike continues questioning.

"Don't worry about it!" the agent snaps. "Deputy Scott, we can't keep him here, we'll use your car to get him to your little station until my back up arrives."

"Fine. My car is still unlocked I'll help you take him out."

"I'll get him into the car, you grab some waters! Your busted non air conditioned vehicle is the reason we had to stop here midway anyhow!" he adds while maneuvering the dazed but walking prisoner out the door.

"Yessir," Deputy Scott says through his teeth. "Bobby, get the door. And Gus, could you hand me some waters, and a towel or two? I don't want this nasty ass convict getting his blood all over my seats."

"Busted door, broken bench, now my water. Anything else?" Gus asks indignantly.

"Gus, just send me an estimate for the damages, the feds will pay. They have plenty of money."

"Yeah, our money!" Mike laughs.

Gus hands Deputy Scott two bottles of water, "One for you, one for the convict. And I'm fresh out of clean towels," he says with a smile as he gestures towards the blood all over the floor and his desk.

Deputy Scott sighs and makes his way out the door that Bobby is still holding open. Outside, he does not see the agent or the convict in his car. The bottles of water fall to the ground as he draws his 9mm. Quickly he makes his way to his squad car under one of the flickering lights. He wants to call out, but he does not want to alarm the convict of his presence. In the dim light, he can make out a blood trail curving around his car. He cautiously moves to see the other side at a safe distance, and he is horrified. The agent is laying faced down gun still in hand. The convict is clutching a splintered off piece from the broken bench in both hands. He is stabbing the agent's neck into a scattered bloody opened purse of flesh, which reveals the bones of his neck and sinew as its contents.

"Get your hands up!" he shouts.

The convict looks up at him. His entire face and the front of his scraggly hair is coated in thick layers of sticky blood and dirt. Except for his eyes, his wide, wild eyes with their tiny pupils. In the sputtering green security light, his blood soaked face appears as if it is covered in a shiny blackness, which only contrasts his crazed expression even more. The convict starts hysterically laughing again, and rises up still holding the blood soaked piece of wood. He begins walking towards Deputy Scott.

"Oh hell!" the deputy opens fire. The sharp pops from his gun echo through the quiet sleepy town. Eight gunshots later, the convict is on the ground.

The garage crew runs outside and over to the deputy. Upon seeing the gruesome sight, Gus immediately vomits and Bobby takes off his glasses while walking away in shock.

"How did he?" Mike starts to ask but stops.

"Mike, go see if Bobby is alright."

"Gus?" the deputy motions to Gus who looks like he is readying to throw up again. "This is a damn crime scene now, go do that somewhere else! All of you get inside! We have to start calling people."

The shocked men head back inside.

The Deputy puts his gun away and turns to the others. "Gus, get the mayor on the phone! Get him down here but do not tell him why, just tell him we have a situation. Mike, I want you to move your truck between my car and the road. I don't want anybody having to see what's out there. Bobby?"

"He's gone, man," Mike answers. "He'll need a few."

The Deputy adjusts his hat, "Okay Gus, you're gonna have to suck it up. Lock this place down and keep an eye on Bobby until help gets here. Can you do that?"

"Yeah, I can do that," Gus answers, still on the verge of throwing up again.

"I'll get the Sheriff down here. Dammit! This means more feds. Boss is gonna have my ass anyways."

The two men step outside, and Mike quickly stops.

Still shaken himself, Deputy Scott asks, "What's wrong Mike?"

Mike points towards the agent's truck, "I parked my truck right next to the agent's after I unhitched it. It's gone."

The deputy turns around and looks towards his squad car where he dropped the convict and starts reloading his gun.

"No way! Get behind me Mike."

"Are you serious? I thought you shot him!"

"At least seven or eight times."

Mike sidesteps over to one of the messy outdoor tables and quietly picks up a large wrench.

The Deputy looks at Mike and shakes his head, "He could have the agent's gun."

The two slowly come around the car as the deputy had done before and they find the agent, just like before but the convict's body is no longer there. Just a huge puddle of blood had soaked into the gravel and dirt.

"This is not real. All that blood! And he just, leaves?"

The deputy lowers his gun and looks around just as confused. "He was only ten feet away. I didn't miss once."

CHAPTER 2

In the dim light of the tiny bathroom, Jake splashes away the remaining soap from his face. He looks up into the mirror and strains to see in the dim orange light making sure he has cleaned away the rest of the blood. After a few moments, he reaches up and removes the smoke stained plastic light cover from above the mirror. And there is light. Brighter, although the bulbs are dirty as well, he keeps inspecting himself. He stares at himself unimpressed by his haggard appearance but confident that he is at least clean again. His fear of contracting some form of prison hepatitis or worse starts to fade. He tries slicking tuffs of his hair down and flattens his thick eyebrows a few times with the excess water. After gathering his toothbrush and other toiletries into his grungy burlap backpack, he puts on a dark grey shirt and bags his stained white one along with the rest of his possessions. He thinks of the crazy scene he was just in, about how strange that prisoner looked and wonders again, why the he snapped like that.

He says out loud to his reflection, "I gotta get out of here."

After a few more minutes, he replaces the dirty light cover and steps out of the closet of a bathroom, into a bright and thankfully cleaner diner.

"Two grilled cheese, an order of fries and two bottles of pop." The young woman in her old-fashioned blue server uniform calls to him from behind the diner counter.

"Yep, thanks." Jake reaches for the grease stained paper sack.

"Your order has been sitting for awhile. I can have the cook heat it up for you."

Jake cannot help but to notice how attractive the waitress is, with her dark eyes and hair. He wonders if the women in that crazy old man's story look as good, better even. To Jake, the country women out here have been just as good looking as the city girls Jake is used to, in their own way.

"I'm sure its fine, thanks again though." He takes the food from the counter and heads towards the exit, only to stop and turn around. "Hey, you wouldn't happen to know how far a placed named—" Jake pauses as he struggles to remember the name, "named, Prudence is from here would you?"

The waitress' right eyebrow rises, "Is that a city, town or a county?"

"You know what, never mind. It's not important."

"Hold on, let me ask. Chef? . . . *Chef!*"

"What?" a gruff middle-aged man pops his head up and shouts through the service window.

Still yelling she continues, "A customer is looking for a place called Prudence. It's supposed to be around here."

"Prudence?" the chef snorts. He takes a long drag from the cigarette hanging off the side of his mouth in deep contemplation. Seeing that makes Jake begin to contemplate his dinner.

"Yeah, the old boomtown."

"The what?" Jake curiously steps closer.

"Boom town, oil." He pauses to take another drag. "It got big off of oil a long time ago, then I think the oil dried up. I guess it just became regular after that." He exhales his smoke towards the waitress, who wafts it away. "Never been there though."

This is confirmation enough for Jake, and he smiles thinking of his odds in a backwards town full of women.

"It is a little out of the ways though," the chef continues. "It should be, . . . keep heading west then take the Rooksville exit, go north for about an hour, hour and a half."

"Alright, thanks man!" Satisfied and with a kind wink at the waitress Jake exits the diner.

Walking back to his car Jake realizes, briefly, that he has been thinking about Prudence ever since he left the garage.

Maybe it's just to keep my mind off what happened in there, he thinks to himself.

Jake stares far west down the highway, his last thoughts had escaped him again. Now maybe he might have something exciting to talk to his brother about. It would not hurt to have some fun while on his crazy road trip.

An hour of driving later Jake wakes up on the wrong side of the road. Just in time to avoid crashing head on into a rapidly approaching curved median. Slamming on his breaks Jake yells and yanks at the wheel. He pulls right and wrangles his car from spinning out of control. White knuckled and gasping for air, he clutches at his heart after he evens his car out. He slaps himself hard and mad for being so stupid. Accelerating again he rolls down his window and pitches the garbage from his dinner into the wind, letting the fresh night air whip around inside the car.

The nightscape of the rural American highways becomes surrounded by a thick sea of dark forests. The drones and growls of the lone speeding semi trucks are snuffed out by an intimate silence. A short time later Jake continues in vain to try finding a decent radio station. He yawns again. He knows he has been yawning too much and starts to worry. He is supposed to be halfway to his brother's place by now, sleeping somewhere. Wishing the starry night were a colder and less cozy one, he rolls up his windows and turns on his air conditioning, trying to snap out of his sluggishness. He feels around for his second bottle of coke, then turns to look for it in the dark of his car. His imagination drudges up an image of a massive deer crashing through his windshield and he returns his eyes to the dark road. He decides to focus on getting somewhere he can sleep, or at least pull over and nap for a bit.

Smash!

Pieces of glass and sparks explode past him. Weightless in the split second, he watches spider cracks slither across his windshield from the impact. He bounces inside his seatbelt and his head is wrenched to the left and sent crashing through his side window. The splintering glass takes small stinging bites from his head. The shockwave causes everything to buckle and shift in the instant and just like that, Jake is again locked onto his steering wheel, twisting at it for his life. Confused and struggling with the inertia Jake fights to stay on the road. He glances to his left and sees a large black pickup truck passing him by. The truck's windows are too high for him to see into, giving him no target for his furious death stare but he hears rock music blasting from inside. He also sees that his left mirror has been completely off torn. He mashes his horn cursing but the truck continues accelerating past him.

Its lights are off but from behind Jake sees that it is a tow truck. Although the plates have been rusted away, he can still read the faded yellow letters, 'Mike's Towing' on the bumper.

Furious and catching up, Jake continues mashing his horn and flicking his high beams on and off.

"You son of a bitch!" he yells.

The tow truck responds by mimicking Jake's sound and light show.

Jake tries to pull up on the wild truck's right, sacrificing the already damaged side of his car to get closer. The truck swerves in front of him blocking his path. Angrier now, Jake accelerates into the back of the pickup causing more new damage to his car than the truck.

"Is this how you get repeat business? Son of a bitch!" Jake continues ramming the tow truck.

In response, the tow trucks large crucifix shaped boom animates and threateningly extends close to the hood of his car. It forces him to back away and the metal cross drops low behind the truck and presses into the asphalt. With a horrible grating sound, it sends a brilliant shower of sparks up from the ground. The bright embers obscure Jake's vision and he backs off even more. Suddenly the truck slams its breaks and cuts a hard right, sliding almost perpendicular in front of Jake. As dirt and dust flies through he air Jake chances again to see the driver of the truck while he defensively breaks to avoid t-boning the vehicle. He figures it is Mike, or one of the other jokers from the garage but he wants to see the driver's face to make sure. The truck peels out and accelerates again, off the highway and onto a side road. Without any thought, Jake follows the truck into the darkness.

The road is wild and riddled with large cracks and holes. With the absence of streetlights, Jake can only follow the reflectors of the truck as they flicker in the swirling dust. They swerve from left to right and he fights to stay behind, hoping to keep ramming it until the truck stops or wrecks. The dust starts to thicken and with another crashing sound, the truck hops as it bursts through a large iron gate. The gates swing wide, then bounce back nearly clipping Jake's car as he passes between them. Jake leans his head out of his missing window ready to shout profanities again when a sudden sharp pain flashes through his head. Stunned and seeing spots he grunts and begins breaking hard. The pain intensifies. He grips his head with both hands, trying to steer by slumping over the wheel. Roughly, it finally skids to a stop. His face tightens in sharp agony. He looks up to see the tow truck has stopped as well.

The pain begins to dilate time and a long moment passes. Slowly the truck begins driving off into the dust again carrying the distant sound of rock music with it. A hum begins in his ears, becoming louder in volume as the pain increases. He clamps down on his head even harder against the sudden migraine. He tries to think if the truck hit him harder than he realized, but the thoughts he tries forming fall apart. The pain in his mind ramps up crushing his remaining incoherent thoughts and the stinging bright spots are snuffed out rapidly by darkness.

CHAPTER 3

Jake opens his eyes and sees the pale overcast sky through his cracked car window. Sluggishly he leans back peeling his face from his steering wheel. He reaches his hands up to his head. The pain is gone but he inspects his head and body for cuts or bruises while shaking the glass out of his hair. After getting out of his car and checking himself further, he notices around him how gloomy and cold the day is.

The air is damp and there is no breeze. He turns around to see a heavy black gate, crooked and open. He also notices that the tree line of the forest stops abruptly where the gate does and is replaced by a wild and dull colored grass. Scattered throughout the grassy fields are equally dull willow trees. However, the semi straight road he is standing on is lined with equally spaced birch trees. Their leafless branches are motionless. They line the path a good ways down where they turn off behind a series of the large willows. Beyond that, he sees nothing else but what looks to be the top of a small forested mountain.

Jake inspects the damage to his car while estimating the damage in his head. As he finishes looking over his vehicle, he decides to continue in the direction of the tow truck driver. Even if the guy is long gone, he still wants to get to a phone. He knows who Mike is and someone was going to pay.

Back in his car, Jake reaches in his pockets for his keys and his shoulders slump at his realization. He grabs his keys that were left in the ignition, and not expecting anything more than disappointment he tries turning it. His car is dead. He tries to start it a few more times in vain. After a few good moments of venting his anger on his steering wheel he gets out.

He retrieves his backpack and the extra bottle of soda. Digging through the trunk of his car he pulls out a scuffed up black leather jacket and puts it on over his hooded sweater. He fishes around through the mess in his trunk for anything else that might be useful. There is a milk crate, a loose jack, an old spare and a plastic bag full of dirty clothes. A forgotten flashlight reveals itself from under some oil rags. The plastic yellow flashlight works fine and Jake debates for a moment if he would be that far from anywhere to need it after dark. It goes in his bag. Jake thinks of the guy in the tow truck, whether it is Mike or not, and retrieves a tire iron as well. He closes the trunk and thirstily drinks his soda then smashes the bottle against the damaged part of his car. He takes another look around and makes his way down the birch lined road.

A desolate town. The majority of windows had been boarded up long ago. The words, 'CONDEMNED' are spray stenciled in faded red and black across the old plywood boards covering doors and windows. Here and there, the carcasses of randomly burned buildings and homes still stand. Rusted cars rot away, littering the streets and sidewalks. Some are even still stopped at various dangling and fallen traffic lights that are so ruined they seemed to have never functioned. All things glass, not broken or burned are coated by layers of dust and dirt. Things crafted from wood had long rotted away while the brick and cement that had not crumbled had been assaulted and split by nature itself. Garbage and leaves do not blow as they had long since caked into corners and gutters, stamped down as if the town had begun to absorb them.

No people are seen here. The only entity with voice is the wind that wails and whispers through the derelict constructions of its long absent residents.

And then echoes.

Footsteps approach, a voice calls out for things no longer there, things that were almost forgotten to this forlorn place. For a moment the eerie winds stop, as if to allow the town to hear and be sure that something has trespassed into its open dead arms.

"Hello!" the echo of Jake's distant voice calls out again.

For the first time in a long time, someone new has come to Prudence, and the winds blow ever so slightly in excitement. Tattered awnings wave, doors and shutters creak and sway. Deep within the bowls of the many dead structures of the town, things begin to stir.

"Anybody here!" his voice has started to become horse.

"Mike!" he looks over his shoulders as he grips his tire iron.

Jake looks around, wondering what the hell happened to this place. He wades through the tall weeds that had punched through the cracked riddled streets. Unnerved, he starts walking down their middles to avoid the crooked half-parked cars and to keep his distance from the darkness within the cracked open doors. Broken and boarded up homes give way to narrow densely packed buildings. He slides the tire iron into his shoulder bag and blows into his cold hands. He notices a dark layer of film on his fingertips, and tries rubbing it away. It does not and Jake looks up to realize he has made his way into what must be the downtown area. He concludes the town must have emptied out a while ago.

Three wide streets converge into a spacious 'Y' intersection, with Jake having come up from the south running street to the junction. More of the cable suspended traffic lights either sag or lie on the ground next to toppled and wrecked streetlights. There are no trappings of any modern businesses, none of the typical invasive fast food joints or coffee shops. Outstanding amongst the monotony of flush and semi spaced shop bottomed two flats is a movie theater sitting on the west corner. The theater's large and once grand marquee sags dangerously over its entrance. The ashen husk of what was a very large church sits on the east corner of the intersection. Directly in front of him on the north corner is a large nondescript building. It is not as formerly ornate or even old fashioned as some of the other downtown places. Windowless and staring past the weathering and neglect, Jake can tell it was once reddish and had been affected by a fire in some parts. The town had abruptly stopped aging, and started dying a few decades ago.

With just a charged car battery, not even directions just a decent battery he could get going. Many of the old vehicles had been left collided into one another, a panicked aftermath. After inspecting a few dozen of the ruined engines, he realizes none of the abandoned rides will provide him with a suitable replacement. He walks down the eastbound road and comes upon another intersection, where he looks up and down the streets again. He is looking for a garage, Mike or his truck, even a decent looking car. He spots what looks like a store and the tattered door is open.

About to walk into the store, he is startled by a strange noise in the distance. It is not another person or an animal sound that Jake has ever heard. He pauses but there are no other sounds. He stares across the street, trying to look within the many exposed cavities of doors and broken windows, but he cannot see into the darkness and instead feels like he is the one being watched. He continues quietly back to the store, stops outside the doorway and stares inside. After a brief pause, he takes a breath and enters.

Just as Jake expected, the shelves are completely bare with the exception of a few corroded cans of food. Other items, shopping baskets, old signage, broken glass and random dirty papers lay strewn about covering the floor. As aerated as the store is by its ruined facade the place still smells like a musty old attic.

"Hello?" Jake announces himself quietly.

He walks behind the register, and satirically picks up the receiver of a faded green rotary phone. Not expecting anything, he listens for a dial tone. He puts the dead receiver down, and begins messing with an old cash register, half-joking around.

Ding!

The drawer pops open and there is cash inside of it. He stops playing around and stares down at the old wrinkled cash. He stares long and hard at it, and becomes very unnerved as to why cash is actually in the drawer.

There is at least sixty bucks here, his thoughts race, what could have happened to make everyone leave so fast? The food and other supplies are gone, but the money is still here. If this store was looted or left, the cash would have still been taken.

Still looking down Jake closes the cash drawer, when he notices some items lined up on the shelf beneath it. He crouches down and finds half a dozen dusty bottles of alcohol and a few old cartons of cigarettes. Next to them is a neatly folded stack of old newspapers, but they are soiled and blackened beyond legibility.

This is even more bizarre to Jake.

Jake looks over the store from behind the counter. He stands and sets a couple bottles on the counter, and opens one. One swig from it and his mouth puckers from the taste, it is barely decent. He places them in his bag, wrapping one in his dirty shirt to keep the bottles from clinking together and keeps inspecting the store. Making his way to the back of the store through the dim light he finds more empty shelves and containers, an office desk covered in old cigarette butts and dust. After rummaging through the desk drawers and finding nothing useful, his search continues then stops at the sound of a distant rustling. He turns and lifts his iron up defensively and moves further inside the store, towards the sound. Down a hallway lined with more empty shelves, Jake sees that the back door is open. It is actually off its hinges and laying flat on the overgrown grass outside. The rustling starts up again. The sound is from grass and leaves. Someone is running around out back. He moves behind the corner of the hallway and nervously stares down just enough to see out the back door.

He would call out but he is inside a store, abandoned or not, basically stealing. The noise stops then starts again, the person seems to be moving back and forth, but very quickly.

Maybe it's a dog, he thinks and relaxes a bit.

A large shadow bolts across the doorway, part of it slapping the doorframe with a thunderous whack.

The hallway shakes and scared, Jake shuffles backwards away from the door and makes his way to the front. A heavy thud sounds from above and freezes Jake in place. Wisps of concrete dust scuttle down from the cracked and stained ceiling. The sound came from the floor above, he is sure of it.

Lingering nervously for a while near the front door he listens for any other noises. He leaves, creeping close to the front of the building to avoid detection by anyone on the second floor. Luckily, most of these stores are built row style, so he does not have to worry about anyone coming around the building at him through the narrow gaps between them.

He thinks the smart thing for him to do would be to find someone that can help get to a working phone or car battery. Taking from the store is not really stealing to him, it is abandoned, but he does not want to risk a bad confrontation with the people in the store. The weird set up with the money and liquor still being there bothers him. He would come back later he thinks to himself.

Hours pass and the day seems timeless. Jake had cautiously explored more of the town without incident, but frustratingly without having found any help. He guesses that the town is no larger than just a couple miles wide from its center, appearing to be around four miles across. Following the east bound road for about a mile, he leaves the houses and passes through a park and a school. The road stops at more forest and splits in two with the roads curving back towards the town. One heading north, the other south. At the outer circle of road, Jake looks back at the town and sees that it may be completely encircled by forest. He also notices a rusted water tower in the town's far west side, and the tips of some other wiry structures beyond that. They are mostly obscured by the downtown buildings and the large rocky and wooded hill north of the town, that he assumed before was a mountain.

He returns to the town's center and takes a break sitting outside on some weed ridden stone steps. Across the street, what looks like an old fire engine is lodged head on inside the burnt carcass of what looks to have been a library. Jake chuckles looking at the absurdity of the image and wonders what turn of events could have caused the truck to plow into there like that. He takes another swig from his appropriated bottle of rum, attempting to sate his growing thirst. From the empty homes he had ventured into, to even outdoor spigots, none of the faucets worked. He notices his dirty hands again and pours a bit of the rum on them. Surprisingly the grime still does not rub off. At least they are cleaner now, if not visibly. He pulls his hood over his head and crosses his arms.

It's going to be colder tonight, he thinks to himself as he looks down. He wishes for a minute that he hadn't quit smoking. Then at least he would have a means to light up a fireplace somewhere. His eyes drunkenly roll over the town. Driven by growing worries his mind starts looking at things differently. He focuses on nook type areas, hidden areas he could sleep. He begins wondering how difficult it would be to gain desperately needed sleep and safety if he had nowhere to live in a regular town, with people. Gaining new appreciation for the state of being homeless, he takes a larger swig of the liquor to dull his new uncomfortable thoughts.

But no, he frowns, he can't think like that. There would be no staying here long term, he has to get back to civilization. He also knows he will not make it back to the main road before nightfall. He takes another drink, looks at the dated whiskey inside and scowls. He throws the unfinished bottle across the street, sending it crashing against the wreckage of the fire engine.

He sits there for a few moments more thinking, when he hears the faint echoes of footsteps. He perks up looking around and listening but sees nothing. Making his way to the nearest intersection, he squints down each street. He hears a distant tell tale sound of a screen door flapping shut. Still seeing no one, he hesitates from calling out. He wants to know how messed up of a person this is before he gives himself away. Minutes pass as he anxiously continues rubber necking and listening for sounds. He hears the screen door again, and turns down the street to see a distant figure exiting a house.

Still not calling out, Jake begins speed walking towards the figure, which is making its way across the street, oblivious to him. As Jake gets closer, he sees a man wearing a zipped up jacket and a trucker hat. It is neither Mike nor any of the other people he remembers seeing from the garage.

"Hey!" Jake calls out.

The man stops and turns to look at Jake. The man is expressionless and begins walking towards him. Jake in turn, cautiously slows down. To his relief the strange man stops a good ten feet away from him. He does not speak, but stands there with his hands in his pockets. He can tell from the short distance that the man is very tall, at least a good head taller than him. They stare at each other for a few moments and Jake feels uneasy.

This is not the type of homeless or crazy person Jake was expecting to find dwelling here. The man is in his early thirties or hardened late twenties. He is wearing a faded dark blue work jacket over a brown flannel shirt, jeans and boots. His hat is dusty and faded black, its bill shadowing his eyes in the gloomy daylight. To Jake, other than his odd behavior the stranger seems remarkably average, almost stereotypical to a small town.

"Do you live here?" Jake asks while composing himself.

"Not recently," The man slowly replies, slightly gesturing with his head to the abandoned state of their surroundings.

The man's speech is not what Jake had expected either. He has no drawl but there was something about the way he speaks or his voice that unsettles him for some reason.

Propping himself for a confrontation Jake asks, "Hey, you drive a tow truck?"

The man tilts his head back a bit and walks closer, still blankly staring at Jake. "I drive a rig for a living," he says.

Jake simply stares back, unsure how to proceed with this slow and awkward conversation.

The man smiles, and for an instant a glare flickers over his eyes. "Are you from around here?"

"No," Jake contemptuously answers the absurd question.

"Why are you here?" the man asks, his smile gone.

Rather than going into the details of the crazed tow truck driver, who may be this man or a friend of his. He thinks about the confrontation that would ensue if either was the case and decides to answer with a different question.

"My car died outside of town, I was just passing through and came here to get some help."

Jake watches him carefully for any reaction to his story. He watches the man forming his next set of words carefully but also without any sign of real concern or nervousness.

"Trucker friend of mine dropped me off at the highway, yesterday. I had a few days off, and my mother wanted me to check in on some family members. She lost touch with them awhile back."

Jake does not like that pause in his response, and presses him. "You walked here from the highway? That seems like a ways to walk, don't you think?"

"I have nothing but time."

"Have you found your family?"

"No. Not yet. I had spent a few summers up here as a kid, of course things looked different then."

"You didn't call ahead?" Jake keeps pressing the seemingly lying man.

The man pauses again and just stares at Jake, a slight smile reappears. "No. Look at this place man," he gestures around again, "no working phones, no power, not even flushing toilets. This is probably why we lost touch with them to start with."

Jake is caught off guard by the man's ginger response, and relaxed by the rational explanation for his presence here.

"Then, what were you doing going from house to house?" Jake lightly prods.

"Same as you were probably doing. Looking for someone, something I could use. My relatives left no forwarding address for where they must have moved to, so I thought maybe someone who still lives here knows where they went."

This makes sense to Jake, and he decided to stop with his interrogation for now. But he still has one burning question.

"Any idea what happened to all of the people here?"

Hands still in his pockets he shrugs, "Your guess is as good as mine. But it looks like whatever happened, happened some time ago."

"Looks like it," Jake nods.

"I found a house with an old wood burning stove and some decent well water."

"Really?" Jake perks up.

"Yeah, come on, I'll show you were it is."

"Ok."

"What's your name anyway son?" the man asks, seemingly warming up to him.

"Jake."

"Well Jake," he reaches his gloved hand out and Jake in turn

31

does the same. They shake and Jake's hand is clasped firmly by the man's icy cold grip.

"Call me Kenneth."

* * *

The voices of the two men resonate within the near empty house. Pale light glooms in through open tattered floral curtains and fills the dusty barren living room. Jake sits at a once white speckled laminate kitchen table. The yellowed top is riddled with ancient coffee stains and other spills. Kenneth sits in one of the rickety chairs as well, facing away from Jake exposing him mostly to his right side and back. The comforting smell of crackling firewood pushes away the stagnant musk of the house as Kenneth stokes the guts of the old-fashioned heater.

"So you haven't come across any other running cars, or anything I could use to jump a battery?" Jake asks as he stares at the dingy glass of water sitting in front of him.

"Nope," Kenneth replies.

"How did you plan on leaving here?"

"Well, I was going to call my buddy in a few days. Let him know when to pick me up."

"No phones though," Jake adds.

"Yup."

"I guess we could walk back to the highway tomorrow morning, and hitch a ride," Jake suggests.

Kenneth remains silent, and continues poking the fire, feeding it with smaller pieces of wood.

"No shortage of dry wood here," Kenneth replies after a few moments.

"It *is* strange that the summer turned so quickly, it seems more like fall," Jake raises the glass of water up, watching the particulates swirl around. "Like something just sucked all the summer out of this place."

"Sure does seem like that."

Jake looks over to Kenneth and notices he has turned towards him smiling.

"What's so funny?" Jake asks, becoming irritated by Kenneth's awkwardness.

"You just have a strange way of wording things, where are you from, east coast?"

"Close," Jake is taken back by Kenneth's comment. "More like the mid east side as opposed to the Midwest, but no one calls it the 'Middle East'," he jokes.

He had travelled around the country and never thought that he had any particular speech habits. He thinks that this guy has a strange way of speaking himself. He takes Kenneth's distraction with the fire as a chance to look at him closer. The man's oily black, shoulder length hair pokes out from under his cap. He had shaved a day or so ago, and he has a slightly dark, dull complexion, but he is also extremely pale except for the dark rings under his wide shifty eyes. Kenneth closes the door on the heater and scoots his chair close to the window, but still does not bother to turn towards Jake. He opens the window a crack and produces a pack of cigarettes and a steel gas lighter from his jacket.

"Do you mind?" raising his gloved hand up he shows Jake the cigarette held between his fingers, still looking out the window.

What the hell is wrong with this guy, Jake thinks.

"Knock yourself out," he says, before he thirstily forces more dirty water down in large gulps.

Bored, Kenneth takes a few long drags, making no effort to direct his smoke towards the cracked window. He unzips his jacket and looks down, seemingly examining his stomach while Jake continues watching the floating gunk in his water as he drinks it.

"Are you sure this water is safe?"

"Cleanest I've found so far," Kenneth says calmly still playing with his flannel shirt. "From what I remember, the water here was never really that clean to begin with."

"Why is that?"

"It had something to do with . . . I think they had to route the water funny to keep it safe. It involved the drilling a while back. There used to be a lot of oil here."

Jake sits back in his chair, "Oil drilling? Doesn't that mess up the water?"

"It can. Don't worry, I doubt that's why this place is deserted," Kenneth teases. "You've never had well water?"

"Not really," Jake distastefully swishes the remains of the water in the glass. "Wait," he pauses, "what's the name of this town?"

Kenneth turns his head to Jake, about to laugh as he zips up his jacket, "You don't know?"

"I didn't see any town specific signs anywhere. This place is so weathered, even the words in the stonework are crumbled away.

Kenneth turns away with a chuckle and takes another long drag, pulling the embers down to the butte then flicking it into the fire.

He looks back to Jake and calmly says, "You are in Prudence."

"This is Prudence?" Jake slams his hands onto the table and jumps to his feet.

"You've heard of this dump?" Kenneth lights up another cigarette.

"Well, no. Not really," Jake hesitates to answer. Explaining how he first heard of Prudence would lead him to the embarrassment of why he considered coming here. He would also have to explain the incident at the garage with the convict, and he still is not sure if Kenneth is affiliated with Mike, or whoever was driving that tow truck. "Just heard what you mentioned, that is was a big oil boom town that died out."

Kenneth rises from his seat and walks across the creaky floorboards to look out another window.

Jake paces around the room stunned at how bad his luck has been and mad at himself for being duped by that crazy old prisoner.

"Well, Jake. Are you hungry?"

"Starving," Jake replies.

"Yeah," Kenneth says as he walks towards the door. "Well, I'm gonna head back out and see if I can find someone out here before it gets dark. Maybe I'll find someone with cigarettes too."

"Actually," Jake awakens from his thoughts of food, "there's a general store, first intersection east from the center of town."

"Yes?" Without Jake noticing, Kenneth has stopped and is hanging on his every word.

"It was weird. The store is empty but under the cash register someone left a bunch of bottles of liquor and cartons of smokes. But I could tell the rest of the store had been looted."

"So you think someone is actually running the store?" Kenneth cynically asks.

"No," Jake sighs, "I heard people moving around there. One was upstairs, and someone was out back."

"Really," Kenneth says slowly, a devious grin pushes its way across his cheeks.

Jake notices that hungry glare has returned to Kenneth's dark eyes from earlier.

"Did you see them?" Kenneth asks him.

"No."

"Huh. Well, thanks for the heads up, Jake."

"I guess I'll just stay here and keep the fire going."

"Here, take this," Kenneth tosses something to Jake. The toss is intentionally low and falls short almost causing Jake to trip trying to catch it. Caught between wanting to snap at Kenneth and show gratitude, he focuses on the object.

It is a steel gas lighter. It has a crisp image of a sexy, pin up style devil girl riding a rocket on it.

Jake looks up, "Don't you need this?"

"Go ahead, keep it. I have my own."

"What?"

"I found that one," he stares at Jake, expressionless again.

Jake looks down at it shining in his hands. It is in great condition compared to almost everything else he had come across so far.

"Thanks!" he looks up but Kenneth is already walking out of the house.

* * *

Jake sits back down and examines the lighter further. He snaps the lid back, watches the bright sparks ignite the gas and takes in the lovely smell of the lighter fluid. He notices tiny chips are cut into the area where the red devil girl's eyes are, making them flicker as the fire dances above.

Still feeling dehydrated, he grabs his cup and makes his way to the kitchen looking for the container Kenneth had said he used to bring in the well water. In the empty kitchen, he sees a large soup pot with a ladle in it sitting on the oven range. It becomes apparent as he gets closer that the container is filthy. Disgusted he looks down into the pot of water. He sees his reflection easily with the help of the slimy black sediment collected in the bottom of the pot.

"What the hell!" his shout echoes through the empty house.

He raises the plastic ladle from the pot and watches as the black sludge plops away in globs back into the water. The site causes him to begin gagging. He covers his mouth with his left hand. Still able to keep looking at the pot, it looks as though the sludge had tried climbing out on its own at some point, and then stopped to dry into a black barnacle like form.

"Son of a bitch!" he yells again.

Sickened, Jake knocks the metal pot off the range and onto the floor, where it shatters. Jake stops, confused at what just happened. He lifts a broken piece of the filthy pot up. Sure enough around the edges of those barnacles is rust. He brings the piece over to the window's light and discovers they are nothing like barnacles. More like a growth. He taps the growth against the windowsill. It is soft. It reminds him of something but he cannot place it. Still confused as to how and why something metal could break as if it was glass, he drops the piece of metal again and it breaks into smaller pieces.

As his thoughts wander back to the filthy water he drank, a slight pain shoots through his head. That migraine from before has started to stir. Wanting to sterilize his mouth, he rushes back to the living room and takes another swig from his rum, swishing it in his mouth and spitting it out on the floor. While taking a larger swig and downing it, he thinks of how stupid he was for drinking the dirty water.

He slumps against a wall by the wood burning heater, massaging his aching head. Tired again with eyelids beginning to grow heavy, he begins to allow his body to relax.

Crash!

Interrupted by the loud noise, Jake scrambles to his feet almost dropping the rum on the floor. He can hear someone running around upstairs, every step a loud thud. Not from boots, the thuds are accompanied by the smacking sounds of bare feet. He can see the stairs leading up from where he is standing. The rickety banister shakes with the slam of one of the doors upstairs. Confused and worried he crouches down and moves towards his bag again, trading the bottle for his tire iron and the flashlight. From upstairs, a door slams open with a rattling bang and the entire house seems to shake again.

Weapon raised, he tries to steady himself and inches over to the bottom of the stairs. He peers into the dark. Aiming the flashlight up with a shaky hand he flips the switch. The flashlight does not work. He shakes it, quietly bangs it against his leg and tries again. Not even a sputter. Angered he mouths a curse word, and lays the flashlight on the stairs as he slowly makes his way up. The thudding footsteps begin again and the banister vibrates with each step.

This has to be that damned guy messing with me. That's okay. Whoever it is, they're barefoot and I've got a tire iron.

Every silent step of his is undone by the obnoxious sound of each filthy carpeted stair. The footsteps upstairs suddenly stop. Halfway up, there is still nothing much to see other than more shredded water stained floral wallpaper. There is a distant light source, probably an upstairs window. Figuring the person upstairs is aware of him, Jake takes a few deep breaths.

"Hey!" he shouts up the stairwell. "Whoever's up there . . ." he lets his words hang in the air like a threat.

There is no sound of movement from the upstairs.

"I'm not a burglar! I just, *we* thought this place was abandoned."

The response from upstairs is more silence. Jake continues up and inhales some thick and horrible tasting air. He wants to gag, but he holds it in. At the top now, he looks up and down the dim hallway. The stink is worse and his eyes begin to water making it even harder for him to see in the dim light. He would try to cover his nose from the offensive stench but his white knuckled grip on his tire iron supersedes his comfort.

The top of the stairwell opens into the middle of a hallway that runs the length of the house. Two doors line each long wall and there is a window at each end of the hall. Where the street facing window on the right is boarded up, the window down the hall on the left has been broken inwards. Shards of window and splintered wood lays spilled in the hallway and the two doors by it are wide open. Jake stairs into the darkness to his right for a moment, then heads the other way to the light of the broken window for want of fresh air more than anything else.

"My car broke down outside of town." Jake times his words in between his movement over the creaking floor, listening for any responses or sounds. "We sure would appreciate any help. I don't have any cash on me, but I can pay."

He sidles up to the wall as he nears the two open doors, when behind him in the darkness at the other end of the hall, a tall figure silently steps out of the room on the left and stops to look at Jake.

Jake looks back and forth into the two rooms trying to see if anyone is in either. Both of the rooms appear empty with the exception of one having a heavily shredded mattress lying propped up on its side. He enters the room on the left and sees an open closet door and that another mattress has been gutted as well. The bad smell lingers but is not emanating from the area although dust has been recently kicked up. Inside the closet there is nothing but scraps of paper and old scattered clothing. Making his way to the room across the hall, Jake stops to look out the broken window. Outside is a straight drop to the backyard. Carefully he places a hand on the busted sill and leans out to look down.

The figure watching him from the dark end of the hall has not moved. Haphazardly sitting in the center of the overgrown yard is a dilapidated rusted boat of a car, empty bottles and other garbage. The car looks like it smashed through the privacy fence from the alley then came to a sudden stop. Assumption's assured Jake begins to wonder how the window could have been broken inwards from the drop.

BANG!

Jake jumps at the sound almost stumbling out of the window. He whips around cringing but cannot see into the darkness. Breathing heavier and scared, he forces his body forwards and thinks only of making it back to the stairwell. Passing the two doors he hears rummaging and breaking sounds coming from the end of the hall and realizes the other person must not be the owner either. Less guilt ridden Jake stands up straight and a bit more relieved.

"Hey buddy, why don't you come out so we can talk?"

The noises stop.

"I don't want trouble, just looking for help," Jake continues peering into the dark.

A loud guttural squeal cracks through the silence followed by another crash and the sounds of the bare feet begin again rushing towards him. Jake's heart comes to a sharp stop. His body locks and time slows down. For a split second, Jake thinks of a time when he and his brother were kids. In the subways, they would dare each other to stand near the edge of the platforms and wait for the coming train with their eyes closed. The rushing wind bringing that particular subway smell and the roaring sounds getting louder and louder. It was unstoppable and terrifying and he wishes he were there now.

As the continuous squealing grows, he manages to look away to the top of the stairwell and dashes towards it although only in his mind. An internal fight on whether to run and jump out of the window behind him or to charge into the darkness swinging rages within. But he can do neither.

As the screaming figure charges at him, the person, crazy or not, bursts from the shadows and his internal battle to fight or flee is lost.

A flood of tears rushes down Jake's bloodless cheeks as he feels his mind give way and snap. Of all the things to see of its shape, of all the details he focuses on one, its face. Its face is upside down.

The sight of the thing that no human being could or should ever have to protect its mind from seeing paralyses him. In that second, his body is assaulted as well. The force of impact from the rushing thing knocks him backwards through the air and hard onto his back where he continues sliding down the hall through broken glass. Jake's tear filled eyes stare blankly at the ceiling. Unable to move his eyes, he can only listen as its heavy steps crunch over the glass as it walks closer. It steps into his view, lumbering over him.

He beholds it again.

This grotesque creature lies on the boundary between the hallucinations of the utterly insane and the kind of mistake a child would make when first attempting to draw a human being. Its eyes, despite having been slapped where the corners of a mouth should be are still uneven. Milky white or filled with puss they are almost on the sides of this thing's head. They do not blink, have no lids and seem to have been mashed into the skin. And the skin, a dark mottled gray, it is shiny and appears greasy or wet. It is wrinkled and twisted like celluloid on an unhealthy person. A sunken cavity is only a slight reminder of where a nose should be and the mouth is the worst of all. Wide and jagged, it appears to have been axed into the creature's head as opposed to some intentional type of organ. The skin around the mouth or the lips, are blackened and crusted. Within the mouth are long and sharp gray teeth. Some are missing with jiggling black exposed nerves hanging from them. The creature is thin and has a grotesquely elongated neck. Its limbs are long as well, all crooked.

It stands over Jake, its twisted upside down face looking at him while vomit like noises spatter from its mouth. Unable to scream or call for help, Jake can only release choking noises of his own in response as he struggles against the paralysis of fear. It slowly squats and curiously looks over him, seemingly with its mouth. Suffocated by its stench Jake can only stare back at the creature, into its horribly wrong visage.

It crouches down more, hovering over his chest and bending far over to look at him closer. It is naked with the exception of a small tattered garment failing to cover the area of its genitalia, although it has none that are apparent. It is wearing various dirty twine necklaces around its crooked neck. Some are nothing more than beaded straps, some strung with teeth, human or animal Jake does not know. But half of them look like they had grown into its skin. Some parts of its wet leathery flesh also have burn marks in them, and what looks like open wounds, that are filled with some kind of filth. Some of its ribs protrude through its skin but not as though from decay. It seems like the ribs grew outwards from its flesh, like an animal trap with the intent to grab something. Lost in his mental turmoil, he stares at it. Its stink is not of rotting flesh but worse. Despite everything he sees, he does not believe this is something dead. This thing is alive, but all wrong. He watches its chest heave up and down, in sync with the low wheezing sounds it is making now.

Its face looms unavoidably over to his, with the short distance of an impending kiss. It breaths, but Jake does not feel or smell its breath. The sounds it makes, it makes when it breaths inwards. It is only inhaling, sucking the air in.

He stares at it hard as his thoughts continue dashing around, trying to understand what he is seeing, if it is real at all. He tries to make a fist but he cannot and he realizes he must have lost his tire iron when he was knocked down. Quietly in his mind the tiniest spark flashes. It is anger. And it starts to show. The creature reacts and brings up its right hand towards Jake's face. Only the first two long fingers and its thumb are spread open. Where those three digits are disproportionately large, its remaining outside fingers are shriveled and seem vestigial. The hand looks birdlike and again the bones of its fingers had burst through the tips and are blackened like sharp claws.

The oversized hand clamps down hard around Jake's neck pressing him into the floor. It throws its head back and screams its pig like scream again by inhaling the air. As it continues wailing, it rises lifting Jake up by his throat like he is a ragdoll. Now suspended above the creature with his head bumping the ceiling he struggles to breath through his crushed throat. The scream winds down and Jake notices something else, from the back of its head a large black feather stands up. Crooked and filthy like the rest of it, the feather looks grafted to its skin, like it grew from the back of its head. The creature shakes him violently then slams him into a wall. A darkness begins outlining Jake's sight and as his vision begins to blur, he realizes he is passing out. He is going to die, no, be murdered by a thing. He tries to resist and manages to gain control of his arms. He uses his anger to drive his quivering limbs up and grabs at its slippery wrist.

This thing . . . what *is* this thing? He thinks as he tries kicking at it.

The creature slams him against the opposite wall and leans towards him making throaty barking noises but Jake keeps trying to push its hand away.

Jake begins completely regaining his senses and he knows he has to get away and to do that he has to fight. He sees the humanoid only has one arm. There is just a stump of mangled and folded skin where its left arm used to be.

Drawing on all the strength and anger he can, he manages to kick at the creature. Briefly stunned it becomes angrier and howls and grunts back at him but Jake just keeps kicking at it. He manages to knock it back and it angrily tosses him away towards the brighter end of the hall. Jake hits the ground and immediately starts scurrying to the window, to the light. When he feels the thing's hand grip him around his ankle, the hope in his eyes vanishes. It drags him back and flips him over with a slap. Jake squirms but it stomps its mangled bare foot into his chest, winding and pinning him. It reaches to its side, and pulls what looks like a weapon from the solitary strap of its worn tunic. Jake had not noticed it before, how could he with the way this thing looked. It is holding what looks like large bone that had been sharpened at one end. It has leather wrapped around the top where it is gripped beneath the wider ball joint section of the bone. The wicked bone is entirely covered with strange dirt filled carvings. It kneels down crushing him with its full weight. The creature stares at him again with its giant mouth, the quivering lips pull away displaying the length of its crooked teeth. The thing raises the bone dagger to its mouth and seems to suckle on the sharp end. A black sticky fluid begins oozing from its mouth and dripping down its own misshapen body.

Jake keeps squirming. He grabs at its leg but cannot get a grip on its rancid and slippery skin. Still gagging as he struggles to hold back his disgust, he tries removing the foot from his chest. The creature drops its knee down onto Jake's jaw twisting his head to the right and locking it at a painful angle. He loses his grip on the leg and begins slapping and kicking away. The creature begins making more sickening sounds in protest, but brings the slime covered dagger closer and lets it hover over his eyes. Jake looks at the wicked dripping tip and growls through his clenched teeth. The creature presses it between the corner of his left eye and his temple and slowly carves a deep path down his cheek.

"You son of a bitch!" he curses at it as he winces from pain.

His cheek feels like it is burning and being ripped. His teary eyes dart around in a panic and he sees the tire iron sticking out from under his back. Fervently he begins struggling more, trying to maneuver it closer to his hand. He can hear the smacking noises from the creature and assumes it is licking the dagger again. He does not look, he cannot take his eyes off the tire iron. He manages to get it to his hand, but suddenly the creature slams its knife down on the floor right in front of him.

I'm done, he thinks to himself.

The creature wraps its hand around Jake's head and turns it to the left pinning it again with its knee. Jake hears the creature pick its dagger up again.

It didn't notice, he realizes and smiles through the pain. He feels the dripping bone dagger making its way over him and with a deep breath, he swings the tire iron solidly connecting with the creature's head.

Black blood from the fresh opened gash on its head sprays against the wall as it flies off him. He continues swinging as he shambles to his feet and it falls back, dropping its dagger.

He does not stop swinging and begins cursing at the thing, as it now tries to get away from him. Even though it is strong and has longer limbs, it struggles with its one arm to get back up. It manages a shove at Jake and knocks him back to the ground. Jake quickly gets back up just as the creature starts to. He realizes he cannot beat whatever this thing is and backs away. He sees the stairwell is behind the creature. He watches as the furious thing grabs its knife and begins to rise. Jake turns around and runs for the window. He wonders if he will break his leg or worse from the fall, but does not care. He has to get away.

With a leap he flies out the broken window into the back yard and crash lands on top of the big old car. Winded, he looks up at the window. He knows he has to keep moving, and tumbles off the car in a daze. He stumbles away from the house towards a broken section of the wooden privacy fence.

Still gripping the bloodied tire iron he feels a burst of energy and takes off wildly down the graveled alley, leaving the screams of the creature far behind.

CHAPTER 4

Jake feels like he has been running for hours, ducking in and out of abandoned homes, listening, even smelling for any sign of what attacked him. He is becoming more and more confused. He had tried several times to get back to the highway but found no way out of the town. He tried going south but somehow got turned around a few times, even though he had started from the town's center. All of the residential streets started looking the same to him. Except for the house he escaped from, that house he would never forget.

Still just as bright out as when he first awakened in his car. He is angry with himself, knowing if he would have known the time he could have walked straight back to the highway. Exhausted from running he tastes blood in his mouth and still shaken, his hunger and thirst is killing him. Not to mention his intense migraines have been coming and going since he escaped, the latest one is only now subsiding.

What he has been thinking of the most, is that thing with the horrible face. For the hours he ran, he tried rationalizing what happened. Something like that cannot be real. But he knows something did happen. He is bruised and cut. A nauseating stink is lingering on him and the whole left side of his face that is not numb is painfully throbbing. Jake looks around and sits down between some cars to catch his breath.

I must have been drugged, he continues trying to make sense of what happened.

Something in the air, something in that dirty water, he only knows for sure he was in a fight. He massages his sore throat and looks around some more only to begin rocking back and forth. He decides that the people all must have left here because of chemicals in the water, and worries that he beat someone down with his tire iron. Jake lifts the iron up to check it for blood. There is none but it is covered with the same black *moss* like substance he saw on the metal pot that shattered. He quickly stands up examining the thing he gripped so tight for hours and just as fast, he drops it to the ground, watching it break into pieces with a clank.

His breathing picks up again and he examines his hand after wiping it off on his jacket. None of the moss is on him, but he notices his hands are darker than before. He crouches down and examines the pieces of tire iron. It is rusted up pretty bad, which it had not been before. He holds a piece of it up in the ever gloomy light of the sky. The black moss appears to have leached from the metal, making it weak and brittle. He has never heard of anything like this happening, rust of course but not this fast and by this means.

He bombards himself with scattered fearful thoughts, of if he is hallucinating or loosing his mind. He wonders if he ever even left his apartment or if he wrecked his car and is in a coma or dead.

Trying not to allow his mind to drown in doubt Jake tries shaking it off and looks around again, not expecting to see anything new. But he does. A one-story house down the block has a few large random tubs on the flat part of its roof. Jake looks all around again and does not see them on any other home. He thinks of how the ground water is shot and how using water catchers would be ideal for fresh uncontaminated water.

Closer to the light blue house, he sees that it is more secured than the other homes. Windows are covered with nailed up doors and other random pieces of wood, which are also scattered around the property. He sees more covered tubs around and hopes they are filled with clean water. The most outstanding feature about this house is that it is covered in crucifixes along its fence and throughout its wild yard. It looks like every cross in the town was brought here. Even a big weathered gold one stands crammed onto the porch that looks like it came from a church altar. And there are not only crucifixes. There are crescent moons with stars, Stars of David, Asian characters and other symbols that Jake has never seen before. If they are not carved, makeshift or from scrap they are painted all over the house in white and grey. Meticulously because not one of them overlaps another.

He walks to the house's crooked reinforced wooden front gate and sees its heavy door is open. He steps into the yard and hears the distinctive racking of a shotgun. Jake freezes. He realizes there is a man sitting on the porch. The man is camouflaged, painted the same faded blue of the house and covered in the religious symbols, but perfectly blended into the wall behind him.

"One more step and it will be the last you take with that foot," he says in a deep grainy voice.

Jake raises his hands. Surprised he scrambles to find appropriate words but only manages to coax a few mumbles from his parched throat.

"Hell did you come from?" the man croaks out, both angry and confused.

Staring at the barrel of the shotgun Jake is speechless and has no idea where to begin explaining the day he has had so far.

"Where?" the man shouts, now shaking and visibly upset.

"Car broke down this morning!" he quickly answers with his hands still out defensively, "been looking for help all day!"

The camouflaged man does not believe him and the two stare at each other.

"Are you alone?" he asks and Jake tenses up, debating if he should lie or not.

"I came here alone, but I met someone else here."

"Oh?" the man leans forward in his camouflaged chair, "and where is he?"

"I don't know. We separated a few hours ago."

"You separated in the dark?" the old man's eyes narrow, causing more of the paint on his face to crack.

"No. It must have been over a few hours ago, earlier today."

The man leans back with his shotgun still carefully trained on Jake. The man is still upset with Jake's sudden appearance, but now he seems confused as well.

"Boy, the sun just came up just an hour ago."

Jake's eyebrows crumple together and with a grimace, his jaw pushes forward. "No. I got here this morning, and I have been looking for help for a while."

The man just stares at him.

"I have been running all over town looking for help, it's been at least an entire day." Jake feels like he is trying to convince himself more than he is trying to convince the religious nut with the shotgun.

The man balances his shotgun on his knee, still aiming at Jake he bites down on his left sleeve and pulls it up his arm. He reveals a series of thirty or more watches running up his arm. Some are plain, others gold and silver.

"Boy, if there is one thing I know for sure, it's what time it is," he says as he brandishes his watch laden arm to Jake.

Jake is once again speechless.

"How did you get here?"

Jake's eyes begin darting back and forth. He has a terrible feeling, like there is something very important that he has forgotten. Something is just missing. And there is another thing he cannot place, that should make sense but it has been eluding him since he arrived.

How *did* I get here, he asks himself.

A fear sends shivers through his racing heart. It is a different fear than from when he was attacked by that thing, this is deeper.

"I," Jake stutters out. "I fell asleep driving and—"

"Bullshit!" the man shouts and rises from his matching camouflaged chair.

"I don't remember!" Jake shouts back in defeat.

"Last time I'm gonna ask, where did you come from?"

"Back East! I was heading west and some asshole ran me off the road!" Jake pleads as he slowly drops to his knees.

"I'm so sorry boy, but bad things have been going on. I don't

48

think you came from anywhere but here." With that, the man begins raising the sites of his gun and looking through them.

Does this guy think I am one of those crazies from the store, his thoughts race. "What? No wait! I can prove it!"

Not listening, the man takes in a deep breath, sternness and sorrow looms on his face.

"Check my wallet!"

The man stops but keeps his aim, "Throw it over here."

"I have to get it from my coat pocket," and Jake slightly moves his raised hands.

The man sneers, "Slowly."

Shaking he slowly fumbles for his wallet and tosses it over by the man's feet.

Keeping his aim he bends down and flicks it open examining it and looks at Jake to verify. Satisfied the man sighs with relief. He looks up and down the street, long and hard.

"You can get up man. I think you should come inside for a bit."

Jake's arms slump to his sides in deep relief and the man lowers his gun.

"You look sick, are you alright?"

"Yeah," Jake replies. Clean water and that gun being the only reason he would think of going anywhere with this guy. Jake takes a step towards the yard.

"Wait!" the man says, and tosses Jake's wallet back where it falls short into the tall grass.

Wachinkt!

Jake hops back surprised and sees that his wallet triggered a rusty bear trap that was hidden in the grass.

He looks up at the camouflaged man who seems more concerned for the trap.

"I'll get it when I reset that trap later, come inside for now."

Jake examines the lawn carefully and sees more traps hidden throughout the yard.

"Walk left in a half circle, towards the side of the porch."

Jake hesitates but begins making his way in.

"Keep left to those sets of hexagrams there and you'll avoid the other traps."

Jake looks from the man to the myriad of different symbols in the yard, confused.

"The Jewish stars, keep left of those there, walk around them and those red flowers to the side of the porch," he makes an arcing motion with his gun. "Then climb over the banister to get on the porch. The stairs are rigged too."

Jake does as he is instructed and makes his way through until he becomes face to face with the strange camouflaged man.

* * *

The inside of the house is even more chaotic than the outside. Religious symbols cover the walls and ceiling both drawn on surfaces and as physical objects. They hang from the ceilings and other furniture, mostly makeshift as well. Woven in between the symbols are unlit candles of different colors melted over one another. The house is sunken in and uneven in some parts, so much that a large beam of wood is angled through the center of the living room. It is apparently holding the crooked structure up. It is also just a bit warmer inside the house than it is outside.

Other than the more notable odd things the place looks like a crazy yard sale. However, everything is extremely organized and densely packed. The man bolts the dozens of locks on the front door and finishes by heaving a huge crucifix against it, which he uses to bar it.

"Have a seat," The breathless man says. He gestures to a set of large wooden cable spools that would make more sense on a construction site than in a house. The middle one is turned on its side and is apparently meant to serve as a table, while the other two have blankets and such strapped to the center spool sections.

Jake sits in one, his feet barely touch the floor and despite the events of the day, he relaxes.

Jake gets a better look at strange man as he begins, ritualistically taking his camouflaged clothes off and hanging them up. The man's paint disguise is so well done, that Jake had not realized he is wearing a bandana and gloves. He can see the man is taller than him but skinner. Jake could tell before by the man's voice and features that he is black but he cannot tell his age. He assumes by the way the man speaks and his demeanor that he is at least twice his age.

The man turns around and looks at Jake, then looks around his home and pauses as if he was about to say something. He walks away into a kitchen and returns with a pitcher of water and a tall empty glass. He fills the glass with water before handing it to Jake.

"Thank you," Jake says as he carefully examines the water. Both the water and the glass are immaculate and he thirstily guzzles it down.

He places the pitcher on the spool table near Jake then takes a seat on the cable spool. Jake nods in thanks again to the man and begins downing the second glass of cool delicious water. The man does not say anything else as he sits in his chair watching him. As tall as he is his feet could easily touch the floor, but instead he has his booted feet up close to him, the bottoms flat against the curve of the chair. He perches there leaning his arms on his knees, now with a rifle in his lap instead of his shotgun. The sound of the thirty plus watches on his arm ticks away loudly in unison. The man soaks in the situation, contemplative and a bit excited. It is hard to tell with his face still covered in the paint and symbols.

"Sam," he says after a few minutes.

"Nice to meet you, I'm Jake."

"I know," Sam says, calmly staring at the front door.

After another few moments, he turns to Jake, "Memory still fuzzy?"

"It's not so much fuzzy as much as . . ." Jake trails off lost in his disjointed thoughts again.

"Looks like you got banged up pretty good. Did you wreck your car too?"

"No, I was hit by a tow truck," Jake sits up, "have you seen one anywhere?"

"I don't leave my property much. And I haven't seen one," he replies.

"My car will run, but it needs a new battery."

"That's not good."

"You don't have a ride?" he leans toward Sam.

"Not for a while. And finding a way to jump a car ain't gonna be easy."

"I know," Jake sighs, "there's no power here, and most of the electric stuff is hosed."

"You sure figured out plenty for someone who just got here this morning."

Jake realizes that Sam is still interrogating him.

"I said before man, I have been here almost all day."

"Yeah, that doesn't explain why in the hell you seemed to have missed last night, or maybe even a couple of nights."

"I don't know either. I do know something is up with this place."

Sam silently polishes the long bayonet mounted on his rifle.

Jake has so many questions shuffling around in his head, but he hesitates, and tries to ask the right ones.

"Anyone else live here besides you?"

"Yes," Sam replies without looking up. "But nobody you would want to meet and definitely no one who could help you with your car."

"Why do you still live here?"

"I lived here most of my life, so did my family. I stay here because . . . close to their memories is where I want to be."

"What's with all the crosses?"

Sam's eyes dart up to look at Jake. "Look boy, I know how this looks. Let's just say, this is what I do."

"Which is?"

Sam looks at him with a slight agitation showing through his camouflage.

"Jake. This how we are going to go about this," he flexes his head from left to right, "and I will have no missteps in how this is done. Are you with me?"

Jake nods apprehensively.

"There are things *I* do not talk about. Which makes them things *we* will not talk about, especially in my home. I do what I do for my reasons and these reasons, I will not explain. Ok?"

"Yeah." Jake replies not trying to suppress his discomfort.

"Good. There's a bathroom down the hall, you can wash up in

there, and hopefully get all that oil and stink off of yourself."

Jake knows that Sam does not mean that as an insult, but he knows what stink he is talking about and understands.

"There's no running water of course, but I'm sure you can figure out the set up I have in there. When you're done, I'll take a look at that cut on your face."

On his way to the bathroom, Jake sees that a shrine of sorts has been set up inside a nook in the hallway. More candles sit wedged in between an array of pictures. Staring at a picture of a young soldier with a sad smile standing in front of a muddy river, Jake sees what must be Sam's real face for the first time.

Many of the pictures are family photos, but most are of other people and their families. Jake even recognizes some of the locations he had been from the pictures despite their ruined states now. It seems like everyone got along great back then, like there was a strong sense of community. So much more than in places nowadays. There are quite a few pictures of very beautiful women too, but the fewest of the images are of Sam himself.

"Which war was this?"

Sam wanders over and manages a smile, "So you found my little piece of heaven."

"Yeah. Looks like really good times back then," Jake says as he taps on a square instant film print. In the picture there is a group people in front of an antique mirror, leaning over a lit birthday cake and smiling up at the camera. Standing out in the group are a few attractive young women who are holding the cake, and angling the top toward the camera.

The cake reads, 'HAPPY 20th Sam!!!'

"Yeah, there sure were some beauties around back then," Sam says with a reminiscent smile, which looks eerie with his paint still on.

"If this was your birthday, where were you?" Jake asks.

"Here," Sam taps the sad photo of himself standing next to a helicopter, "in 'Nam."

"Those silly girls did that for three years straight bless their hearts. It helped remind me that I had somewhere good to get back to."

"What is this, Thanksgiving?" Jake points to another picture.

"No," he says coldly.

"No what? Everyone's done up kinda like a pilgrim, even your folks."

Sam stares at the photo with a grimace for a few seconds.

"This was a local holiday. A once a year thing I don't remember what it was about."

He walks away from the pictures and Jake takes that as his cue to proceed to the bathroom. Other than being brighter, the bathroom is no different than the rest of the house. Sam has some type of camping shower set up inside it, using an elevated water filled barrel. The water is cold but it is clean and feels great. The mirror has drawings of religious symbols on it, and when Jake looks into it, he understands how Sam gets the camouflage on his face to match up just right with the house. The symbols on the mirror overlay on Jake's reflection in just the right places.

Jake examines the cut and reluctantly it does not look nearly as painful as it feels. In fact, a scab had formed in a clean thin line the length of the cut even though the skin around it appears inflamed. It looks to be the length that it felt when it was carved into him though. It runs from the corner of his left eye, arcing back and down to the corner of his mouth. He presses against it and feels that the cut runs deep. Jake sees his hands are even blacker and he scrubs them vigorously with what he surmises is a homemade soap solution in a coffee can.

Nothing happens. Whatever this stuff is, it will not rub off his hands.

"Are you hungry?" Sam's asks through the door.

"Yeah sure," Jake replies.

And with that, the bathroom door locks.

"Hey man! What the hell?" Jake tries and fails to open the door.

"I'll let you out when you're finished, call me but don't yell," Sam's voice fades as he walks away. "Heading out to reset the trap and to get your wallet. I don't want you messing with my shit."

Frustrated Jake slams his fists into the old porcelain sink, wriggling it from the wall. He does not like being at the mercy or kindness of strangers. Nothing about anything that has been happening to him has made any sense. He looks up into the mirror, struggling internally.

In his mind, he tries to connect the random dots of what has been happening to him and every time he comes close, it is like his thoughts unravel again.

Getting attacked on the road, the state of the town and the weirdos living in it! Was any of it real? The black moss and that *thing*! That damned thing that tried to carve my face up.

The strain of thinking shoots a pain through his head again, sending him to his knees. After catching his breath, he stares blankly around the tidy but old bathroom until the pain in his skull subsides. He gets up to look in the mirror again and inspects the part of his head that went through his window when the tow truck struck him. He shakes away more crumbles of glass and finds what he guesses is a split bruise beneath his blood stained hair.

Maybe it's all just a concussion, he thinks to himself.

Hours later, a cleaner Jake stands on the enclosed back porch to Sam's house. The rear matches the rest of the house, as does the back yard mirror the front. Especially as far as the condensed cemetery's worth of symbols of faith. Rifle in his lap Sam sits with his back facing the house stirring a can of beans, which he is heating up over a hobo stove. As he cooks, Sam recounts a few stories from his days in the war and what his function there was. He is excited, as if he had never had a chance to tell anyone his war stories before. Jake does not mind at all, he always enjoyed listening to people tell stories about interesting things that really happened in their lives. He wraps up the tale of his last adventure and adds more bits of wood inside his stove to keep the small fire strong.

"I normally only cook at night, but its not often that I have a guest," he leans back against the house smiling. Once again blending into the house with his camo.

"Why only at night?"

"Because the nights here are safer."

"This place is safer at night than during the day?" he yells in disbelief.

"Keep your voice down."

The wonder of why Sam goes through so many precautions the way he does baffles him. To be invisible, and protected from something with these symbols and the guns. Only to not want to speak a single word of it. If it was not him hitting his head, then it must be something in the water that is affecting them both. Making them see things. But Sam does not drink the ground water. As far as the person or thing that had attacked him, he definitely wanted to ask Sam about it. But he is sure it is one of those things that would set him off. The thing he could not ask about but both of them may be fully aware of.

The many unaskable questions lead Jake to ask one thing, related but not, that would be permissible to speak about under Sam's strange rule.

"Hey Sam, can I have one of your guns?"

"No," he replies with a chuckle at the ridiculousness of the request." How do I know, you won't shoot me after I give you one?"

"I wouldn't, I have no reason to."

Sam replies only with a slight shrug.

"I could pay you for it, I'm gonna pay you for helping me out anyways."

"And what would I do with your money? Take it down to the Forks, watch a few movies and go for some ice cream?" Sam teases and goes back to stirring the beans.

"The Forks?"

"Downtown. You missed that with all the running around you said you did?" jokingly, he gestures north.

"I did see that, I didn't know it was called the Forks though. Why not just call it downtown?"

"That's what it was always called. Wait you got that far? Shit, I'm impressed." Sam catches himself from speaking further, instead focuses on the perimeter with a seriousness.

Jake looks around and sees nothing, "Why is that impressive?"

"Here, yours are done," Sam says as he scoots the hot can of beans over to Jake. "Let's eat these inside."

Back in the house, the two are on the spool chairs again enjoying the meal.

"These are great Sam, thanks again."

"They're just beans man, save the parade."

Jake pauses and stares at the beans, "How are these beans still good?"

"I have them delivered," he states and continues scarfing them down.

"What?" Jake jerks up. "How often does the delivery guy come here?"

Sam just shakes his head, "Four times a year and you missed him by two weeks."

"Damn!" Jake slumps back down. "Do you call him?"

"No. I have an arrangement."

"Then why do you have them just bring beans?"

"Hell is wrong with beans?"

"Nothing."

"I have different things to eat. I just felt like having these today."

"Sorry I didn't mean anything by it. It's just that this place is so cut off from the world."

"I see what you're saying, kid. Let's take a look at that cut."

Sam stands over Jake and inspects it for a few moments.

"Looks like it might be infected Jake."

"It feels that way. Want to know how I got it?" Jake looks up at Sam, for a reaction.

Without skipping a beat, Sam responds, "Not really. I do wish I had some alcohol to sterilize this."

"Hey, I know where some old liquor is."

"How so?" Sam says as he steps back from him, still not comfortable with Jake's sudden movements.

"Yeah, it was strange. In one of the stores, it was all cleared out, except someone placed cartons of cigarettes and booze under the register."

"Oh, that was me," Sam says excitedly.

"What?"

"That was years ago, so long ago I forgot where I left it," he crosses his arms. "I could have used that last winter."

"Why did you leave it there?"

"I don't indulge in smokes and liquor. So I left it there incase anyone else needed it."

"Oh."

"Well, where is it at?"

"It was," Jake strains to remember, "east of the Forks, first intersection."

Sam snaps his fingers, "That's right! I left it at Chuck's."

Jake stairs at the milky sky through the narrow gaps in the boarded up windows.

"I have to leave soon."

"You should stay until after dark, it's safer," Sam cautions.

"But how will I make my way through the dark? My flashlight died the moment I got here."

"I just think it would be better if you waited until dark."

"Sam, how many people are still in this town?"

"Why do you care? I thought you wanted to get out."

"I don't know. The only *people* I have run into are you and that guy from earlier."

Sam ignores Jake's stressing of the word, people. "Besides myself, one, maybe two others," Sam nonchalantly seems to guess, "I haven't seen wither of them in years. And what about your friend, any idea where he went?"

"He's not my friend. He said he had lost touch with some family here and arrived earlier today."

"I don't believe there would be anyone else still coming here for anybody."

"Well," Jake shrugs, "he is here for something. Tell me what happened here Sam, why is this place like this?"

He glares at Jake for a long hard minute, then looks away. He tilts his head back and with his watch laden arm reaches up and pulls a rosary out from under his shirt while he stares at the ceiling. Jake had not had a chance to notice before but Sam has a myriad of necklaces around his neck besides the rosary. No doubt each of them attached to a religious pendant as well, but Jake cannot tell. Sam takes a long deep breath then sits down only to slouch over.

"The people here always kept to themselves. The town itself had a basically troubled past. But they moved on. Found a lot of oil one day. And that's when my family showed up. There were more jobs here than there were people and my great grandfather was one of the best drilling engineers in the region."

"So where did everyone go, did the oil dry up and everyone just left?"

"That's exactly what happened Jake," Sam says with a dangerous finality.

For what feels like an hour to Jake after Sam's last statement the only sound in the gloomy living room is the ticking of Sam's watches.

"Well," Sam says examining those watches, "it's almost noon."

Jake stares up at the strange old man. "Yeah, thanks again for everything man, I appreciate it."

"I enjoyed the company too, kid," he says as they both stand up from their spool seats.

"I guess I'll just go out on the road I came in on."

"Which road was that?"

"The south road, south of the Fork," Jake says with a grin.

"Well, the west road will get you closer to the highway, there's less forest there."

"Really?"

"Yeah, you didn't see all the oil derricks?"

"No, actually."

"I guess your best bet will be to stick with the way you went before, seems like that was the luckiest for you."

"Ok, I probably won't be seeing you again," Jake reaches his hand out to shake Sam's, but Sam just stares at Jake's soot covered hand.

"Yeah I know," Jake says. "I don't know what I touched, but it won't wash off," he says, slightly embarrassed but still keeps his hand out.

"No problem Jake," and Sam gives his hand a good solid shake. "Hey, you know what, take this."

Sam removes one of the watches from his arms, "For good luck. Besides you seem to need help telling what time it is."

"Wow, Sam I don't know if I can."

"Just take it kid, its okay. I knew all the owners."

He is surprised by his strange statement and Sam notices.

Jake begins to mouth another question but he quickly manages to relax instead and smile.

Sam plays his misstep off as well, "Remember to walk in that half circle to avoid the traps," he tosses him back his wallet.

"Sure thing," Jake replies and makes his way through the front yard.

As he does, he wonders for a moment if he would be feeling a bullet in his back but quickly dismisses the thought. Sam had helped him out a lot and it didn't matter where he got those watches. Jake was just upset that he couldn't learn more about the madness here but it didn't matter right now, he was getting out of this place. After making it through the front yard he turns back to wave goodbye but Sam is already invisible again, camouflaged. Jake waves anyway then rapidly makes his way, south of the Fork.

* * *

It was not long before panic began stirring in Jake's mind. Outside again in the cold his thoughts still try to clarify the strange things that have happened. An unshakable eerie feeling of being watched permeates him further and hastens him along. In the distance he sees his car. He crouches down at the base of one of the thicker birch trees lining the road and observes his surroundings for a bit. He thinks about how helpless he would be regardless if anything like that shadow were to come barreling towards him across the open fields.

What a horrific sight that would be he thinks, still clueless as to how he outran it to begin with. Regardless, he now knows a simple hike will return him to the highway. Scurrying from tree to tree, he returns to his car and slows to examine it. Rust has begun eating away at it that was not there before.

"Impossible," Jake utters the words out loud and cautiously continues passing by it.

The majority of the corrosion is centered around the hood of the car, which has been popped up. Jake looks around again and lifts the hood then stares down in shock. The entire engine is rusted through to the point that it looks more like a pile of dirt sitting inside the chassis. That, and more of that black mold is all he can see. Jake jumps back accidentally allowing the hood to slam down, and send echoes throughout the empty gloom of the fields. The dark willows motionlessly stand there as witnesses to another in a long line of bizarre events since he awakened at this very spot. His panic returns in full and he begins racing south down the road, and hopefully out of the town forever.

At least half an hour into the woods and breathing hard, Jake presses on switching between running and speed walking while he catches his breath. There are no sounds of animals or insects coming from the forest but there are random and close sounds of crunching leaves and breaking twigs, which keep him from calming down.

A short distance away he sees a large broken gate standing over the road. He vaguely remembers this from the night he passed through them behind the rabid tow truck. Relief washes over him as he speeds to the gate. Closer now, he sees a wooden pillar standing off to the left of the gate. At least three stories tall it does not sway in cold gusts and stands planted firm in its rocky base. The base is stained with red and forms a ring around the pillar. Inside the ring of the base is a dip in the center like a fountain and apparently is where a red dye pooled at one time. It is dry and looking closer Jake sees it is not blood, as it is still a very deep red. The pillar itself is carved from base to tip with animal and human faces, one stacked upon the other. Jake knows this is some type of totem pole even though he has never seen one with his own eyes. This one looks more simple than the elaborate ones he has seen in pictures and films. Its darkness contrasts with the pale sky and against the dull trees behind it. He stares at the faces longer and an ominous feeling presses against him. He struggles to look away. He forces his attention back to the base and kneels down to inspect the curious stained rocks again.

He reaches his hand out to pick one up and feels heat coming from it. He pulls his hand away, then returns it near the rocks to make sure and the same thing happens again. There is no sign of a fire, recent or old having ever been there. Staring back at the totem pole Jake remembers the thing that assaulted him earlier. The details of the thing that remained from the encounter had blurred, with the exception of its stench and that face. He thinks back and tries focusing harder. Vague details come to him, something on its head or its clothes.

Could it have been an Indian? Someone pretending to be an Indian, or was it one before it became that thing? Unless it is some crazy bumpkin in a mask, it and this totem might have something to do with each other.

Jake stares blankly up at the totem but whatever connection there is to the weirdness he does not believe that he is the one to figure it out.

Snap!

A branch breaks somewhere nearby and sends him speeding south again. Through the gate, his rush of fear is interrupted by dizziness. He stumbles nearly diving headfirst into a tree but catches himself and keeps running. He glances around as his knees weaken and his hands begin to shake. Another *snap* from around him and he forces himself into an awkward sprint. He bounds down the crumbling road and sees a few mobile homes and trailers scattered within the edge of the forest. They look as uninhabited as the homes back in the town. One of them may be a good place to hide long enough to catch his breath again. Jake passes and stays on the path a little while longer, hoping the highway is not far. His heavy breathing worries him and the pain in his head worsens. He comes across a once burgundy house and falls back against it. He looks around the corner of the house down the road and sees a complete town laid out before him. Jake just stares catching his breath, he had not noticed this the night he was attacked on the road. He quickly looks back to the worn road and the forest, but it is all gone and replaced by more decrepit houses. Hopelessly confused, he looks back and forth down the road and creeps to the center.

"What the fuck?" the words escape from between his gasps for breath.

The town is old and abandoned, but Jake recognizes it, because it is the town he just left. He sits down looking around in disbelief, again. His grip on reality weakening even more and he returns to doubting whether he is here or not, sane or not, living or not. He does not bother trying to make sense of anything. It has been too much. So many unexplained and terrifying things have come up for him to handle. He is tired of events and questions that confront him at every turn. The hours slowly pass by again, but he remains motionless as he stares up at the unchanging pale sky.

He guesses that this is how he has been spending his lost days. Leaving the town repeatedly only to walk back into it. But his hopelessness is finite, as it has been his entire life. And whether he is aware or not, his despair has always been conquered by one thing. Fortunately for Jake the signs of that one thing begins to show. He tightens up, his breaths deepen and become healthy as his anger rises.

Jake's only goal is to leave town, but with all of these bizarre things working against him, he obviously cannot. He doesn't care about the details or how they fit together, he just wants out. And to do that he needs answers, strait answers. So far, there is only one place he knows to get them. Sam is going to answer these questions regardless of his rules or fears. Determined, Jake picks himself up and begins walking towards Sam's house. He feels no need to run because apparently, time here is relative.

Because so many of the street signs have rusted away, Jake has to return to the Forks to make his way back to Sam's house. Only a few minutes away he hears laughter in the distance. He spots a man walking towards him from one of the alleys a few dozen houses down. Jake tenses up but he forces his boiling temper to a simmer.

"Hey buddy!" the man shouts. "Where've you been?"

Jake stares at the shady figure through the gloom and sees a familiar shit-eating grin on Kenneth's face. Thinking of his little joke giving him that contaminated water makes Jake angrier and he begins moving towards Kenneth with intent. Closer now Jake sees Kenneth has become dirtier than before, and a slick muck covers his legs up to his knees.

"I thought you were going to stay at the house?" Kenneth asks, still grinning.

"Son of a bitch!" Jake responds grabbing Kenneth's collar and shoving him to the ground.

Kenneth sits there on his ass oblivious to Jake's affront, still smiling.

"What's gotten into you?" he leers up at Jake from under the brim of his hat.

"Drop your shit! You know what you did making me drink that dirty fucking water!"

"I didn't make you drink anything," he replies coldly, but still smiling. "All I did was give you some water man."

"I saw the pot of that nasty water!"

"What are you talking about? I told you I gave you water from the well, not from a pot."

Jake thinks back trying to remember if he saw a well at anytime in the yard but quickly refocuses on Kenneth. "And why did you attack me?" Jake angrily points towards the cut on his face.

"I attacked you?" Kenneth's smile wavers for a moment as he pulls himself up to his feet.

Jake's anger wanes and he hesitates from blurting anything out, as he is unsure of how to accuse Kenneth of something so inexplicable.

"Let me see," Kenneth steps forward and uncomfortably clasps his hand under Jake's chin, to which Jake responds by batting his arm away.

"Easy there Jake," he steps back poorly feigning innocence and concern.

"Here!" Kenneth quickly lobs an object into Jake's stomach, winding him and allowing him to realize that Kenneth is a lot stronger than he appears.

Jake clasps his hands around the painful object and sees it is his backpack. He thinks the bottle inside must have banged right into his ribs.

"You left that back in the house. I'm going to take you back there so you can see the well."

"I don't think so."

Kenneth chuckles as he adjusts his hat and layered collars, "So I poisoned you with some stink water, then prettied your face up with a knife, why?"

Unable to come up with a good answer Jake just glares back at him. He cannot put a finger on it but everything about Kenneth gives him a bad feeling. In fact, he is much more like the opposite of camouflaged Sam in many ways. But both of them are hiding things from him about this place.

"Just stay the hell away from me man."

Kenneth watches Jake back away and casually lights a cigarette, "Where do you think you're going?"

"Don't worry about it. You just keep doing whatever the hell you were doing and I'll be on my way," Jake replies while turning away. He needs some answers but realizes that nothing true or helpful will ever come spilling out of Kenneth's crooked mouth. His distrust for Kenneth makes him decide not to head directly to Sam's house. He looks back again and sees Kenneth is still just standing there smoking. He thinks again if he really had been poisoned by him.

Why go through all the trouble just to slash me up with a knife?

Jake keeps marching away as his own logic falls apart then he realizes, why would Kenneth assume the water was poisoned and how did he know his face was cut with a knife?

Jake spins about and Kenneth is gone except for his lingering cigarette smoke. Having made a few crooked cuts around the neighborhood Jake decides to head around the back of Sam's house to be extra cautious. A few steps through the alley and Jake doubles over in pain. He grunts through his tightened jaw and clamps his hands over his head pressing inwards. The pain in his head is back, abrupt and worse than ever. He feels like a giant white-hot nail has just been hammered into his forehead. The humming noise becomes louder and he can think of nothing else but the intense pain. He issues a pitiful croak of a scream through his quivering jaw and falls down, thrashing in the gravel and dirt like a dying rat. The pain spreads to his eyes and with the pain comes an intense light. Fighting back the pain and blindness, Jake gets up and stumbles towards Sam's house. Desperately struggling forward he has forgotten that he has no idea how to move around the traps in the backyard. It was too late. Jake was falling forward into the yard. The sensation of falling and falling fast comes over him. Until he is swallowed by the pain and blinding light.

CHAPTER 5

In the darkness the pain is gone. From his mind and everywhere else that was aching. The cold is gone and well replaced by a hot wind that blows over him. There is a soft sweetness in the air and Jake feels like he is waking up from a long sleep, unable to remember a time before when he felt so comfortable. Jake opens his eyes and groggily stares around to see stars shining in the night sky.

"It's night?" he mutters.

He smiles and realizes he is in a well-lit garden and lying on his side. Yawning he tries to roll over and stretch, but he can't. Something is binding his wrists. He hears voices from behind him and squirms to roll over. Above him stands an older black couple. The man casually holds a shotgun while his wife stares down noticing that Jake has regained consciousness. The older man is talking to a cop and both men stop talking to turn and look down at Jake once she has their attention. The cop beams his flashlight into Jake's eyes stinging them. He walks over to kneel down by him.

"Well, good evening sir. You mind telling me what you're doing on these folks' property?" the cop asks in a humorous tone.

"Its night," Jake mumbles again, still trying to sit up.

He grabs Jake by the back of his neck and pulls him upright,

67

"That's right, its night time! Do you know this man had every right to shoot you for trespassing?"

Jake tries squinting past the blazing flashlight. "Huwhut? No. I wasn't breaking . . . Sam."

"What did he say?" the gravelly voiced old man steps in closer to Jake.

"Something about Sam?" the cop says.

The older couple begins a heated and hushed conversation with each other.

"How did you get here?" the cop asks while shaking the still groggy Jake up.

"The Forks."

"No shit smartass where did you come from?" the cops pale gray eyes beam at him.

He drunkenly rolls his eyes around some more, "Car troubles, was looking for Sam just now."

"Come on," the cop maneuvers Jake to the alley to his squad car and throws him in the back.

Jake stares around the inside and becomes startled as he wakes completely up. He does not know where he is or how he arrived. He watches the cop return to the older couple and speak with them a few minutes before he returns to the car and begins driving away.

"Hey, am I under arrest?"

The cop ignores him and keeps driving.

"Why am I handcuffed?"

After a few minutes of the silent treatment, Jake sits back and just stares out the window listening to the mundane cross chatter on the cop's old-fashioned radio. Jake knows what to do in situations like this, his brother is a cop after all. He knows he is not under arrest, yet. So all he has to do for now is be polite and figure out how he ended up in this town. More importantly, he wants to know how he got out of the other. He sees this is yet another smaller town, but this one is at least alive. It seems like the sun has just gone down because people are still bustling about. They slow down by a concrete building that is painted a faint lime green color. The cop pulls into one of two street facing garage doors and parks next to an old model fire truck.

Inside, a grizzled old firefighter with a dirty shirt sits on a milk crate reading a newspaper and smoking a thick cigar. He looks up to scowl at Jake then back to his paper. When the cop takes Jake out of the back, he sees that the old squad car even has the bucket style light on top. He is led through a grimy and beaten set of glass double doors and down a long yellow hallway to a cell. The cell door is slammed behind him. The cop removes the cuffs through the bars and walks to his enclosed office, not ten feet away from the cell. Jake remains silent and tries to appear calm while looking around. Flakes of the creamy yellow paint are chipped away from the bars of his cell. It has a small cot that does not seem to have been used in a while. The only other cell he can see looks like it is used for storage more than anything else.

Another much older and rounder cop, a sheriff enters the building, pauses and stares at Jake for an awkwardly long time. The man is wearing the same tan and brown short-sleeved uniform as the deputy that brought him there, except he wears a large white sheriff style hat. The two men talk to each other while periodically looking over at Jake. The younger of the two, the man who brought him in, appears to be in his forties and is on the phone. He seems to be getting frustrated and hands the phone off to the sheriff, exits the office then stomps towards Jake's cell.

"Take off your shoes!" he barks at Jake.

Confused by the strange request he replies with a shrug, "Am I under arrest officer?"

The cop tiredly sighs trying to calm himself and steps up to the bars, "Just give me your shoes."

Jake debates rebuffing the cop and repeating his question with a matched sternness of his own, but he sits down on the cot and reluctantly complies. He removes his shoes and pushes them through the bars.

The cop picks them up, "Let me see your feet."

Jake leans back and casts a questionable look, then raises his feet up to the cop. Satisfied the cop walks away with his shoes, halts and looks curiously closer at them then keeps walking.

Jake stands up and grabs at the bars, "Hey, I'm not suicidal!" he shouts, but is again ignored.

Alone in his cell again, Jake leans his head forward against the coolness of the bars and tries to retrace his steps. He has no idea how he managed to get out of that weird town or end up on that couple's porch. He worries about what the two cops are discussing about him in there. But he has done nothing wrong, as far as he can remember. The bad feeling in the back of his mind starts up again.

A door opens and Jake looks up to see a girl stepping into the building. She is in her late teens, with long brown hair spilling out from an ornate red headscarf and she looks good. Jake slowly lifts his head while staring her up and down and she in turn, notices him. She was heading to the cop's office but she changes her direction and heads towards Jake. She is wearing a red blouse that hangs loosely off her shoulders and a very short denim miniskirt. Her suede knee-high boots have tassels hanging from the tops and around her neck and wrists, she has various beaded jewelry jiggling around. She actually looks like a hippie to Jake, an extremely beautiful one. Everything about what she wears accentuates her finely developed body and bounces with her every step towards him. He is helplessly mesmerized, trapped in her big warm smile.

"You must be the stoned guy they found at the Dixon house, huh?" Her voice is loud and melodious at the same time.

Jake stares into her large hazel eyes. She is almost as tall as him and not that she needs to, she is barely wearing any makeup with the exception of her dark red lipstick.

"I guess you're still high," she laughs.

Back to reality and remembering he is in a cell Jake stutters in response, "Uh, I don't do drugs," he says defensively.

"So why were you passing out in people's backyards?" she smiles.

"I didn't. And how do you know where I was?"

She throws her head back and laughs, truly amused by Jake's poor situation.

"Small town. So, how'd you end up in the yard?"

Slightly irrigated Jake shrugs, "I had been travelling a while and just got tired I guess."

"Oh, you poor thing!" she teases then leans close. "You don't happen to have anymore doobies hidden anywhere you do you?"

"What? I said I wasn't smoking," he grins. "But I did have some whisky on me."

"I can dig that," she gets excited, "and where's the booze now, did the fuzz take it?"

"Actually, I don't know. It was in my bag but I didn't see that cop with it."

Jake realizes her hands are on the cell bars near his. She is so close he could kiss her through the bars.

"That's groovy, maybe I'll have to take a look around," she keeps flirting.

"Maybe you should," Jake flirts back.

He cannot believe how close she is to him. There is nothing she could know about him, other than he is the type of person to end up in a cell. She appears to be attracted to the entire situation and appears to be the fearless type of bad girl that Jake had always been hopelessly drawn to. And she is so beautiful too. He pauses admiring her as she smiles back at him. Her skin is smooth and does not even seem to crease around her big bright smile. She is white, or mostly Jake thinks. She seems exotic in a way, something about her and her features are just different. Her skin is fair, but there is something else. She has a tint, but unlike a tan, it appears to be a very light shade of gray.

Jake does not know why, but he has a sudden urgency about his situation.

"Hey, what town is—?"

"Sophie!" the two cops exit their office and the younger one keeps shouting. "In the office!" He rigidly points to the office door with Jake's shoes in hand.

The girl, Sophie pulls herself away and starts walking to the office in an intentionally sexy way.

"Now!"

She jumps to attention and scrambles into the office.

The older cop pulls a stool up next to the cell and sits down facing Jake with his wallet in his hand.

"I'm Sheriff Yates if you didn't know and this is one of my

deputies who runs things locally in town, Harris. As I am assuming he did not introduce himself."

Unconcerned with their names and titles Jake stares at his wallet, mentally kicking himself for not having realized he did not have it on him.

The Sheriff leans forward, a straight but curious look in his eyes. "Well Mr. Walker, it appears you may have us at a disadvantage."

He opens Jake's wallet and pulls out his driver's license to hold it up comparing it to Jake for a moment before handing it and his wallet over to him.

"Could you explain to us what this is?"

Jake stares at his driver's license and matter-of-factly answers, "My driver's license."

"I told you he was a smart ass!" Harris barks and rests his hands on his belt.

The sheriff motions a calming hand towards the deputy his gaze not wavering from Jake.

Jake looks at both men, his eyebrow raised, "What do you want me to say? That's what this is."

"Well, we figured that," the sheriff points at the card. "Those colored reflective patterns on the front and the black lines on the back, what are those?"

Jake looks closer at his driver's license and flips it over a few times, "What? You mean the holograms and the bar codes?"

The two men look at each other and Deputy Harris shrugs.

"A holo-what?" the sheriff leans back on the stool, and removes his hat revealing a balding ring of white hair, which he scratches in confusion.

"The holograms," Jake says turning his driver's license in the light. "So they can't be faked."

Jake becomes nervous about their specific line of questions and that the two veteran cops look more confused than he is.

It is then that Jake takes a good look at the deputy's uniform. The black patch on his shoulder has a simple yellow type at the top that reads, 'ROOKSVILLE COUNTY' with what looks like the image of an eagle's claw in the center. Jake's eyes drift down and lock onto a supplemental patch below it that simply reads, 'PRUDENCE'.

The blood drains from Jake's face with a stinging slap of coldness as he becomes physically petrified, whereas his mind floods with hundreds of colliding and half-formed thoughts. Overwhelmed he pitifully tries to make sense of at least one thing, but he cannot. The cops notice his sudden change and call out to him, but to Jake their voices trail off and are replaced by a loud painful hum as his mind checks out.

I'm really dead, he thinks. I was right when the tow truck hit me. I'm in hell! But why would this be his hell? If this is Prudence now, where the hell was I before, he frantically tries to think straight.

The lights go out along with the warmth. He finds himself still in the cell. The cops and their voices vanish completely and he is sitting in the shivering cold except the door to the cell is missing and dust and cobwebs cover everything. He looks around panicking because he cannot see beyond the rusted bars of the cell into the nothingness of solid black. His eyes bulge and every beat of his heart becomes stronger and more painful. He grabs at his chest and falls off the ruined cot, onto the floor and gasping for air. The humming sound drones in his ears and he closes his eyes as he tries to scream, but nothing comes out. He tries again feeling it would be his last and opens his eyes.

The lights are on and the two cops franticly open the cell door while he is lying on the floor loudly screaming a horrible scream. The pain in his chest and the humming fades away. The officers help him back onto the cot. Sophie reappears behind the men and stares at Jake with a look of fear and sorrow.

"Calm down son, calm down," the sheriff tries relaxing Jake.

"Sophie, bring some water!" Harris shouts.

"Deputy, don't yell."

"Sorry Sheriff," he replies and looks down to Jake for the first time with a bit of mercy in his eyes.

Jake's hyperventilating slows but his eyes continue darting around frantically as he keeps grabbing at his chest.

The Sheriff stands up and backs away from Jake, "Calm down,

it's gonna be alright."

Sophie returns with a cup of water and hands it to the deputy, who in turn motions her away from the cell. As Jake begins to calm down, as best as anyone could in his situation, he feels a flush of embarrassment, then shame. The officers give him a few private moments to collect himself. Jake downs the water and looks out of the cell to catch Sophie peeking at him from the office. She abruptly turns away. Jake thinks long and hard trying to understand. Now he feels like he needs to know everything and how it all fits together. For what is left of his sanity's sake. All of the recent strange events make him realize that his perception of reality and its rules have been changed, rewritten.

Is this what it is like to lose your mind, he wonders.

As his breathing finally normalizes he reaches deep within himself to find a calm. Often when he would find himself at an impasse, he would think of his brother and one of the major differences between the two of them.

"Slowly but surely," he mutters to himself.

Jake understands he cannot figure everything out but he knows that right now, this place is real. These people are more than figments of his mind and he is in a jail cell. He thinks about the strange questions the cops asked him about his driver's license but cannot figure out why it is so foreign to them. Jake knows he will have to be smarter and learn the rules of what has been going on around him. Before he can form a solid plan, the cops return with more water which he thankfully takes and swallows up.

"So," the sheriff waits to see if Jake is responsive enough to keep answering their questions.

"Sorry about that," Jake gives an uncomfortable reply.

"That's fine, we understand," Deputy Harris says as he assumes a non-threatening stance.

What is it they understand, Jake wonders.

"You said you were looking for Sam," Harris states.

"Yeah. I was trying to get to Sam's house," unsure about everything Jake says it with ease because that at least is true.

"You two were in the war together then?" Harris continues.

Jake stares back, doing his best to hide any reactions.

Harris points to the drivers' license on the floor, "So, that some sort of military identification?"

Jake looks down, rubs his eyes and contains himself. Pieces finally begin clicking into place. The town, the old cars everywhere even the hippie girl. They think he was in the war with Sam and they have never seen a regular driver's license. Jake realizes that he never left Prudence. He woke up this night, right where he passed out by Sam's house, but decades in the past.

He heaves again but keeps his breathing in check. Whatever else snapped in his head causing his freak out earlier somehow allows him to handle this more insane revelation a bit better. Or his sanity has simply checked out for the night.

"Yeah, it's a military I.D.," Jake says, unflinching into the deputy's eyes.

"But it doesn't show any rank or unit information," the sheriff softly chimes in, and Jake knows the interrogation is on again.

"That's because I'm a civilian now, I don't have any of that anymore. I still have a special ID because I still have certain benefits."

"And the black bars on the back?" he leans forward with genuine curiosity.

"Those are barcodes, for scanning into a computer," Jake answers again, his confidence returning.

"Scanning?"

"It's . . . how the computers see. A camera is hooked up to the computer." Jake sighs.

"Well, your I.D. says that you haven't even been born yet," the sheriff adds, his gaze once again unwavering.

"It's a typing mistake, that's been happening a lot with our new civilian I.D.'s. All the new systems are still being developed."

The sheriff removes his hat and begins scratching at his head again. "And what about that fancy plastic card, what I guess is a bank card. It has one of those holo-things on it too."

Jake hesitates and tries to keep acting as though there is nothing unusual about his possessions. "Holograms sir, all for security. And what about my bank card?"

"Well, we tried calling the numbers on it and it doesn't lead to anything. The card doesn't seem to expire until the next century. In fact, no one has ever heard of that bank or anyone named Jacob Walker that is your age." He returns his hat to his head and stares at Jake with his curious and new predatory look in his eyes.

Jake knows that he cannot miss a beat and that this man is no amateur.

"Those two things are kind of tied together. The bankcard is a special issue card. It is how I get paid my disability from a private government bank. The number on the card is only part of the entire number, the rest I have memorized. You know, like a pin number, in case it's stolen."

"And what does that have to do with you not existing?"

Jake almost has the sheriff sold, and dares not avert his eyes to see how well the deputy is responding.

"That probably has to do with what one of my functions in the service was."

"Yes?"

"Not that I am fully at liberty to say sir, but it had to do with gathering intelligence."

"No shit," the Sheriff says, more sarcastic statement than question. "So how did you meet Sam?"

"When we met he was with the 173rd Airborne, Sky Soldiers. His team escorted us for three weeks. Sam saved my life and we became friends."

"And you didn't know he was still over there?"

"No actually. I thought for sure after what we went through he was done, his tour was ending too."

The sheriff motions to the deputy with a phone hand signal, after which Harris returns to the office and makes a call.

"So you finished your tour before him?"

"I was in intelligence, I was never meant to see the things or do the things I did when I was there. I was given an honorable discharge."

Harris returns to the cell, "According to Mr. Dixon this guy is right about the 173rd."

The Sheriff grunts, "Why come all this way to visit a man you didn't know was here?"

"I was just stopping in. I was on my way to visit my brother, out west."

Satisfied the sheriff nods and places his hand on Jake's shoulder.

"I want you to know that we all appreciate everything you boys have done, regardless of the garbage they say about you on the television."

"Thank you very much, sir."

The sheriff stands up and begins making his way out of the cell. Jake feels bad about lying like that and pretending to be someone he is not. But he is thankful that his deception worked.

"Can I have my shoes?"

"Oh yeah. Harris, get this man his shoes."

Jake remains in the cell as he puts on his shoes and listens in on the two officers' hushed conversation.

The Sheriff leans forward adjusting his belt beneath his portly stomach, "When was the last time you took that long walk?"

"It's been a few days boss. I've been busy with the missing persons."

"Don't worry about it, I'll take it tonight."

"Are you sure? I was going to."

"That's alright, just take care of your family and keep an eye on the fields."

As Jake keeps listening, he is almost disappointed they had no extra reason to concern themselves with him. He had gotten off lucky though and it will be easier for him to learn more about how he ended up sliding back in time. The seriousness in the sheriff's voice when he mentioned taking a walk, like it was something more, sticks with Jake. He also wonders if the missing persons have anything to do with it as well.

"Did you plan on staying at the Dixon house?"

Jake looks up and realizes he has spaced out again. The deputy has returned to the cell and the sheriff was gone.

"Do you have anywhere to stay?" he asks again.

"Ugh, no." Jake replies.

"We have one motel in town. It's more like a bed and breakfast. You can find it if you go back to the Forks."

"Thanks officer," is Jake's only reply.

"You can't make him pay for a room. This is a friend of Sam's!" Sophie says as she walks towards the cell.

"Sophie, don't you have anything better to do?" Arms crossed Deputy Harris stands there blocking Jake from her sight.

"Yeah! He can at least come out with the gang and tell us how Sam's doing over there."

"I don't think so Sophie! You know what's been going on and you are not hanging around with an outsider until we have this figured out."

"Dad! I can take care of myself!"

Jake quickly becomes more cautious of where his eyes wander.

"I said *no* Sophie! You're lucky I'm letting you hang out with your friends this late. If you keep at it, you won't be!"

Sophie grunts and slams her hands into her curvy hips with a quick stomp to the floor.

Her father, the Deputy replies by sternly pointing to the door.

She turns and stomps away uttering, "Such a drag!" before exiting and slams the door behind her.

The deputy turns to Jake shaking his head, "She's just like her mother."

Jake nods back smiling, "So, people are disappearing here?"

"You heard that?"

Jake notices how this bothers Deputy Harris, "Yeah, sorry. Old habits I guess," he says, pleased with himself for his improvisation.

"Yeah, that's why we had to take a good look at your shoes."

"Oh?"

"Yeah, we've been finding an extra set of boot prints around where people have gone missing."

"Wow, this town isn't that big, you could probably find the maker of the shoe, then try and see how many people in town bought that shoe, at that size."

"Huh? You are an interesting guy Jacob, but how would we find out who bought what shoe?"

Jake stops to remember, transactions would be mostly cash or check in this time. "Ugh yeah, usually the military keeps a data base on that stuff."

"What's a data base, some kind of record vault?"

"Yes."

"Well, that probably wouldn't help in this case anyway. More than half of the men that work the fields are outsiders. We think it may be one of them, we just don't have enough to go on."

"An outsider huh? Wouldn't people notice a stranger hanging around?"

"Well yeah, they noticed you immediately," Harris says jokingly.

"That's weird."

"Yeah," the Deputy replies mimicking his daughter, "it's a real drag."

"If I see anyone stranger than me creeping around, I'll come and get you."

"Alright funny guy. Take a left and you'll hit the Forks."

"Thank you, and have a good night," Jake exits with a cocky smile.

Outside he welcomes the gusts of warm wind and the sweet summer aromas they carry with them. He is giddy, in good and bad ways about what has happened to him. He wonders if any other human experienced anything like sliding through time before. He had always thought a person's heart would give out if they ever slid through time or saw an alien or anything like that. Like his episode in the jail cell, except ending in death. He figures that whatever is going on, his mind and body may not have had a chance to catch up to it yet. He remembers his watch and quickly looks at it, expecting it to have stopped or be doing something strange like running backwards. It ticks away as if nothing were wrong.

Jake stands at the center of the Forks and turns around taking in all of the sights. It still all looks old fashioned to him but it is vibrant. There are less people out now, he guesses that he was only in the police station for about an hour. The downtown is teeming with the sounds of life and nearly unrecognizable from what he had seen of Prudence before. The lights of the theater's marquee are animating and it looks brand new. Every building has a personality, either by structure, the stylish colors or trim. Even the tall steepled church with its stark white color gives off a sense of warmth. All except one building, the large block structure that stands on the north corner of the Forks. It looks pretty much as solid as it did before and is a thoroughly red color

Such an odd color for a big square building like that, he thinks. He keeps looking around while ignoring the curious stares of the local residents until he spots the motel, a few stores down west of the theater. Walking under the dazzling but quaint marquee of the theater he stares at the old movie posters in the 'now showing' frames and remembers his plastic money would be useless here. He hopes the cash he has on him will take care of him long enough to figure out what is going on. He realizes that he has not slept in a bed for over a week. He cannot remember sleeping at all other than coming to from his black outs.

"Hey space cadet!" Sophie slams her body against him and locks her arm around his. Jake is startled but happy to see her. "So are you going to get us a room for the night?"

"What?" Jake stammers for the second time.

"Too easy!" She laughs and playfully pushes him away.

"Ha, ha," Jake shelves his nervous thoughts of the last time he was surprised the best he can. "Didn't your dad tell you to stay away from me?"

"Nope. He said you couldn't crash with us, he didn't say we couldn't hang out."

"Wait, he *did* say we couldn't hang out."

She laughs.

"I don't know. I don't want any trouble."

"Don't be such a square."

Jake smiles at her. Normally he was the one flirting and joking around with women but Sophie is beating him to every punch.

"I guess my bag wasn't there?"

"Oops, forgot about that. All that booze might go to waste."

"That's alight, I can always get more."

"Are you hungry?"

"Yeah, I am," as he says it, he becomes aware that he is actually starving.

"A bunch of us are hanging at Buck's tonight, you should come with me. You can tell us all how Sam's doing."

"Buck's?" Jake poses the dumb question to give himself a

moment to think. He wants to avoid having to give a bunch of people who know Sam information that could definitely be wrong. Especially if Sam or *young* Sam were to show up. He had done so well with the cops but things would quickly unravel for him if he were to slip up.

"Well duh, it's a food joint. Buck's Burgers, it's the best!"

"I really want to get a room before this motel closes."

"What? The motel is open twenty four seven silly."

"Oh yeah. Well I still have to get cleaned up, and take a look at this big cut on my face."

"What cut?" She leans forward inspecting him.

"You don't see this?" he draws a line down his cheek with a finger.

"See what? You need to shave, but I think you look cute all rugged like that."

"You seriously don't see this? And the blackness on my hands?"

Jake stretches his hands out palms up towards her and sees that saddened look on her face again. He looks down to see there is nothing wrong with his hands, the dark soot that would not wash off is gone. He runs over to the movie poster display and stares at his reflection in the glass. He sees no cut or scrapes or bruises at all. Confused but happy, he feels a hot flush of embarrassment coming over himself again. That's twice he's looked crazy in front of this girl and he figures she'd be gone when he turns around. Instead, he feels her small hand squeezing his shoulder.

"The war was hard on you guys, huh?"

Jake does not answer. He debates if being in a war would have been worse than the madness he was going through now. "I'm surprised you're still standing there."

"My mother used to tell me, never be afraid of anything you can see, grab and punch. That's why you should come and talk to us about Sam, so when he gets back we can be there for him more, you know?"

"Yeah."

Sophie slowly locks her arm with his again her eyes alight under the marquee. Jake drifts away staring at her. He wouldn't have spent a second around anyone acting the way he had been. How can she be so fearless and comfortable with him, he wonders.

She winks then looks away, leading him to Buck's Burgers, "Don't worry cool cat, I'll let you buy me dinner."

"Really?" he jokes. "Thank you?"

She covers her mouth and giggles, "You talk funny Jacob."

"So do you Sophie."

"I do?"

"I noticed people from here like to say, 'well' at the beginning of their sentences."

She pauses then starts laughing again, "You're a space cadet, who would notice something like that?"

"Well, I would. By the way, call me Jake."

* * *

With the exception of the excessive wood paneling and orange pleather covering the seats, the inside of Buck's Burgers looks more like a fifties style diner. Not very wide it tunnels through to the back of the building. Bar style seats line the eating counter on the left while cushy benched tables sit on the right by the windows. At the back of the restaurant a classic song plays on a jukebox and competes for musical reign for the diner's atmosphere with two arcade game cabinets.

"What do you think Jake?" she says and turns back smiling at him.

"Looks like it only half made it out of the fifties."

"Yeah, things here change slowly, it's a drag."

"But it smells great!" he excitedly squeezes her hand in his.

Jake tries not to be rude with the maelstrom of thoughts thrashing around in his head. Through it all he tries remembering what other facts he can about Sam to maintain his story. There are just a few people scattered around the place and at the last bench sits a girl. She is beautiful as well and about Sophie's age. She does not have any particular expression, but her pupils, which seem more like floating dots of ink, follow them. Her hair is shoulder length and hangs around her round face in large dark curls that contrast her smooth skin.

"You sit here." Sophie points to the seat across from the girl. He sits across from the new girl, then Sophie sits on the outside of Jake, successfully trapping him there. The girl raises one of her dark and angled eyebrows questioningly towards Sophie.

"Where's Ralph Junior, running late again?" Sophie playfully taunts her friend.

"He had to work late," the girl says, unphased by the jab.

"Again?" Sophie smiles.

Jake notices the girl is different in the same way as Sophie. She has the same exotic features and completion, except for dark circles under her eyes and a very cold stare. But she is still very beautiful. She dresses completely different from Sophie. More formal and covered, favoring dark green and white over Sophie's red. She wears no make up either, except her lips are slightly stained red.

"Who is this?" the girl says as her eyes dart from Sophie's eyes directly into Jake's.

"Oh, you haven't heard?" Sophie wraps her arm around Jake to his surprise and giggles, thoroughly enjoying taunting her apparent friend and rival.

The girl responds by bringing her drink up and sipping it, her eyes not wavering from him.

"Well, I just busted this hunk out of jail. He's the new guy who was passed out drunk in Sam's back yard."

A sign of life flashes in her eyes, followed by an accusatory look of scorn, "What were you doing by Sam's house?"

"Relax Evelyn, he's a friend from the war."

"How is he?" Evelyn leans forward and sets her cup down.

"He was fine when I last saw him. I am sure he will come back in one piece."

"How can you be so sure?" her stare hardens.

"This is Jake," Sophie adds in.

"Sam handles himself well, trust me."

"He said Sam saved his life."

"Trust you? Why?"

"Whoa!" Jake leans back, "I don't know what you want me to say. He was okay and I hear from some of the other guys that he's still okay."

Angry at being ignored Sophie jumps to her feet and slams her hands into the table. "Evelyn! Why do you always have to be so intense?"

"I'm not being intense I want to know about Sam!"

"I know. That's why I brought him here!"

As the two friend's argument escalates, Jake stares out the window and tries to get back to digesting his situation. The cut on his face, his scuffs and the darkening on his hands have vanished. Most incredibly sliding backwards like this, and to the seventies of all times. Something must have happened here and whatever has been messing with him may want him to see or do something before sending him back to where he came from. As bleak and terrible as future Prudence will become, it is still a hell of a lot closer to his home and family.

"What do you want?"

"Huh?" Jake looks up to see Sophie still standing and angered.

"I'm gonna order the food, what do you want?" she asks again.

"Burger and fries I guess."

He watches her stomp away then turns back to see Evelyn as calm as she was before. Apparently, Sophie's plan to rile her friend up had backfired.

"Sorry about that Jake, normally I do not become so *intense*," and she stretches out her hand to shake his. "You already know but, I'm Evelyn."

"That's cool, nice to meet you."

Their hands touch and to Jake the world suddenly stops. Nothing moves and he is unable to look away from Evelyn's piercing stare. Her beady black pupils sit alone in her wide eyes and an uncomfortable but familiar feeling shudders through his bones. Jake sees that she seems to be experiencing the same as she fights against it. She physically strains, manages to blink then look away, breaking them from their strange trance. Leery about making eye contact with her again, he looks down and sees her long hand and fingers wrapped completely around his. Her hand is soft and looks delicate, but it is also strong and cold.

"I'm sorry!" she quickly jerks her hand away.

"What was that?"

"I don't know," she says still avoiding eye contact. "I get dizzy spells," she blurts out.

"Has that happened to you before?"

"Has what happened before?" Sophie asks suspiciously eyeing the two.

"Ralph Junior. If he's ever stood us up before," Evelyn snaps.

"Oh," she giggles, "well, he's never stood *me* up before," and returns to her place right up against Jake.

Jake stares at Evelyn considering her evasive answer to her friend. It surely could not be to spare Sophie's feelings about the moment they just had, not that it was a good moment. Evelyn knows something and she might have some answers. Jake knows he would have to start being more bold in figuring things out. He turns sideways to Sophie's dismay to peel her away from him but also allow him to gauge both of their reactions. He also wants to look more casual and would play a bit dumb while asking the two young women what he believes might be awkward questions.

"So, you two look different from most of the people here, why is that?"

The two women go silent and stare at each other.

"Do we now? How do you mean, different?" Evelyn asks, staring down at her drink, her long spidery fingers wrapped around the cup.

"You both have slightly different features about yourselves, and your complexions too."

He looks over to see Sophie has a narrowed dangerous look in her eyes that he had not yet seen, "And this difference bother's you?"

"Uh, no." He clears his throat and worries he has quickly gone too far. "I have travelled around different parts of the world and you both still look so exotic to me. I've honestly never seen any women nearly as beautiful as you two."

Sophie's narrowed eyes waver and her cheeks flush red. Her lips spread into a smile and both of the women burst out laughing at him. He sighs internally and relaxes while keeping a clueless demeanor.

"Real smooth, you're not as square as you act!" Sophie covers her mouth as she laughs and he is reminded that she at least has normal hands.

"Well, it's true," he adds.

"Aw, such a nice guy," Evelyn adds. "Do you want to tell him Sophie, or should I?"

"No, I saved him from jail, I get to tell him."

"You did?" he asks.

"Shh! I have to think," Sophie nibbles on her bottom lip as she organizes her thoughts. "Ok. So, once upon a time..."

"Hey! You can't start it like that!" Evelyn butts in, now laughing at her friend instead of Jake.

"How else should I start it?"

"I don't know, not like that!"

"Fine! Back in the old days . . . , is that ok with you, Evelyn?"

"That's swell, hurry up before the food gets here."

"Don't rush me," she whips her hair over her exposed shoulders. "Back in the old days, before Prudence had its name, it was just an isolated colony, or a small town," she shrugs. "One day a plague swept through and killed a bunch of the women and children. A few years later a tribe of Indians—"

"Indians?" Jake blurts out.

"Yeah, do you have a problem with that?" Sophie tries making her smooth face frown.

"Of course not," Jake calms himself. The past Indian presence at least explains the strange totem poll he saw on the edge of town. Worse, the thing that cut him was reminiscent of something native.

"The Indians came into the area and the tribe had just been at war with another tribe, so most of the men were dead."

"All of the men were dead," Evelyn corrects.

"Yeah, whatever. So, the Whites needed women and the Indians needed men and here we are! The end."

"But, I've known," he pauses, "Native Americans, before and they still didn't look anything like you two."

"Native American?" Evelyn sips her drink again and smiles. "Sounds so, proper."

"I don't really know what term to use," Jake apologetically

raised his hands.

The girls laugh again.

"But still, you two look different than other ones I've met."

"It's not just us two, there are a lot of people in town like us. Some just have more Indian in them than others."

"They were a special tribe," Sophie adds, "they were very dark skinned."

"Oh," Jake nods. "You mean they were Black Indians?"

"No, they were gray," Evelyn returns to her serious self. "They say there are two things that are unique to this part of the world. The rare, red variant of the 'Meadow Death Camas', a flower which I am drinking as a tea right now and the gray skinned Indians."

"They said their skin was originally as gray as slate," Sophie adds. "That's why we have this lovely and *exotic* complexion."

"I don't know, gray people?" he raises an eyebrow, "were they from New Mexico?"

"Get real! You're the space cadet here, Mr. Walker! Besides, I even hear there were *blue* people who lived in the south. They were called the . . . what were the called, Evelyn?"

"I don't remember."

"That explains the totem pole I saw on the edge of town," Jake mutters.

"Yeah, we've got six of those! They're supposed to protect the town from bad luck. Foods coming!" Sophie excitedly rubs her hands together.

"Then why are the faces on it aimed towards the town?"

"Huh, never thought about it. Do you know Evelyn?"

"No. And I would rather talk about Sam anyways," she curtly says.

"But, what was the name of the tribe?"

"It was forgotten!" Evelyn snaps.

Sophie reaches over and puts her hand on Evelyn's. "Evie relax."

"I didn't mean to push," Jake shrugs. He figured out that at least Evelyn knows more than she is willing to speak about. Not just because he is a stranger but because Sophie is apparently ignorant to the details as well. Evelyn definitely looks like she has more of that gray blood in her veins. There was also the weird experience he had when they shook hands. The feeling reminded him of how he felt when he was in the cell and had his momentary slip back into the present. Jake wants to spend his time with Sophie, but he will have to get closer to Evelyn to find out more. He decides that lies or not, talking about Sam would be easier than waiting for the girls to start asking him specific questions.

"So, I am sure you heard that Sam signed on for another tour," he starts.

Evelyn regains her posture and stares down into her tea, "Yeah, he wrote to me that he was thinking about doing that in his last letter.

"I think he'll be fine. He was pretty good at camouflaging himself. He fooled me a few times when he was escorting us."

"Yeah, Sam's a smart guy. He used to go out hunting with my dad."

"Eat your food Sophie!" Evelyn chides her in between bites.

"You look like you've been back awhile Jake. Sam just wrote me three weeks ago and he never mentioned you."

Jake had his next comment ready but is caught off guard. "That's because I was collecting intelligence. He wouldn't be writing about classified missions."

"How long *have* you been back, Jake?" Sophie gently asks.

"About a month, I was making my way west to visit my brother, that's when I thought I would stop in."

Evelyn is looking into Jake's eyes again with her deep stare, "Why come when you weren't sure he would be here?"

"Geez Evelyn, you sound like my dad!"

"I figured it couldn't hurt. Besides he had shown me a picture of some cute girls holding a birthday cake for him. So even if he wasn't here I knew I had a good reason to come."

"That was us!" Sophie blurts out.

The girls are both pleasantly surprised and Jake feels safe in his lies again. He is glad that had already happened, but then again old Sam had several photos of the people holding the cake from different birthdays hanging up in his shrine.

"I knew you had a good idea with that Evelyn!"

The smell of the food causes Jake to look down at his plate and he cannot believe how starved he is and how he has been able to keep forgetting his hunger. He takes a huge bite out of the burger and moans at its goodness. He continues eating as the hot juices spill down his throat while periodically shoving the fries in his mouth. The food actually tastes different back here. It seems more real, better. In less than a minute, his plate is empty and Jake looks up to see the shocked expressions of the two girls staring at him.

"Geez Louise!" Sophie gasps.

Like a slob Jake speaks while still forcing the last few bites of food down his throat, "That was awesome!"

"We can see. Do you want another?" Evelyn asks.

"Sorry, but yeah! I, *we* kinda had to chow down over there."

"You don't have to apologize Jake, that really was *awesome*!" Sophie happily repeats as she adds Jake's expression into her vernacular.

As Evelyn gets up to order more food, Sophie turns to Jake and slides a napkin over to him.

"Oh thanks," he raises it to his mouth but Sophie snatches it away.

"It's not for that! It's my number."

Jake reads the napkin, carefully folds it up and places it in his pocket.

"Sophie, I don't know how much longer I'll be around."

"I know," there is hurt in her voice. "You don't have to be around just to talk to me."

"I guess you're right," his smile cheers her up.

"Just don't call after nine. My dad would flip!"

"That's fine. I usually like to call people at two in the morning."

"Better not!"

"So these six totem poles, I saw the one by the south road. Where are the others?"

"Huh? Oh, just follow the path."

Jake stares at her blankly and shrugs.

"There's a road that circles around town," she draws a big circle in the air.

"Oh yeah, I think I remember being on that a bit."

"It's easier to see in summer when the red meadow camas blooms."

"Are those the flowers that Evelyn mentioned?"

"Yeah, she just calls them red meadow death camas or red death flowers all ominous to impress people. But anyways, they line the entire road around town. We even have a festival for the totems in fall, it's really groovy."

"I would like to see that. What's the meaning behind the festival?"

"I told you, for good luck. We pick the red meadow camas and use them and their roots to stain the totems. It's supposed to rejuvenate them for another year of good luck."

Jake remembers the red stains he found at the base of the totem and how the base emitted heat for no reason. The totems . . . he wonders. They surround the village and when he walked out of the circle, he ended up appearing back in another part of town again.

That must be it! It was either the shadow in the house that marked me with that cut or it was drinking that water. Sam must be cursed too, why else would he be hanging around. If I can break the circle then maybe I can get out of this town, he wonders.

"And what's left over you make into tea?" he gently presses on.

"And other stuff, I don't like the taste of it, but I wear it as a perfume."

"I thought I've been smelling somethin' good."

"You're no stranger to the whole sweet talkin' thing are you," she laughs.

"Not when you keep giving me so many reasons to keep trying."

"Oh, you're so bad!" she flirtatiously sips on her straw.

"Get a room already," Evelyn returns to her seat with another burger and two cups of her tea.

"Thanks Evelyn," Jake forces himself to eat the second burger a little slower while the girls watch on expecting another show.

"Aw, now you're being a drag, I missed half of the show when you did it before."

Jake just focuses on his food, while Evelyn slides a receipt over to him.

"Here's the bill."

"What's the damage?"

"For you two, three dollars and change," Evelyn slides a cup of the tea over to Jake. "This is on me."

He looks at the cup of hot red fluid ominously. He wonders, if I really am cursed somehow and this flower has an affect on keeping me trapped, what would happen if I drank it? Could it be like the heat from the totem, or hotter and enough to burn? That shit could be poisonous or make me slide back to my time in a poof!

He is not ready to go yet. Not with so many questions. Sophie's warm soft body pressing against him is not helping either.

"Evie, don't make him drink that."

"It's a tradition Sophie, you know that."

"Really?" he nervously asks.

"Yes, its how we welcome strangers to town," Evelyn says as she sips from her own brew.

Jake pulls the cup towards himself and stares into its thick red depths. It smells good, like Sophie, a musky sweetness. He raises the cup, then lowers it. He looks up and sees Evelyn watching him closely, while Sophie focuses on her burger. He takes a finger barely dipping it in, expecting to be burned but it is just hot tea. Rubbing the fluid between his fingers he looks for any blistering or tingling, there is none.

"What's wrong?" Evelyn asks.

Jake looks up at her and sips the tea in the same way she has been doing. He had never tasted anything like it before. It is good but strong and as he swallows, it burns and feels like he just gulped down cognac.

Jake coughs hard a few times then grunts it down.

The girls erupt into laughter again.

"Burns don't it?" Evelyn chuckles.

"Yeah!" he continues coughing. "Is this even tea?"

"All natural," she says.

A warming sensation fills his chest, and he feels lighter. He takes larger gulps of the tea and fights against the burn. The more he drinks, the better he feels. His deep hunger that even the burgers and fries could not take care of washes away. Halfway through he leans back and realizes he is so hot that he has started to sweat. Looking over at Evelyn again, he sees that he passed her little test but a sense of urgency distracts him.

"Hey, is the bathroom back there?" he points past the noisy arcade cabinets.

"Why, are you gonna spit the tea back up?" Sophie jokes, but Evelyn is not amused.

"No, I gotta use the toilet. That's some strong tea though!" he reassures.

In another cramped bathroom, Jake looks at his reflection again. Everything still looks normal to him. He does not even look worn out. As he stands there relieving himself someone knocks at the door.

"Jake?" Sophie speaks through the door. "Hey, my dad's outside to pick me up."

"Does he know I'm here?"

"I think so. He has his cherry light on."

"What should I do?"

"Nothing, just open the door so I can say goodbye."

He finishes up and flushes quickly to open the door for Sophie. Instead of letting him come out, she pushes her way in, pressing up against him in the small bathroom.

"This is a real bummer. I didn't want to say goodbye like this."

"That's ok," he stares into her big eyes passionately, her soft body on his exciting him again.

"Tomorrow night?" she asks.

"I don't know," he says sadly.

"We can meet for breakfast at least?"

"Sophie, I don't know."

"What?" she becomes a little angry.

"Sophie, I'll try, but I don't have a lot of control over where I can be," He moves his lips close to hers.

"Not like this!" she hides her disappointment beneath a laugh and smile. "You make sure I see you again, and you will have earned a kiss, deal?"

"Deal."

"Well, goodbye for now Jake Walker."

"Goodbye Sophie Harris."

Sophie slowly backs out of the bathroom, still smiling a sad smile, then walks away. Jake sees the flashing lights from her father's car from outside. A car door opens and closes then the car drives away. After washing his hands and cooling off with the water, he comes out of the bathroom and finds Evelyn still sitting in the booth.

"Evelyn, why are you still here?"

"Is that a problem?"

"No, I figured you would have gone with Sophie."

"Nah, still eating," she places a book she was reading back into her rustic tote bag. "Don't just stand there. Aren't you going to finish your tea?"

"Yes," he sits back in the booth across from her.

"So you and Sophie really hit it off. I've never seen her so smitten."

"Really?" Jake smiles. "Wish I could stay longer."

"Do you like her?"

"I just met her a few hours ago."

Evelyn half rolls her eyes at him.

"Yes, so far I do like her. I've never met anyone like her before."

"That's good, because I love her like a sister."

He looks out the window into the emptied streets. "So that guy never showed up, huh?"

"Who Ralph Junior? He's never been reliable. Probably at the road house getting drunk with the other workers."

"The oil field workers, right?"

"Yeah, they are mostly out of towners that come in for the work. They've gotten rowdy a few times in the past, so they are discouraged from coming too far into town."

Jake says nothing but continues drinking his tea. He wants to ask more about the town's lore, but finding the right words has been difficult. It is a similar situation to when he had attempted to get information from Sam, as if just talking about these things were taboo.

"Sophie told me you guys have a festival coming up soon."

"We do," her discomfort returns. "You should check it out, we start it late at night and we light up the town and party until dawn."

"I told Sophie it sounds like fun, the whole lore of this town is so interesting," he watches her discomfort grow.

"What else did she tell you?"

"This and that, a few things about the importance of the totems and how the red death flowers are linked to them."

Evelyn calms again and smiles. He wonders if he just slipped up.

"Strange she would say they were linked. The flowers are used to stain the totems for good luck, but linked?"

Jake senses a slight deception in her voice, a hesitant waver but he plays along. "That's what I meant."

A skinny old man calls from behind the counter to the two, "Hey guys, want to settle up front, we're closing soon."

"I have to go anyways," Evelyn says and she stands up from the booth.

As she starts digging through her bag, Jake sees that Evelyn is close to a head taller than him. Even though Jake is almost six feet tall, he has begun to feel short around the residents of Prudence. He looks at her feet out of curiosity. They were normal for a woman her height and not as disproportionate as her hands.

"Hey don't worry about dinner, I'll get it," Jake offers.

"No, thank you. I pay my own way."

Jake places a twenty on his bill and slides it over to the skinny man.

"What the heck?" the man says, squinting at Jake's twenty.

Jake looks down at his money. He had completely forgotten the bills looked different now, very different. Evelyn is startled as well as she eyes the bill, then Jake.

He conceals his surprise as he stares down at his future bills and mentally kicks himself for having left the old cash in the register of that derelict store. "What's the problem, sir?"

"Are you tryin' to con me boy?" the old man squints. "What the heck is this?" he presses the bill under is ruffled nose, smelling it.

"Those are the new twenties," Jake states casually. "See," he produces his I.D. and bankcard from his wallet and lays them out on the counter. "I was in the service. All of the new stuff looks like this. There should have been some mention of the new bills on the net—" he coughs, "television."

Almost having made another mistake he thinks of how taxing it has been holding up this charade. He looks over to Evelyn who has the strangest expression as she eyes the articles he laid out for the cashier. It is different from her suspicious paranoid look she gets when pressed about the town, she looks more interested.

"Well, I guess. These sure do look fancy. Probably cost more to make than they're worth."

He is still collecting his change when Evelyn rushes out of the Buck's Burger.

Her long legs are carry her away quickly and he has to speed walk to catch up.

"Hey, what's the rush?"

"No rush, I just want to get home," she says, not looking back.

"Let me walk you there at least."

"I'm a big girl, I can take care of myself."

"I know but, the Deputy said people have been disappearing, you could at least let me walk you for a little while."

She stops and turns around, "Just a little while. But I don't feel much like talking." A few minutes later, he guesses they are in a western part of town.

"Oh yeah, thanks for the tea."

"You are welcome," she strains to reply.

They keep walking in the half moon's light and Evelyn keeps her purse clutched to her chest. No longer appearing comfortable at all.

"Do you have any idea where I can buy some of that tea? You know to take with me," feeling bad he hopes more conversation will relax her a bit.

"I get mine from the Fork's Apothecary but try Chuck's general store."

"Chuck's and Buck's, that's funny."

"They're brothers."

"Really? Was that Buck who we just talked to?"

"No, you'll know Buck when you see him," she stops walking and turns around. "Thank you for walking me home. It was a very gentlemanly thing for you to do."

Jake looks around at the intersection they are standing in, "This is an intersection."

"I know. This is my block. I don't know you and I don't feel comfortable with you knowing where I live."

"I understand," Jake pouts. "I didn't mean to pry about things. I just, have been going through a lot. I've been having a hard time with things."

"I hope you pull through Jake, you seem like a very nice guy."

From behind them a boat of a car sloppily turns down the street. Its headlights glare at the two as the car slowly shudders towards them. It stalls for a moment as it approaches then reluctantly pulls past them to stop. A young long faced guy with buzzed red hair leans out of the driver's side window and drunkenly stares at the two.

"Evelyn . . . hey. I was at Buck's and didn't see you anywhere."

"That's because you blew us off Junior," Evelyn says, disappointed but more annoyed than hurt.

"Yeah, well I was," he pauses when he notices Jake, "who is this?"

"This is a friend of Sam's."

"Oh." Junior angrily stares at Jake. His drunken mind fruitlessly tries to establish some connection between Jake and Sam.

"From the war," She adds.

Junior's bravado slides away at the mention of Jake having been in the war. "Then, let me give you a ride home Evelyn, you don't know this guy."

"I don't know who that guy is either," she points with her chin to Junior's passenger.

Jake had not noticed anyone sitting in the car with Junior until then. Between the patchy beard and the oversized shades, his face is almost completely covered. Most notable though, is his black nylon foam mesh cap with its dirty orange brim sticking out, competing for room with the sunglasses. Motionless the man stares at them from the seat, more than likely drunker than the driver.

Junior sluggishly looks at his passenger then back to Evelyn, "What? Oh, Joe. He's the animal control guy for the fields."

"I'm already at my house Junior and you're drunk!"

"But no! He could, he could be the one taking people," Junior loudly whispers in protest.

"He just got into town Junior!" Evelyn turns to Jake, "thanks again, but I have to get going."

Jake looks up into her eyes and stretches out his hand, "Alright, good bye then."

She glances at his hand then him, in that brief moment he watches her become nervous again. Staring at her with a serious look, he dares her to take his hand again.

"Nice meeting you." She turns and begins walking away,

Jake watches her leave, still arguing with Junior who follows in his big yellow car. He takes a few steps back to the center of the intersection, as a sharp pain shoots through his head. *The* sharp pain. An icy cold shiver runs through him. He embraces himself and sees the moisture in his exhaled breath as a thick fog, as if it were winter outside. He tries to leave the crossroads but everything begins to spin and he falls down on the street. The humming and the pain are intense. He presses against his head and closes his eyes tightly while fighting for control of his breath. As the cold intensifies, the pain recedes and he looks up and sees it is day. Once again finding himself under the gloomy skies in the ruined town of Prudence.

CHAPTER 6

Jake sits up shivering and looks around. He cannot remember being so cold when he was here before, if he really left. The never changing milky skyline stretches out above him, stinging his eyes. The sense of comfort and security he had before the pain is replaced with thoughts of the screaming shadow.

He crawls over to a nearby car and leans his back up against it. He begins rubbing his cold hands together and sees they are stained again, blacker than before. The discoloration has spread under his fingernails and he imagines if this is what frostbite looks like. As cold as his hands are, he can still feel them. If it were frostbite, it would not make any sense because he had not been exposed to any extreme cold for long. He pulls his hood over his head and sighs.

Jake wonders if he was just dreaming of being in the past. It was a nice dream towards the end, if that is what it was. With all of the inexplicable things happening to him, sliding back and forth through time was still a stretch. Nevertheless, he had appeared in the past where he had fallen down, Sam's house. And if the experience was not a dream, he would be by Evelyn's house now.

He leans forward and looks across the intersection. Everything is like the rest of the town, just rows of rotten houses. Nothing looks familiar. He looks left to see where he saw Evelyn standing, minutes and decades ago. More of the same, except one thing is standing out and Jake rises to his feet. Barely sticking out from between two of the houses sits a very familiar vehicle, Mike's tow truck. Jake crouches down and weaves his way through the few scattered cars and stray trash barrels towards the truck.

The houses that the truck is parked between were both once white and like the others do not seem lived in. All of their windows are shattered and the doors are either gone or half open. He looks around for a street sign and sees the names on them rusted away a long time ago. Cautiously he creeps over to the driver's side of the truck, noticing that the windows are rolled down. Rust has been unnaturally eating away at it, just like his car but he still wants to see if it has power. Jake slowly rises up to look inside and is met with a horrifying site.

What appears to be the skin of a man has been shed and is sprawled across the driver's seat. The mouth of the human skin suit is stretched open as if that was where whatever had been inside crawled out from. The skin is still intact and looks rubbery. Matted gray hair pours from the distorted, sunken in head and curls around the gaping mouth. The smell hits Jake next. It is that same disgusting smell from the shadow. He gags and covers his mouth. The skin suit wears its own clothes as well, a bloodied orange prison suit. Jake feels like ice cold water was just slapped across his eyes and he winces.

The crazy bastard from the garage.

His bizarre behavior, his grayish skin even his stink. Jake reaches up and touches his forehead with a trembling hand. The reason why he felt compelled to come to this town, why he is trapped and seeing things. It was this guy. This bastard marked him with his own nasty blood back at the garage then made extra sure Jake ended up in Prudence by attacking him with the stolen truck, leading him here.

"But why?" Jake asks the sagging bloody mess, numb from his realization.

He stares at it a while longer, then looks away to see if the keys are still in the ignition. They are not. However, in the passenger seat Jake sees a familiar pearl handled gun. It belonged to the agent who was transporting the crazed convict. Jake opens the door half expecting the shed skin to jump out and try swallowing or strangling him with its elastic arms.

Skriscrunk!

He jumps back while some heavily rusted shackles spill out of the truck. They weren't too loud, but he looks over his shoulders. He takes a deep breath of the fresher air away from the inside of the truck, then quickly reaches over the emptied skin and snatches up the gun. He inspects the gun as he backs away from the truck. It is tarnished now except for the pearl handle. He presses his thumb against the cylinder release and the gun cracks in his hand. He stands there staring at it, not surprised but angry. He squeezes the gun harder, crumbling it away. Demoralized again he looks back to the white house and thinks of the secrets and terrors he might find within. He is thirsty again and was already getting hungry but he would not venture into the house without a way to protect himself. He knows where he can find food, answers and guns. Once again, he heads to Sam Dixon's house.

Jake quickly makes his way back to the camouflaged man's house, determined to get answers this time. Slowing down he stares at the porch and after a while spots where Sam is hiding. He walks right up to the fence and tries to remember the path around the traps hidden in the weeds.

"Sam." he calls out. "Hey Sam!"

Sam slowly rises to his feet, and begins lifting his rifle up as well.

"Sam?"

"Jake?"

"Yeah, it's me. I gotta come in."

"What the hell are you still doing here?"

"I made it into the woods but ended up downtown here again."

"What?" the old man shouts.

"I can't get out. I think it has something to do with the totem—"

Blam!

Jake drops to the ground and scrambles around for cover, but there isn't any. Of all the streets with cars strewn about them, this is not one of them and Sam must have set it up that way.

Blam!

Another shot sounds and a bullet whizzes right passed his ear. He panics and his fast crawl breaks into a run.

Blam!

A bullet bounces off the street right next to his foot and he starts running in a haphazard zig zagging line.

He dashes around the nearest house and tumbles back to the ground. For a good while, he waits trying to listen over his frantic breaths for any sounds of pursuit, then heads away from Sam's house.

Wandering aimlessly and no longer as cautious, Jake debates what he can do. He wants to grab Sam's old ass and just start shaking him but he couldn't even get close to him. He also thinks that something bad would happen if he tried destroying one or more of the totems that mark the barrier that is keeping him sealed inside the town. Then there is the shadow thing with the knife and Kenneth. The one thing Kenneth did not seem to be lying about was that he in fact was from Prudence as proven by his peculiar skin aberration. Kenneth knows more than he is letting on but he is much larger than Jake. He would have to sneak attack him somehow to get the upper hand and sneaking is something he is becoming very good at.

Jake looks up and sees he has stumbled into an undiscovered part of town. He must have been heading west because he is less than a dozen feet away from the derricks. The field is huge, at least the size of the town itself. Most had collapsed or looked like they were burned up some time ago. A few rusty blue barrels are sloppily stacked near the side of a road. Jake walks up and examines them. A black fluid leaks out of a few weak spots in the metal. He looks out over the oil fields again. Even this oil must still have some value but these people just left it and never came back. He gets a little on his fingers and smells it. It has a petrol smell with a hint of sweetness. He half expected it to smell like the things, seeing as how their blood and the oil look so similar. If any of it were in the barrels, they would have been reduced to nothing by corrosion a long time ago. The similarity is a strange coincidence that he does not like.

The westbound road breaks off to the north and south just like the east road. And as Sam mentioned, it also continues west and is closer to the highway. Stacks of rusted corrugated containers and rotten wood is piled on the westbound road as it continues into the forest. Despite the tall weeds and small trees that have sprouted up through the broken asphalt, a car could still fit through the old barricade. Just before the dead end where the west road curves south, a large block looking structure sits on the corner. It is three stories of smoky looking wood. The bottom floor looks like an old saloon style open patio that runs around the whole building. More old beer cans, broken bottles and gravel serve as its lawn. He squints and makes out from the faded yellow letters along the side that simply spell, 'ROADHOUSE'. With its absence of windows and doors, it looks vacant as well.

Jake looks up across the road and sees he is also very close to the rusted old water tower. It is tall, he figures maybe eighty feet tall. He had noticed it at different times hovering over the city with its bulbous head. Jake stares at it closely and sure enough, it is nearly consumed by red and brown shades of rust, the name 'PRUDENCE' looms in once bold letters.

It was then that he remembers Sam saying there were other people in town, that would not be helpful but then again, Sam was no longer any help. He came upon Sam by chance because he noticed the water catchers around his house. He heads to the tower hoping he can safely make it up high enough to see more from above. The tower appears sturdy enough to Jake, not that he has been having any good luck with metals in this town. Weeds have consumed the base of the tower and the safety gate around it is in shambles. Empty old beer cans and cigarette butts litter the ground as well as a particularly stained old mattress.

This must have been the oil workers' hangouts, he thinks.

He reaches up to the metal stepladder and pulls hard. The corroded rings of the safety chute running up around the ladder do not look like they will be much help, but he begins ascending anyway. He stamps down hard on the first few steps to check the integrity then keeps ascending. Halfway up he begins to strain. It is not just his poor fitness, it is his hunger. He thinks of the burgers he ate a few hours ago and stops himself from drooling.

But those burgers were not real, or were they?

His body certainly was different in the past, it wasn't scarred or stained like now. But if that past is real, could he have taken the food in his stomach back with him. As wild as it is, he wishes that his slide to the seventies *was* real, that Sophie was real.

Another thought pops into his head as he rushes to the top. Once there, he heaves himself onto the catwalk, but does not bother to look around. Instead, he reaches in his pocket. His eyebrows raise and he withdraws a napkin. He grips it tightly so the wind does not take it and carefully opens it up. The words read as they did before, "Sophie 215-1891".

"No way!" he says, amazed.

He really was in the past and everyone there was real. Not only that, he can take things with him, possibly change things. Did he already change things when he went back, he continues wondering. Before, Jake thought Sam opened fire on him because he mentioned the power of the totems, something he said he really did not want to hear or talk about. Now, maybe the people he met in the past told young Sam about his visit and old Sam now thinks Jake is a ghost or worse. And Sophie. How did the thing that happened here affect her? He worries and hopes that she and Evelyn had left long before whatever event occurred that ruined this town. By the look of when things in town stopped changing and started dying, his visit to the past was not far away from that event. And maybe that is why something had pulled him back there.

Jake places the napkin carefully in his pants pocket again and looks over the town. He creeps along the rickety catwalk that wraps around the top of the water tower. Prudence looks just as desiccated from above as it does from the street. Worse, because the small grimy details mesh together. In the far distance, he spots another of the totem poles and wishes that he had something to write with. From what he can see, the town is indeed encircled by an outer road pegged with equally spaced totems. There are three inner circles of streets each one smaller than the other. He sees the three semi straight roads flow from the outer ring and come together making the Forks' 'Y' shape at the center of town. North of the Forks, there just appears to be empty space but it is obscured by a growth of larger gnarly looking evergreens. North of that but still within the bounds of the outmost circular road is the large rocky hill, also heavily covered by trees. It looks like the mini mountain was the reason for the forks to split the way it does. It tapers off quickly at the top and looks like it could be a dangerous climb, but it would afford a better view of the town.

Jake had not noticed before how the elevations of this town are uneven and contradictory to the accurate placing of the roads. It looks like laying out the town a different way would have made more sense, but it was painstakingly laid out specifically to cater to the roads. There are four main circle roads, three wide streets merging into the Forks and six totem poles.

No number coincidence there he thinks, but it may still have something to do with what is keeping him trapped in the town.

Was everyone in town in on it? He wonders.

Burning or chopping down the totems seemed like a weak plan now, especially if he would have to tear up parts of the roads. There would still no guarantee the seal would be disrupted.

A windless chill rolls over his body and he feels weak and hungry again. He scours the town looking for anything different. The water tower stands in the upper west of town, between the two outermost circular roads. He sees a bit of Sam's house to the southeast near the second to smallest circle and the south road. Taking a few steps to his left, he looks north. He walks around and looks south when something catches his eye. Along the third largest circle is a burned house, flanked by two more burned houses. Even the houses behind those three on the other side of the alley are burned and sunken in some way. The detached garages for those six homes are all intact. Not just that, plants and tall grass flourish in the back yards of the houses and in the middle, a large willow lumbers, draping its branches over the center garage. Jake leans forward on the safety bar and sees that the doors to the garages have been either covered or reinforced.

"Gotcha!" he smiles.

Khurunk!

The flimsy metal banister breaks sending him falling forward to the ground. He shouts and spins around grabbing at the air. He manages to shoot his left arm around the lower bar of the banister, but the force of his fall and body weight causes him to swing out over nothingness. Loudly the banister begins bending and popping off bolt by bolt from the tower. Frantically, he scrambles up the warped old metal and to the catwalk. He struggles for a few split seconds that seem more like minutes while his movements cause the banister to loudly tear away more. As he sways back and forth, he looks down the long drop. At worst, he could try for some bushes that would not help with a seventy foot drop. At best, he could fall and get cut in half by the rusty fence and hope he dies quicker. Maybe even swing under the water tower and chance a landing on the nasty mattress. Still from this height, he thinks he is done for. The swaying calms down and hand over hand he makes his way to the still anchored part of the banister. Weak, with his arms giving, he can only stare at his black hands as they maneuver up the lower bar. He has torn a good four feet of metal off the tower and is halfway back to the catwalk when not so far away he hears a familiar sound.

The guttural squeal cracks through the ambience, it is long and it is loud.

"No!" Jake gasps, trying to look around the ground. His movements agitate the tower and another bolt noisily pops off.

How could I have been so stupid, he curses himself, climbing up into plain site, and making all this noise?

In a steady panic he makes his way back to the catwalk and pulls himself up with a heavy grunt. Before he can stand, he hears the creature again, closer than before. He presses his back to the tower, his faith in the monolith's integrity gone as he tries to ascertain the creature's location. Jake realizes he has to get down to the ground to make a get away. He side steps to the ladder and quickly begins his decent, but it is too late. The creature smashes into the base of the ladder with a sickening howl and shakes the entire tower. Jake looks down and the thing answers his frightened look with a nod and a gasping chortle, which could only have been the creature's poor attempt at a laugh or chuckle.

Jake is only a third of the way down and starts scrambling back up. The shock of seeing it again super charges his desire to escape. The creature leaps a good distance up the chute and latches on to the ladder. Despite having one arm, it gains on him quickly. With the advantage of distance gone so fast, he debates letting go and coming down on top of the creature to try and knock it off the ladder. He looks down to aim his release and sees the creature's large hand already slashing at him. The tower begins shaking violently as the two scuffle inside the chute. Jake sends powerful kicks down at the creature's hand and misaligned face. He realizes the one armed wretch is highly disadvantaged now. He presses on hoping he can beat the thing out of the chute and leave it wounded enough to make another getaway. The thing squeals and gasps. Black juices spurt and mist from its large hideous mouth. Jake smiles and yells down at the creature stomping it further towards the ground.

Luckily the chute is narrow and humanoid is larger than a normal person. The creature tries to cover itself with its one arm as it keeps getting bashed against the chute. Jake does not relent. With a barrage of profanities, he sends his frustration into its head kick by kick until finally a section of the chute gives way as it is knocked squealing backwards fifty feet down into the cold hard dirt.

Jake smiles, but his victory is short.

Before he can take another step down, the thing is already coming to its feet. It releases an angered roar and shambles to the base of the ladder. Staring up at him, its upside down face twists in a horrible way, making an expression that Jake interprets as anger. With that look, the thing pulls its knife. *The* knife. And flicks it back and forth through the air.

As animalistic as this thing is, it shows Jake a very human intelligence. He keeps looking down at it over his shoulder, returning his own angry stare. In defiance, Jake takes a step down the ladder. He has no other choice but to get down. To Jake's surprise the creature jumps back.

His confidence grows. He has beaten this thing back twice now and is determined to live. It keeps slashing at the air with the knife but Jake does not stop. It stomps the ground a few times, like a child throwing a tantrum, then starts exhaling deep backwards breaths.

It inhales making a sound Jake has not yet heard. It is a loud squeal like before, but interrupted by the creature opening and closing its mouth. He gets a bad feeling and speeds up. Before the echoes from the first squeal ends, the creature repeats the sound then places the blade in its mouth. It begins ascending the ladder again, slowly this time. Halfway down, Jake readies himself for another kicking match.

As they move towards each other, it stops and pulls the blade from its mouth. The thing exhales again, but before it can suck its scream inwards, a new sound breaks through the air. Almost like a dog's yelp from being bitten or kicked by its wicked owner, the new sound answers the call. The source of the noise is close and the creature below removes the blade from its mouth long enough to reply with a short version of its own call. Jake glances away from the thing below him and looks around needing, not wanting to see what new horror has joined the assault. And he does. Another creature rushes towards their direction from the oil fields. It appears to be running on all fours and it is fast.

Jake tries convincing himself that their numbers do not matter. One or two in the chute and he could still try to keep them at bay.

The new thing leaps to the base of one of the still standing derricks and nimbly makes its way to the top.

"This one climbs," he gasps.

Apelike, it hangs from the derrick and looks around until it spots them. It barks its twisted dog bark and scrambles down the derrick in a flash.

He guesses this thing can scale the tower without the ladder and cut him off at the top. He looks back down to the first creature who is moving faster now that its help has arrived.

"Fuck you!" Jake yells down at it, then begins racing back up the ladder.

A jittery weakness takes over him but he fights it and tries to come up with a plan where he doesn't end up dead or wanting to die. He scurries up and chances to get a better look at the new thing.

It also looks like it was human once, naked and filthy. Its arms are long and massive, but its legs are shrunken and malformed. The legs bow out from its sides and curve back under the thing's body, tapering into small points and making a crab like claw. Its movements are jerky but fast. This creature strides by pushing its legs in unison between its elongated arms, like most fast land animals.

Already at the base of the tower, it leaps up using its curved legs like hooks and begins effortlessly swinging its way up along the lattice of support struts.

Jake pulls himself back to the catwalk and hears the thing clattering its way up the shaking tower. Quickly he runs over to the torn banister and tries yanking a piece of the metal off. He figures his best advantage is also his greatest disadvantage, the long drop from the catwalk. He knows these things are tough but one of them is missing an arm so they can be hurt.

He wrenches a decent size piece of metal off that he can use as a club. The one who screams slaps its large hand onto the catwalk and begins pulling itself up. Jake rushes over and bashes its large fingers a few times until it withdraws. A sucking hiss threatens him through its blade clamping mouth and Jake smacks it good and hard in its mouth, knocking the knife out and onto the catwalk.

It thrashes in defiance chaotically batting its arm around but Jake times his blows to its head. The thing slips up and falls, banging its way down the chute. The creature's stench is so pungent he has to pause to quickly wipe tears from his eyes. With a thud, the one who climbs bounds onto the catwalk and immediately charges. It scrabbles at him more crablike than anything. Its wicked face is upside down as well, almost, because its head is cocked at a crooked angle. The contorted climber has the same overdeveloped two fingers and thumb, with the rest of its digits withered away. The new creature is actually smaller than the screamer, closer to Jake's size but with longer, more powerful looking arms. he notices that the thing's neck appears to be stuck in a broken state as the wretch angles its body to see. From a blackened mouth a bloated sickly tongue samples the air like a snake's and every movement of its broken body jerks with a popping sound. Jake sees the knife he dislodged from the other one's mouth lying on the shaking edge about to fall. He rushes towards it and the climber.

It leaps at him knocking him to his back but Jake holds out his weapon sideways in front of him, hoping the thing will grab at it instead of him with its claw fingers. It does and Jake rolls back and kicks up at with both legs, sending it over him and through the broken area of the banister to the ground.

Flailing wildly through the air it releases a garbled whine then slams into a section of the fence on the ground. Jake sits up and scrambles to get to the dagger just in time to see the one who screams half way out of the chute again. Jake roars and with an overhead caveman swing, bashes its skull. The creature does not fall back this time. It shakes off the blow and continues to pushing onto the catwalk. Jake leaps over it and lands with his left hand on the blade. It feels unnaturally cold, painful even, but he grabs onto it as hard as he can. The screamer rises to its feet and lumbers towards him. Jake charges and stabs it with its own weapon. It squeals again as the black blood feathers out from the wound.

"You like this?" he shouts and continues stabbing it while protecting himself from its one armed strikes with his metal club. He is actually forcing it back as he belts more profanities at it. The groaning tower's shakes worsen and he knows the climber is on its way up again. He pushes the screamer harder to the edge.

The screamer glances back seeing with its mouth, as it does. It figures what Jake is planning, but too late as it is batted off the catwalk. It flies back but manages to grab hold of the bent out banister's end. The force causes the metal to loudly unravel more and cause the tower to sway back and forth. Jake takes a step to the edge to see if it has fallen off as his ankle it grabbed hard. He looks down to see the climber instead hanging onto him and the rusted metal walkway. It jerks his leg and he falls onto the catwalk. Instinctively he looks and jabs the metal club into a space between the catwalk and the actual water tank. Just in time or he would have been yanked away. His wedge holds and he starts kicking at the creature, but it is too strong. Its grip is so powerful Jake fears his ankle will be crushed. It pulls at him with its entire body, but screaming Jake will no let go. The creature growls and changes from pulling, to climbing up his body.

Jake looks around and fears the screamer has made its way back to the catwalk by now. If he were to see the other rushing towards him he would be done. Jake looks back to the climber, who has gotten halfway up his body now. It dribbles its filthy fluids over him. It had let go of his ankle and has grabbed onto his jacket, its other hand is reaching over him for his wedge. Jake shouts at it and jabs the blade into its exposed bent neck, and twists. The creature screams and to Jake's horror, it sounds like a child's scream. He sees its grip on his jacket waiver and notices deep ligature marks on its wrists. He almost feels sorry for the broken wretch but he is not going to let it kill him. He twists the blade the other way while kicking at it. It gives in and reaches for the knife as it is once again, knocked from the catwalk to the ground.

Jake pulls himself up to his knees his body exhausted. He catches his breath while moving to where he last saw the one who screams. He holds his club in both hands and staggers to his feet. Over the edge he sees the screamer hanging from the banister. Its gangly legs sway back and forth as it makes pitiful squealing noises. It cannot pull itself up with one arm and the scene looks comical to Jake.

Jake does not know how he manages to do it, but he laughs at it.

The creature reacts, its whimpering tone angry again. On the ground the one who climbs limps around below it. It has pulled the blade from its neck but it finally appears to be hurt. They both do. Jake looks at his metal club and sees it has already started weakening from its exposure to the things. His most effective weapon against them has been that blade, probably because it was carved from the same evil cloth.

He figures if he were to dash down the ladder right now, he would not have the strength to fight or outrun them. He is stuck up here and his hopes are that there are not any more of them. So far his plan has worked though, he is still alive.

"Hey, I can do this all day!" he tiredly shouts down to them.

The climber hisses at him and the screamer's metal corroding grip has weakened the banister. It sounds like a dropped plate instead of metal when it snaps dropping it once again to the ground. Jake sees that it recovers more slowly this time. The two creatures make their respective noises towards each other. Jake does not hear any words but he knows they are communicating.

What could they be planning now, he thinks. Tempted as he is to make a run for it, a part of him just wants the nightmare to be over with, and that part yearning for an end is growing.

Shuffling back to the ladder Jake watches them and hopes the screamer does not call for more help. The second he backs into the stairwell, the two stop and look up at him with their gaping mouths. He climbs back out and watches them from the catwalk. Each of the things walks over and places their hands on one of the main support legs for the tower. He crouches down to see what they are doing.

The creatures start taking long, deep gasps of air and slowly a strange mist starts rising from the metals and is sucked into their mouths. Jake watches the act intently. The already rusted metal of the water tower begins to deteriorate rapidly. He thinks of his engine and the tire iron. Like the black moss that comes from their blood, they are leaching the very essence out of the metal. He looks on and realizes that because they cannot bring him down from the tower, they will bring the tower down. Jake stands up pacing back and forth as they continue leaching away at the base.

They are draining the two east facing supports, the tower will fall that way. Jake looks east and sees the crumbled road he came running down between over grown empty lots. The fall will cripple or kill him and they will have him. Unless the tower falls slowly. Jake looks around and notices the roadhouse across the street, directly south. If the tower falls into that building, he might have a chance at getting away. Redirecting his attention to the two below, he sees they have begun tearing away at the leeched metal, sending rusted chunks and dust to the ground. The tower begins shaking and violently, twists back and forth. He stares at the still attached section of the banister to the west and hopes that it stops him from falling. He runs to the west side and slides foot first to hit the base.

It rattles but holds and he gets up to do it again. As he slides to crash into the banister this time, the entire tower shakes just as he hits. Jake believes the two support legs have been completely separated now. The tower shakes worse than before and moving around the catwalk is more difficult. The tower will fall east to close the gap in its supports but Jake still hopes his weight can offset the fall. He just needs to nudge it west a few inches, and gravity will do the rest. He doubles back, slides and slams into the banister again and the tower stalls. He creeps back and slides into it again. The tower groans long and loud. It teeters then starts tilting west. Jake stays there, not wanting to have his weight sway the tower anymore. He can hear the creature's guttural excitement below and hopes they have once again not caught on to his plan. The tower stops shaking for a moment. Then like someone having been shot from behind, it begins to turn around as it falls, its two remaining legs bend and buckle from the weight. The force of the fall pins Jake's back against the now upright catwalk as the rapid decent blasts his body with wind.

With what may have been the loudest sound ever heard in Prudence the behemoth crashes into the top of the roadhouse, sending Jake bouncing across its collapsing roof. Tumbling through the air with wood and glass, Jake slams into the edge of the roof and is winded, only to be dowsed and almost drowned by the stagnant water from the tower. Now it is the building's turn to shudder and the squeaks and snapping of wood joins into the cacophony. He muffles his coughs in the dust while trying to catch his breath and looks around for the creatures. He is lying on the outer edge of the roof, a few inches away from the large jagged hole created by the tower. Jake rolls on his left and sees that it punched through all of the floors of the buildings.

The tank is busted open at its seams. Broken wood, pipes and snapped cables still landing on top of it. He rolls back when he sees the two already clambering over the tower and knocking the debris around looking for him. He keeps rolling away from the drop until he is stopped by the edge of the roof. Carefully, he rises to a crouch and looks over. He is in a better predicament now, but still trapped by height. He looks at his improvised club and sees the black moss thriving on it. It has completely leeched away the metal's integrity. It is worthless.

The creatures were becoming agitated, he peeks back into the disaster area and sees that he could climb down to the second floor, then make his way out if he can run along the tower's legs without slipping off.

Looking around the roadhouse from the roof again, he sees mostly forest behind it. A few boulders are scattered here and there, then he sees a large tree stump, surrounded by empty bottles. It is farther away than any of the other boulders, but it is still the most likely to get their attention. Jake adjusts his grip on club and takes aim. He hears them making their way up the floors, but focuses on the bottles.

He quickly stands straight, throws it and drops down again. He knows he has to move fast if they fall for it.

Tinkt!

Jake's waits. It is not at all the sound he was hoping for, but the roadhouse becomes silent. He hears them gurgling back and forth to each other, then a ruckus starts and ends with a window being smashed. He chances a look through the hole again and sees that the things speeding off after the noise.

Jake wastes no time and instead of climbing, leaps from the roof and lands hard onto the third floor. He hustles down some solid larger pieces of debris to the second floor. From there he climbs off the edge and drops onto the water tower as gently as he can, muffling the hollow drum. He makes his way out of the roadhouse along the slippery support legs and finally drops back to the ground. He takes off south immediately, frightened but with a true smile. He makes sure to keep the roadhouse between him and where he threw the club as best as he can, disappearing again into the endless decay of Prudence.

CHAPTER 7

With no signs yet from any pursuit Jake slows down to catch his breath. He notices his increasing endurance despite the beatings he has been taking. With the adrenalin fading his hunger returns, stronger. He is still wet and smells like the foul water, which is still less offensive than the stench of the creatures. From the alley and through the overgrowth of weeds, he sees the formation of the six burned houses with the great willow looming between them. Jake slows down to a walk and looks for any traps, snares or tripwires. He is sure that if any of the other residents were like Sam there are bound to be defenses in place. He also knows it could be dangerous and maybe even pointless to talk to any of the people here but he needs answers.

He wishes that he at least had a gun.

Jake stops and examines the center garage nearest the willow tree. The garage door does not look fortified at all. In fact, the nearby garages look no different from the others. He inspects a small hole on the edge of one of the garage doors. And sees the doors are bricked from the inside.

He forces himself not to rush as much as he wants to get indoors somewhere out of sight from the creatures. Carefully he makes his way around the garage by the willow and inspects its house facing side. He comes upon a smell, a pleasant one that makes its way past his own foul body odor. The yard looks more like a garden. Plant life creeps across the yard and fences here unlike anywhere else he has seen in town. Most of it looks like wild growth, except one type of plant. It is laid more even spaced than the others are and grows along the fence and around the garage. They are foot high sprouts of a dark purple plant, with long tapering leaves sprouting from the base. The stems are purple as well and some of the tops look like empty grape stems. He approaches a few that still have deep red flower pedals hanging from the stems, the sweet musky smell is coming from them. He had seen the purple plant around the outskirts of the town but had not noticed any blooming. He gently caresses the red death camas and takes in its scent again.

The fortifications he saw from the water tower are on the sides of the garages that face their burnt parent houses. A passerby would see nothing unusual from the alley and have no reason to go inside the destroyed houses. Jake starts feeling better about finding someone here. This person appears to be more subtle in their ways, possibly less likely to have booby traps or guns at the ready. An overgrown dirt path leads from the back of the house to the thick, yard side door. The handle is missing, removed, and even layers of wood have been nailed across the door.

He looks around and listens for a moment but hears nothing. Worried about having bullets fly through the door killing him, he crouches down by the side of the door and pushes against it. It does not budge.

He quietly knocks, waits then says, "Hello?"

A shuffling noise comes from inside garage, followed by a grunt. Jake goes over his recent unsuccessful attempts to introduce himself since he has been here, but knocks again.

"Hello? My car broke down outside of town, and I think I was being chased," he lies with a forced calmness.

A deeper grunt resounds followed by a clicking noise. He leans back against the garage and stairs up at the milky sky. An orange flicker catches his eye. He turns around and sees a periscope looking contraption sticking out from the upper corner of the garage. He stands, looking at the orange flickering mirror in the corner of the 'L' shaped pipe.

Jake thinks of how he and his brother used to make things like this as kids to see around corners.

It is small but he sees a blurry shadow moving away from the periscope. He stands and tries to look as harmless as possible while looking for other peeping contraptions.

"Were you the one who made that loud noise?" a parched but deep woman's voice pushes its way through the door.

"Ugh, yes?" Jake replies.

More grunting accompanied by the sounds of stone sliding against stone, the rattling of chains and sliding of bolts riots from the doorway. The door opens wide and Jake jumps back at the site of the woman standing there. She looks very old and terribly haggard. Her skin is filled with deep cracks like drought stricken earth and it has that tint. Mostly white hair splits off to the sides of her gnarled face and runs down the front of her body in wild crooked curls. The ancient woman's eyes are the most frightening. The creamy gray pupils, bright against the thin circles of her black irises are almost swallowed by the large eyeballs floating there in her sunken black eye sockets. The expressionless woman squints at Jake for just a second before the lines of her face contort into a wicked visage of hatred.

"You reek!" she hisses and raises a long barreled shotgun from behind her drab robe.

Jake may have been too exhausted or may have had death aimed at him enough for the day, but he does not raise his hands. Instead he clenches his fists and snarls back, "I smell like this because those things attacked me!"

"After all this time, this is how you finally try to kill me? Pathetic!" she sneers.

"I don't know who you are you old bat! I came here looking for help!"

The woman's leathery face shifts, still angered but a bit more curious. "So you've said."

"Can you point that thing at the ground?"

"No."

"Do you want to see my I.D.? I'm not from here."

116

"I'm practically blind you idiot!" she barks. "But with this," she grins and hefts her shotgun, "you try, you die."

"If you don't want to help me, I'll move on."

"You stink like those damned things!" her jaw quivers and her body winces.

"So you've seen them?"

"As well as I can," she says with an abrupt calmness. Her stony expression breaks into a wicked smile, "But I don't think you would get so close to them and live."

"Well, I did. A few times."

"Oh? So you're a badass?" she taunts him.

"No, they're just very stupid."

The woman belches out an unsettling cackle.

"Come closer, boy."

Jake hesitates. As old and slouched as she is, she is still a bit taller than he is and scary as hell. She looks like the classic witch from fairy tales except she has a shotgun.

"Come!"

Jake takes a few slow steps forward, "What for?"

"Come, and raise your hands."

Jake does as he is told, his eyes now on the end of a gun again, he is just a foot away from her. In contrast to her appearance, she has a pleasant smell and Jake sees small pouches hanging from her rustic necklaces.

"Higher now, raise your arms, palms out."

He does as she tells him.

"No!" she shouts, "press your fingers together."

Jake looks at his hands, aimed up, palms out with his fingers pressing together.

She takes her left hand from the barrel of the gun and grabs one of his hands inspecting it for something. Her leathery hands with their dark pointed tips are half covered by the sleeves of her strange robe, but they are warm, hot even as they press against his.

What she is doing is strange, he thinks, but maybe she knows what the discoloration on his hands might be.

But here he is with his hands like this, introducing himself like an Indian stereotype from some old cartoon, to an actual Indian.

One of his notoriously dumb for the sake of humor thoughts crosses his mind and he feels a bit like his old self. He thinks maybe some humor would ease some of the tension and he cannot resist.

"How." he says with a stupid grin.

SLAP!

The old woman wraps him across his face. The powerful smack stings his skin and he feels more like he had been kicked in the head. The force knocks him down to one knee and he lingers there, stunned. He shakes his head and looks up to see the butte of the gun crashing painfully into his jaw. There is darkness again.

The old witch towers over Jake's crumpled body. She looks around the yard and listens as Jake had, muttering to herself. She reaches down and her long birdlike fingers easily wrap around his dirty pants. She drags him with ease into the garage, locking the many locks on the inside behind her.

* * *

Different pains compete for their place in the forefront of Jake's mind as he regains his consciousness. His cuts and bruises from his battles and falls, his stinging skin and aching bones. Above all, the pain in his gut from his hunger. There is a new sensation, a tightness around his neck and wrists. His vision still blurry, a haze and small fires dance around a dark small space. He tries to move but the tightness constricts around his throat. He gags and leans back, away from the tension. A rope is tight around his neck and his wrists are bound. He kneels on a stone floor his knees are numb from pain. The ropes binding him are tied to a wooden beam. A murmur bubbles out of his tired body and he jerks when he realizes he has been stripped down to his underwear.

Ice cold water splashes across him and he yells while straining from the shock, choking himself again.

"Oh, I didn't know you were awake."

Jake looks up to see the old which leering down at him.

"You fucking bitch!" he shouts angrily but still sounds pitiful.

"Such a mouth!" she exclaims with feigned offense. "I just

118

wasted a whole bucket of water on you."

"Why are you doing this to me?"

"Because you stink! Like one of them."

Jake squirms and tries breaking free.

"Stop that! You will only choke yourself."

"Untie me!"

"No! Not until I know what you're about!" she snaps.

"I came looking for answers!"

She blankly stares at him.

Jake examines the long narrow room. He doubts he could be inside that garage because the dimensions are much larger. The walls and floor looks to be made from a combination of slabs and assorted bricks. He sees no doors or windows from where he is tied up and the only sources of light are from a few dim lanterns. He keeps straining and the witch sits down a few feet away on what looks like an outdoor picnic bench. The room is over crowded with books and other random things. Some of it is junk, some of it tools. Other things appear to be tribal paraphernalia.

She watches him strain against the ropes with no expression and lights up a tobacco pipe, her eyes unblinking in the dark, glow in the flame from Jake's devil girl lighter.

After ten or more minutes of struggling, Jake slumps down. Now at least sitting on the cold hard floor instead of being on his knees.

"Strong will, I'm impressed," she cackles.

Jake angrily stares past her.

"Do as you wish. I don't mind staring at a supple young body all day."

He winces at the thought.

"I thought you were blind," he says through clenched teeth.

"Not entirely, not yet."

"Where are my clothes?"

"Over there," she gestures to a steamy section at the end of the long narrow room. "I am trying to boil that nasty smell out of them."

"That's my lighter."

"Is it? You had no smokes on you."

"So! It's mine."

"I kind of like it though. Its nice shiny luster, hard to find good metal around here," her withered fingers smooth over the lighter.

Jake looks at her and in his discomfort, kicks himself for taking the risk of seeking someone out.

"Will you help me?" he asks, sincerity in his voice.

It is a sad sounding plea and the woman turns her head away to hide the brief wash of emotion that comes over her.

Jake looks at her, only seeing another puff of smoke rise from behind her wild gray hair.

"This doesn't look like a garage."

"Why would it?" she turns to him, "You are not in that garage."

"Are you here alone?"

Her eyes narrow, "Are these the questions you want to ask?"

"No."

"You claimed you sought me out to get answers from me," she says suspiciously.

"No. I came to find answers from anybody, I don't know who the hell you are."

"Then why not ask?" she says impatiently.

"Because you have me hogtied in my underwear, and the last guy I started asking the real questions, tried to shoot me even though he had just helped me!"

"Heh. Who was this?"

"The old war vet, Sam."

"Ah ha!" she cackles again. "That old fool! He didn't want to talk about *them*, huh?"

"No," he was dead set against mentioning anything about . . . you know."

She laughs again and shakes her head, "I told him so many times, those rules don't apply when they're already out."

"What?" Jake gasps. "So you know what they are?"

"I would like to think so, but with these things. . ." the witch spaces out for a moment while taking another long drag from her pipe.

"Okay then," Jake perks up, "how do you kill them?"

"Kill them?" she smiles. "Have you tried?" she swings her long legs over the bench she is sitting on, leans forward and rests the backs of her hands on her knees. Jake sees she has the lit pipe in her left hand and a curved knife in her right. The knife looks handmade and does not have a metal blade. Regardless of what it is made from, it is covered in a dark red wetness and a single drop beads near the tip of the blade.

Jake hesitates and looks back at her. She seems oblivious to the knife and curious about what he has to say. He thinks of the creatures and how they at one point seemed to have been Indians, and then of the ligature marks he saw on the one who crawls' wrists. Here he is tied up in front of a strange Indian witch doctor.

Jake can only think, this is too bad to be true.

He leans back from her and sinks. His drained body is beyond shock or dread and he looks away from her at the sloppy gray brick wall.

"Just, just fucking kill me already," he sighs.

"Whaaat?" the witch leans back and notices the knife in her hand. "Oh!" she throws her head back and cackles, "I stir my stew with this knife!"

"Bullshit," he mumbles. "I'm tired of the games. I know you are with those things. I'm not doing this anymore. Just kill me."

The witch looks upon Jake with sadness. She groans as she stands up and shuffles away from him towards the seamy dark end of the long tunnel like room. There, on what looks like a cooking range from America's frontier days, she tends to a series of pots, all boiling away. She opens one and stirs something deep red with the knife, then swipes the blade over her tongue, smacking at the flavor. After adding in some obscure seasonings, she stirs it again while puffing at her pipe in deep contemplation.

Eventually she returns to Jake, but instead of sitting down she stands next to him. Jake looks up with a defeated grimace and sees the witch staring down at him, holding a black container full of something hot.

"Drink this," she says in her rough and serious tone.

"Why? Is this how you turn me into one of those things?"

She squats down over him and presses her knife to his throat. "Drink it!" she growls.

"No! If you are gonna kill me, kill me!" he presses his throat against the knife.

She presses the blade back against him, slowly cutting into his throat. A few drops of blood smears from his neck onto the blade. The witch looks at it and moves the knife away from him. She still squats there eyeing the blood on the knife intensely. Even in his anger Jake stares at the blade to see what is so damned interesting. She angles the knife in the air allowing his blood to mix thoroughly with the red fluid on the blade. Nothing happens.

"Huh," she says and takes a swig from the container she is holding. "I guess you're alright."

Confused again Jake stares eyes wide open at the old witch.

"What the hell just happened?"

"Nothing happened."

"Nothing?"

"That's a good thing, boy. If something would have happened I would have slit your throat and you would be bleeding out on my floor right now."

"What could have happened?!"

"A reaction, between your blood and my concoction."

"And if I would have drank that stuff?"

"A bigger reaction, if you were like them, you would have suffered violently, if you were not . . . "

"Then no reaction," he finishes her sentence.

She leans over him offering the hot beverage again, "Will you drink now?"

"Your stew?"

"No. Stews not ready yet."

Jake's face tightens but he nods and she presses the container to his mouth. He sees that the strange container is a hollowed out piece of tree branch. Its outside is still covered in bark but it has been treated in someway. His eyes turn towards the mysterious fluid he is about to drink. Through the drink's rising steam he sees it is dark red, the familiar smell is the same as her tobacco and the flowers outside. She tips the cup back and he drinks. The fluid is hot but it burns in a different way. It is the drink he had before, in the past. He takes a few swigs, remembering how it chased his hunger away before, and it does. It burns again but his body becomes invigorated and feels like the rays of a hot sun are spilling over him. He takes a few deep breaths and relaxes. His hunger is finally gone again.

"Good?" the old woman asks, watching him for any other reactions.

"Yes, very," he says while catching his breath.

She backs away and returns to her seat at the bench again. Sits sideways and drinks from the container.

"So neither of us are monsters," she says.

Jake stares at the ground, "Will you untie me now?"

"No," she looks over to him and smiles, "not quite yet. I want to know what you're doing here."

Jake tries to make himself comfortable as best as he can.

"I was driving out West to visit my brother. I had some car trouble and a bunch of crazy things started happening then I woke up here in my car."

"No."

"No, what?"

"It's the crazy things I want to know about. There's no reason you should ever have found this place. Something led you here, that's what I want to know."

Jake's eyes shift over the floor as he tries to organize his crazy experiences enough to articulate them. He takes a deep calming breath and begins.

As Jake discloses his story to her he tries to gauge her reactions, many of which she could easily hide by turning her head away as if she were more worried about her cooking. He understands why she sits almost sideways towards him in that strange way, because it is perfect for her to hide any reactions or expressions. He lays everything out starting with the bizarre incident with the convict and everything that happened to him up until the first encounter with the one who screams. Jake notices that despite her listening technique she seems very disturbed at the mention of a few things. Particularly of the convict and of Jake subsequently finding the convicts shed skin in the tow truck and later of his encounters with Kenneth.

Jake sees the woman has stopped smoking her pipe and appears nervous. She turns to finally look at him and her eyes are so filled with terror that Jake feels like his soul just got knocked out of his body. They share one of those eternal moments together staring at each other in fear. Her look confirms the dread Jake has been forcing to the back of his mind since his arrival in Prudence.

The old woman wanders back to her bubbling pots, Jake watches her fishing what must be his clothes from the largest pot, and slinging them over an old radiator. He watches the steam billow from the clothes into the cold dank room, thankful that her drink has given him a reprieve from the cold, inside and out.

Wiping the steam from her wrinkled forehead, she returns. This time, periodically stopping and staring out of different periscopes she has throughout the room.

"Go back to your first encounter," she asks while still staring out one of the peepholes.

"Yeah? With the one who screams."

"An appropriate name for that one," she turns to him, trying to smile through her worry. "How did you get away from him?"

"Him?" Jake huffs. "*It* seemed to want to torture me first. Started cutting at my face. Luckily it only has one arm and I beat it down with a tire iron that I brought from my car."

"And then?" she kneels down by him again, inspecting his cut.

"Well, I ran for my life!"

"Smart move. You know now, they do not die like we do."

Her long hard fingernails roll over his face especially his forehead, then the scar running down his cheek. She mumbles to herself as she does this, as if she were going over some old recipe book. Her brow furrows and Jake stares at her, expecting her dried up skin to literally crumble away.

"What the hell are they?" Jake barks, his patience spent.

"Maybe I should start there," she says. "But first."

She moves behind him and he feels her fumbling with the ropes. Just like that they drop away from his neck and wrists and he is unbound. "Here," she tosses him a towel before he manages to fully stand on his numb legs. "Go over there and put your underwear in that large pot."

Jake stares at her uncomfortably.

"What? They're filthy, or would you rather wear a pair of mine?" she teases him.

Jake quickly turns about and makes his way to the end of the long room.

She set him free but he still looks around for an exit or a gun or something, incase she changes her mind or worse, those things come crashing in.

"Eyes forward smart ass," she nags him from across the room.

With the towel around him he drops his soaked underwear into the bubbling pot and makes his way back. The old woman's place looks like an alchemist's lab, just what he would expect to find in an old witch's hut. He sees her books and trinkets and jars filled with who knows what. Along a wall are illegible newspaper clippings and various photos. It reminds him of Sam's shrine and many of the same people from his pictures appear to be in them.

"Sit here," she gestures to a small leather armchair.

It creaks and its springs pop when he sits down, but the patch covered old chair is a lot more comfortable than the cold stone floor. Even with them both sitting she looks down to him and hands him a blanket and the container of the hot red drink. Jake remembers it is the same red death camas tea he got before from Evelyn and wonders if this old lady ran the apothecary that she had mentioned getting hers from.

He takes a large swig and the heat fills his body again.

The gnarled old woman takes a long drag from her pipe and collects herself. Her pose is serious and her cloudy eyes flicker from their dark sockets in the lantern's light.

"Although they are truly monsters now, I do not believe that they were ever really human. They are now as they were in their first life, vicious and hateful. Like locusts, they travelled these lands killing and mutilating everything in their paths. And with their insatiable hunger consuming all their eyes could see, the Devourers were then as they are now, a plague on life itself."

"Devourers." Jake slowly whispers the word. "First life? I have no idea why, but I assumed that they were somehow alive, or are they dead?"

"Neither. Like all abominations, they are not subject to the simpler rules of nature," the old woman's mouth twists in disgust.

"Then they are undead."

"No."

"So they just decided one day they wouldn't die?"

"Something like that."

"No, sorry no," Jake shakes his head. "That's just bullshit."

The old woman sighs a stream of smoke into the air and watches it swirl and fade away. With her pipe in hand she makes gestures in the air, like she is trying to sculpt the words in her mind so Jake could understand.

"They are like dreams or nightmares but also physical," she tries to simplify. "What you have seen of them is a glimpse of how they perceive themselves, but within the confines of their bodies as they were before the end of their first lives."

Jake is still skeptical, "So yeah, they just decided one day they didn't feel like dying."

"Yes and no," her shoulders slump in defeat. "It's not that simple."

"I'm not going anywhere without clothes, so explain away."

"Look boy, not everything can be known or explained!"

"I guess."

"Hey!" she snaps. "Have you seen anything normal since you got here?"

Jake thinks about his behavior. He of all people should no longer be skeptical. "I'm sorry. I believe in monsters now. I never believed in magic or anything until I woke up here, but I do believe. I just wanted more."

"More what? Did you expect me to weave some story of an ancient curse or tell you how you are part of some prophecy?" she barks.

"No!"

"What then?"

"Well you know, are they some type of ghost? Are they like vampires? I've never met one but I kinda think I would know how to kill a vampire!"

"Nothing like that, like any of those."

Thinking hard, Jake itches away at the slight beard that he has grown, "Where did they come from?"

"I do not know how they came to be, but when they came to this area, Prudence wasn't even a town. It had a different name. The tribe started with its killing, eating. The townsfolk tried killing them off but to their horror they could not." She stops to tap the spent leaves from her pipe and stuffs it with a fresh batch lighting it again with the devil girl lighter. "This went on for a few weeks, until one day the founder of the town left only to return a few days later. That's when the totems were carved and erected and the Devourers vanished."

"Just like that?"

"Of course not. You know who has the answers."

Jake sits forward in the chair, leaning his head on his left hand and pressing two fingers against his temple, fidgeting.

"So they're not alive like we are, but they don't die. Their bodies are all messed up like that, because they get stuck with what they had when they died the *first* time."

"Yes, boy."

"Well," Jake shifts around uncomfortably in his seat. "Do you have any thoughts on um, why their fucking faces are upside down?"

The crone winces at Jake's mention of their faces.

"They were cannibals as that was not so uncommon in their time, but they fed voraciously. And they marked their faces in a peculiar way."

She leans over to Jake, touching his forehead with her long boney finger and draws a single line from right to left.

Jake shudders and jerks away.

"They consume what they see," her words sound distant as Jake relives the moment when the convict marked him in the same way.

He clenches his fists, "When I told you about that crazy old prisoner and that Kenneth guy you gave me a look. What do they want from me?"

The old woman straightens her back, stern and serious, "The old prisoner and Kenneth are the same person."

Jake jumps up in his seat, nearly dropping his towel and steps back, noisily bumping into a shelf.

"What?" he says in a weak voice.

"You know. You told me what you found in that truck, the cast off skin."

Silently, Jake replays the find in his head.

"Don't boy. Don't try to make sense of this wickedness, you will lose yourself to it."

"What do they, what does *he* want?" he says in a shaky voice.

"He was a man who helped bring them back. He was a man responsible for the tragedy that ruined and claimed many lives in this town. In fact, I thought you were him outside, come to finish me off."

"So, everyone did get killed?" he feels the terrifying reality expanding around him on all sides. He visualizes their black blood rising up around him in giant tidal waves under the pale lifeless sky. Coming for him.

"What do I do?" he pleads.

"I know that he has lured you here. I know he is keeping you here. And I know that twice you have been marked by them."

"What do the marks mean?"

"This makes no sense!" she shifts in her seat, agitated. "You are not from here. But your parents, where are they from?"

"Not here."

Your parents, grandparents are you sure?"

"Are you asking if I'm Indi—" he catches himself, "Native American?"

"Just say Indian you fool!" she snaps.

"But earlier you slapped me!"

"Because you were being a little smart ass! Your people?"

"No Indian blood, look at me."

"That means nothing."

"European, I'm pretty sure of that."

She looks at him, gently raking her fingers against her skin, the tips push into the deep cracks running down her cheeks.

"Why, why, why?" she quietly repeats to herself.

She shakes her head, "This is what truly confuses me, more than his return. Those marks are a right of passage for them, they are welcoming you as one of their own."

"What?"

"Yes! This is all far beyond what I know of them. But I think, if they mark you a third time then . . . "

Visibly distraught, the cold beads of sweat on his face begin to melt. He reaches up and touches his glistening pale forehead, "The pain, the hunger."

"So they can!" she rises towards Jake. "They want to make you one of them!"

Her vocal epiphany causes Jake to feel even worse and he sees the black tidal waves rise higher above him in the pale sky. He tries to talk but only stammers. The room begins to spin but a sharp slap brings the dim room and the witch into focus again.

"Pull yourself together!" with a strong grip her sharp fingers dig into the back of his neck and she shakes him once, as if he were a disobedient child.

"If you fall apart this easily, you might as well just walk to the center of town and bend over!"

The slap had brought him back but her words wake him up. He casts an angry stare at her as he tries breaking out of her powerful grip.

"That's better," she smiles her wicked smile and shoves him back towards the seat. "Ah, stews ready." The woman turns away from him and waves for him to sit down again.

Jake breathes heavily thinking about Kenneth being the old man. How uncanny it all was. Looking back, Kenneth had been toying with him. His whole demeanor towards him had been off. But how was he to know? How could he have conceived any of this to be possible? The witch had told him so much but he still feels like he knows nothing, in fact he has even more questions.

She returns with two cheap looking plastic bowls, a large contrast to her tree branch cup. Inside is another deep red concoction, with chunks. His hunger had abated but he still digs in. It contains beats, roots and other vegetables. It is predominantly the color and taste of that flower again.

"Thanks."

"Oh, the first thank you all day," she says sarcastically which seems to help her savor her meal. "So, have you figured out what makes you so special to him?"

"No," he somberly replies.

"What do you do for a living?"

"This and that, nothing out of the ordinary."

"A slacker then," she says with disdain.

"I mean, I went to college."

"For what?"

"Just took the standard classes. I can do different things, I just don't see myself spending my whole life doing the same thing."

"So just slow in the head," she teases.

"Thanks. Do you ever eat anything besides this?" he pantomimes with a spoon full of the stew.

"It beats the alternative of nothing," she grins.

"Can you leave this place?"

"What would I do out there? And why do I get the feeling you are trying to set me up for more of your sarcasm."

Jake looks up and smiles at her.

"I know, I'm pretty sharp for a blind old witch."

He is surprised, but he likes that she is familiar with his sense of humor and smart mouth.

"Go ahead, get it off your chest."

"I was going to say," he wipes some stew from his smart-aleck grin. "Slow as I am, at least I know there's a simple operation to get that cataracts fixed."

Her head whips over at him, her expression blank.

Jake leans back, once again having gone too far with his humor.

She blinks a few times and he watches her dull eyes move around the room.

"Really?" she asks with earnest curiosity.

"Yeah," he answers in an uncertain tone.

"Huh. It *would* be nice to see better again."

"You really can leave?"

"I believe I could if I wanted to."

"Why stay?"

"To keep them sealed and to help a friend."

"Sam?"

"Him too, that fool. He thinks his little crucifix garden has been protecting him. Had I not planted my flowers in his yards he would've been done for, years ago."

"Can I kill them with that flower?"

"Not likely. It's like acid to them. and when they breathe or suck at the air, whatever it is they do, this flower is like poison to them."

"That's only fair. Their stench causes me to gag."

"And you boy. You cannot leave because you have been tainted by them?"

"I tried. If I pass between those totems I just wind up back in town."

"Interesting. To them it is a solid barrier, painful to touch."

"If I were to push one against the barrier, through it even, what would happen?"

"You would have better luck pushing one of them through a mountain. But if one of them manages to get out, an awareness of them would spread and they would become too powerful for the barrier."

"What do you mean?"

"Boy, what fuels them is our knowledge of them, our thoughts. Remember they are like dreams and you cannot have a dream without a dreamer."

"But Kenneth was outside of the barrier for decades."

"I know. He escaped from here when he was still a man, or mostly. He was caught too far away for the town's survivors to enact their private justice. So he sat rotting away in the system. For the longest time it kept me up at night. But I would take the long walks and keep the barriers strong while he was far away."

"But he could have been telling people about it, sending them here with his lies."

"A few have come over the years, mostly other ex-con's looking for whatever false promises Kenneth had poured into their ears. The people who escaped that night have taken great care to keep this place hidden. And besides, not many would listen to a madman."

"And that's also why Sam wouldn't talk about them."

"Yes, but it doesn't matter now. And I do not know how Kenneth's power grew in such a way to slip his old skin. What dark pacts he has made and secrets solved. But somehow back then, he set the Devourers free causing the calamity that destroyed this town. I do not how he accomplished that either."

"How many were there?"

"Too many. I still hear the screams from that night. We were being drug off into the smoke and shadows by them as the town and oil fields burned."

"So there's more than two," he groans.

"You have only seen two? That's good. But there will be a third."

"What?! Why?"

"Even the descendants of the colonists knew little of the Devourers, as it had to be. Absolute knowledge of them was never meant to be passed down, but future generations had to know and believe in the rituals that kept them sealed away. The situation would always cut both ways. So brilliant and insidious was the tribe that became the Devourers, that they may have planned it that way from the start. Immortality gained from the thoughts of others who have no choice but to think of them. There have been only two for many years, two of them because of Sam and me. Now you are here and you believe, so there will be another."

"But if the whole tribe showed up that night, why are there only a couple of the things left?"

The witch's demeanor changes, she even twirls a lock of her wild gray hair in her fingers.

"I'm not entirely sure, but there was a man. The man who helped me escape the town that night. He went back in to help others."

"Did he take a bunch of them out? What happened to him?"

"I stayed outside of the town for a few days. That's when Sam returned from the war and he wanted answers. Only a few of us went back in with him, the fewer of us the better. But when we did, all but three of them were gone. Many of the bodies from the people who were taken were never found, neither was the man who helped me."

Jake sees tears well up in the old woman's eyes, then recede.

"Lady, what did he do to get rid of the other creatures?"

"I . . . maybe they took him and the others away to wherever they came from. He did have knowledge of a tool that was used by the founder to stop them before. Maybe he got to it and used it on them."

"A weapon?" Jake stands up surprised.

"Of sorts."

"Why are you mentioning this now?"

"I spent my adult life in this town just looking for it! It's been lost since before you were born!"

"Where exactly are they sealed up? If they're trapped inside the barrier, it can't be far."

"You will have to get Sam to talk about that, he found it."

"And he came back? Maybe he has it!"

"I wouldn't know."

"Why, didn't he tell you?"

She shuffles over to the end of the room tending to his clothes.

"Sam was different when he came back from where they are and what he went through in the war didn't help. He blames me for what happened."

Jake stares hard at the old women's back and wonders. Her appearance is frightening and she is a hard ass, but she does not strike him as someone so malicious. "Were you?"

She ignores his question and continues working in the steamy area. He walks over to one of the peepholes and looks out. Not surprisingly it is daylight outside but he does not recognize the area. He tries to think of how the old woman could have carried him so far, unless she was getting help. He looks out another peephole and sees part of a willow tree with a burnt house behind it.

He has not moved far, but this cannot be the interior of any garage.

"See anything?"

"Nope."

"Your clothes are dry enough to put on."

"So soon? Thank you."

"I didn't want to ruin your leather jacket, so I tried smoking the stink off."

The old woman returns to the bench and starts smoking while Jake gets dressed. His clothes are soft and mostly dry, but they have the heavy smell of that flower. He looks around but does not see his shoes anywhere.

"Shoes?"

"Oh yeah, smoking them with your jacket. I'll get them for you later."

He returns to the seat where she is waiting for him and feeling a lot better now that he is not naked.

"The founder started a group called the Lamplighters. Sam's was one of them."

Jake is caught off guard by the importance the woman put on this, it sounds like she is confessing.

"They were the ones who were taught the methods of keeping those monsters bound and they were often outsiders or newcomers to the town. The founder was the first of them. Sam was from the third generation of Lamplighters in his family."

"That sounds backwards using outsiders for something so secretive."

"It was a matter of trust."

"He didn't trust the other townspeople?"

"At first, of course. But as time passed," she pauses then starts over. "Because the existence of the Devourers had to remain unspoken and especially kept from their descendants, the bloodlines of the people here became ineligible to become lamplighters."

"What? But you said that they were all sealed away!"

"Yes, the adults were, but not the younger children."

"Those things had kids?" he says out loud to himself.

"Why wouldn't they?" the old woman defensively asks him. "They were still people, the savagery was taught to them."

She stops to smooth the wrinkles out of her clothes.

"So in time, many of colonists ended up having kids with the surviving tribe members. And although Sam was a Lamplighter, he never really believed until he saw. And once he did, for that and other things I could have gone about better, he hated me."

"Wait a minute!" Jake leans forward in the chair and presses his hair back while trying to digest what he just heard. Another obvious piece he failed to put together sooner. It makes sense to him, but he is compelled to confirm, "So. The tribe that became the Devourers and the gray skinned Indians were the same."

The old woman's large eyes pop open then flatten in confusion.

"Yes," she answers in a strange, uncertain tone that Jake fails to notice as he gets up and paces away still rubbing his head.

"The gray Indians killed most of the men but they still let the kids hang around?"

She rises from the bench, quietly tucking her knife up her sleeve and slowly approaches Jake from behind.

"The founder couldn't bring himself to harm the children," she says. "And that may have been the reason why they weren't sealed away forever."

"At first I assumed that the gray Indians were the ones who helped seal them," Jake pokes at the soreness of the cut as he keeps thinking out loud.

"Sam told you about the gray Indians?" she slides the blade from her sleeve back into her hand.

"Huh? No."

She holds the blade up high while Jake is still mired in his thoughts.

"Then who?"

"Sophie."

The name hits the old woman like a shockwave and just as Jake turns around realizing she is that close, she turns away concealing the knife from him. She is overwhelmed and breathless, slowly shuffling back to her seat and away from him. In that split second, her world is turned upside down. It had been over forty years and the man who saved her life, the man who went missing so long ago is right here, right now.

"Are you ok lady?"

"Yes!" she stammers and drops back onto her bench. "It's just, I didn't know anyone outside of town still knew about them as being called the gray Indians."

"Yeah," he slowly says. "There's something else I haven't told you yet. Because I was still wondering despite everything if it was real or if I was going crazy. But I have—" he reaches into his left pants pocket and withdraws some damp bits of tissue. "Damn. It got washed."

"What was it?" she tries to hide her curiosity but she is sure she will believe anything he is about to tell her.

Jake sits down on the edge of the seat leaning towards her. "For one, I haven't seen the night since I've been here. It's like I have been stuck in one long day. But I believe I have been here for close to a week now."

"That may be how they see things. Your perception is influencing actual time?"

"I don't have any control over it, but it gets weirder. I actually slid backwards in time, into the seventies!"

The old woman had been a great poker player in her time but today she is pushing her blank stare to its limits. She is pretty sure about what this boy, who she knew as Jake, was going to tell her. She also knows about the things he has yet to do. She fears that if she were to say anything to him, it may alter everything for the worst. She decides on caution for the moment, but already begins the complicated task of finding a way to manipulate time for the better or to let things happen as they are meant to.

"Really?!" she feigns shock.

"This never happened?" he asks half surprised.

"No, this is all new to me! And you cannot control it?"

"I just get a terrible pain in my skull and pass out. There's a humming as well, but that's it."

Jake continues on with the story of him lying his way out of the police station then going out to eat. The old woman struggles internally, listening to this was not as easy as she thought it would be. She strains her weak eyes trying to see him better and hopes she will have an opportunity to get close again, just to see him.

"Then Sophie introduced me to Evelyn at the diner. Did you know them?"

The old woman freezes. She did not expect to answer any questions. She keeps her posture but puts her mind to work quickly to place herself somewhere back then that Jake would never have had a reason to go to.

"What, just because we all have that *tint* as you call it, we are supposed to know each other?" she stalls with fake irritation.

"No, I didn't mean anything like that. I figured you might now their parents. I mean, you were what, ten, twenty years older than the girls back then?"

She is taken back. Surely, she had been scarred by her experiences and lifestyle, but she does not think she looks that old.

"I kept to myself mostly but their names sound familiar. One of them was the sheriff's daughter right?"

"Kinda' yeah. Sophie was the deputy's daughter."

"I don't think I had either of them in any of my classes. I taught at the grade school there."

Having no reason not to, Jake believes her.

"What did you think of the girls?"

"Hm? Oh, well they were both very beautiful. I had never seen any women like them before."

She smiles inside, it was a selfish question for her to ask but Jake has redeemed himself. "I meant, how did they react to your cover story?"

"I didn't mean to deceive them. Like I said, I thought I was losing my mind. Or that they were ghosts, but they were great girls. Sophie really liked me but Evelyn, she was a little off."

"How so?"

"She seemed to be going through her own personal stuff. I didn't spend that much time with her, but it was like she was scared of something."

She feels like she is watching a movie from a completely different point of view. All of the strange things about Jake, how he knew the things he did and his motivations back then were becoming clear to her. It must have been so hard for him going through all of that in the past on top of what was happening to him here.

"Do you think she suspected you?"

"Kind of, but that wasn't it. I don't think it had anything to do with me, but a strange sensation would came over me when I touched her, like I was sliding again. I don't know, maybe she knew something about the Devourers."

"Possibly, but you should be careful about drawing attention to yourself and alienating people who normally would have helped you."

"That's true."

"So you just had diner with them."

"Yeah, that's all that happened that night. Sophie's dad picked her up and I walked Evelyn home. Then I woke up here, in hell again." He looks up at her and pauses as he braces himself for an answer, "Do you know if they made it out of town?"

The old woman stares with her nearly blind eyes for a moment, her mind decades away. She wants to scream but she remains calm and shrugs.

He looks away, saddened.

"Do you think you will go back?" she tries to keep his morale from dropping any further.

"I have no idea," he crosses his arms still thinking about the girls. "Another strange thing, I don't look like this when I slide back."

"Like what?"

"Like this," he moves his face close to a lantern.

She leans forward squinting at him.

"You might have to get closer," he says.

And just like that, she gets her opportunity to see him. If she was still young she may have blushed. Instead she acts as though it is a bother to get up to look at him.

She hovers a few inches away from him in the lamplight. It really is Jake, in the flesh. She remembers his bright blue eyes with their hazel centers. He does look different. He is pale, haggard and looks sickly. Jagged dark circles cover his sunken eye sockets and along with the myriad of bruises and scrapes, she sees the black cut running down his cheek more clearly than before.

"Eh, you just look like you've been to Prudence," she tries cheering him up. "So, what do you look like when you go back there?"

"Better. The way I looked before that crazy bastard wiped his blood on me."

She remembers the way he looked when she first met him, "Maybe when you stop Kenneth, you'll go back to the way you were."

"Do you think I can?"

"I think you can," she pats him on the shoulder.

She walks back to her steamy kitchenette, to a bare section of wall and presses against it, sliding what reveals itself as a door to the right. She turns to Jake, "Wait here," then steps into the dark new room.

Jake hears her bustling around in the room for a good few minutes and passes the time by looking through more of the peepholes. His watch claims it is half passed two in the afternoon. He does not trust its accuracy seeing as how it carried on as usual when he was in the past. He wants to know where all of his lost nights have gone. He did only slide back that once, as far as he can remember.

If he were to be here until nightfall, he wonders what the old woman's perception of him would be. What would she see him do when the night came? Faint, become catatonic or just fade away?

"Anything?" she calls, staring in his direction from the dark doorway.

"Nope."

"Come over here," she says as she disappears into the dark.

By the time he rounds the corner she is lighting up the room's second lantern. He enters into the new room, which is completely different from the last. Here, the ceiling and walls are a gray corrugated metal, all slightly rusted. Wooden latticework supports the walls and ceiling while also obtrusively running along the floor.

"Watch your step."

He reaches out and touches one of the metal walls, it is cold. "A shipping container?"

"Yeah," she states casually. "It was before we knew what they do to metals."

"This is all underground?" he says, astonished.

"Where better to hide," she yawns and sits down on a quilt-covered bed.

"Awesome."

"Sam and a few others built this and a few more like it before they left Prudence behind." Realizing she has mentioned Sam too many times to Jake she adds, "I figured, I would let people much younger than me do all the work."

"How far does it go?"

"Just two containers running beneath the alley, between the garages. The rest is excavated tunnels beneath the four garages."

"That's a lot of work for those things not to have noticed."

"We kept them distracted and as you said, the two you encountered aren't that intelligent, but they learn. They also do not come out at night."

"Sam said something about that."

"They may be sleeping or feeding at night, maybe it's just their backwards nature."

"Feeding on what, animals? I haven't seen a bird or rat since I got here."

"Pay attention, boy! You will have to start thinking ahead and not just reacting if you are going to beat him. They feed on dreams, energy, life!"

Jake crosses his arms kicking himself for his stupid question, "Sorry, you're right. I was never any good at planning ahead."

"Don't shit on yourself like that either!" she snaps. "I doubt anyone else in your situation could have made it this far. The way you have been thinking on your feet is fine, you just have to learn to push that ahead. Anticipate."

Jake nods, "Got it."

"If you want to shave, I have an old straight razor by the sink over there, in the top shelf."

Jake looks to her and sees her sitting, staring at him and pointing to a lit back corner of her room, past her bed. He reaches up and pulls on a thick tuft of his rapidly grown beard and thinks of the benefit of having some facial hair as cold as it is out. It ceases to matter though, because the coldness he has been feeling recently was coming from within.

"Doubts?" she asks. "If you end up sliding back again, to the old Prudence, you might want to try and look the way you did the last time," she says as she shifts to sit cross-legged.

"I wonder what excuse I should give anyone who recognizes me from before. I told people I was just passing through."

The crone groans as she sifts through her memories, trying to remember what he actually said when he returned, then hides a smile. "Just don't say anything stupid like you left your wallet in a motel that you never checked into."

"Huh, I was just thinking that," Jake says innocently to her amusement.

As he walks by, he notices her shotgun from before lying next to her on the bed and wonders if it is the same or if she has one in every room. On the bed is a haphazardly stuffed box filled to the brim with down facing picture frames and other junk. It looks out of place.

"What's with the box?" he asks while searching the dresser drawer.

"Stuff collected from the neighborhood. I've been meaning to go through it."

"I guess, Sam does the same. He gave me this watch," he shakes his wrist.

Loaded dressers and shelves line the room as well as other comforts that were lacking in the previous area and he surmises the first room is more like her workshop. He steps up to a dirty cracked mirror that hangs over the sink and sees that he looks even worse than he thought. He turns the faucet and nothing happens other than the sound of her chuckling at him. Further inspection brings his eyes to a bucket filled with clean water sitting next to the sink on a small worn dresser. An empty bucket sits underneath for the unattached sink to drain into. He wets his beard and with the newfound straight razor, begins carefully shaving.

The strangeness of his current situation does not escape him. He instead keeps working on a plan to undo what has been done to him as escaping is no longer an option.

"I've been wondering what *is* up with them and metal?"

After he hears no response, he turns around to see she has slumped against the headboard and passed out. He stares at her for a bit and feels sorry for her. Jake knows today must have been a hell of a day for her.

After he finishes, he decides to let her sleep and uses the privacy to quietly inspect the room. More picture frames of people line the shelves, apparently taken from their homes. A dragon's horde of jewelry lays scattered throughout the shelves, intermingled with other trinkets and a few knives. Books are stacked and lined up along the wooden support structure. Some of them look so ancient they could be worth more than all the jewelry. What catches his attention more than anything else is an unfolded map of Prudence. He grabs the lantern from the sink and brings it back to the map. It looks basic but it confirms what he has seen of the town. Certain areas and homes are marked on the map, but the handwriting is illegible, if it is even in English. They could be stash locations and some are marked by dates as well. He looks over the room for something to write with, but sees nothing. After a while of searching, he returns to the knives. He doubts she would mind giving him one, but with his success of using metal on the creatures, he imagines he would only get one or two useful stabs in, tops. A knife in his hand would be nothing more than a false sense of security. The bone knife the one who screams has, that was another matter. The old woman appears to have just that one non-metal blade of hers, for cooking.

The information he received from her was invaluable and this place is a treasure trove. Another of the ancient books catches his eye. It is sitting open on a nightstand by the old woman's bed. He sets the lantern next to the large tome and examines it. The thick paper is waxy, maybe preserved in a special way and has that old book smell. The ancient pages crack and buckle defiantly as he turns them. He tries to read the handwritten words but the perfectly aligned characters are unknown to him. He checks the first and last pages for a cipher of some type but finds nothing. Instead he comes across pages of notes that have been placed throughout. The chicken scratch does not help him either. He looks at the black book's hard leathery cover. There are no words on the outside, just a simple raised image of a box with a lit candlewick in the center.

"Lamplighters," he whispers and thumbs through the thick

book stopping on the intricate and wild pictures of symbols and diagrams. The strange highly detailed images are inked with red and black. The style of the images is neither Indian nor European. If he had to guess, they remind him more of Sumerian or African art.

"I guess my non specific education might be good for something after all," he mumbles to himself. He closes the book and stares long and hard at the cover again. He realizes this is where the old woman gained her knowledge of the Devourers.

"Come up with a plan yet, boy?"

Jake looks to his right to see the old woman staring at him from her rigid sleeping position.

"I didn't mean to wake you."

She responds with a light shrug and with what sounds like a hundred cracks and pops, she rises out of the bed and heads back into the other room. "You should get ready. Waiting here until the safety of the night to leave is not an option for you."

He follows her, "I need a way to defend myself better."

"That's obvious, what else?"

"I need to talk to Sam again. Before I make a wrong move. That book in there, is that from his secret club?"

"Better. As far as that book, I doubt he ever saw it. He still would have been too young when he went off to the war. Besides, he never really believed, he put his faith in other faiths," she chuckles at her joke. "That's why the truth offended him so. I on the other hand, spent years learning the truths in that book."

"Did you need it?"

"Of course! The secrets in that book had nothing to do with the nameless tribe, the gray Indians who became the Devourers. Those secrets came from beyond the tribe."

"That's right. The surviving tribe members were little kids when that all went down, so they wouldn't have known anything. So how is it you have the book?"

"I have my ways. Here take this."

She hands him a hollow branch container similar to the one he drank out of. It is longer though, with what looks like an actual wooden twist on cap. No wider than a coffee mug, he wraps his hand around it noticing instantly how the ridged bark exterior provides him with a sturdy grip. The container is also varnished to a beautiful dark shine. A thin hemp like cord is looped through wooden cut-ins at the top and bottom of the container. The cord is thick and sturdy. More than likely made from the fibrous parts of that special flower. He pokes his head and left arm through the cord and slings it across his body.

"I filled it with a very concentrated reduction of the drink you had before."

"Thank you, this will help me out a lot."

"We'll see. The corruption in you will grow, as will the hunger. If you allow things to continue, this fluid may very well go from staving off your hunger to becoming a poison to you."

He makes a worried look thinking of if he could handle becoming worse, "I guess a gun wouldn't do much for me?"

"Oh, would you deprive an old woman her only means of defense?" she teases.

"Huh? No. I also used the one who screams knife against it, it seemed to hurt it."

"Hurt it? Try insulted," she cackles. "This might get you further, and I have plenty. She hands him a plain wooden stake. At least two feet long, a quarter of which is shaved down to a point. It has a lanyard resembling the cable from the wood thermos.

"It's been treated appropriately, but keep it wet just in case."

Jake admires the red varnish of the smooth smoked stake. He looks into the old woman's cloudy eyes and smiles, "So they are like—"

"Don't say it, they are not!" she gently punches his chest and it still almost winds him. "They have no hearts as we know, trying something like that will set you up to get your head bitten off. Until you find a way to kill them, run."

"Got it."

She steps close to him and places a corded pouch around his neck.

"Medicine bag?" he chuckles.

"Ha!" she laughs, "Yes smartass! Seeds. The seeds from the red death flower, for good luck."

He inspects and hefts the small leather bag, "Well Lady, I wish you would—"

Abruptly she presses two of her long fingers over his mouth, "Shh!" she silences him and turns her head to the side, listening.

A few intense minutes pass as they stand there listening. Jake fears that like an idiot he'd left some sort of trail for the creatures to find the woman who had remained hidden for so long. She motions for him to look out of a nearby peephole while she makes her way to another. His stares out of the hole but sees nothing. He quietly moves to one after another. He looks over to the old woman who has her ear to one of the holes, and shots ring out. Two, three more shots ring out and she grimaces.

"Sam?" he whispers.

She shakes her head, "I think I hear a car."

"What?" Who could it be?"

"You better get up there!" She quickly shuffles away from the hole and across from the other secret doorway. She slides another door sized piece of wood, this one with a faux brick paint job. Instead of entering, however, she backs away.

"Up the stairs, you will find a locker. Your shoes and Jacket are smoking inside. Finish getting dressed then toss some of the dirt you will find over the embers."

Jake does not question her and goes through the new exit. He enters a stairwell the steps themselves are cinderblocks. Pale light from the outside spills in through scattered holes as he steps up and into a garage. A dust covered old car sits there and he sees the bricked up garage door from earlier. Sure enough, there is an actual row of rusted high school lockers. Slight wisps of brownish smoke billow from one. The locker door opens without a creak and through the haze, he sees his jacket and hiking shoes hanging from their laces. He quickly gets his shoes and jacket on just as the old woman steps up into the garage, leading with her shotgun.

"Here!" she says in a hushed voice and tosses his lighter to him.

He pockets it and follows her to the bolted and covered door. She points upwards, "Be careful."

Jake looks up and sees a complex wood contraption that resembles an *arm*. Its *hand* is composed of more wood, a section of tire and a series of sharpened jagged pieces of red stained wood. If their enemy was anything other than what it is, he would call overkill on her deathtrap. She disarms the trap, which could be set off by either the door opening or a weight release on the floor, by moving cinderblocks into appropriate places as stoppers. She then proceeds to unlock the various chains and bolts on the door.

"Sounds are coming from the northwest, maybe even by the forks."

"What are you going to do?" he gives her a sorrowful look.

"Come on," she gestures for him to leave. "I don't like having this door open during the day."

"Why can't you just go to Sam's?" he pleads.

"Been fine on my own. So has he," she says stubbornly.

"Then just leave town tonight."

"Are you stupid?"

"Look, I've got this now. You told me everything you could right? Either we all win or we all loose. So you might as well get as far away from here as you can and never come back!"

Jake sees that his words shake her.

She recovers quickly and she becomes a rock once again, "This is my home, I'm not running anywhere boy."

Jake sighs, "I'll come back then."

"Keep that confidence handy, you'll need it," she smiles.

"I never asked your name," he shamefully says. "If I slide back—"

"No!" she interrupts him. "I would remember if I had met you. And if a stranger had told me about any of this back then, I would have called the cops."

Jake is torn, they had come a long way in the short time they spent together.

"Thank you for all of your help then, Lady. For what it's worth, I'm Jake," he reaches out his dark gray hand.

She reaches out and shakes it, "See you around Jake. Now get the hell out of here and draw those things away from me."

"Got it," he smiles and starts sprinting in the direction of the last resounding shot.

The old woman finishes securing the door and resets the trap. She stops to snuff out the embers that Jake forgot. Making her way back underground she begins trembling and does something she had not done in over thirty years. She drops down as the waves of tears spill down through her ancient and cracked hands, alone again.

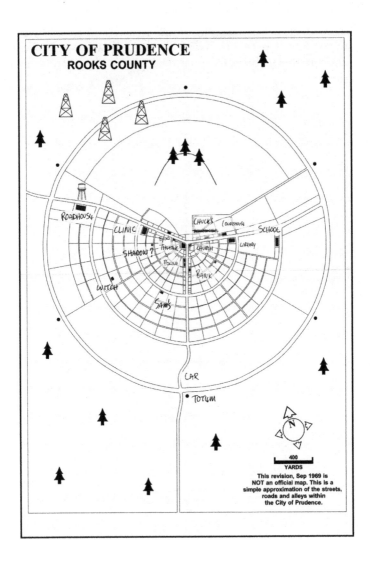

CITY OF PRUDENCE
ROOKS COUNTY

ROADHOUSE

CLINIC

CHUCK'S
COURTHOUSE
SCHOOL

SHADOW ?
SCHOOL
THEATRE
CHURCH
LIBRARY

POLICE

BANK

WITCH

SAMS

CAR

TOTUM

N

400
YARDS

This revision, Sep 1969 is
NOT an official map. This is a
simple approximation of the streets,
roads and alleys within
the City of Prudence.

CHAPTER 8

He dashes off again down another alley intersection trying the puddles that have formed in the gravelly dips. There must have been a downpour while he was unconscious in the old woman's hideaway, which may have also helped cover any tracks or scent he left that could have led to her. He is not as nervous as he was last time he headed out and away from safety. He is better prepared now, informed and armed.

A few spaced shots echo again through the empty town leading him closer to their source, which is still moving. He hears a vehicle speeding up, skidding around on the street and the terribly familiar call of the one who screams. Jake starts running faster, to his surprise, towards the sounds of the battle.

He comes around the left of a paint supply store and onto the street that forms the inner most of the concentric circle streets. To the right, his view opens up to a large silver pickup haphazardly swerving around the abandoned cars towards him. A man is hanging out of the passenger window firing a rifle at the one who screams who is closing in over the obstacles fast. The man fires again hitting the screamer in mid leap, knocking it out of the air and into the ground. Jake's eyes pop open with surprise briefly, because it tumbles back to its feet and re-engages the truck.

He sees the front of the truck is damaged and covered in the blackish fluid of the devourer's blood and he knows the vehicle is done for. The black moss will grow from the blood and will eat it away in no time. There is something else stuck in a few places on the truck. They look like long jagged rods.

He does not see the one who crawls and figures now would be the best time to try to take out the screamer. He grips his stake in a downwards position and bounds towards it. His heart sinks when in the background he sees a dark figure leaping along the rooftops of the two and three story buildings. It is large. Taller and thicker than the one who screams and has both arms. It shakes the windows of every building it lands on as it gets closer. He sees its wretched upside down face and three large black feathers protruding upwards from the back of its head.

Abruptly, it reaches up and pulls one of the feathers from the back of its head. It cocks its head back and draws the feather against a large bow and fires at the truck. The arrow tears through the air and hits the bed of the truck, barely missing the tire well. The impact is enough to cause the rear end to skid sideways a few inches. The truck straightens out and accelerates when Jake starts waving his arms to the driver, "This way!"

The panicked driver's jaw drops when he sees Jake and he swerves the truck, breaking hard in a wide left arc around the paint store.

"Get in!" the man shouts.

But Jake is already hoping into the bed of the truck as it takes off again, "You guys need to get the hell out of this town now!"

"Who the hell are you?" the man in the passenger seat says, now back inside the cab and reloading his rifle.

Jake recognizes him, it is the tow truck driver he had thought was the one who ran him off the road, "Mike?"

"What?" the man says surprised. "Who the hell are you?"

"Doesn't matter, you guys have to leave now!"

"We've been trying since those things attacked. We keep driving out and then ending up here again."

"Oh shit! You guys?" Jake shouts.

"We're almost out of gas, do you know where a bank is?"

"Why?"

"It should be fortified!" the driver yells.

Jake clenches his teeth, I should have thought of that myself! "No idea, how about the police station?"

"It'll have to do!" the driver says.

Jake looks around, "Turn right up here!"

Something heavy hits the vehicle, Jake turns around to see the one who screams in the bed of the truck with him already slashing at him with its knife. Mike shoots it point blank, knocking into the back of the truck bed. It lunges forward again. With both hands on the stake, Jake plunges it into the creature's desiccated stomach. To both of their surprise it screams. A scream of true pain sucks into its mouth. Even though Jake feels like his eardrums will burst, he enjoys knowing he caused it so much agony. Again the car swerves as the driver and his passenger reel from the sound. The shrill high pitched squeal causes the truck's windows to explode outwards into a crystal mist.

"Take another right!" Jake crouches down and yells.

The truck whips to the right, sending the screaming creature out of the truck and crashing into a storefront.

"Green building!" he shouts.

"Where?" the driver calls back to him.

"That one!" he points to a pale bleached building with a wide shuttered garage door.

"Turn it around!" Mike yells and climbs from the cab into the back with Jake. He pops open the truck's toolbox and grabs a large bolt cutter then hops to the ground.

"Hurry!" the driver calls back.

Mike begins snapping away at the orange rusty chains keeping the garage door sealed.

Jake does not see any sign of them yet, but he doubts the garage doors will stop the creatures from coming in. He looks at the tip of the stake and sees the creature's black blood evaporating with a sizzle.

"Gimmie a hand!" Mike calls up to him.

Clouds of dust spill from the station as the men lift the garage door. Other than even more dust, scattered tools and stacks of boxes, the garage is empty. The truck backs in too fast and hits the wall while Jake and Mike pull the garage door shut. The driver hops out and secures the inside of the door using its sliding locks.

Jake recognizes the pale round headed driver, "Deputy, we have to block off the front doors!"

Trembling, the plain clothed man looks at Jake puzzled.

"This guy knew who I was too," Mike says as he gasps for breath.

"Where are the doors?" the deputy asks.

"This way! I don't know if there's more in the back." Jake takes off through the dirty glass double doors.

"Keep the engine running Mike and horn it if they start knocking!" the Deputy pulls his pistol out and heads after Jake.

Jake checks the front doors, two solid green metal doors aged far more than he remembers. They are both locked and chained up from the inside.

He turns around and runs into the deputy.

"Doors?" he eyes Jake cautiously with his gun at the ready.

"They might hold for a bit."

"A bit?" he says surprised.

"Deputy, do stations like this have backdoors?"

"Let's check. Ain't a deputy anymore either. Name's Scott."

Jake remembers the man's heavy drawl and the two men rush down the faded yellow hall that ends in darkness.

Click.

A simple sound and a cool blue light illuminates their path.

He looks at the deputy surprised but happy.

Tiles have fallen and crumbled away while web covered cables sag in the lightless hallway. Within a few frantic minutes they ascertain that the thankfully windowless building as well as its back doors are secured and had been barricaded some time ago. They return to the garage, each of them dragging a metal file cabinet with them.

"Anything?" Scott asks Mike.

"Yeah. But they're not making a move," he points through one of the small grimy garage door windows with his rifle.

They push the cabinets against the garage door, the beginning of a barricade then carefully peek out of the window.

Jake sees the new large one, the one who shoots, standing

motionless on a three flat across the street.

"Have you seen any of the other ones?' Jake asks.

"Not besides that one and the loud one armed thing," Scott says. "Cut the engine Mike, we're gonna make a wall here. I want to make it so we can clear space in front of the truck quickly."

"What's it waiting for?" Mike stares at it through his sights.

"It's either scared or it's waiting for help," Jake says.

"Hey, who the hell are you anyway? You a local?" Mike asks.

"Yeah, how do you know who we are?"

Jake looks at the two men, "We met at the garage a few days ago, when that prisoner attacked me. Name's Jake." He guesses although it had only been a few days for him, it could have been weeks from their point of view.

"That was you?" Mike says stunned. "You look like shit man!"

"That was over a month ago," Scott nervously adds.

"What?"

"Yeah man, what the hell is going on here, what are those things?"

Jake slams his fist against the garage door and glares up at the creature on the rooftop. "That Son of a bitch!" He breathes deep and calms himself angrily, thinking about the rules of his strange new reality.

"Did that convict mark either of you? Wipe his blood on you anywhere, like he did to me?"

The two look at each other worried and confused, "No," they answer together.

"Good! Do either of you have a knife or something sharp."

Both men pull out decent sized hunting knives. Jake slides his thermos around his body and unscrews it, "Bring them over here."

The men are hesitant but they comply, he dribbles a little of the red syrupy fluid over the knives, "Don't wipe that off, in fact keep that on them and sheathe them."

"What is this?" Mike smells at it.

"It's like poison to them, but not fatal. It may even protect the metal from them."

"What does that mean?"

Jake directs their attention to the silver truck, specifically the areas spattered with the thing's blood and where the arrows have struck.

"Right before their eyes they see the metal is oxidizing through bubbling fading paint. What Jake knows as the black moss spreads cancerously.

"Are you fucking kiddin' me?" Scott says.

"That's what they do," Jake says somberly.

"This shit can't be real," he says.

"Hey!" Jake shouts. "Did you not just see the things that attacked you? Did you forget you were stuck in a loop, unable to leave town? This is happening. If those things come in here, and they can, don't bother shooting them. You saw," He holds out his stake in front of them, "this red stuff does affect them."

"Oh man, oh man," Scott squats down with his hands to the sides of his head.

"How did you guys get here? And why?"

Mike gets upset and starts pacing back and forth, "How about we talk about it while we build up this wall?"

"Alright." Jake dreads what the implications of the two being here means. Now he has to assume there are at least five Devourers creeping around town and he thoroughly understands Sam's dilemma. As the old woman said, it is too late to bank on silence.

"Scott!" are you alright man?" a concerned Mike asks.

"Don't know man . . . I don't know."

"Give me the flashlight. Me and Jake will grab some more stuff to pile up. Can you call if they start moving?"

"Yeah," he stutters and hands the flashlight over.

"First, let's cover this garage door. Then I'll tell you guys everything I know. But it's a long crazy story and I may not have time to tell twice."

The men scavenge for sturdy objects to use for a barricade. He steps into the sheriff's office and starts looking for any logbooks or anything else that could tell him the day of the disaster. After all the questions he asked the old woman and he still forgot to ask a few.

The office is cleaned out so they begin moving the empty desk.

He looks over to the cells and a cold enough chill reaches Jake's spine. He remembers his flash forward when he was sitting in there before.

"What's the matter, man?"

Jake drifts to the cells, "I have to see something. Would you mind shining the light over here?"

"Have you been here?"

He ignores the question, "Maybe we can get the cell doors off and use them."

He comes upon the cells and sees that one of the doors has completely rusted away. Uncomfortable with the scene he pushes his way into the cell and sits down where he sat before. The view is just slightly different from what he saw before, but this is what he saw and it as just as cold. The corrosion looks like it occurred some time ago, there are no signs of the black moss either.

Did someone catch one of these things in the past? He can only wonder what happened.

Mike pushes the sideways desk out of the office and into the main hallway. As he does the flashlight rocks and shines into the next cell. Jake looks over and sees tarp covered boxes and the file cabinets from before.

"Hey, it looks like they stored things in the next cell here," he calls to Mike.

"Is it open?"

Jake walks around to the front of the cell, "No. Have you seen any keys anywhere?"

"Nope. Forget about it, this should be enough."

"Wait," Jake sees that the corruption of the metal had spread from the first cell to the second. "The lock looks rusted up. Do you have a tool that could break it?"

Curious now, Mike makes his way over and inspects it with him. "We might not need one, this thing is rusted badly. Was it them?"

"Looks like it, but it looks like it happened a while ago."

Jake steps back and kicks at the lock hard. Dust and crumbles of rust fall from the bars as the whole thing shakes. He kicks it a few more times, each one harder than the last. Some of the weakened bars have cracked and fallen away, but Jake keeps kicking. After a minute of creating a ruckus, he leans forward, out of breath.

"What the hell's going on?" Scott rushes in startling the two.

"We're trying to get the goodies from the cell," Mike answers. "Anything new outside?"

"Damned thing's just standing there," He walks over to the cells, "Are you trying to kick this in?"

"Yeah."

"You know they open outwards?"

Despite the situation Jake cannot help but to laugh at himself. They join in.

"Looks like you banged up the lock pretty good though," Scott grabs at the door and jerks, cobwebs stretch as the door flies open with a defiant creak.

Jake steps in covering his mouth while he pulls the dusty tarp away. "We can use the file cabinet, but I want to have a look at these files. There might be information we can use."

"I looked around and found some other stuff we can use. Got some paint thinner, blankets, some old road flares and other stuff."

"Blankets?" Mike says with disdain. "I don't plan on being here that long."

"We may not have a choice," Jake adds. "I've been stuck here since the day I met you guys at the garage."

"What?"

"Yeah, and even though I feel like I've been here as long as you say, I only have knowledge of just a few days. You guys said about a month has passed right?"

"Are we in hell?" Mike sighs and Scott begins to show signs of stress again.

"I think there's a way to stop this craziness. Let's just finish securing this place."

The three of them build up a secure enough wall. The truck has become useless and there is no longer a point to having a fast, moveable section of wall. If they leave the police station, it will be on foot.

"What the hell are you guys doing here anyway?

"We're out to get that fucker, Tanner," Mike tells him.

"Who?"

"Kenneth Tanner, the convict that attacked you. He escaped shortly after he did that."

"How?" Jake asks angrily.

"You remember how that bench shattered?"

Jake nods.

"He used a piece of that to shank that agent, then took off in Mike's tow truck."

"That makes sense," he says aloud, more to himself.

"How so?" Mike steps up.

"That night, he attacked me with your truck. I recognized and chased after it. I thought it was you, Mike."

"Fucker ran down a mother and child as he made his shitty getaway. On top of that, the feds that came down on me like a ton of molten shit because of what happened to their guy. Made things so thick for me I left the force then decided to track his ass down. And not just me, he ruined Mike's rep."

"All over the news, my name and my business were associated with that murderous mother fucker."

"How did you guys find the town?" Jake asks them.

"It wasn't easy. We had to dig deep to find out where he was born and figured he might come home. Then we had to ask around a lot 'cause this place is just gone from every damn map."

"And when found where it should be, we spent all day and night looking. There is a maze of roads leading back out of the area and to dead ends."

"We were heading the wrong way again, when we heard this loud, and I mean loud, crashing explosion coming from the south of us. We cleared a path through empty barrels and fallen trees. Next thing you know, we are driving through an abandoned oil field."

"Well, I promised you guys a story."

Jake begins giving them the short and sweet version of his trials so far. He is getting better at telling the story although it is longer each time. The men's reactions shift from fear to confusion to doubt. Towards then end of the story Jake does see a glimmer of hope has begun to shine in at least Mike, whereas Scott continues reeling against his shock. He finishes and watches them still struggling to digest everything he has just told them. A sharp bark sounds from outside denying the men even that.

Because of their barricade, they are forced to look through one of the small uncovered windows. The one who shoots is still where it was before, on the roof of the three flat and it is no longer alone. The one who climbs has appeared and it franticly scurries around the large shooter, while the screamer remains unseen.

He figures he must have hurt it bad. Good.

The climber barks and yips at the one who shoots, even grabbing its legs and pulling at it. With it's his gaping mouth, it just stares at the police station, ignoring its smaller accomplice.

"The little one seems to be trying to get the big one to come with it," He tells them.

"Come with it where? They have us cornered."

Jake has no answer. He looks at his watch and sees that it is five in the afternoon.

"They haven't been seen at night, well, just the night they showed up and wrecked the town. I'm thinking, maybe they have to be somewhere else at night."

"Like a home base?" Mike says.

"Yeah. I've been thinking they recharge there at night."

"How about we follow them 'em and light 'em up in their sleep?" Scott says as he re examines the coating on his knife.

"And what if they just turn around and attack again while we are following them? From what Jake said, there might be five of them now because of us. Six if Tanner caused one to show up."

Mike is right. If the one who shoots was set free in response to him, he dreads what creature Kenneth could have riled from beyond, unless he is just the foot in the door.

"Besides," Jake adds, "maybe only six have gotten out. We don't know how many are in their home base or if fire even burns them."

"What do you mean, if fire does anything?"

"I mean, what if they just suck it up, its energy right? Let's see."

Jake steps over to the truck and with the devil girl lighter tries to burn some of the black moss and part of the wicked looking projectile embedded into the truck. The moss quivers and tries to evade the flame. It releases a miniscule squeal causing the men to jump back. The projectile liquefies into more of the moss and drops from the rusted cavity to the ground where like a millipede, it tries to slither away as it squirms and turns to ash.

"What, the, fuck!" Scott yells. "That shits alive?"

"I figured as much," Jake says as he closes the lighter.

"I think I'm just gonna go sit on the porch with that vet," Scott says, while he squats down again. "I can't believe any of this shit. I can't."

"Hey, where did you get that lighter?" Mike asks.

"The young version of Kenneth gave it to me when he was trying to buddy up to me."

"That was mine, it was in my truck."

"That guy is something else," Jake holds the lighter out for Mike to take.

"Keep it man. I found it myself in a burnt up wreck. It was the damnedest thing, because it was the only thing untouched by the fire."

"Great! More creepy shit," panicked Scott yells. "I can't listen to the noises those things are making, I'm, gonna go look for anything else we can use."

"Try to calm down man, the lighter always brought me good luck!" Mike calls out to him as he heads into the hallway.

"Then take the lighter back, Mike."

"No. Sounds like you need it a lot more than me."

Jake looks at the lighter and places it back in his pocket.

"It's getting late. Remember I told you I haven't seen the night since I've been here."

"Yeah, you said you wake up in the past."

"Just the one time. The other nights, I do not know what happens to me. If I vanish, pass out or sleepwalk."

"So, what are you saying."

"I just don't know what happens. My plan was to get to Sam, because he knows things that can help me take 'em out. But then you guys showed up."

Mike begins talking but Jake cannot focus on his words as his view of Mike blurs. The shapes Jake sees bleed together and dim, leaving a hazy green outline in Mike's place. The outline brightens and sharpens, becoming what looks like thousands of tiny sparks firing away from his body. They are white at their base and bright green at their ends, reaching out like electricity in slow motion. They illuminate the areas of his clothes where his skin shows, like his collar and sleeve ends, even the edge of his hat. The breaths coming out of his mouth as he speaks looks like a bright living vapor. Mike's pupils have become bright white pinholes and a swirling glow pulses from the center of his chest. Within Mike's outline, he sees self illuminating glimpses that flicker like lighting flashes in thick clouds, revealing what appears to be his skeleton. His image reminds Jake of a shifting x-ray or a burned afterimage from staring at the sun. He feels the warmth coming from the lights and is reminded of his own painfully cold body. He moves his hands in front of his eyes and sees that his aura is quite different. His outline is colorless and thin compared to Mike's and within his own outline is a solid black void. He realizes how empty he has become. Jake looks back at the image of Mike, of his life force, and becomes transfixed on the glowing parts that flicker and swirl even brighter and more beautiful.

"Hey!" Mike shouts him back to reality. "Why the fuck are you looking at me like that for!"

"Huh?" he shakes away what he was seeing and rubs his eyes. "Like what?" he asks innocently.

"I don't know man, you were looking at me all pissed and bug eyed."

"Sorry, I tuned out. I was thinking about Kenneth Tanner."

"I'll bet," Mike says as he tries covertly to move away from him.

Jake was starving already and as he feared, he was changing. He takes a swig from his thermos. It burns going down, but his hunger abates. Not wanting to be locked away or shot, he had omitted from the two of them that the Devourers had tainted him. He is surprised that neither of them asked him about his darkened hands and thinks that they assumed it is oil or dirt.

"I was saying, maybe we should lock you in a room or something, chain you up in that cell back there."

"What! Why?" Jake shouts, wondering if he was thinking out loud.

Mike stares at him the way the two cops did when he had his episode in the cell. The unmistakable look that the sane give the insane, "What's wrong with that? Incase you sleepwalk or they bust in here and you are still passed out."

"Oh. Sorry," Jake rubs his eyes again. He tries acting like it is fatigue that confused him. "I don't know. If I do slide back, how would I explain how I ended up in a cell. In fact, I shouldn't even be in this building, especially if I pass out!"

"Damn. Where can you go? Hotel?"

"There's one up the street, but it's small. The owners might notice me creeping out and call the cops. And again, I would be unconscious for a few."

"Park bench? Just get some newspaper."

Jake groans, unsure. "No, this place wasn't like that back then. I didn't see any bum types, besides my cover story—"

"Rooftop!" Mike says with excitement. "You'll have plenty of time to wake up."

"Getting down would be tricky, but that's not bad. But still, there has to be somewhere."

Jake walks over to the window again and sees the creatures still arguing with each other. The large one bats climber away but it gets right back up again.

"Aha!" Jake moves away from the window as he turns to Mike, "The movie theater."

"That'll do. Different people would be coming in and out of there all the time. And it's no big deal if you fall asleep in there."

"Hey Guys! I found something back here!"

Scott leads them back to the cells.

"First, when I was moving the rest of this crap out of the way I found a box with ledgers inside. Recent ones, or recent for them. There's mention of weird things going on, then they stop abruptly."

"That's awesome!" Jake says.

"Just wait, then I found this under all the stuff!" Scott steps back and aims his flashlight down.

Cut into the floor is a hard stone square. It is three by three feet with hinge bolts apparent at the top. What stands out the most is a square cut in with an embossed image of a lit candlewick inside it.

Jake rushes to it and drops to his knees examining it.

"There's what looks like a keyhole near the bottom," and Scott focuses the beam of light on it.

Sure enough, Jake runs his fingers over the strange 'V' shaped keyhole.

"This was the same image from the book I found."

"Is it a safe or a trapdoor to somewhere?" Mike probes the stone slab with his hand.

"So what, the police here were part of that group?"

"Apparently," Jake answers. "I'm guessing no key anywhere?"

"Nope."

"For now lets get these logs back to the garage where there's more light. If you guys are planning on staying here, you might want to set up some lights and a way to keep warm."

"Where are you gonna go?" Scott blinds them with his flashlight.

"He can't stay here, incase he pops up in the past."

Scott just frowns at the mention of sliding through time.

"I really want to know what's in here," Jake blows some dust off the stone plate.

"You think that tool that can kill them might be in there?" Mike asks.

"It couldn't be that easy, could it?" Jake replies.

Back in the garage, the men sit on the dusty chairs relocated from other areas of the small police station. They take turns watching the street and the rooftops for any new movement while Scott pours over the ledgers.

"They kept good records here. Pretty standard except for a few things. It was quiet here, not so different from my last job."

"Any mention of Tanner?" Mike asks.

"No, at least not in these last ledgers. They had petty fights, mostly from rowdy oil workers. Biggest thing here was that church there on the corner burnt down. They suspected arson but they had no actual suspects."

"And the weird things?"

"Yeah, people were going missing."

"I remember the cops back then mentioning something about that. They suspected me when they picked me up, but their suspect had bigger feet."

Scott looks up shaking his head, "I still can't believe this man, waking up in the seventies? Come on! Mike do you believe this shit?"

"I think anything's fair game right about now."

"Well, ok. Alright dammit I'll try," he thumbs back a few pages in the ledger. "So, six people total went missing over a period of nearly two months. They think, because no one exactly knew when the first ones disappeared, probably older people. There's a note that leads back to a page when the first person that went missing. And they put a 'G' by the name, then by all the names of the missing people in a different colored ink."

"Just a 'G'? What does that stand for?"

"It's new to me, but not just that. In this ledger here," he grabs another of the opened books, "once a month, like clockwork until the disappearances started, they did something and marked it with an 'LW'."

"It doesn't say anything else?"

"It says nothing at all about it. It's just that as a former deputy, it stood out to me."

"Riddles within riddles," Jake leans back in the chair with his hands behind his head and sighs. "Does it mention the incident that hit the town, when that was?"

"No. And the last date entered here wouldn't tell us anything either."

"Why not?"

"Because this is a duplicate ledger."

"How can you tell? Mike asks.

"Look," Scott turns the inside of the book to the others. "See how clean the pages are, how it's always with the same color ink and no revisions?"

"Yeah?"

"Every ledger I've ever seen has edits, different colored ink, sometimes even pencil. There's also wear and wrinkles on the paper, coffee stains, etc. A real ledger basically looks like someone wiped their ass with it. We do the same thing nowadays except we type into a computer. So we don't know if this copy was updated after the last event."

"Hey! Check around August, see if I'm mentioned in the ledger."

Scott huffs and doubtfully starts flipping through the pages again more irritated than interested. He comes across a page and slowly reads it. His demeanor changes and he rereads it, this time carefully moving his fingers along the bottom of the words.

"Holy shit!" Scott says, then looks from Mike to Jake dragging his jaw behind as his head turns. "Holy shit!" he repeats leaning back flustered.

"Spit it out!" Mike says.

Scott leans forward again, now giddy and reads with his fingers from the ledger.

"August 28, Picked up a strange man named Jacob Walker who was passed out in the Dixon's yard. Thought he could be a suspect in disappearances, but feet too small. Is an outsider. Had strange identification and way of speaking which confirmed his claims to be a former government spook. Had flashback in cell. Did not seem dangerous."

"Wow!" Mike stands up and begins pacing back and forth again.

"I'm for sure sold now!" Scotts says apologetically. "This is nuts!"

"And you can bring stuff there and back?" Mike asks.

"Yeah, I'm pretty sure of it," Jake answers.

"Here!" Mike reaches into his wallet and hands Jake forty dollars. "Buy me all the baseball cards you can carry!"

"This ain't funny man!" Scott shouts.

"I know, but we might as well make the best of it!"

"Best of it! Do you have any idea what all this means? Magic being real, an afterlife! This ain't a joke!"

"Calm down Scott, I see where Mike's coming from. We can't give up on getting outta here."

Scott tries to contain his stress and looks back at the ledger.

"This day is also marked with an 'LW'. Did you see or hear anything special that day, maybe the officers mentioned something?"

Jake goes over what happened that day. His eyes narrow but he cannot think of anything. "Nothing as far as the 'LW'. But if we look at everything in terms of the Lamplighters and Indians, the 'G' could be for gray Indians. It may even fall in line with the creature's existence being dependant on people's knowledge or belief in them."

"So Tanner must be the kidnapper! But why his own people?" Scott adds.

Jake shrugs. "Stronger ties to the tribe?"

Mike returns from the truck and tosses bottled water to the men. "This doesn't add up though. If Jake goes back and Tanner is creeping around, wouldn't they have met and wouldn't he have recognized Jake at the garage?"

"Maybe he did. Maybe that why he was so smug," Jake says. "He could also have no idea I slid back, because if he knew, he probably would never have let me get away in the first place. Because I could screw up his plans."

"Whew, then you may have one advantage."

"Yeah, that's a hell of an advantage!" Mike says. "All he has to do is kill Tanner."

The simple thought never occurred to Jake but it is true. Killing Kenneth means that none of this ever happens."

"Yeah, just kill him before he lets them out!"

"Damn, you guys are right!" Jake shoots up and starts looking through the boxes. "Have you guys seen a phone book anywhere? That way I can just look him up!"

"I was all over these boxes and didn't see one, Jake."

"Doesn't matter. I can look him up in the past," He looks at his watch, then out the window again. "Do either you two have a sturdy container?"

"For what?"

"I'm going to leave this container with you guys, but take a little of the red stuff for myself," He takes the wood thermos off and carefully sets it on a box.

"Won't you need that?"

"Yeah but I can't walk around town with it, besides I could buy more if I end up there."

"And if you don't?"

"I'll come back here, or the old woman's house. Whichever is closer."

"I emptied this right after we saw the first of those damned things." Scott pulls out a faded brown leather bound hipflask from his coat pocket and rinses the inside with some of his bottled water.

"And take this." Mike reaches behind himself and brandishes a beautiful silver .45 revolver from under his shirt.

"I can't take your gun man."

"I've got a few more in the truck. Besides were you planning on killing Tanner with your stick?"

"Do you know how to shoot?" Scott asks.

"I've been to the range a few times, but never owned one."

"Then just get real close to him. Mike, how many bullets do you have for that?"

"Six loaded and," he sifts through his pockets and pulls a handful of bullets out and hands them to Jake, "another six in change."

He holds his stake out to Mike and cannot help but to think of how ironic the situation is. He thought he needed a gun for the longest, then when he is finally armed with things that will help against the creatures, he has to leave them behind.

"No man, you hold onto something. You still have to make it to the theater."

"What's your plan for getting past those things?"

"May I?" Jake reaches his hand out for Mike's rifle.

Mike obliges and Jake chances a closer look outside through the scope.

"How about you guys distract them and I run like hell. I saw before that one of the doors to the theater is open."

"What if you don't vanish into thin air though? Scott asks as he dares a glance out the window.

"What do you mean if I don't vanish?"

"You know, you said in the past that you don't look all jacked up like you do now. What if your real body stays here and in the past it's your ghost double or something?"

"Ghost double?" Mike smirks.

"You said anything's fair game, so I call ghost double!"

Jake cracks a smile at their banter. He wouldn't mind hanging out with these guys on weekends. As they engage in a mildly comical debate about the nature of their enemies, Jake plots out a path that would avoid obstacles and provide cover for a run down the street. With the police station about six buildings away from the Forks, it would take him less than a minute to dash down and get inside the theater. As long as he doesn't trip up on the cracked uneven ground or any of the debris. Dodging those nasty arrows would be the main problem. There are about six derelict cars scattered along the street and sidewalks. Garbage, weeds and the fallen traffic signals from before line the ground. He moves the scope up the rooftop across the way and centers it on the one who shoots. It is like a larger complete version of the screamer. The skin on its chest appears to have been cut open down the middle. The skin's frayed edges hangs there loosely, like its using its own skin as a vest. From the rot underneath, its ribcage juts out further. Over developed and broken outwards like a bear's two clawed hands reaching out to maul something. This one is accessorized much like the others. Around its long neck, bone necklaces dangle partially grown into the skin. And from the sagging flaps of its ears, hang human jawbones partially lined with teeth as earrings.

Its bow is as thick as a leg at the center and gnarled. At least six feet long, the thing holds it tight with that signature birdlike grip. Three slimy feathers sprout high from the back of its head, but Jake swears it fired one of those off.

He wonders if the gun would still work fine if he covered the bullets with some of the extract, but figures it would burn off as the bullet was fired.

Although the creature's large toothy mouth had remained aimed at the building, it realizes it is being watched. It cocks its head back and to the left like it did when it was firing before and Jake sees that unlike the blind pupils of the thing's counter parts, its right eye appears to work. The large overdeveloped pupil the size of a horse's glares at him. The gaze is full of hate but with a terrifying non-human intelligence. In that split second Jake drops and pushes away from the small viewport.

"Look out!" he screams just as an arrow blasts through the hard plastic window.

Scott throws himself backwards as it whizzes by. The projectile shatters into the cement floor with a thud that shakes the room.

Jake darts into the hallway, "Guys! I don't think that garage door will slow those arrows down!"

Scott does a clumsy barrel roll into the hall with Jake but Mike climbs inside the cab of his truck.

"What are you doing?" Scott shouts.

Mike ignores him and wrenches off the rear view mirror before sliding towards the hallway at their feet.

"Dammit!" Scott yells again, pointing at the wickedly destructive arrow. "You think you can outrun that?!"

"I guess that's a gamble I'm going to have to take, unless you know a secret code word that will get me out of any trouble with the police if I pop up here."

Scott nervously shakes his head.

"Was the back door locked?" Mike asks.

Scott holsters his handgun and drags the truck's toolbox closer to the hall to retrieve a second rifle from inside it. "That thing is completely barricaded. The door's barely sitting in its frame. We'd be better off leaving it as is."

"Why was the back door barricaded and not the front?"

Jake tops off the flask with the red death flower extract and places it in his inner jacket pocket. "I've noticed that in a few places. I'm guessing when they attacked they used the alleys to get around."

"So, the gauntlet is the only way then," Mike stares at the garage door.

"Yep," Jake takes the last swig of water out of the bottle. "I was thinking. What if we got oil from the truck, mix it up with some of that paint thinner and dump it into a container with the road flares? Maybe add in some tire rubber and other garbage to get like a smokescreen going. Then, if it works or not, you guys snipe at the one who shoots and I try to outrun them."

"We'll get everything ready, when do you want to go?" Scott asks.

"I'll wait as long as I can. The times I've slid back always start with a really bad headache. But the other times I've skipped, I wasn't even aware of sun down. Maybe I'll notice this time because I'm focused on talking to you guys instead of wandering around similar looking parts of town."

"Its going on seven now," Mike looks at his watch. "Skies don't seem any darker."

Scott gathers up some of the loose components. "I'll pack that stuff into this paint can and pop a bunch of air holes in it. That way I can roll it out a ways from the building. Maybe see if it will light that car in the middle of the street on fire."

"Think one of us could toss it into that car that is between us and it from the front door, so it might catch on the seats?" Mike chances a look through a view hole.

"We can try that too," Jake shrugs.

Scott goes to work on the impromptu smoke device. He cuts sections of the trucks tires and seat padding into strips and bundles them up in the can with some old flares. He adds motor oil drained from the truck and lets it mix with the other liquid chemicals. The smell of the accelerants is toxic enough, it was definitely going to smoke. He taps the lid back on and gashes it up with holes using the back of a hammer.

"Who volunteers to throw it?" Scott looks up and presents his work.

"I'll do it, so you guys can try and keep it from firing," Jake takes the bucket by its handle.

Mike inches over to the window and angles the mirror to look outside.

"It should only have two shots left at least," Jake says while watching its last projectile lose its stiffness and slowly liquefy into black moss.

The two men watch Mike's reaction as they look from the melting projectile to whatever he sees in the reflection of the mirror.

"Ugh. More bad news. It looks like it's growing a new feather."

"There's just no breaks with these things!" Scott pouts.

"Doesn't matter if it has one or a hundred, we get hit with one and it's all over."

Jake looks at the crater in the ground and wonders. The Devourers want him alive. At least the other ones do. Maybe its shots are only meant to scare and cripple. If they see living things the way that he saw Mike, the smokescreen would be useless. Hiding would be pointless. But then again, his own aura or whatever that was, is far dimmer than what he saw of Mike's. His plan could go either way.

As he thinks, a familiar pain begins in the front of his head, "It's starting."

"Yeah," Mike adds, still looking with the mirror. "It looks like the smaller fucker gave up on the shooter and took off across the roof tops."

"Which way did it go?" Jake asks.

"Towards the Forks," he shifts the mirror for a moment. "I didn't see it cross the street into the theater or anything. The big guy hasn't budged. Come get a look at where the car is, Jake." Mike hands the mirror over and readies his rifle.

Jake sees the car. It is an old station wagon. He thinks a hatchback or convertible would have been better. This would be a tricky toss, especially with the bucket on fire.

Quietly they slide open the bolts on the garage door and clear a small space for Jake to crawl out under the door when they lift it.

"Headache's getting bad, let's do it."

Mike dashes to the other side of the garage, and maneuvers through gaps in the barricade. "Okay, I have a view of him through this window over here."

Jake snaps open his lighter, takes a deep breath and ignites the contents. He takes a last look at car through the mirror then swings it out the window. Smoke trails behind the bucket as it flies through the air. He looks back through the mirror and watches as he hears it hit the hood of the car. His heart slows as it spins around on the hood. He hopes it will somehow bounce or roll into the car's interior. An arrow's sound comes through the air and a black bolt strikes the bucket, pinning it to the hood. There is no chance of the can going anywhere now. The shooter throws its head back and barks once, triumphantly.

Jake lays down on his back and Scott takes his place with the mirror.

"Is it smoking?" Jake asks.

"That it is, at least."

"I can't wait to shoot this thing again," Mike scowls at it.

"How's the smoke looking?"

"Almost, Jake. I'll give it a bit more and you should be covered."

"Scott, this thing shrugged my shots off before. I'll try for its bow this time, you wanna go for its center?"

"Sounds good but I really want to pop that big assed eye," Scott slings his rifle over his shoulder. "Alright Jake, take some breaths. As soon as I crouch to lift the door, you push the door up and pull yourself through."

Jake just nods as he strains against the pressure and his growing headache.

"Now!"

Scott drops the mirror, squats down and begins lifting the garage door. Jake gets his hands under it and pushes as well, while Mike fires off a shot hitting it in its elbow. Unfazed it spots Mike and fires at him. Mike falls left barely avoiding the shot. Jake rolls underneath and scrambles behind the smoking car. Crouched down with wide eyes he looks to Scott for instructions.

Scott shouts, "Go!" and fires at the creature.

Jake bolts down the street behind another car, then cuts right, closer to the row of buildings the creature is on.

The creature perks up, looking at the scene and snaps its head to the right directly at Jake. It gurgles out a roar, only twitching as the two men continue firing at it.

It readies another arrow and crouches on the edge of the roof. It looks over, and spots Jake.

"Go left Jake!"

Jake jumps left and slides behind another car. The arrow cuts through the air right by his ear. The shooter takes after him along the rooftops.

"It's coming!" Scott shouts out again.

Jake is already halfway to the theater but his heart and head is pounding. He pushes himself faster, crossing back to the left side of the street. The two men keep firing, but the smoke has become so thick and wide that it is their view that is now obscured.

Jake hears the sound of another arrow coming at him and pulls to his right. The arrow grazes the side of his neck and the force of the shot jerks his body left sending him tumbling over a car.

"Ack!"

Is the only sound the two men hear from down the street. They see the creature has stopped shooting its arrows. Now it is standing with its long arms reaching upwards, and belches in a victorious roar to the sky.

Scott and Mike look at each other through the barricade. Mike scowls and screams, "Damn you fucking monsters!" And follows with more direct hits.

With a quivering jaw, Scott fires with him and nails it in its left knee. The creature loses its balance and falls from the roof to the ground. Immediately, as it impacts head first into the sidewalk with a loud crack, it snaps back up to its feet and charges at the men. It leaps through the smoke and crashes into the garage door, almost breaking right through it. As Scott jumps back its long arm shoots through the window. Its claws reach out to gouge his eyes. It misses and flails its arms trying to grab at him while pushing its way through the garage door.

Scott drops his rifle and pulls out his pistol while Mike reloads. He fires a few times but it keeps coming, wrecking more as it does. Scott pulls out his treated knife with his other hand and while holding the blade pointed down he angrily hammers into the thing's arm. He opens a large black gash across its ruined flesh as it releases a thunderous roar. Lighting fast the arm withdraws from the window and is replaced by the creature's one good eye. The eye darts around the garage and focuses on Scott. He can feel the rage in its piercing stare and is stunned. Too paralyzed to move, Mike fires at it again, tagging it in its head but missing the evil eye.

Within a blink it is gone from the window and there is nothing but silence.

Blood spurts through Jake's fingers as he presses his hand against the gash on the right side of his neck. Whether from the intense burrowing pain or the loss of blood, dizziness comes over him while he stumbles back to his feet. Unable to turn his head, he twists his entire upper body to see. He dares a look back to the police station and sees the creature halfway through the garage door. He hopes they survive their encounter. He turns back to the theater and even though he is running a hundred miles an hour in his mind, his shaky legs slowly plop down one after the other. He glances down the east path of the forks for any signs of the crawler or screamer. Gunfire echoes from behind him as he steps underneath the sagging marquee then finally through the opened door. The inside is as expected and he walks past the ticketing booth hoping to find old tissues or anything that could help him stop the bleeding. His head feels like its going to split open again. Starving, in pain and bleeding to death. He continues into the pitch black of the next door. After bumping around a few times, he realizes he is in a narrow hallway but there is a light at the end of this tunnel. The hallway opens up to the theater. Streams of gloomy light pour in through the large room's caved in ceiling. Near the front he sees a weathered seat free of debris and sits. He looks up at the tattered movie screen and for a moment, swears he sees a flicker of a film playing on it. His headache rages but his body is giving in to the numbness. His eyelids quiver as he fights to keep them open and a long quiet moan leaves his mouth. His eyes roll back and he gives in to the painless bliss of darkness.

* * *

A single flame floats through the starless dark streets. Metal noisily rolls against ragged asphalt as the two men take turns pressing the corroded barrel forward. The furthest reaches of the makeshift torch's light begins to flicker against the stores of downtown Prudence.

"Do you think it's safe to check inside?" Scott holds the torch out towards the ruined marquee.

"As loud as we've been, I'm sure he was right about them not being around at night," Mike says, giving the barrel another shove with his foot.

Scott lowers the torch to the ground revealing the trail of blood Jake left during his escape. "He lost a lot, but it doesn't look arterial."

"How can you tell?"

"There's no consistent spurts of blood. You know, per heartbeat."

Mike examines the splattered sidewalk, sadly shaking his head. "There's no way he would be conscious after loosing this much blood."

Scott moves the torch around the area then returns to Mike's side, "Shouldn't we go in?"

"Would it matter? If he slid back, then he slid back. If he's dead there's nothing we can do about it."

"Or he's turned into one of them, gone zombie or worse."

"I don't think it works like that."

"How do you know?"

"Cause then the whole town would've turned!"

"Maybe they did. Maybe they just ate each other 'til there was just a few left."

"Shit man, don't start that again! Let's just finish what we're doing."

A few minutes later, near the still smoldering car from before, they tilt the barrel upright to maneuver it through the bank's front door. Scott carefully places his torch into a different barrel sitting just outside the front door, wherein a small fire burns. The vault is not the large steel room with a two-foot thick round steel door like either of them had hoped for. The size of a small bedroom, its averaged sized door is a few inches of steel. It has a thick glass view window while its secondary, inward swinging door is made square iron bars. The walls are solid concrete lined with dingy deposit boxes and a heavy wooden table bolted to the center of the room. They drag the barrel into the vault and unscrew its cap. Mike begin siphoning its black contents into various glass bottles, partially filled with scavenged liquor and gasoline. Scott stuffs rags into their tops, allows them to soak up the crude, then corks them off with various snug fitting objects. He lines the black molotovs up on the teller's side of the counter.

"How many is that?" Mike calls from the vault.

"Eighteen. Think its enough?"

Mike silently debates while he ties one of the legs from an old wet pair of jeans to the lock of the inside door. "Yeah. I want to stash a few around some of the other stores later. We can't run with all these."

Scott tosses Mike a sack of clothes which he starts piling in a line around the inside door's path. Scott takes a large wrench and bashes away at the vault's glass window. "I know it didn't scream when we lit the torch, but do you this oil is similar to their black blood?"

"It looks the same but I don't think it is. I think it hides inside the oil or feeds off it the way it does metal. I think that might be how those things stayed alive while being locked up all those years."

Scott shakes his head as he thinks about it, "I keep wondering what other things could be out in the world."

The men keep working, preparing themselves until the early morning's dreary dawn sky is just beginning to lighten.

Out of breath, Mike rushes inside the bank and half closes the door behind himself, "They're already coming!"

"Did you get everything?!" Scott asks from his hiding spot across from the front door and behind the counter.

"Yeah. I even found a few supplies at the clinic." He places the torch upright in a waste basket and grabs a sharpened broomstick, treated with the red extract. "Remember, pistols then sticks."

Scott looks at him and hesitates for a moment, then slings his rifle over his shoulder like Mike and draws his pistol.

They listen to the sickly wheezing of the creatures accompanied by thuds and strong impacts with stray cars and debris rapidly getting closer.

"Shit!" Mike jumps up, "I forgot to tip it!" He rushes into the vault and shoves the oil barrel over on its side. The black liquid begins glugging onto the floor but is kept from running out into the bank by the dam of clothes.

Instead of relying on the single straight view of the barred bank display window and the front door, they placed angled mirrors at the ends of the walls.

"See any of 'em?" Scott whispers.

"Yeah, here it comes," Mike squints as he uses his mirror.

The large creature dashes by from right to left, shaking the windows as it does.

"Which one was that?" he nervously calls over to Mike.

"It was that damned archer. What if it just pins us down until the others get here?"

"I see it now. It's hopping around the car we burned all pissed. Any others?"

"Not yet," Mike responds, "It's gonna run into the station soon, try now?"

"I'll do it," Scott whispers, then yells, "Hey Fuckface!"

A pitched gasp comes from outside. The one who shoots rushes back to the front of the bank with its bow drawn. It begins sucking at the air with its broken gash of a mouth and tilting its head back to make better use of its one large eye.

"This way asshole!" Mike bates the creature.

It draws back and fires faster than Mike ducks behind his side of the counter. The black arrow crashes through the glass and penetrates halfway into the concrete wall behind them.

"Fight like a man!" Scott yells out, "You can't hit shit from out there!"

The creature inhales deeply and makes a sound like the cross between a bear's roar and a giant garbage disposal. It drops its bow and charges through the door, smashing away a large portion of the frame with its head.

Mike is amazed by Scott's show of courage as he hops up in front of the vault door with his spear ready. It bats away the safety wall on top of the teller's counter like it is nothing and steps completely over it with its thick gangly leg. Overwhelmed by its speed, Scott slips to the ground but has his spear ready. Mike stands up and shoots it in its knee, off balancing it before its back leg comes down. It drops down on Scott but impales itself on his treated spear. It screams again, in pain this time. Its roar is deafening. Mike jabs its side with his spear and while it is still off balance, both men force the creature tumbling forward into the vault. Scott grabs the jeans tied to the vault door and pulls it closed, trapping it inside. It slips in the spilled oil and scrambles to its feet in a flash. Beyond enraged it grabs at the bars and pulls. Scott strains but it does not matter, both men see the bars in its hands immediately start dissolving into a rusty sand.

"Do it!" Scott shouts.

Mike lights a black molotov with the torch and hurls it at the one who shoots. It smashes against the bars, coating the Devourer with the oil, which ignites violently. It falls away and Mike slams the outer door closed. On his feet Scott tips a heavy cabinet sideways across the door.

The men look at each other half terrified, half elated and it flails inside the vault. Both men close their eyes while bracing against the door. Like a dragon's breath, the fiery explosion bursts out of the vaults square window. The creature's roars are now high-pitched screams, interrupted by the sporadic flapping of its mouth.

They share a laugh and Scott hops over the counter then turns back to Mike, excited that their plan worked.

"Hold on!" Mike shouts and bends down to retrieve Scott's spear. He looks up and tosses it to Scott who reaches out for it.

Just as it leaves Mike's hand, he yells to warn Scott who could already tell by the horrified look on his friend's face. Scott catches it and turns around just as the one who screams hacks its knife crookedly downward across his chest. Scott's eyes widen in disbelief as if the blow knocked his soul right out of his body. It squeals in delight and bites down around his face. Scott's head disappears into its expanded mouth and viciously wrenches at him. Ribbons of elastic flesh stretches then snaps away, tearing his head off above the jaw. In fine crimson feathers, Scott's blood sprays up against the ceiling and into Mikes' face as his convulsing spastic body falls backwards. Shock and rage blend and Mike looses himself. He Jumps onto the counter then leaps spear first at it. It grabs the treated end of the spear and snaps it off before he lands.

Mike quickly pulls his pistol and begins shooting its blood spurting mouth as it crunches down on skull. It slashes at the air a few times and misses, before Mike slashes back at it with his treated knife. With both of the things in agony, a sick happiness comes over him and he keeps stabbing and slashing at it. It shoves him back and sends him flying to the floor. The vault door smashes open and the screaming shadow engulfed in black smoke bursts out. Its arms whip around unnaturally fast as it rushes forward, plowing into the one who screams, knocking it out of the bank and into a building across the street.

Mike is focused, ready to die fighting but as the opportunity to escape again opens in front of him, his death wish flickers out. The rush of thoughts and emotions cause his body to shake violently. He looks down at Scott's blood soaked and slashed body, replaying what he just saw in his mind. He reaches up and wipes Scott's blood from his mouth then stares at it dripping down his quivering hand. He turns around in time to see the one who screams awkwardly bounding towards him from across the street. He looks down and calmly picks an unlit Molotov up from the floor. He waits until the thing is right in the doorframe, so it cannot dodge left or right and he nails it. Mike grabs the torch and swings at it. It hops back fearfully and smells, in its way, the oil covering its body. Mike rushes it but it leaps backwards again. It crouches down scooping up the one who shoots' wicked bow and hisses threateningly at Mike. Mike does not stop advancing and it cuts away towards the Forks. He exits the bank in time to see it leap and scurry along the buildings and disappearing over the rooftops.

CHAPTER 9

"Shows over."

Jake opens his eyes seeing large white letters reading "THE END" floating in blackness.

"You ok?" a bright light stings, as it shines into his eyes.

He hisses at the light.

"Hey buddy, you want to watch it again. You gotta pay upfront."

Still pressing his hand against his neck he looks around. He is warm and pain free and better, no longer bleeding.

He is back.

He looks up to see a curly haired kid with small round glasses holding a flashlight in one hand a broom in the other.

"Ugh, I was just leaving," he starts to stand but realizes the stake is swinging from it's lanyard around his slumped hand.

"You one of the field workers? Never seen you before."

Jake's stops to think as he leans forward trying to conceal his weapon, "Ugh, no. Just passing through town."

The kid just looks at Jake, waiting for him to leave the theater.

"Where's the bathroom here?"

"To your left when you come out of the hall," he turns around and points to the exit.

Legs no longer shaky Jake stands up and turns the stake

upwards, hiding it in his jacket.

"Make sure you turn off the lights in there when you're done!" the kid calls out behind him.

Jake enters the small bathroom and looks at himself in the mirror. He looks fine. Other than being hungry, he feels great. Better than great and remedies his hunger with a swig from his flask. He takes off his sweet smelling medicine bag and stares at it for a moment and chuckles before placing it into a jacket pocket. After a few attempts, he manages to fit the stake into his free inside pocket without it looking conspicuous.

He sighs with relief, exits the bathroom and inhales the ambient smell of stale and fresh popcorn. He looks at his watch and sees that it is seven thirty.

"I must not have been out for that long," he says out loud to himself.

He walks out of the theater and looks out at the Forks from beneath the beautifully lit marquee. Under the purple skies of dusk, the hot winds continue to blow even though it appears to be late September. Like before, people are still bustling around despite it being late. He notices a few people staring hard at him and ushering there kids along past him. Almost all of the kids are dressed up like little pilgrims or puritans. The girls are wearing detailed, quilted red silk shawls over their shoulders and the boys are wearing matching red sashes. The boys also have little black brimmed cone topped hats with ornate gray cloaks and large collars that curve outwards. Their knee-high boots have pointed tips that curve upward and back. Without trying to be to obvious, Jake watches the kids and their parents walk by. He notices specific details in their costumes, the designs and cuneiform he saw in the Lamplighter's book.

Jake remembers Sophie mentioning the festival they have for the totems. That must be what is going on and he worries that this might be the night they escape. He looks down all three roads that become the Forks, and sees miniature versions of the totems. Two each have been placed on the three corners at the intersection. They stand only twelve feet tall and fresh red flowers are strung from them, draping over the three main roads. He watches the people for a while longer and wonders how many, if any of them know about the cross continental origins and purpose of their festive customs.

He spots an old phone booth on the lone sidewalk across the street. It is in front of the large nondescript red building that stands on the north corner of the forks. He walks over hoping to learn Kenneth's whereabouts from the local white pages. Standing outside its closed doors, he sees the occupant of the booth is using it as an office. The scruffy man is reading into the phone from various small books and papers and keeps either adding quarters from his large stacks atop the phone box. He keeps hanging up and dialing new numbers. Jake lingers for a few minutes then decides to knock on the door to hurry the man along. The bearded man looks back over his shoulder and almost does a double take. The man's large shades sit awkwardly under his black, orange billed hat and his face is almost completely concealed. He turns back away and continues operating the booth like it is his personal area.

Jake tugs at the front of his hoodie a few times trying to cool off. He hefts his jacket wishing he could remove it, but thinks about his concealed stake and the revolver within his inner jacket pockets. After a few more minutes he knocks again. The man does not turn around but holds up four fingers to Jake, apparently signaling it would be a few more minutes.

Jake turns away and his mind wanders back to the dark task he has ahead. He probes his neck with his fingers where the arrow struck and wonders how painful returning to the present would be this time.

He spots Chuck's general store and sees that it is still open. He gives up on waiting for the man in the booth. He steps inside of its brightness and again the dim light stings his eyes.

To the left, a middle-aged man with a meticulously trimmed beard looks up from the small and loud television. He stands up, leans on the counter, and gives Jake a nod hello.

Jake casually picks up a shopping basket and walks through the living version of the store he had been in when he first arrived in Prudence. Tall simple wooden shelves line the walls and reach up to the ceiling. They are packed with medicines, canned goods, boxed supplements and stuffed burlap sacks. Wood barrels are scattered throughout containing everything from grains to fresh produce, peanuts and candies. The back of the store is lined with tools, spare parts, sewing machines and cleaning products.

As he makes his way further back into the store the man calls out to him, "I'm closing up soon. Can I help you find anything?"

"Yeah," Jake wanders back to the front. He tries looking at what medical supplies the store carries. He knows what he needs, but tries to ask for them in the least suspicious way he can. "Could I get some wraps, like bandage wraps?"

"Any in particular?" the man presents the appropriate shelf to Jake.

"I'll take a few boxes of the thick rolls and I'll take a bottle of that rubbing alcohol."

"Are you hurt?" he asks him.

"No," he answers plainly but is annoyed. "Needle and thread?"

"Yes. What kind of thread?"

"Green. Regular for clothes I guess."

"Anything else?"

Jake's eyes move over the counter top and shelves, "Hey, how much is one of these packs of baseball cards?" He tries to throw the nosy store owner off.

"Huh? Oh ten cents."

"I'll take about thirty."

"Well, I've only got this box here, looks like there's about twenty three."

"That's fine." At least Mike will be happy, he thinks.

The man moves the baseball cards onto his stack.

"What's the best painkiller you have right now?"

"Without a prescription it's, this one. Anything stronger and you'll have to go to Doc Clifton or the apothecary in the morning."

"That's alright," Jake shrugs him off again but sees the man is looking out of his store window for someone.

"Sure you're not hurt?" the clerk repeats.

"No, I'm fine," Jake forces a smile. "On my way to my sister's. I'm taking my nephews camping and they're both accident prone. Oh yeah, any super glue?"

"Sure," The unconvinced clerk walks to the end of a shelf and returns with the glue.

Jake looks out the window to see what is so interesting to the clerk and sees Deputy Harris walking down the other side of the street. His eyes widen but he turns back to the clerk with a cheesy calm smile. The clerk is still watching Harris.

"So, let me make sure I didn't forget anything." He vocalizes his thoughts for the clerks benefit. "I got the rubbing alcohol incase they gets scrapes, got them ball cards, got a few wraps for her tennis elbow, needle and thread for her torn curtain and pain killer for the headaches the boys will give me."

"Oh?" the clerk says relived. "Is it that bad?"

"Not really, but I've done this a few times. I think there was something else though, oh yeah." He feigns realization and pulls the devil girl lighter from his pocket. "Do you have any lighter fluid?"

The clerk stares down at the shiny and beautifully designed lighter.

"That's a beautiful piece, may I?"

"Sure," Jake hands it over to him.

"I collect these, but I've never seen one like this before." The clerk cradles the lighter gliding his thumb over the raised image of the devil girl.

"It was a gift."

"Any idea where he got it done?"

"My friend said it was custom job. I can ask next time I see him."

"Oh, that won't be necessary," He returns the lighter to Jake.

Jake turns and sees that the deputy has passed them by.

"I hear there's a special flower grown locally, supposed to make a great cup of tea?"

"Yes, actually, it's quite expensive though but our community is very proud of it. I am surprised you have heard of it. How much would you like?"

"How much is that tin there?"

"Five even."

"I'll take it. I'll also need a note pad, a few pens and about six of these chocolate bars."

The clerk puts his hand on the side of the old-fashioned register and stares at Jake. Jake stares back at him confused for a moment then realizes the guy wanted to see if he had any money before he starts ringing everything up. He opens his wallet and also produces the forty dollars Mike gave him for the cards and quickly places that inside the bill sleeve. He hopes he doesn't have to use his modern bills with the already suspicious man. He holds out the change in front of the clerk he got from before in the diner and hopes it will be enough. Satisfied the clerk begins ringing everything up on the ancient cash register.

"That comes to, nine dollars and seventy seven cents."

"Really?" Jake says surprised.

The clerk becomes flustered and defensive. "What? Well, you can't get prices better than mine anywhere here!"

"No, I meant. I'm just shocked that's all it costs," Jake explains.

"Oh? I'm sorry then. It's still the largest sale I've made all day."

He hands the clerk his old-fashioned ten and they complete the transaction.

The clerk pops out a thick paper bag and carefully places everything inside.

"Well, sir it's been a pleasure, I should have more of those cards in by next week if you're passing back through."

"I'll definitely stop by again if I can," he turns to leave the store then stops. "By the way, would you happen to have a local telephone book here?"

"Of course. Got one for all of Rooks County."

"Would you mind if I had a quick look? An old high school friend of mine might have moved here, thought I would look him up."

"No need to explain."

He produces a phonebook from under the counter, sets a rotary phone next to it then turns away to watch his television again.

The phone book is basically a pamphlet and he hopes that Kenneth Tanner has a listed number. He quickly thumbs through the pages. There's only one Tanner, not a Kenneth tanner though.

Elijah Tanner, possibly his father. He retrieves the pad and paper from the tightly packed bag and the clerk looks briefly at him to make sure he is not stuffing anything extra into it. He writes down the name, address and number. A thought crosses his mind and he looks up Harris as well and writes Sophie's number down again.

He knows it is stupid for him to hope, but he has been thinking about her more than he feels comfortable with.

"Do you have any maps of the town?"

"No. This is a pretty small out of the way place. Most of the people here were born here. Plus it's laid out pretty simple."

"Could you tell me how to get to Little Willow road?"

"Sure, what's the house number."

"Does it matter?"

"Of course. Prudence is laid out in circles and each circle counts as one big road. So, with the main circular roads, Red Pine runs around the entire town, followed by Red Oak, Red Willow and Red Birch. The size of the road is relative to the size of tree it is named after. The smaller roads in-between the main ones are named, Little Pine, Little Oak and so on. And then they're all just spilt by our East, West and South roads."

Jake hesitates, assuming Kenneth is only just a screw up now. Jake does not want to be associated with him as a friend.

"House number twenty two," he lies. With my luck, it's probably this guys house, he thinks.

"Hmm, not sure who lives there, but if you take west fork and turn right at the third street, you can't miss it."

"Ok man, thanks a lot."

"Have fun camping," he smiles and turns back to his television show.

While looking out for the police, Jake heads to the house hoping that Kenneth is there and hoping he will have the strength to put him down.

Jake analyzes his possible courses of action. If Kenneth is at the house, he will have to shoot someone in cold blood, because the bastard may still be innocent at this point. Then hope that after he does, he is immediately transported back to his time. He may never have a recollection of ever having come to Prudence. On the other hand, he could kill him and be trapped in the past. In that case, he would have to make sure there will be no witnesses. Jake might have to talk his way into the house somehow. If he isn't even there, he will have to come up with a reason for being at the house and asking about Kenneth.

By the time he arrives at Little Willow number 27, he has a solid plan if Kenneth is not there. The neighborhoods are still bustling with their Halloween style festival apparently just getting started. Jake approaches the white house trying to conceal himself from any onlookers with his hood. He sees lights are on in more than a few rooms in the house. There are just a few families out on the street but he kneels down as if to tie his shoe and transfers the revolver from his inner jacket to his outer right pocket. Jake steps onto the well-lit porch and places his hand in is pocket and slides his finger over the trigger. He stands there thinking of all of the horrible things that happened to him, that will happen to all of the people here if he fails. Still nervous but committed, he takes a deep breath and rings the doorbell. He has become clammy and especially his face heats up. Time slows down as his heart pounds and he keeps trying to take long deep breaths. He hears someone coming to the door and a sensation of shame over what he is about to do comes over him.

He just wants to run away.

It unlocks and the door swings open. Standing there is a beautiful teenaged girl with short curly hair and the darkest eyes.

"Evelyn?" he gasps and quickly pulls his trembling finger off the trigger.

Evelyn was smiling when she answered the door, now she is wearing a confused expression. She takes a step back into the low lit hallway and Jake sees a hint of her worried look from when he met her before.

With an eyebrow raised she looks him up and down, "Sophie didn't say she invited you."

Jake is speechless.

"You really are a space cadet. Are you going to come inside or not?"

"Ugh, do you live here?"

Evelyn rolls her eyes at him and walks away, leaving the door open, "Lock it behind you."

Jake looks down at the powder blue carpet on the inside of the house, but it feels more like he is looking off the edge of a cliff. He looks around the neighborhood again and debates still running anyway. He wipes his feet off on the doormat and cautiously steps in. In front of him is a stairwell leading up. To the left is a hallway with the sounds of a party coming from one of the rooms at the end. He closes the door behind himself and locks it, then quickly eases the hammer forward on the pistol and places it back inside his inner pocket.

Slowly he walks down the unlit hall towards the lights and the source of the classic songs playing. He observes a photo collage along the wood paneled walls. Family pictures. Jake sees the progression of Evelyn from a new born until now. There is a man in the picture who must be her father. He looks average, of European descent and cheerful. Evelyn is more adventurous than he thought. In many of the photos she is doing some different activity from horse back riding to shooting or winning some award.

Finally, he comes to an image that makes an absolute connection between Evelyn and Kenneth. It is a family photo taken in front of one of the totems. It looks like it is the entire family, Evelyn and her parents and Kenneth, her older brother. He must have been in his early teens when this was taken but it is definitely him. The mother who could pass as Evelyn's sister stands with her hand on Kenneth's shoulder. The both of them stand a distance away from Evelyn and her dad. The mother has that same foreboding look as her son.

"Jake?"

He turns to see Sophie's excited eyes beaming into his. Her miscellaneous bracelets rattle and clang when she wraps her arms around him and squeezes with a grip far stronger than to be expected from a woman her size, "How've you been, cool cat?"

His heart flutters, "I've been alright, you?"

While she tightens her crush on him he sees four other people in the living room. Kenneth is not among them.

"Hey guys, smile!" A blond girl steps up to them with a camera.

Sophie grins instantly but Jake looks shaken.

"Ok, smile," she repeats.

Sophie looks back at him causing her large feathery earrings to whip him in the face, "Not happy to see me?" she teases.

"I'm happy," he says. He really is happy to see her again.

"Then smile," she looks back to camera.

Jake smiles just as the camera flashes. The camera's gears whir as it spits out the square floppy print. The blonde hands it to Jake but Sophie excitedly snatches it up and begins fanning it back and forth.

"My names Jennifer by the way," The blonde reaches her hand out to Jake.

"Hello," He shakes her hand.

The rest of the party introduces themselves to him and one by one he shakes all of their hands. A guy the girl's age with glasses, flat black hair and the taller guy that showed up late in his car the night when he walked Evelyn home. Her father steps forward and introduces himself as well. Other than Junior's, all of their names breeze by him. He was never good at remembering names. After the introductions, everyone resumes their conversations and Sophie backs him into the hall. She is wearing a loose almost transparent white blouse, embroidered with red swirls and flowers. Her thigh length skirt sways as well revealing her long shapely legs to him.

"It's been over a month, why didn't you call me?"

"Accidentally left the napkin in my pants and the laundry got it," He lies apologetically.

"It was that important, huh?"

"No, I felt terrible and really wanted to call."

"Then how did you know about the party?"

"Small town," he says. Something she told him when they first met.

"You gonna be here long?"

"I don't know" he answers her somberly.

Sophie makes a pouting expression for a moment but smiles again, "You're here for the night at least." She pulls him closer and whispers in his ear, "I have a present for you."

"What's that?" he smiles.

"I'll give it you later tonight."

Her warm breath against his ear causes a flood of goose bumps to run up his neck.

"Huh? Jake, are you blushing?" she teases him.

"No," He smiles. Jake cannot fathom how despite Sophie being years younger than him she is making him feel like a little school girl.

"You didn't have to bring anything. Do you have something that needs to be refrigerated?" The two of them jump when they see Evelyn's tall backlit silhouette in the hall with them.

Having forgotten, Jake looks down and sees his hands tensely gripping the top of the rolled up paper bag.

"Ugh, just some personal stuff."

"Oh yeah! I found your bag by the Dixon's house."

"You did? Is that the present?" he asks innocently.

Sophie's eyes pop open and dart at Evelyn then back to Jake, "Yeah." She smiles nervously.

Evelyn stands their silently for a few awkward seconds, "Well, the cakes all lit."

Jake follows the girls back into the living room where the rest of the party has crowded around a lit cake.

"You should get in the picture Jake. Sam will flip out when he sees you in it!"

"What?!" he blurts out. Suddenly the entire scene becomes familiar to him and he realizes that these are the other people with the cake. One of the wall photos from Sam's collection.

"Yeah Jake, get in the picture!" Jennifer calls out.

"No, you guys are his friends, I should be the one taking the picture," He says his mind trying to figure out the implications of being in the photo.

Jake concludes that if he was in the photograph, Sam might have recognized him as being from the past. And with him not having aged when they meet decades later, Sam would more than likely have shot him. Possibly thinking he was a ghost or a trick the Devourers were trying to play in order to kill him. It would not be t different from Kenneth's trick of making himself young again.

But Sam had no idea who Jake was when they met and he was not in the picture. But then again, he also shot at him later, possibly for this very reason. This reinforces that Sam returns after the town goes to hell. Jake realizes he has to get his hands on the picture of himself and Sophie, as well as the picture that was about to be taken.

"Come on Jake, don't be such a square," Sophie moans.

"Alright fine, but you have to let me take one with all of you in it."

He places the paper bag on the floor and they group together, somehow with Sophie and Evelyn flanking him, he holds up the cake.

Right when Jennifer says "Cheese!" he jumps and nearly drops the cake during the flash.

One of the girls had grabbed him from behind.

"You alright Jake?" Sophie asks him.

He cannot tell if this is a prank or, . . . he turns and looks at Evelyn who is looking at him with the same coy expression.

"Alright my turn," he quickly hands off the cake and gets the camera from Jennifer. He takes the print from the camera and casually places it in his pocket. The group gets ready, this time with Evelyn holding the cake. Jake looks through the viewfinder and notices the antique mirror. A thought crosses his mind. Although it brings the same risk he is trying to avert by keeping the pictures of himself, it might be a worthy gamble. It could also be the only way to gain Sam's trust and something similar helped him get former Deputy Scott to believe him about his time sliding experience.

He starts maneuvering while aiming the camera. He positions himself so he is barely in the bottom corner of the mirror's reflection. Trying to make his image as less obvious as possible.

"I'm hungry Jake, let's go!" Junior calls out.

"Ok, nobody move," he lines up the shot then raises his head up from behind the camera.

"Say Spaghetti!"

They say it together and he snaps the photo.

"Are you sure that came out? You were looking through the view finder," a concerned Evelyn places the cake on a coffee table.

"Here," he hands her the fresh blank image and she begins fanning it.

He gives the camera back to Jennifer, hoping she would not take any more pictures of him.

"Well, I'll go get plates," Sophie offers.

"Hey, how did the picture of us turn out?" he asks before she turns away.

"You want to see? Here," She hands it to him.

It is a nice picture of them Jake cannot help but to smile.

"What a cute couple," Evelyn taunts while she picks up his bag.

"What are you doing?"

"Relax. I'm going to put it away before someone trips over it."

Jake subdues his stress about her taking it, "Ok."

"Got the plates!" Sophie returns from the kitchen.

Jake looks to Sophie as he pockets the first photo of them. He does not notice Evelyn turn back to look at him, with her peculiar look as she walks away with his bag.

"I'll cut the cake," Evelyn's father steps in.

As slices of cake are passed around, Jake looks over more of the living room for clues of where Kenneth might be. He sees nothing helpful.

"Here you go, Jake," Her father hands him a plated slice.

"Thank you, Mr. Tanner."

"You're welcome."

Jake studies the father and still sees no strong resemblance to Kenneth or Evelyn, "Have you lived here long?"

The man sits down across from Jake, "Almost twenty-five years. The city boomed when they found all the oil."

"You're an oil worker?"

"No," he laughs. "I'm a mechanic. With all the workers showing up back then they needed people to work on all the drilling equipment."

"And you decided to stay?"

"Yeah well, I met Evelyn's mother and settled down here," a sad look comes over him.

Jake pushes a little. "I heard she has a brother, is he around?"

"Hm? No, he and I," the man pauses for a moment, "we never

got along that well, he was always closer to his mother."

"So he doesn't come around too often?"

"No," the man pauses again. "I'm gonna grab a beer," he stands and heads out into the backyard.

"Wow dude, bad move." Junior says as he and his friend slide over to Jake.

"What? Did I do something wrong," By her father's reaction Jake knows he had but he plays dumb.

"Yeah. You couldn't know, but never bring up Crazy Kenny around Evelyn or her father."

"Crazy Kenny?" he leans back.

"Shh!" Tim, the slick haired teen with glasses glances around the room, "He was kind of—"

"Run out of town," Junior finishes.

"No shit?" Jake asks, unsurprised. "What did he do?"

"What didn't he do, the guy's an asshole," Tim pushes his black thick framed glasses back up his nose.

"When was the last time he was around?"

"Another slice?" Jennifer pushes in with more cake.

Jake looks down confused and sees that he finished off his slice without realizing and he has licked his plate clean.

"Uh, sure."

She swaps plates with him and walks away.

Tim continues, "I think it's been a few years, right Junior?"

"I don't know. Evelyn started acting funny a few months ago, like before."

"Funny how? She doesn't get along with Kenneth?"

"Oh no, never have," Tim shifts his beady eyes around the room again. "He beat her up pretty bad. That was the last straw for their stepfather, he came close to shooting Kenny right there."

"Should have shot him," Junior adds.

Jake can only agree and wishes that he had been put down already, "So you think he's hanging around again?" Jake lowers his voice further when he sees Evelyn enter the room.

"I'm not gonna ask. But why do you care?" Junior's voice has become laced with a hint of jealousy.

Jake looks at him with a firm reassuring look, dismissing

Junior's misplaced concerns, "If he's around town, where do you think he might be?"

Junior crosses his arms and tries staring down Jake, Junior loses.

"Nobody in town likes that guy, so we would've heard if he was seen anywhere," Tim adjusts his glasses again. "And no nearby towns would put up with him for long, whatcha think Junior?"

Junior remains silent but a thought does come to him, "The outskirts maybe?"

"What's that?"

"Yeah, he used to always camp in the woods," Tim says in a whisper as Evelyn approaches.

"What?" Jake's shoulders slump. If Kenneth were camping somewhere, it would be next to impossible to find him in one night, let alone get the drop in on him, "Any idea where?"

"Where what?" Evelyn joins in. Eyeing Jake more curiously than before.

"Where is a good place around here to go camping," Jake states plainly to the two boy's surprise.

Evelyn looks at him without any expression, except for her dark eyes, which have become intense, "You? The outdoors type?"

"Got to liking it in the war," he smirks.

"I guess that explains the weird combination of stuff you have in your bag."

Jake's smirk melts into a scowl.

"Oh, I'm sorry," she coyly apologizes. "The contents accidentally spilled out when I was moving it out of the way."

The two boys back away and exit into the yard while Jake and Evelyn maintain there subtle stare down. Jake is glad that she at least does not seem to be helping Kenneth, and he wonders if she may know where he is.

Sophie innocently pops up between them looking to and from their faces. "Okaaay. What time should we leave for the festival Evie?"

Caught off guard Evelyn fumbles for an excuse, "Ugh. I'm not going out till later."

"What?" Since when? We've always done the walk together."

"I have to clean up after the party. Besides why don't you go with Jake. I'll catch up."

Sophie immediately agrees with the idea of being alone with him.

Jake watches Evelyn rejoin her party guests and his attention is pulled away from her by Sophie.

"You're coming, right?"

"To the festival? I don't know if I'll have time Sophie."

"Oh come on! Don't be such a pansy! Everyone in town should be there."

Jake doubts someone as notorious as Crazy Kenny will be out for the festivities.

"Have you got something better to do tonight?"

"I did want to find out if there was anywhere good to go camping around the outskirts here. Do you think a camping store could still be open tonight?"

She stops and thinks, "Lots of stores stay open late for the holiday, but we don't really have a camping store. We'll see a lot of people who camp while we're on the walk though, you could ask them."

"Where are we walking, to check the totems?"

"Yeah!"

"Have you ever gone camping with Evelyn's family?"

Her flawless face tries to scrunch, "No way! Camping's not my thing, I would rather live in the big city, like you Jake."

"How do you know I'm from the city?"

"My dad saw your outer spacey I.D.'s remember?"

Jake is torn. With the abductions, Kenneth has to be around and he has no way to find him. But he also wants to be with Sophie and enjoy not being in pain. He knows win or loose, this could be the last night he will ever be with her.

"Ha, ha! Will you stop that?!"

Jake realizes again that he is licking another plate clean and wonders if his unconscious eating could become a danger to people around him.

"Sorry," he shrugs.

"That's ok! I'll forgive you if you come with me tonight," she leans in with a huskier voice, "You wouldn't want to miss out on your surprise, would you?"

"Of course not," Jake sadly smiles.

"Well, I'm gonna say goodbye to everyone incase I don't see them tonight. I think Evelyn stashed your stuff upstairs."

"Ok." Jake looks around and sees Evelyn is still busy with her friends. As he makes his way upstairs he studies the family photos again, looking for any camping trips, cabins or boats they may own. The top of the stairwell opens in the center of a hall that stretches equally left and right. Standing in the hallway, he sees two doors facing each other down each side of the hallway and he freezes.

He whips his head back and forth. It could just be a result of repeated housing construction but the connection between Kenneth and Evelyn, even the tasteless floral wallpaper is a giveaway.

He is in the house where he first encountered them. He remembers the one who screams rushing down the hall with that sickening noise and smell.

All of the doors are closed save one. He walks down the hall wishing he could at least warn the people here, but mentioning the Devourers now could be what sets them free. It could be the reason why he has slid back to this time. He is not about to play into Kenneth's hand like an idiot, again.

He looks through the half opened door and sees what must be Evelyn's bedroom. It looks normal for a girl who is almost twenty. It is plain except for a carved mural in her headboard. He pushes the door open a bit more and tribal furnishings come into view. A vast collection of dreamcatchers covers the room, dangling from the ceilings and walls. An incense, the sweet husky scent of the red meadow death flower floods his nostrils and he sneezes.

He thinks all the room needs is some mounted antlers and a couple black velvet paintings of wolves howling at the moon.

Not seeing his paper bag in the room, he walks past it and to the window overlooking the street. He leans forward on the sill and sees more people are walking around outside, some of the adults have started dressing up as well.

"Looking for your stuff?" Evelyn's voice quickly turns him

around.

"Yeah," he cautiously leans back.

She is standing near the other end of the hall holding the paper bag in her arms. He can tell she is trying her best to be either spooky or intimating, but he is too frustrated to care. She walks towards him too and notices her bedroom door was pushed open, but she says nothing. She holds the bag out in front of herself as if to keep him at a distance. He reaches forward but closer to her hand than the rolled paper grip and she pulls away.

"What's the matter?"

"Nothing," She frowns and tosses the bag to him.

"Evelyn . . ."

"Whatever you're going to say, don't."

"I'm not your enemy."

"Who said you were?" she tosses the bag to him.

Caught in another precarious situation, Jake cannot think of an easy way to come out and ask her what is going on. Either way, he will blow his cover somehow or mention her brother's ties to the Devourers. He did not even want to chance thinking about them. The risks are too high and he decides that Evelyn will have to be a dead end for now.

"Thanks for the cake, Evelyn and for having me over."

Defeated, he heads downstairs where Sophie is leaning against the wall, listening to their conversation with her arms crossed. Her homemade purse hangs from her shoulder and she looks ready to go.

"Ready?" she opens the door before he can answer.

Jake steps through and Sophie closes the door behind them.

"You're not going to say goodbye to Evelyn?"

"We'll see her later," she snaps.

Jake can tell she is upset, jealous even.

He is upset as well. He hoped he could have prevented everything from happening tonight, with one bullet. He laughs at the thought, ending it all with one bullet.

"What's so funny?"

"Hmm? Nothing. A lot on my mind, I guess."

"What were you talking to her about?"

196

"I went up to get my bag. I don't think she likes me. I was going to ask her if I said something to make her all weird around me."

"Oh. that's all?" she smiles again. "Don't worry about that, she's like that with most people."

"Really? I didn't notice. That's at least settled."

"Jake, you're so sensitive." She laughs.

"Shh, don't let anyone find out."

She laughs again and wraps herself around his free arm.

"Where was the rest of her family?" Jake asks naively.

"Uh oh. I hope you didn't ask her about that?"

"No, I saw from that one picture."

"Yeah, don't mention it to her," she shakes her head.

"Oh, did they die?" he feigns seriousness.

"No, her mother walked out on them about ten years back."

"Walked out? Where'd she go?"

"Nobody knows. She just left this bummer note saying it was over. That's okay. Mr. Tanner is too nice for her. She was a bitch."

"Sophie!" he laughs.

"What? She was."

"And her brother?"

"Oh, he was a piece of work. I never liked him."

"Did he walk out too?"

"Not by choice. My dad and a few others got tired of dealing with him, so he got the boot."

"What from the town?"

"Oh yeah!"

Jake does not like misleading Sophie but he would try what he could to get information. "Huh, that must have been what Junior was talking about."

"What do you mean?"

"Junior said something like, Evelyn was acting strange, like she did when her brother was around."

"I noticed that."

"Really, did you ask her about it?"

"Nah, she's a big girl. She knows she's got me to talk to."

"If he's in town, do you have any idea where he could be?"

"If he is in town, my dad or the Sheriff would have kicked him back out by now."

"Camping maybe, in the outskirts?"

"Hey, that's a good idea! I'll tell my dad about that!"

Jake starts to feel better. At least the people here would be on a better look out for Kenneth.

"So, where does this party start? Is it like a parade?"

"Yeah, we walk around the town and stop at all six totems. I'll show you."

"And after that, is there a feast or something?"

"Is all you think about food related?" she smiles, "Didn't you just have a bunch of cake?"

Jake shrugs.

She pulls him close, "After that, is your surprise."

Jake smiles again.

The two head off to the center of town laughing and talking all the way. Jake is having such a great time with her he does not care about his surroundings until they are at the forks again.

"Hey, there's my dad!"

"What?" he jumps. He sees Sophie's dad coming across the street and staring right at him, not angrily, but not happy either.

"Hey Dad! Do you remember Jake?"

"Deputy Harris." Jake says as formally as he can.

"Where'd you come from?"

"Just uh, passing back through, heading home."

"And you just happened to run into my daughter?"

"Dad! Evelyn invited him to Sam's birthday party."

"Oh, that's where you've been," He says sternly. "You're supposed to let me know where you are at all times after curfew."

"But Daddy, the birthday party has been the same day for the last three years," she pleads.

"Don't Daddy me tonight!"

"I'm sorry Mr. Harris, it's my fault. She was with Evelyn and the others. She wanted to show me the totems before I leave town tomorrow."

Sophie cast Jake a hurt look but does not disagree.

"That's alright I guess. You couldn't know. We've had some

missing persons and we're not a damned step closer to finding what happened to any of 'em."

"The missing persons from before? That's still going on?"

"Yeah," the deputy says as he tiredly removes his hat and rubs his neck. "Forgot we talked about that."

Jake starts thinking about the ledger.

A squad car pulls up next to them with the Sheriff leaning back behind the wheel, eyeing Jake.

"Any problems, Deputy?"

"No, Sheriff."

"Who is this? Oh, I remember. What brings you back to Prudence son?"

"Just stopping in on my way home sir."

"Hmm?" the Sheriff watches Jake with narrowed eyes from the car.

"Well," Sophie cuts in, "we were just—"

"Hold your horses, girl. Deputy Harris why don't you bring Jake to the station."

"Why?" Jake and the Deputy ask in unison.

The sheriff waves a calming hand at the group, "Just want to get his opinion on things, get that fresh pair of eyes we were talkin' about."

"Hear you loud and clear Sheriff."

"What's going on?" Sophie asks in confusion.

"We're just gonna have Jake take a look at something. Don't worry," he stops her before she can protest. "It won't take more than a minute."

Sophie leans against a wall outside the office waiting impatiently while the two officers lay out papers and notes in front of Jake. He was worried at first that he was going to be locked up as a suspect again. Their worried expressions tell him how desperate they are.

For the next fifteen minutes, Jake goes over all of the paperwork looking for any information that could lead him or them to Kenneth in anyway. Again, he finds nothing helpful.

"And this was taken a few days ago?" Jake holds out a police report detailing a vehicle theft.

The officers nod.

"Something this big and no tracks?"

"It was taken hours before a downpour. Any tracks were washed away."

"So, they know the area and at least the area's weather." Jake adds trying to nudge them towards Kenneth as a suspect.

"Possibly. Could have been a coincidence that it rained," Harris adds.

"Do you think it's related to our missing persons?"

"Could be. I mean if bodies are missing, it would make sense to me that an excavator goes missing as well."

"You think they could be dead?" Sophie shouts from the hallway.

"Has anyone been buying more food than usual?" he asks them.

The sheriff removes his big white hat and shakes his head.

"And there's nothing that connects these people?" Jake leans his mouth against his steepled hands.

"We've been over it," the deputy explains, "all five of them are different ages, professions and only two of them really knew each other."

"And there's no person they all knew other than the abductor who was no stranger to them?"

"That sums it up," the Sheriff sighs, disappointed.

"There's got to be something," Jake says as he gets ready to give them their break.

"That's why we wanted a fresh pair of eyes."

"Any religious affiliations, clubs or ethnicities?" he pauses but the officers continue drawing a blank.

"I noticed there's an exotic Indian nature, if you don't mind me saying, to some of your people here in town, like Sophia," he gestures to the blushing girl. "Could they all have had that in common?"

The two officers look at each other and pause. They shove Jake out of his seat to look over the papers. One by one, they put a 'G' by each of the names of the five missing people.

"Damn boy!" the Sheriff rubs his balding sweaty head.

"Am I right?" he asks, knowing he is.

"That's it, that's the connection!" Harris slams his fist down excitedly.

"So, would the person who knew the victims also be part Indian?" he pushes.

"We can't know that. We haven't had any crimes here like that in a long time," Harris explains.

"Besides it was never really a cultural thing here," the sheriff says and Jake worries his plan is loosing steam.

"I can't think of anyone local who would even care about something like that. Let alone take people from their homes," the Deputy adds.

"What about that one guy?" Jake gets ready to play his last card.

"Who?" the men perk up.

"I just heard about the guy at Evelyn's party that's supposed to be living in the woods around here. Would he have a beef with the town or people he could be related to?" He knows it would normally be a ridiculous conclusion, but if the two cops are Lamplighters they should not think twice about a connection.

Jake's eyes shift over to see Sophie's beautiful hazel eyes wide open.

"What guy?" the Sheriff barks.

"Someone said that guy is actually Evelyn's brother, right Sophie?"

The sheriff reddens in anger. Jake worries he's gone too far but he wants Kenneth badly. The officers stare at each other nervous and angered, but in silence.

Deputy Harris turns to him, "Jake, you helped us out a whole lot tonight. Could you do me one more favor?"

"Anything sir."

"Get my daughter home safe, right now."

"But Dad!"

"No, Sophie! This guys snatching people like you and your mom up! I want you home safe!"

"Could he take me home after the festival?" she pleads. "There's people out everywhere, it'll be the safest place to be tonight!"

"She's right," the sheriff calms Harris down. "Tonight on the long walk is the safest place to be. That's where we'll be until the morning when we head out into the woods with Jimmy's dogs!"

Dogs? Jake thinks. Good! He also discovers what the 'LW' annotation in the logs was for. The 'Long Walk' must also be the Lamplighter's perimeter check. Things are finally looking up.

"I don't know. Is your Mother at the festival now?"

"Her and my wife are already there Deputy. Said hello to them right before I came across you three." The sheriff calms Harris further.

"Alright, you find your Mom and stay with her."

"What are you gonna do, Dad?"

"Special police business."

Special indeed, Jake thinks.

"You two better get going," the sheriff gestures them to the door. "Thank you again for your help, son."

"No need to thank me, sir."

"Yeah thanks, Jake. Get her home safe."

Jake nods and leaves with Sophie. He looks back to see if either of them are going for the secret floor safe in the vacant cell, but they just watch him leave and lock the door behind him.

"Sorry to pull you into that," He turns as he apologizes and catches a warm wet kiss from her. He wraps his arms around her tightly and everything else ceases to exist. Eventually she breaks away and stares into his eyes with her perfect smile. Neither of them say anything, but they head to the Forks to join the others in the festival.

* * *

Almost the whole town is parading around the outermost street. More people are dressed up in the festive costumes, carrying ornate lanterns and flashlights. Not that they need them, the entire road is lined with yard torches, illuminating the circular path. A horse drawn carriage makes its rounds giving treats to the kids, selling handcrafted holiday paraphernalia and shots of the brew naturally derived from the red death flower. Jake nervously looks around either for Kenneth, the deputy or even a younger version of the old witch. Sophie continues leaning on his arm as they make their way south to their first totem, the first one he originally came across.

"So, how many times do we walk in this circle?" he jokes.

"Just once," she smiles, "we stop when we come back to the first one we visit, to close the circle."

"Ahh, does it matter which one we start at?"

"No, I usually start at a different one every year."

"See your dad anywhere?"

"No, why? Are you gonna kiss me again?" she bends down to pick some more of the special flowers that are growing in abundance on the sides of the road.

His smile wavers, "Aren't you worried about the kidnapper targeting the descendants of the grays? No one is even sure Kenneth is working alone."

"I'm not scared of that punk," she assures him. "Besides, I've got my Dad and my neighbor's family who loves guns. And . . . I have you."

"Sophie."

"I know, you don't know if you can stay," She looks around disappointed.

He tries to explain, "It's a complicated, messed up situation."

"I used to think getting older meant I would know more, so things would be less complicated," she pouts.

Jake is pleasantly surprised by her words. This was not the first time she has said something that he thought himself at one time.

"But then again, what's so important where you have to get back to?"

Jake thinks about her words for a few moments, "Right now, it is important for me to be here. I want to be with you. But as far as me leaving, I wish I could stay but I don't really have a choice."

"Well, how about I come and visit you?" Sophie tries to act like she is joking but Jake can see a seriousness in her eyes.

She has also given him an idea that he will try out as soon as they reach the first totem. Her eyes are asking him for an answer, that he cannot give. "Visit me?"

"Yeah, I'm done with high school. I'll be twenty in a few months."

He stops walking and puts his arms around her again, "Sophie, I would like nothing more than to take you away. If I had one wish, it would be that I could, but I can't."

"Jake, I'm just messing with you. I can't runaway anywhere, I start college this fall."

The hurt in her eyes is unmistakable. She ruffles his hair and turns away from him, hiding her grief and they quietly walk along the path until they come to the totem. When they arrive, the crowd that was there begins to break up and move onto the next, allowing them to get a better look at it.

"Okay, get down here." Sophie kneels at the base of the towering wood pillar, shamelessly as her short denim skirt hikes further up her smooth thighs.

As before, Jake finds it hard to look away from the thing. Candles and lanterns are placed around its piled rock base. Highlights from them flicker off the wet red lacquer, giving the impression that the eyes of the crudely carved animals are glowing.

Jake kneels down next to her and feels a vibration as well as heat coming from the totem. "What's causing those vibrations?"

"What vibrations?" she looks at him confused.

He touches the ground around the totem, then the stone base. He recognizes the vibrations are definitely coming from the pillar, though only he is aware of it either because of his condition or his displacement in time.

"You can be so weird!" she giggles. "Maybe the vibrations are just after shocks from my kiss."

He smiles, "I'll show you some aftershocks."

Sophie bashfully shakes her head, "This is all you do." She pulls some of the flower's petals off and rolls them in her fingers crushing them. A large amount of fluid bleeds out of the pedals. She closes her eyes and rubs it against the totem.

"Is that it?"

"Yup. Oh, you're supposed to wish for good luck onto the people you care about when you do it."

She hands him some petals, "Your turn."

Jake stares at the petals in his hand. Before arriving in Prudence he was never much of a person for faith. He figures if there is some consciousness working behind the scenes in this town it would already know what he would wish for. He crushes them and presses his hand against the totem.

A painful shock shoots through his arm.

"Argh!" he shouts and falls back.

"What's the matter?" she cries and leans over him.

"Nothing," he strains and sits up nursing his arm. "Arm's still healing."

"Oh, I'm sorry!"

"Why are you apologizing?" he forces a smile.

"Need me to get you some water or something?"

"No, I got something on me," he pulls the flask from his jacket and takes a swig.

"You brought booze? Gimmie some!" she playfully grabs at his flask.

"Its not booze, besides, you're not old enough to—"

She snatches it from his hand and takes a swig, only to spit it out.

"Yuk! this is—" she coughs.

"I told you!" he laughs.

"But it's pure! How can you drink it like this?"

"I like it like that," he makes a reference that is lost on her.

"Gross, now I need water. And I thought your booze was raunchy."

"My booze? From my bag?"

"Sorry, I didn't know if you were coming back."

Jake shakes his head, "Finders keepers I guess. You drank it all?"

"No, me and Evie couldn't finish it. We think it was spoiled."

"Oh well, at least you found my bag. I won't have to carry things around in this anymore." He taps his paper bag with his knee.

"What's in that grocery bag anyway?"

"Groceries, candy, baseball cards and some band aids and stuff."

"What?"

"Long story. What do these faces mean?" he distracts her back to the totem.

"Oh, um. Well, there's the bear, the bird on top, the snake the cougar, um . . ."

"You don't know do you?"

"No," she says relieved and laughs. "I think they're just standard animals."

"This still doesn't look like some of the totems poles I've seen before."

"Other totems? How many have you seen?" she leans close to him with an inquisitive stare. "Do you have a thing for Indian girls?"

"Not really, just for one," he smiles.

"Interesting," she raises her eyebrow. "What's so different about this one?"

Jake stands up and looks closely at the carvings. "This one is, well, it's very shiny but the carvings seem kind of crude and I've never seen symbols like the ones carved in it before."

"Oh?" Sophie stands next to him and leans forward.

Jake watches her intently to see if she even can walk around it. Even though he brought Sophie's number with him to the present, a small part of him still wonders if the people and this version of the town here in the past are real or ghost doubles as Scott refers to them. If they are ghosts, and he really hopes that Sophie is not, then she shouldn't be able to pass through the barrier. If she can, then she is alive right now and there is still a chance that he can save her.

She passes behind and around the barrier to Jake's deep relief, while exploring the statue and returns to his side.

"Weird, I've always liked the symbols but I never wondered if they stood for anything before." She looks at him with her eyes wide, "Hey!"

"What? Do you remember something?"

"No, but these would make great tattoos!"

He shakes his head and laughs again, "Anything else?"

"Yeah, I think I see what you're saying about the carvings being crude. And you should know the answer to this Mr. Walker." She mock places her fists on her hips.

He shrugs.

Sophie rolls her eyes, "You were busy stuffing those burgers when I was telling you, but anyways. The gray tribe didn't have any men or elders left after their war, the settlers made these."

"That's right! They wouldn't have been experts at carving tribal stuff like this."

"That's the reason," she looks at him seductively and reties her head scarf. She allows more of her silky brown hair to spill out from around it than before. "Are you ready to go to the next one?"

Jake stares away from the totem wondering what would happen if he would step through while being in the past. He wonders if he could stay here with Sophie or if he would explode. Worst of all he does not know if he would let the corruption inside of him out. He looks at his hands again, they are still not black and the taint had not slid back with him. The hunger remained though. That too could just be from loosing track of days gone by. He steps close to the invisible barrier and remembers the reaction from slapping his palm on the totem. He pokes a solitary finger out slowly to where it should be.

The closer his finger gets, the stronger the vibrations become, until—

A soundless tap.

His finger presses against the air but does not pass through. He chances using his hand and like a mime, he stands there with his hand pressed flat against the air, pushing with no results. He thinks of the witch's words telling him he would have better chances forcing a Devourer through a mountain than the barrier.

He knows now, this is what she meant and he debates if this means he has become more like one of them or if the time difference the issue. Maybe allowing him to get out while in the past would cause too many ripples in time. He decides to test this and picks up a small rock then tosses it at the barrier. It collides with nothing and passes through the barrier, bouncing across into the forest.

"Interesting."

"What is it? Do you see someone in the woods?"

"Huh? No." I was just thinking about this town's history."

"C'mon lets get going, Evie should be out here somewhere by now."

Jake backs away from the ominous monolith and heads off to the east with Sophie to the next one.

As they approach their fourth totem, the north most one, Jake finds himself in a part of town he never explored. Sounds of the wind and the crickets are the loudest in this area furthest from civilization. The forest outside of the barrier is the thicker than anywhere else, but what interests him the most is seeing the mini mountain that occupies the north side of town from a new angle. Its thick trees sprout defiantly from the exposed rocky faces. No lights from cabins or homes glow in the night, no campfires.

"Anyone live up there?" he points it out to Sophie."

"There? Not really. I don't think there's even a way up there. Its just rocks and tress."

"How do you know if you've never been there?"

"Look at it during the day, you can tell it's not that big."

"I bet someone would have a great view from up there though," he notes.

"Oh, you want to sneak away up there with me?"

"I was wondering if Kenneth could be hiding up there."

"Ew, creepy. You think Crazy Kenny's watching us?" she rubs her upper arms and shivers.

"From that far at night? I doubt it. But he could be watching people living closer to it. Singling them out when they're alone."

"Jake!"

"What?"

"Your mind goes to dark places sometimes."

"I don't want anything to happen to you, Sophie."

She leans in and he kisses her again, more passionately than before.

"Come with me," she backs away and pulls him along.

"What about the next totem?"

"It's not going anywhere, but you are. I want to show you something really far out."

As she leads him west, he sees the self-lit water tower growing larger. He keeps his eyes open as they pass in and out of the crowds of festival goers. He takes a precautionary swig from his flask, which he jokingly offers to his companion. A section of the oil field opens up to their right. The derricks stand vigilant over the hammer-like pumps moving up and down, all bathed in the orange glow of the hundreds of sodium vapor lights.

He can see the roadhouse less than a mile away. It looks good, but not at all as lively as he assumed it would be right now.

"Are we going to the roadhouse?"

"No, somewhere special I like to go. Are those people still behind us?"

Jake looks back, "Not really, they headed off the road to the totem."

"Great! Keep up with me!" she dashes off into the oil fields.

Confused, Jake takes off after her. She is fast. Her delicate body nimbly makes its way over stray barrels, around and through the derricks. She even dangerously speeds underneath the moving pumps. Jake tries to catch up but clumsily collides and stumbles while watching her in awe of Sophie's speed and agility. She laughs and teases as she widens the gap between them. He sees a clear opening and a chance to cut her off so he rushes towards it.

Bam!

Stunned for a split, second he slams into nothingness only to bounce and fly backwards through the air. He ran too far and hit the barrier. He crashes into the dirt with a grunt and continues tumbling half a dozen feet away. More worried that Sophie has seen his stiff impact with nothingness than being hurt, he sits up and looks for her. What he sees instead are glowing red rings in the air. They are expanding across the invisible barrier from where he hit it. Like a stone dropped in water, they ripple away becoming invisible again as they weaken. He stands dusting himself off as the last rings disappear.

"What happened?" Sophie rushes to his side.

"Just fell, I'm not as nimble as you," he gasps in the thick hot air as he dusts himself off.

"I'm sorry, that was a stupid thing to do. How is your shoulder?"

"I'm fine Sophie, just landed on my butt," he sees that she

didn't see the lightshow or hear the loud sound. "I've gotta admit," still breathing hard he leans against a derrick and smiles. "I've never seen anyone run that fast in flip flops before."

"Flip flops! Oh these?" she laughs hard and kicks the dirt from her sandals.

"Well, this is it!" she opens her arms presenting the fields.

"The fields? Isn't this a dirty place for a little thing like you to hang out in?"

She closes her eyes and breathes deep through her nose, "I love coming here when no one else is around. There are no people or cars, just these machines slowly beating like giant hearts. I feel like I'm really part of the earth when I come here."

Jake's heart beats louder while he watches her. She really is different than any of the girls he has known before. So full of life and surprises, playful and relaxed but deep. He thought he was immune to what he is feeling. He had been through a few bad apples, good ones too. But so many women altogether that had amounted to nothing. He knows that what he is feeling can only be love. He feels stronger inside, but worried that he could vanish any second and leave her out here all alone with a monster like Kenneth on the prowl.

Sophie opens her eyes and stares into his. She does not blink or look away, but pulls her red scarf from her head and neatly wraps it around her wrist. He stands up straighter as she starts walking towards him and they lock again in an embrace. They force themselves against each other kissing like tonight is their last. She wraps her arms tightly around his neck and he slides his hands down along her curvy hips. She takes a deep nervous breath and presses her chest against him while he reaches under her skirt and tenderly squeezes her ass. She wraps her right leg around him and pushes him back with her left pinning him against the derrick. He allows them to slide down to the ground along his back. Sophie starts rhythmically pressing herself against him and he takes his right hand up through her hair and firmly grabs the back of her neck. She responds by wrapping her other leg around him tight and pushing up from him with her arms. Her eyes set on him intoxicated with lust, she is almost feral. She presses her open hands against his chest digging deep with her nails, slips his jacket off and flings it to the side. She pulls his hoodie and undershirt off at the same time. With a dirty smile, she continues stroking his bare skin with her nails and he pulls the top of her loose fitting blouse down around her waist. Goosebumps sprout all over Sophie's flawless skin. She shifts her shoulders as she pulls her arms out of her sleeves and wraps them around his head again, pushing her bare chest forward and offering her breasts to his mouth. As he kisses and teases her nipples, she moans and returns his hands to her soft perfect ass. They begin necking again voraciously. She frantically undoes his pants. He lifts her up pressing himself against her. Their breathing heavy, he gently leans her down on his jacket. She gasps in pleasured surprise as he pushes his way inside her. She moans loudly and he kisses her up and down her neck. She digs her nails into his back and he rubs her smooth thighs firmly as he rhythmically makes long grinding thrusts into her. Her moans become louder as the circular thrusts intensify. They passionately stare into each other's eyes and begin kissing again. He reaches behind her back, lifts her up, and presses her back against the angled base of the derrick. They grind harder against each other. In the soft glow of the pulsating oil field, they become one.

* * *

Jake opens his eyes to see the tall wood structure standing over him. His heart skips, then he relaxes and smiles. It is still night. He looks down and sees Sophie passed out with her head and right hand on his chest, her beautiful hair wildly strewn over him. His right arm protectively around her, he places his left hand on hers and looks back up to the stars. He tries to think of nothing else but her and he knows he would be an idiot for doing that.

Despite all this crazy shit, even if I win, can I keep her with me? I still don't know how or why I've been sliding through time. I wound up running into Sophie and Evelyn twice! Could one of them be pulling me back here to stop this? Or is it the fucking evil inside giving me the power to slide back for what I want? The witch mentioned the Devourers might project their own realties or some shit like that. No. Something's been pulling me back here for a specific reason.

He gently squeezes Sophie's hand, then remembers Evelyn. When he touched her hand in the diner, he felt like he was sliding. That did not happen when he touched anyone else. Maybe she did something to pull him back, to try and stop her crazy brother. She might have abilities similar to Kenneth.

He looks at Sophie again and sees she is awake, smiling up at him.

"We passed out?" she whispers.

He moves a lock of hair from her face, "I don't want to move."

"Me either," she kisses him.

She sits up, looks around and shyly covers her chest with her arms.

"I've never done this before," a vulnerable look comes over her as she waits for his response.

"I've never fallen in love like this before, Sophie."

She grabs him and plants a deep kiss on him and they stay that way for a few minutes more.

CHAPTER 10

"Do you see any dirt anywhere?" Sophie twirls around as they cross another intersection.

"I see nothing but beauty," Jake winks and she hops back into his arms for another kiss. "Think your friends will be mad we ditched them?"

Sophie shrugs and twirls around again, "Aren't you glad we did?"

"Of course."

"How's your brother doing?"

"What? Oh yeah, he's fine."

"What does he do anyways?"

"He's a detective."

"Wow, that's pretty cool, so you guys almost do the same thing?"

"I guess."

"I bet you're the sexy one though," she pecks him on the cheek.

"Funny you should say that."

"What do you mean?"

"We're twins. Identical twins."

"Whoa, that's so cool! I've always wanted a twin."

"We had fun with it as kids."

"What's his name?"

"James."

"Oh no!" she laughs. "Did they call you guys Jay Jay?"

Jake chuckles, "No, that might have been better. They called us, 'Slowly but Surely'."

"I don't get it."

"Most people expected us to be the same person because we looked the same, but we weren't. So they would tease us about our differences."

"That's a bummer, but you weren't 'Slowly' were you?"

"Yep."

"No way, you are one of the smartest people I know."

"Why, thank you my dear."

"Did your brother say you were slow?"

"James? No way. That was mostly trash talk from the adults. James was the only one who understood the truth about us."

"So is he just a super nerd?"

"Hmm," Jake pauses for a moment, "It's like this. My brother taught me how to play chess. It took me forever to learn, but once I did he couldn't beat me at it anymore."

Sophie looks at him confused, "I never played chess."

Jake's head slightly bobs as he carefully builds his thoughts in his head. "My brother has like a photographic memory, he soaks stuff up fast. It takes me a while to learn things, but once I do, I can kinda mix and match them, get really creative with what I learned. But my brother isn't really good at improvising or coming up with new ways to do things. But then again, he does not make mistakes. Does that make sense?"

"So 'Slowly' meant, you were slow on the uptake?"

"I guess, but yeah."

"I still think its mean."

"We were cool with it. I like being how I am and so does he."

"Well, you should. My mother always says, twins have a link between them, like they share a soul. That's what makes them special."

The blood drains from his face as Sophie's last words echo in his mind.

That's it! That's what makes me special! When Kenneth went

crazy and marked me I was telling Scott about my twin brother. That fucker's plan can only be to make me one of them, then ride some link between me and James out of here like a backdoor! Piece of shit. Not only does he kill everyone in town, Sophie and everybody else. He is trying to use me and my brother to let those fucking monsters loose!

He drops his bag onto the street and stares down at his open trembling hands. His teeth clench and he holds back an enraged scream. He worries that James could be just as sick and messed up as him on the outside right now and have no idea what is happening to him. Jake swears to himself that somehow in the past or the present, he will kill Kenneth Tanner.

"Jake?"

Sophie's sweet voice brings him back from his hatred. The fear in her voice fills him with shame.

He looks up to her, his eyes on the verge of tears, "Sophie, I'm so sorry."

"Sorry for what?" her worried stare is painful to him.

"I'm all messed up. I never want anything bad to happen to you."

"What's going to happen to me?"

Jake pulls himself together, for her, "This whole thing with people here disappearing. I feel so bad that I have to leave."

"Then don't."

"Ain't got no choice. That's what's killing me."

"Jake, I like that you're worried about me, but I can handle myself."

"I have no doubts about that, but there are some bad things in this world." He takes a deep breath and looks around seeing that the streets are almost cleared out. "Come over here." He picks up his bag and guides her underneath a streetlight, where he huddles close to her.

He reaches inside his jacket and pulls out his revolver. "Do you know how to shoot?"

Sophie gasps, "You had that the whole time?"

"Do you know how?" he looks at her in a kind but serious way. Sophie, more excited than shocked takes the gun from his hand, and in a few quick motions snaps open the cylinder checks the bullets then snaps it back.

Jake's eyebrows rise and she continues examining the quality of his piece.

She looks back to him with a smirk and raised brow, "Daddy's a cop."

Despite everything, Jake smiles again.

"What are these?

Still dumbstruck he shrugs.

Sophie points out the glowing orange paint on the gun's sites and other small details, "I've never seen these on a revolver before."

"Ugh, it's a special issue."

"Far out," her delicate hands keep smoothing over the gun.

"Don't let anybody see you with it, okay?"

"Jake I can't take this," she pushes it towards him.

"Please, just hold onto it until this guy gets caught."

"Well, I have a .22 of my own, but Dad keeps it locked up. But this baby looks like it packs a punch." She admiringly hefts it a few more times.

"So you'll keep it on you?"

"I will."

"Thank you Sophie. Take these," he hands her his loose bullets.

"What the heck are these?"

Jake looks in her hand. He never cared before that they are hollow point bullets.

"Special issue too. The bullets expand instead of passing though."

"Groovy. Do you have any other space stuff on you?"

"My jacket's bullet proof."

"Really?"

"No," he chuckles.

"Aw." She puts the gun and bullets in her purse and wraps her arms around him again, where they kiss for a while under a street lamp.

"Let's keep walking. We're almost at my house. My neighbor's might be watching the house, so it would be better if you stayed outside or my Dad will flip."

"That's fine."

She throws him a worried look, "Where will you stay tonight?"

"Uh, was thinking the hotel by the forks."

"Hmm, that's not far from my place."

On the east side of town again, she leads him to a house that is barely a ten minute walk away from the forks. It is a nice place similar to the Dixon house.

"This is me."

"Nice! Just you and your folks live here?"

"Yeah, we do have a spare room, but my dad would never have it."

"Neither would I," he adjusts his mock tie.

She laughs, "I'll be right out. Want anything to drink?"

"Waters fine,"

"Sophie? Where's your friends?"

She jumps at the sound of the voice. They see a match light, revealing an older man sitting in the dark of the house next door.

"Mister Warren! You scared me!" She cries out.

"Your dad asked me to keep a lookout, so I am," he sternly says from the dark.

She leads Jake to the porch stairs, "Sit here, I'll be right back," then enters the house.

"Aren't you a little old to be dating a girl Sophie's age?" the man on the porch prods Jake.

"We're not dating, just getting her home safe."

"Yeah, I'll bet," the old man growls and stands up revealing a rifle in his hands. "At least now I can go relive myself." He rattles open his screen door and disappears into his house.

Sophie returns to the porch with a cup of water and Jake's bag. "Here," she drops his backpack into his lap. He sees that she patched up the few holes in it.

"It's a pretty cool bag, I've never seen one like it. I washed your funky shirt too."

"Thanks, but you didn't have to," he smiles. "Your parents home?"

"Nah, they're still out." She looks over the porch as she hands him the drink then snuggles up next to him with a kiss when she sees they are alone.

He puts his arm around her and she lays her head on his shoulder. Jake stares into space, his mind trying to formulate ways to prevent the fall of this town and the eminent death of Sophie. With all of the crazy rules and possibilities, nothing concrete comes to mind.

"Leaving already?" she asks in the softest of voices.

"No. But soon, though."

"You're not curious about my surprise?"

"Surprise? I thought—"

"You thought that was my surprise?" she smiles.

"Well, yeah."

"Check in your bag."

Jake opens his newly returned bag. His shirt is cleaned and neatly folded. His toothbrush and other loose toiletries are in a small plastic bag. What stands apart is the new item. He pulls it out admiring it as he does. Neatly folded into small squares is a thick, tough feeling black cloth. It is embroidered with white threading, so neat and shiny it appears silver. Taking it in both hands, he shakes it a few times and watches it unfold to its two by two foot size. The center design looks like the cross between an open winged death's head moth and an inkblot test. The details of the silver embroidery range from thick to delicate, straight to curvy. It reminds him heavily of the patterns he saw woven into the townspeople's festival garb. He is amazed at how thick yet malleable the cloth is and he continues folding it over in his hands.

Amazed, he turns to Sophie, "This is, awesome!"

"You really like it?"

"Yeah! This is really damned cool! Did you make this?"

"Yes," she blushes.

"Wow Sophie. This is the coolest thing I've ever seen!" He pulls the fabric between his fingers. "What is it made out of?"

"Same as mine, made from our town flower."

He wraps both arms around her and squeezes her tight, "I wish I could take you with me."

"Here." She takes the bandana and folds it once from corner to corner, then ties it behind his neck, letting it hang like an old cowboy scarf. Not how he was thinking of wearing it, but he remembers that he may bleed to death from the wound on his throat as soon as he returns to the present.

"There you go my rugged man," she smiles. "How does it feel?"

"Comfy," He reaches up to probe around his neck. "It smells good too."

"I soaked it in my perfume, that way you'll keep thinking about me."

"I don't think I could ever stop thinking about you."

Sophie's eyes open wide as a car rolls its headlights over them.

"Uh oh, my mom's pulling in around back," she rises as she watches the car pull into the alley.

"Should I stay?"

"I really want you to Jake, but this might cause problems for us later. You know, because you're leaving."

"That's cool," he slowly stands up next to her.

"Sophie, please take care until I come back and please, keep the gun on you."

"I'll try. This girl's already got a ton of stuff to carry around with her."

He stares at her with a sad look, saying nothing.

"Jake, you should go," she leans in and kisses him one last time.

Jake wraps his arms around her and up to touch her soft hair. Her mother begins calling out to her from inside the house.

"Good bye, Jake Walker."

"I'll see you again, Sophie Harris." He backs down the stairs still holding her hand.

She turns away but he calls to her, "Sophie, if you do not hear from me it's not because I'm spacing out or being a douche. It'll be because I really can't call you, but I'll be thinking about getting back to you every minute of every day."

Sophie turns back to look at him as the hurt melts away. "I'll be waiting," she steps into her house and waves good-bye as he backs away from the soft light of her porch. Back into the darkness.

* * *

With the festival long over, the streets are empty again. Few lights remain on inside the quiet homes as the town returns to its slumber. He feels more alone now than when he walked through the future ghost town of Prudence, because of the absence of her. A weakness comes over him and his hands begin to shake. He is starving. A few swigs from his flask helps, but he senses it is losing its effect on him. Close to midnight, he wanders down the side streets wanting to only think of Sophie and recount the night he just experienced with her. His mind keeps searching for where Kenneth could be hiding and if there is a way for him not to return to the painfully cold gloom of the town's future.

The festival aftermath at the town's center looks remarkably clean. The decorations remain as they dangle and bounce in the warm gusts of wind. Even though they are all closed, most of the stores' lights remain on.

Probably to help the police enforce their curfew and help with their hunt.

He slouches down on a bench and looks down the three roads. Nothing, as before. He shudders when he sees the spot where the arrow caught his neck. He reaches up to feel where it hit then looks down at his two bags and begins transferring the contents from the paper bag to his cloth sling bag. He sets the bandages and rubbing alcohol to the side and transfers the rest. He slaps his neck with a few splashes of the alcohol and wraps it with a bandage. Next, he dribbles some of the extract from his flask underneath the bandage where his wound will reappear and lets it soak the cloth. Finally, he wraps another thicker bandage around that. He pops a few painkillers, then goes over his possessions again even folding the paper bag and stuffing it inside. Something is to be missing from the bag but he cannot remember.

Maybe one of the decoy items he thinks to himself.

He sits there for a few minutes feeling defeated and useless as he waits to slide back to his time. He still has no headache. He starts jotting down everything he has learned as best as he can in his new notebook. As he fills page after page he starts to become angry again. Angry at his situation and how he should have found a way to spend this free time, with Sophie. A whiff of a burning smell pulls him from his mad scribbling and he looks around to catch a plume of smoke just sprouting from the church. He packs up and slings his bag over his shoulder.

Is this it? He wonders, is this the beginning?

He jogs down to the church and sees fires flickering far behind the stained glass, where the altar should be.

Jake tries to open the door but it is locked so he hammers on the door calling out to anyone who may be inside. Nothing but the sound of the adolescent fire growing responds.

He runs down to the police station and its adjoined fire station. No one is can be seen, nor are there any squad cars and the stations doors are locked, so he runs back. As he runs past the dark gap between the church and another building, he hears glass shatter and stops. He looks into the narrow passage and sees flames licking out from one of the church's basement windows. He looks around for help again and has to laugh when he feels Sophie's gift hanging around his neck. He pulls it over his nose and mouth and rushes into the smoke. He presses himself against the adjacent building away from the flames and intense heat to see if someone was trying to get out or if the glass blew out because of the fire. But the broken window is already consumed. He turns to leave the alley and another window shatters at his feet. He jumps, but looks through the window and sees someone covering their mouth in a panic.

"Hey!" he shouts. "Can you make it to the door? Is there a door you can make it to?"

The person falls away from the window avoiding the spreading fire. He looks at the window and sees that a child would barely fit through. He runs around to the back of the church and finds a smaller door that has been jimmied open. He looks over the street again and still sees no one. He takes a few deep breaths, tightens the bandana around his mouth and charges into the building. In a smoky hall, one path leads to a fire, and through another door two stairwells leads up and down. He rushes down hoping the person can tell him if other people are inside the church. Downstairs the roaring fire has wrapped itself around the doorframe, but he jumps through and sees the collapsed person from before lying faced down to his right.

"Hey!" he calls out.

He slaps out the small fires catching on himself and the person while turning them over.

"Evelyn!"

Once again, Jake is stunned to find her somewhere he did not expect. She is barely conscious.

"Is anyone else in here?" he tries shaking her awake. Her arms are tightly wrapped around her big knitted bag. She shakes her head no, to answer his question. He feels himself weakening now from the fumes, "Can you walk?"

Slowly, she shakes her head again.

He scoops his arms under her and heaves. Even though she is a lot taller than he is, she is still a lot heavier than he expected despite her slender body. He carries her up the stairs slowing as he goes, but makes it back out. Across the street, he lays her on the ground. She is unconscious and not responding to his calls and shakes. He tries a light slap followed by a harder one, but she does not stir. Forcing away his panic, he pries her bag out of her arms and tosses it to the side.

"Evelyn!" he shouts and looks around. "Somebody! Anybody!"

He pulls his bandana away and crouches over her sideways. He starts thinking of a first aid class he slept his way through in high school. Even a few television shows. He tips her head back, presses his lips over hers and breaths into her mouth.

As soon as their lips touch, time pauses just like before. A dizzying and foreboding feeling comes over him. He strains against the sensation. It feels like his mind has awakened while dreaming, leaving his body paralyzed as the dream becomes a night terror. Desperate, he manages to force the feeling away and time goes on.

She does not move so he tries a few more times. Nothing.

"Fuck! What were you doing in there?"

Nervously, he rubs his hands through his hair then crosses them palm down over her chest. In fast steady beats, he presses down counting to twelve. He stops and goes back to breathing into her mouth.

Evelyn jerks awake startled and stunned and slaps him away while coughing violently. It stings. He has had worse but he is happy she is alive.

"Easy, it's me!" he reaches for her upper arms to calm her but she is still panicked.

She responds by coughing more as her teary eyes dart around.

"Evelyn, its ok! It's me Jake!"

She tries sitting up as she backs away from him, snatching up her bag as soon as she sees it.

"Were you alone in there?"

She calms down enough to nod.

"What the hell were you doing in there? What's started the fire?" he tries not to yell and he looks down the streets seeing that still no one has responded yet.

"What are you doing here?" she asks in a shaken but accusatory voice.

"Huh?" he stands up confused. "Saving your ass from a fire!"

"You followed me to get it!"

"What the hell are you talking about? I was coming to get a room at the motel, and I saw the church burning."

"Bullcrap! I looked in your bag, you're with h—" Evelyn stops midsentence looking past Jake and an expression of terror contorts her face.

Jake turns to see what has upset her. Through the haze and thickening smoke, he sees a dark cutout of a large man leaning out from an alley a few buildings away, watching them.

She gasps and scrambles to her feet clutching her bag.

Jake doesn't turn away from the eerie figure," Evelyn, who is that?"

"You know who!" she begins to cry. "You're helping him!"

When he turns to look at her, pain shoots through his skull.

He is sliding again.

"No!" he cries out, but frightens her even more.

She backs away shaking her head, "You can't! You can't be helping him?" she pleads.

"Evelyn, I'm not! I'm here to help!"

She takes off down the street and he reaches out for her and misses. He turns back to see the shadow has stepped from the alley and is running towards Evelyn's direction.

"Kenneth!" he shouts and the figure stops. "Come here motherfucker!" Jake shouts and speeds towards the shadow.

The figure seems confused and turns away, heading into the narrow passage by the church. He rushes in after, it straining through the smoke and fire to see the figure rapidly putting distance between them. He guesses that Kenneth is trying to cut Evelyn off and he wishes he still had his gun. Desperately, he continues his pursuit despite the hot knife in his mind, which is carving out a new depth of pain. His vision doubles then blurs.

"No!" he calls out to whatever powers may be guiding his transitions through time. "I can stop him!"

His next step does not connect with the ground. Air rushes up against his body as he falls into darkness. Then like being awakened by the flip of a switch, the lifeless white sky turns on and burns his eyes. Stunned, he is flash frozen by the bitter cold and all of his collected wounds return in unison. Wracked with pain his body tumbles out of the path and onto a sidewalk. He rolls onto his back clutching his neck with both black hands and thrashes. He tries yelling in pain and anger but instead blood just spurts through his clenched teeth.

CHAPTER 11

Jake's dry lips crack and bleed as he stretches them open. He tips his flask completely back as the last few drops fall into his hungry mouth. He had even managed to stop from bleeding to death, though Jake was worrying now that it was not because of his medical prowess but because his physiology has run off course. Looking at his hands, he sees they have become as black as ink. Both sides, even his nails which have drastically become narrower. He pulls his sleeve down and sees that the black tendrils and veins run down from his hand fading out by his elbow. Jake updates this new discovery in his notebook and returns his shivering hands to his pockets again, the treated stake swinging from his left wrist. Demoralized by his failure to stop the decimation of Prudence and the loss of Sophie, he trudges on through the dead streets.

He spends a good hour downtown looking for Scott and Mike, not really trying to hide from the creatures. The police station had collapsed in on itself, no signs of the two winning or loosing any battles and the car they set on fire just yesterday from his point of view is icy cold as well. There is no telling how many days he has been gone this time. Something had happened at the bank. It was burned completely down as were the buildings closest to it. No smoking embers or warmth came from them either. The festival decorations were gone, not blown away and rotting somewhere but taken down. He stares at the burnt husk of the church he pulled Evelyn from, wondering what she was doing inside.

Maybe Kenneth tried to kill her in there, he wonders.

Staving off his unnatural hunger again, he wants to return to the old witch for more of her extract. But figures all he could do would be to give her a pathetic update and beg for help again. Sam is the one he needs answers from, as dangerous as the confrontation might be for either of them.

Jake arrives on his street without any incident and walks fearlessly through the alley behind Sam's house. Jake wants to let Sam know he is not trying to be sneaky but he wants the garage as cover incase Sam starts shooting again. He makes it behind the garage and peeks around the corner, studying the camouflaged house for a few moments. He cannot tell if Sam is there. As he stares, he begins to pant and his eyes loose focus for a second. As he strains his eyes, his view dims except for a faint outline of man standing against the wall. The green outline glows and slowly more luminescent details begin to swirl within it. Just like before when he saw Mike in that strange way. He ducks back behind the garage and presses his hands against his head, trying to shake away the view. Jake realizes when his hunger is at its worst, his tools to find food begin to ramp up. Quickly he wolfs down two of his chocolate bars.

"Sam!" he calls out. "I can see you standing there."

Silence.

"I know why you don't wanna talk or help, but I'm on your side."

"Sam, please. I know all about the Lamplighters."

A slight ruffle of clothes can be heard.

"It doesn't matter if we talk about them anymore, they're out!"

"Shut the fuck up," Sam voices a quiet, gravelly threat.

"They're out and they are going to get past the barrier if you don't help!"

"You don't know a damned thing, boy! Shut your mouth or I'll come over there and kill you."

"Please, man. You are the only one who can tell me how to stop them."

"Well, I thought about your hands. They got to you the minute you stepped in here, boy."

"You're right. They got to me, but I am still me right now. We can stop them."

"Just poke your head around the corner so I can help you on your way," Sam says, sounding deadly serious and hurt at the same time.

"I might be able to save them, all of them."

Jake hears the gun rattle and click. He tenses up expecting bullets to fly any second.

"You want proof? I can prove it! Is me stopping them from ever getting out a chance you are willing to piss away?" Jake does not know if the rage in his voice is because of Sam's stubbornness or his own hunger.

"Step on out and give me some proof then." Sam's voice is blatantly a ruse to lure him into the open.

Jake begins to laugh, "I've been there, Sam. To Prudence, nineteen seventy three." The ludicrousness of Jake's own comment getting the best of him.

"Oh, I'm sure!" Sam is equally amused in a tragic way. "Just step on out with your proof. We'll talk."

"I don't need to," a sincere smile appears on his cracked lips. "The proof is in your house."

The absence of any threats or banter tells Jake he may have gotten Sam's serious attention. Waiting for a response, he stands up behind the garage. Small creaks in the back porch's floorboards tell him that Sam may be shifting his weight, contemplating what to do next.

"Go look at the picture Evelyn sent you from your twentieth birthday party. Look in the reflection of that antique mirror behind everyone."

Jake wishes he could see Sam's reaction to what he just told him, especially when he mentioned Evelyn from back then, whom he could never have met. He hopes this does not kick start the scenario he was trying to avoid, where Sam believes he is an agent for the creatures. He hopes that giving himself up like this will help him regain his trust. He hears Sam quietly slip through his back door.

Jake looks up and down the alley again as he waits, but thankfully sees nothing strange. His view of things was temporarily normal again. His gold watch glows in contrast to his blackening wrist and still ticks away. He has been waiting at least ten minutes now. Sighing, he chances a peek to the back of the house again.

"Don't move," Sam's voice coldly calls down from above Jake.

Eyes wide open Jake freezes.

"Hands high," he commands him.

Thinking about his radically altered hands, Jake hesitates.

"Now!"

Jake lifts his hands into the air, his stake dangling from his wrist.

"What the hell are you gonna do with that?" he taps his bayonet against it.

Jake chances to look up and sees Sam standing on top of the garage, rifle ready. Sam is looking down on Jake with a teary-eyed death stare. He is torn in a bad way.

With his arms raised Jake shrugs, "It's all I got."

"Eyes forward boy!"

He hears Sam quietly drop down behind him, amazed that the old man can still be so stealthy and agile.

"One twitch I pull the trigger, got it?"

Jake nods and feels the tip of the bayonet poke into the back of his head. Then from his left, he sees Sam's black and white painted hand holding a worn metal spike. Sam presses it against Jake's cheek and keeps it there for a few awkward minutes.

"Which of your religions is this from?" Jake asks in his smartass way.

Sam responds only by taking the spike away from Jake's face.

"Keep your hands up and turn around."

As he turns, Sam holds a photograph up. It is the picture he took.

"How did you fake this?" Sam asks in nervously angry voice.

"You know those can't be faked man, it's instant. Besides, this thing has been hanging up in your house for decades."

"Then how?" he shouts.

"I told you."

"Bullshit!"

"How'd I fake it then? You tell me!"

"They took you back then and figured to send you to trick me."

"What about my driver's license? You remember that, don't you?"

"Maybe you're just fuckin' with my head."

"If that's the case, then both of us are getting mind fucked. Here check inside this jacket pocket." Jake leans the pocket towards him.

Sam keeps his gun trained on Jake's chest and withdraws two more instant photos. He turns them over and backs away to look at them. He sees Jake and Sophie hugging in one and the picture of Jake holding Sam's twentieth birthday cake, surrounded by all of his friends, in the other. Visibly shaken, Sam lowers his gun and holds back his tears.

Jake slowly lowers his arms.

"How?" he asks in a shaken voice.

"I wish I knew," Jake shakes his head. "But, if I can go back again, I kill Kenneth before any of *this* happens," he gestures around with his head.

Sam begins to nod as massive thoughts shift behind his wide eyes. "Tell me everything."

* * *

Inside Sam's fortress of a home again, Jake thirstily gulps down some of the freshly prepared tea he brought back with him. They both sit in the large cable spool chairs and Sam leans back holding the metal spike in his hand. It has thick cordage bound tightly around its blunt end. Sam turns it over in his hands going over it with his fingers while he watches Jake down his third cup in a row. Sam dips a rag into a steamy bowl of water to his side and starts dabbing away his religious symbol camouflage paint. Jake produces his notebook, places it open for Sam and begins retelling his story once again. As the hour goes by, Sam leans excitedly forward during some parts and contemplatively back during others. His most painful expressions show when Jake describes Prudence as it is in the past and interacting with Sam's friends. Curious to Jake, are the few times where Sam held himself back from correcting something Jake said and just let him keep talking.

As his tale comes to its close, Jake sees Sam's real face for the first time. Naturally he looks older than in any of the pictures, but he looks like the kind and serious man that he is. He sits there thinking deeply and handling the black spike while he fidgets. He leans forwards a few times to thumb through Jake's notebook, then leans back again to think. Eventually Sam's changing expression settles into a sad frown and he leans down holding his head in his hands.

He takes a deep breath and sighs, "You can't save anyone from what happened."

With a hurt grimace, Jake turns his eyes to the floor.

Sam's eyes linger up to the sickly man in front of him, "Ask me what you want to know, I'll answer if I can. Then I'll tell you some things that you don't know."

"Let's start with that metal spike you put on me, something was supposed to happen right?"

"You were supposed to start screaming."

"So that's the weapon?" Jake hops in his seat.

"Hey! Don't move around like that!" he shouts and Jake sits back down, "It's all that's left of it."

"What?"

"This piece here was broken off of it," he tosses it to Jake.

Jake catches it, noticing first that it weighs at least three times more than it looks like it should, "It feels warm, heavy too."

"Feels cold to me."

"So it's like the red death flower to them? They're allergic?" he examines the spike and sees the small cuneiform pictographs scattered across it.

"That burns them like its white hot. It probably feels warm to you because of that." He stops talking and points to Jake's hands.

"But they drain away at metal, rusting it up. And why metal?"

"Metal is a conductor."

From Jake's own observations and what he knows of their

nature, this makes perfect sense to him.

"So they suck what, minerals out?"

"Something. Whatever conducts electricity. Maybe something that people don't even know is in metals yet. Something hidden deep between the atoms. But yeah, gold, copper. The more conductive something is the faster they make it waste away."

"And this?" he hands the spike back to Sam.

"This is something special. It seems like it is metal but its not, watch." Sam takes the spike, looks around the room and he sees an empty metal bucket along a wall. He tosses it across the room and it lands inside without making a sound.

Jake taps it against the bucket a few times. It still makes no sound. He holds it in his hand with a peculiar new respect.

"My father said our book referred to it as the silent stone. At around the thirty year mark, after reading through most of the interesting books, I started into what was left of the comic books. That's when I decided to name that metal Parasidium."

"Parasidium, why because it's paranormal?"

"Huh? I never thought of that. No, whatever it is, it absorbs energy. It was because not even fire or sound affects it. I even got mad and shot it a few times. The material sucks it all up, like those things. You know, like a parasite, parasitic. Anyway, I liked the sound of it." Sam raises his hands and shrugs.

"It does sound cooler. How did this piece break off though?"

Sam shrugs again. "Something happened to it. I don't know when, but my father never mentioned it as being broken. I'm guessing it happened the night they broke free, because when I came back all I found was this piece."

Jake examines it more with even more admiration.

"Of course there must have been a way to heat and hammer it. Otherwise it could never have been shaped. Whatever secret methods were used I never knew. But when you stick that thing into one of them," Sam actually smiles, "get ready for a show. They scream, burn, then scream some more."

"So it can kill them!"

"That piece alone will do some serious damage. But I believe only the whole thing can finish them off permanently." Sam stands and stretches out, "While we're sitting around running our mouths, let me take a look at your neck."

Jake takes off his jacket and fumbles around his neck for the beginning of the bandage and carefully, painfully unravels the splotchy blood crusted gauze.

Sam winces when he sees the exposed gash. "Bastard clipped you pretty good."

"Knocked me over a car. Looks that good, huh?"

"Go wash that up in the bathroom, the bandages too. I'll sterilize some things."

Jake returns from the bathroom and finds Sam with a pan of boiled water, some clean towels and other surgical tools.

"I picked these supplies up back then in town," Jake pulls the contents out of his bag.

"Good thinking, now lean over here. Try not to move around."

Jake kneels down in front of the spool table and leans over another empty pan while Sam examines the wound.

"Is it infected?"

"Can't tell. That blackness is spreading from the cut, but it also appears to be keeping the wound from bleeding."

"Burn it out."

Sam goes to work on Jake's wound, carefully removing the smaller infected and dead looking chunks from it. He presses the spike into the black gash and the moss squeals as it bubbles out and into the empty pan. Dead blood and puss oozes out behind it and Sam gags and turns his head away.

Jake's grip on the edge of the table tightens from the pain, "What are these things?"

"Mistakes, rule breakers, just more of, the things which should not be."

"That's your answer?" Jake stares up at him awkwardly.

"That's what we refer to the unnatural as, 'The things that should not be'. From what we know things like this are beyond ancient, older than the dinosaurs."

"Humans didn't exist back then, how could they have?"

"We weren't the first walking, talking killers in the world. But I'm talking about things that *cause* unnatural things to happen. Bad energy. Think of them as toxic waste, except they *mutate* the laws of reality. You and I could have a metaphysical discussion for the next few years about it, but it won't matter. Something affected reality at some point and we're dealing with the result."

"Then how did the Lamplighters know what to do?"

Sam stands upright for a moment, giddy. Like he feels liberated to be able share all of these pent up secrets with someone. "In the seventeen sixties, when all this went down and those nameless bastards attacked the town, people fought back. The grays were crazy and strong as hell but they had never dealt with guns before, so eventually they lost. But they couldn't be killed. So everyone, lead by the founder Caleb, tried for weeks to kill them."

"They weren't monsters then?"

"Just self mutilating giant gray cannibals. But no, nothing like what you've seen. They kept them roped up and even started sealing them up in a stone enclosure. Their howls and screams still messed with people's minds though."

"Fire, drowning, chopping them up didn't work?"

"Nah, they burned but they didn't burn up enough to die, if you can imagine what that would be like. And you can imagine the people's shock when hanging and drowning didn't do the trick either. Weapons sharp enough to chop their heads or limbs off would shatter when it struck their bone. They still wouldn't die and then that evil oil would grow out of their cuts and rust whatever metal was left away."

"The black moss?"

"Yeah, that stuff. So word started to spread that the gate to hell had opened in Marrow and people start leaving. The founder had no idea what to do."

Sam stops to pour himself some tea.

"Town's original name?" Jake asks.

"Yeah."

"Mean anything?"

Sam shrugs and pours the rubbing alcohol over the open and freshly red wound. Jake strains against the pain to keep from moving, almost lifting the spool table off the floor.

"When word about Marrow's problems spread far enough,

three men just showed up one day."

Sam unrolls a suture kit on the table and sterilizes it some more with the alcohol, "There was a young Indian man, regular, not like the grays. He travelled with a very old Moor and a strange European."

"What the heck is a Moor?"

"Moors came up from the African continent and used to travel around Europe spreading science, medicine and stuff. In this case, think of a black guy dressed sorta like Sinbad with a bunch of books and swords. Actually, this guy carried a spear with him. There is a sketch of the three of them in the book."

"So that explains the Babylonian and African stuff I saw in it."

"Exactly. What we learned from the knowledge they gave to the founder was that these three men always seemed to travel together, by bloodlines. By that I mean, sometimes the Moor would be young and the European would be an old man. It's like their kids would take their place. The book they transcribed for us was part manual, part journal, so it wasn't always clear. But that's what we figured out about those three."

"So they show up and put the tribe down?"

"No. Those three might as well have been aliens as far as Founder Caleb and his people were concerned. They were freaked out enough already. So only the European one was allowed into the town."

"Stupid. I'd fight weird with weird."

"I know. The three still offered to take Caleb with them and train him up on what to do. Two weeks later, he returned to the town. All that forbidden knowledge had changed his hair from black to white. But at least he had a better idea of what the hell he was doing."

"And they gave him the weapon."

"No. Just the means to make it. I never got that high up in the order to know what the weapon was or what it looked like." He strokes the spike hanging around his neck, "but this was part of it."

"Was letting the children live really what screwed everything up?"

"Yes and no. Caleb was proud and stubborn. He did things his way and ad-libbed with what he was taught. The right set up was supposed to just drop 'em out of existence. Instead it wound up acting like the barrier that it is."

"And the three? Did they just leave?"

"Yeah, they were pissed. I guess there was no way for them to undo what he did without making things worse. So it was left as it was. And Caleb chose a few of his people to train up, and they became the Lamplighters."

"I wonder why the old lady never told me any of this if it was all written in the book she had."

"There are two books. The one she has was a copy given to the founder by the three men. The details of the accounts that occurred in Marrow were written into a second book, the founder's book. And it was privy only to us Lamplighters."

"That makes sense. So where's the second book?"

"I wasn't high up in the ranks, never really believed until the day I came back."

"How do you think Kenneth knew about any of this?"

Sam shakes his head, "Maybe the secrets were just in his blood. The founder worried about something like that happening. That is why new group members were chosen from the outside, as ironic as *that* is. I don't know. I thought for the longest time that, your witch was working with Kenneth."

They stop talking while Sam begins to sew the gash on his neck up. Jake strains every time Sam pulls the long itchy strand through his flesh even though his hands are remarkably steady. Jake counts at least fourteen stitches being sewn into his neck. Sam finishes and inspects his handiwork. After a few minutes he steps back satisfied. "Let some air get to that until you leave. Bandages need to dry off anyway."

Jake gets up to inspect it in a mirror. It is nearly a perfectly straight line angling downwards from back to front. "Thanks Sam, that's a hell of a lot better than I could have done on myself."

"You're welcome, man."

"I find myself wondering, why I'm sliding back there. Most of the helpful things I've been finding out have come from you and the old woman."

"Back then the secrets where buried the deepest. Maybe it's the connections you are making, to the people, the town. Maybe that's why you're sliding back."

"I don't know."

"It helped you gain my trust, didn't it? And the old woman's too."

Jake reaches in his bag and offers Sam a bar of chocolate. Sam stares at it with a lost look but thankfully accepts it. Jake adds more to his notebook then takes a few moments to think. He flips back to his hand drawn map then looks up at Sam.

"So, where are they?"

He shakes his head, "You can't."

"Let me use that on them," he points at the spike, "I'm not afraid anymore."

Sam sadly chuckles, "I was younger than you. A trained soldier fresh from the battlefield *and* I had this." He lets the spike swing like a pendulum.

"I thought you said—"

"Oh I killed one of them with it. It was not easy. As I said before, I believe you need the whole thing to put them down for good. You have to take out their leader to do that."

"Kenneth?"

"No. The chief."

Jake's shoulders sag again and he presses around the tender stitch job on his neck.

Sam leans forward and rests his chin over his interlocked fingers. "It's not the one with the bow if that's what you're thinking. I'm sure you would have mentioned it if you'd seen him."

"Great. You fought him?"

"Never seen him. Just heard things from the people who got out."

"Shit. What does *that* one do?"

"Probably the worst one to mess with," he looks up to lock eyes with Jake's. "In the book he was referred to as Chief Blackhands."

Jake looks down at his hands, a knot in his stomach turns and he nearly vomits. His nausea is accompanied by dizziness but he holds back the bile.

"I guess it makes sense, to send their boss through first," Jake nervously mumbles.

"Anything I need to worry about?"

"I'm hungry Sam. More than physically, and constantly. And it is so cold everywhere I go."

"Are you in control?" he leans back laying his hand close to his rifle.

"Yes. But sometimes, when I've gotten really hungry or this red stuff has worn off, I see things differently."

"Different how?"

"It's hard to describe. It reminds me of images I have seen before. Have you ever see those images where they used weird equipment to take the picture of a leaf or someone's hand? The objects looked mostly black but were all glowing in different colors around the edges. Like the aura crackled its way from the object being photographed."

"Are you serious?"

"Yeah. I see outlines of I guess, the living things. It's like a million tiny colored sparks are running around them. I see stuff on the inside, real trippy. That's how I knew where you were standing there out back."

"Mothafuckers! You mean I did all that shit for nothing!"

"Your camo? Sorry, yeah."

Upset Sam stands up stomps over to look out the window, "Forty damned years!"

"But you looked cool," he tries joking.

After a few minutes he drops back into his spool chair and rests his chin on his fist, moping. "I wonder if they can see the mines."

"What? You put land mines in your yard!"

"Yeah. They're far enough from the house if they go off though," he casually adds.

Jake walks over to look out the window.

"Do you have any idea who the guy was that saved the old lady back then? The one who knew where the rest of the spike was at?"

Sam does not respond.

"Sam?"

"I heard you."

"Any idea which house he lived in?"

"Dammit Jake! You were that guy!"

"What! No, I never knew that old lady, I mean the old lady when she was less old."

Sam shakes his head and stares at Jake curiously.

"You think I meet her back then? Huh, maybe I save the old lady when I go back and then she tells me."

"She's a year younger than me, man."

"What? She looks ancient!"

"Damn Jake, how the hell did you make it this far?"

Now Jake stares back at Sam confused.

Sam sits up and sighs, but tries to be more empathetic.

"Jake, that old lady is Evelyn."

With a slack jaw, Jake stairs up at the ceiling his eyes dash around connecting the dots. His expression scrunches up and his teeth clamp together.

"I never thought she . . . but then she lied to me. She knew who I was."

Jake leans against a wall arms crossed and stares down. "Evelyn." He says her name, still in disbelief. "I just pulled her out of that fire."

Sam sits somberly allowing Jake to digest things.

"I shouldn't have left her alone in that damned bunker," he swings and knocks a pile of books from a shelf. Angrily he turns to Sam, "You shouldn't have left her all alone all those years, living like that!"

"It was our choice."

"Bullshit!"

Eyes glazing over Sam looks away, "You know who her brother is."

"Doesn't matter! She loved you and stayed here for you!"

"I stayed here for her!" Sam rises. "But I couldn't trust her! She kept that book from me for years while I went out looking for it, risking my life!"

"Can you blame her? Look how you reacted!"

"It wasn't like that, boy! Don't stand there chastising me! For all I knew, she was the one who told Kenneth how to let them out."

"She would never!"

"You don't know her! You know the child that she was, the old bitch that she became, but you do not know her. How do you think she knows what she does, she stole the Lamplighter's book!"

"What?"

"And she lit the church up to cover her tracks!"

Jake begins to calm down. He understands why Sam had blamed her for things going wrong. She had lied to him too. "Then she didn't tell me who she was, because there were things I still had to do."

"She's good at lying, her family has a knack for that. But it was probably for the best."

"And that's why you told me I can't save anyone from the past. Because everything I will do, I have already done."

"Yes." he sighs.

Jake stares hopelessly at the floor thinking mostly of Sophie.

"She never said my name?"

"She might have, it wouldn't have mattered. Jake is not a unique name. And what would I be to walk around thinking I'll meet someone who slip slides through time?"

"But I do have another chance. I will go back."

"And like you just said, nothing different will happen." Sam shakes his head. "She told me about you, the mystery man before our falling out. Hell, I helped look for you or your body. She only mentioned to me that a man showed up the night everything went to hell and then disappeared again."

"And Sophie?"

Sam shakes his head.

Jake slides down a wall onto the floor and sulks.

"You probably don't want to hear this Jake, but I found Sophie's father outside of where they come from. He gave me this spike right before he died."

"Where do they hide?" Jake asks, pain in his voice.

"You can't do it with just this," he places the spike around his neck, with the rest of his charms.

"Where!" Jake slams his fist into the floor.

"We're all damned here! It's not about them, not even about us.

It's about stopping these damned things from getting out. *That*, is not written in stone!"

After a long moment Sam takes a deep breath, stands up and slowly walks to the back of his house. He stops in the hallway and looks at the photographs. "Let's go get your friends and Evelyn."

"Do you have a plan?"

"I think so. If she sent you off after the weapon in the past and you managed to get to it in that chaos, I'm thinking you show up back here with it."

Jake raises his sunken head, a spark of hope shines in eyes again.

Sam stands tall facing Jake. "I think they've sucked enough life out of us."

* * *

As the lantern light dances, shadows shake back and forth across the damp corrugated metal walls. Plume over plume, the smoke blends into the rooms orange haze. Sitting upright on her bed, the haggard old witch stares with distant pale eyes at the dustless rectangular spot on her nightstand.

Wham!

She calmly looks up as the room shakes. The sounds above her continue as bricks crash and wood splinters above. Silently, she mouths numbers, counting steps while she pulls her long barreled shotgun onto her lap.

She cocks her head to the side expecting something and her eyebrow rises in confusion. Another clashing sound of wood and metal followed by a deep inhuman bellow brings a smile to her face as one of her traps is sprung. She sits there gleefully listening. Something in the garage above the room struggles against chains and other painful sounding contraptions. As the thing continues to struggle, a heavy gasping of breath and slight whimpers can be heard as it staggers down into the subterranean burrow. With each of its steps, a heavy slapping noise shakes every side of the room.

She looks into the blackness of a half opened door and waits. The heavy breathing from beyond slows and is drowned out by the snapping of bones and other sounds indicative of tearing skin and snapping muscles. As the sounds quiet down, the witch leans back and takes another puff from her pipe, dispersing its smoke towards the offensive smell coming from the doorway. A few cans and jars crash to the floor next, then after a brief second of silence, the door begins to creak open.

"There you are little sister," Kenneth slowly says as he leans into the room a wicked smile.

With the exception of a tablecloth wrapped around his waist he is naked and covered in slimy black filth. Large black puncture wounds from her traps have ripped open parts of his skin, revealing the rumpled dark gray hide of the devourers.

"You could have knocked," she teases him.

Still smiling, his wide predatory eyes stay locked on her but a wince betrays his thoughts.

He shrugs with his arms opened wide, the rotten punctures and the tears in his skin quickly mend themselves in front of her eyes.

"Of all the places I never thought to look for you," Kenneth walks around the room inspecting her possessions but keeping a good distance from her.

"Just you? I'm surprised you had the balls to come here without your smelly little gang?" she calmly takes a deep drag from her pipe.

"Aw, listen to you little sister. I remember when the sight of me used to make you piss your little panties." His voice continues to be a threatening hiss, "And my smelly little gang? That's family you are talking about."

"All these years and still just a bitter copy of your mommy."

"Our mother!" Kenneth growls, his calm facade already gone. He takes a breath to calm himself and notices a larger piece of the black mold sticking to his chest. Calmly he picks it off and to Evelyn's disgust, sucks it into his mouth.

"Well, I appreciate the visit but I wasn't expecting—"

"A mirror! Really?" he cuts her off and points at the dingy mirror over the sink. "Evelyn, do you have any idea of how ugly you've gotten?"

Despite her poor vision, she notices the skin of his index and pinky finger dangling limply from his hand. Evelyn remembers her brother's short temper and hatred of being mocked. Even now, he is feebly trying to lash out at her. She knows why he has been looking for her. Her deep wrinkles stretch into a smile.

"Of course I have no idea, I'm blind you idiot."

Kenneth begins trembling with anger but he forces it back and props up his false leer again.

"I guess all those years standing around in a cell never gave you that room you needed to grow into a man. I'm sure *Mother* would have wanted at least that from you."

He steps towards her and she responds by turning her gun in his direction. He stops, looking at the gun as his three fingered hands anxiously open and close. He backs away grinning again.

"Your tongue's as sharp as ever little sister. You almost made me kill you earlier than I wanted to."

She huffs a few raspy laughs, "Just kill me now. Spare me having to smell you for another second."

Kenneth drags a wooden chair close to Evelyn and places it a few feet away, between her and the door. He sits down. His eyes darting from her to her gun jokingly, just to let her know it is no threat to him. His small black pupils look into hers while he adjusts the loose skin around his face. Kenneth sucks air in across his long blackened tongue like a snake and looks around the room, pausing when he looks back to the sink and mirror. He leans an arm over the back of his chair then stares back at Evelyn. He smiles again as he uses a dirty thumbnail to pick at his jagged, rotten teeth.

"Evelyn!" he says feigning surprise. "Have you had a boy over?"

She sighs, "If you're gonna kill me, do it now or leave. This old woman needs her nap time."

"No need to lie. I know Jackie boy was here. Even over that disgusting incense I can smell him."

"Someone came by. Wanted to know how to leave town, so I told him. Haven't seen him in over a month."

"That's funny, I haven't either. I would think, for all my gifts and the gifts of my people it should have been so easy to keep track of someone so simple."

"Maybe he left."

"I would have known!" Kenneth snaps. "He's probably curled up in some other hidey-hole you told him about, wondering what's going on with his sad little life."

He watches her very closely. Evelyn fights back her urge to smile when she realizes that Kenneth has no idea that anyone has been sliding through time looking for ways to stop him.

"I shouldn't say he's simple though," Kenneth stops and reflects. "He's been pretty resourceful in postponing the ritual."

She pushes her chin forward in a confused grimace. "Ritual?"

"Please Evelyn, you were never good at playing dumb. I know you saw the mark on him. Even if your blind old eyes couldn't catch it, I can *feel* how much he's changed. I can almost feel his brother too, on the other side."

"Are you finished?"

"Evelyn. Things don't have to be this way," he says in a soft voice.

"What way would that be?"

"You don't have to be all old and blind, hiding down here from the world."

Evelyn responds with another long puff from her pipe. She blows the smoke into his face. His nose crinkles and he coughs but is otherwise unaffected.

"Why deny yourself—"

"That's your pitch? Youth at the cost of me becoming a thing like you?"

"Youth, freedom, power. You don't know what being completely like our people is like."

"An endless hunger, gnawing at me for all time? You're right, death would be a relief."

Mentioning his hunger causes him to gnash his teeth at her. "Everything has a price little sister, why deny what you are. Besides, it's not just your life I'm talking about. Don't you want your love to at least die quickly?"

Evelyn's brow furrows a bit, unsure about what exactly Kenneth knows.

"My love?"

"You didn't think Sam's holy house has been protecting him all this time? He's still moping around, sucking up air because I allowed it."

Smiling she offers him to use her pipe. He sneers and stands up from the chair.

"He and I aren't on speaking terms, haven't been for some time."

"Oh, I know. Otherwise you two would have bundled up together down here, started up a litter."

"I'm flattered that you spent all this time looking for me, just to ask if I'd join your little play group but my answer is no."

Kenneth leans over her, trying to menace her. "You stubborn bitch! You know why I came here. Tell me where it is or I will kill you! I'll kill you but first I'll make you feel so much fucking pain!" his voice is joined by another deeper one that speaks with him.

"Only an idiot like you would threaten a person who is ready to die with killing them!"

A deep gurgle sputters from Kenneth's mouth as he swings at her. She fires her shotgun. The buckshot scatters across the right of his stomach and ribcage. He flies back into a bookcase, then groans as he falls to the floor, writhing.

"You bitch! What is this?" he screams and grunts, shocked at the effect her blast had on him.

She stands over him with a wicked grin of her own, "Pain!" and fires again blasting skin and flesh from the side of his head. He begins thrashing and screaming worse than before.

"Easy now big brother," she drops the smoking empty shells to the ground and loads new ones before snapping the shotgun closed. "We're just getting started."

CHAPTER 12

The sixth block cleared and Jake is happily surprised that his slow jog has not lost any steam. His endurance has definitely increased despite his wounds and he is not lugging his bag around with him. He breathes into his gloved hands and rubs them together. Neither his breaths nor the borrowed leather gloves do anything for the biting cold, but they will help conceal his condition from he others. His hunger is still bearable. He could eat or drink something, but figures allowing his hunger to grow will cause his special vision to kick in allowing him to find Mike and Scott sooner. Finding those two is his top priority and hopefully Sam has made it to Evelyn's place by now.

Jake still cannot believe that Evelyn is actually the old witch. Looking back he sees that their mannerisms were similar, though young Evelyn was understandably not as hardened. Visually they did not even look related with exception of the traits from their shared heritage.

He checks his watch, it is barely two o'clock, giving him a good amount of time before he and Sam's plan to be put in motion. He still has a full hour before he is supposed to return to Sam's house so they can update each other or lead the creatures back there and help each other fight them. He slowly turns his head to inspect another street as he runs by. His neck feels far better now and he re-wrapped it to protect his long line of stitches. Not wanting to have a weak spot on display, he has covered the bandages with the bandana Sophie gave him and pulled his hood over his head. Thinking of her again, he stares in the direction of her house. It was no coincidence he started his search on the northeast side of town. He had glimpsed her house a few times, wanting to stop and run in every time. He is half expecting her to be hiding in the basement somewhere and half expecting to come across some ancient crime scene that would tell him how she died.

He remembers there being a school here on the east side, near the last row of homes and past some willow fields. Some useful things might have remained there enough for the two guys to hole up. It definitely would be affording them a good view around the area and it is more private than the downtown locations.

Still jogging steadily he sees the school a few minutes later. It is surrounded by the open field, which is covered in decades thick layers of dead leaves. Jake chances moving straight for it, exposing himself in the open areas to save time. It is a simple boxy two-story building, the upper floor smaller than the bottom. Just three of the sagging willows away, he runs for it. He passes the second one and hears a rattling from behind that startles him. He stops and stiffly turns his head around in time to see a few of the willow's branches bobbing and swaying. He stairs at the gnarled lazy branches looking for any other movement or whatever animal caused the noise.

As he stares, he keeps thinking of the lack of animals within the barrier. Sure enough he sees a humanoid shape clinging motionlessly to the branches. He looks to its head and sees a black gash snap open revealing sharp crooked teeth. A quick gargled bark and it vanishes deeper into the tree. Jake turns and keeps running to the school. He hears the rustling again and glances back, catching it brachiating from branch to branch. The Devourer's gangly swinging launches it into the third willow ahead of him.

He remembers how fast this one can run and gambles at trying to control where it will end up. Instead of arcing around the last tree he runs underneath. As expected, the thing drops down above him. He sidesteps and thrusts it in the side with his stake just as it hits the ground. It yelps and catches Jake with a jerking backhand that sends him flying into the rough warped tree trunk. Painfully, he bounces and flies arms first into the leaves. He scrambles to his feet but is tackled back down from behind. Quickly he turns to face the creature. His right arm pinned, he socks its crooked dangling head with his left. Its diminutive bowed legs clamp tightly around his waist like the pincers they are. He kicks frantically but in vain, as his free hand becomes pinned down as well. The grip of the thing's large overdeveloped hands cuts away at his blood circulation but he does not stop kicking. In a stalemate they struggle against each other, the creature leers down at him then lifts its crooked head back and releases a loud gritty howl. Jake struggles harder before its help arrives but he is weakening. As the Devourer dangles its head close to him and he realizes its wretched stench is not choking him. Suddenly its long blistered tongue whips out of its mouth and wraps around his neck. Painfully the tongue constricts for a second before retracting back into its drooling mouth. In pain, the one who climbs covers its face with its huge hand. Jake uses the chance to elbow it in its broken neck. It jerks and he elbows it again and follows with kicks as its legs unclamp. The creature is more concerned with its mouth and falls away, gagging. Jake rises to his knees and brings his stake down into it hard. Feebly it screams some more and starts crawling away. Jake stabs a few more times before he is batted away again. Dazed Jake shambles back to his feet.

He reaches around his neck and realizes the one who climb's tongue made contact with the bandana Sophie gave him. Her perfume must have also been protecting him from gagging from their stench.

Jake brushes the leaves and dirt from himself as he runs again towards the school. The windows are heavily boarded up and there are no doors facing him. An old school bus peeks out from around the far side of the building. It is pressed against the building. More crashed than parked, it amazingly has not yet completely rusted.

Again a noise from behind him, the rustling of leaves. He turns back bracing himself for another scuffle with the one who climbs and instead sees Kenneth slowing from his own run. Jake's heart begins pulling a double duty from the rush of fear and trying to catch his breath simultaneously. Kenneth puts on his fake smile and keeps walking towards him.

It was the same kind of walk he had seen once before, back when two men walked up to him on a subway one time just before they tried to mug him. Jake clenches down on his stake with a firm self soothing. Oblivious, Kenneth keeps walking towards him. Jake starts walking backwards away from him and Kenneth closes in. Jake turns and starts running. His eyes dart around looking for somewhere he could escape to. He would have to cross very close by Kenneth to make it back into the cover of the houses. The trees would be useless. He hears him getting closer and remembers how fast he could run from their encounter the night the church burned. He also remembers his fearlessness and rage towards Kenneth when he charged after him and he uses it.

Jake spins around and looks him in the eyes. Just a couple yards away Kenneth slows but does not stop, arms outstretched and the one who climbs limping behind him. Keeping his soulless black eyes locked on Jake, Kenneth turns his head slightly to the Devourer and babbles a few incoherent words. The creature tilts its head like a confused dog then eventually scuttles away. Jake keeps staring back with a stern and angered look. Internally, he struggles not to panic and races to come up with a viable strategy to escape his predicament.

In the distance, shots wring out and Kenneth's psychotic grin intensifies but Jake keeps his poker face as he thinks.

That could be Sam, Mike or Scott. Even old Evelyn. At least someone else is still alive but I'm too far away to help.

"Jake," Kenneth says slowly as he breaks the silence and takes a few more steps closer. "Where've you been all this time, man?"

He is still catching his breath and weakened from his hunger, which grows every time Kenneth steps closer. He knows he cannot kill him, even fight him. All he can do is hope he can get away if he runs for it. If he can gather enough strength. He lets go of the stake allowing it to dangle from his wrist and reaches his other hand into his jacket to withdraw his flask. Holding his hand as steady as he can, he takes a few big swigs. He sees Kenneth's grin briefly shift into a scowl.

Is Kenneth feeding off my fear too, he wonders.

"Drinking that crap isn't good for you."

"Makes me feel good," Jake shrugs.

"I see Evelyn went all out to make a mess of things. But I expect no less from my own flesh and blood."

Jake gambles with a stupid question, he has to know how much Kenneth knows.

"The old woman? What, is she your mom?"

Kenneth's eyes bulge then narrow. He speaks with a low and threatening tone, "Are you fucking with me, Jackie boy?"

Jake stares blankly at him.

"What did that crusty old bitch and the old soldier tell you? That I want to end the world or something?"

"Do you?"

Kenneth crosses his arms and smirks. Jake notices the peculiar limpness of the last two fingers on each of his hands and thinks back again to the emptied skin he found inside the truck.

"They're all full of shit!" he starts pacing around him like a stalking predator.

Just as subtly, Jake backs away to keep from being cut off from the refuge the school could provide him.

"They couldn't tell you about one thing without mentioning the other. I am sure they just glossed over the part where my people were tortured endlessly. Just protecting what was theirs."

His keen eyes spot Jake's reaction despite his intentions to hide it.

"Ah. I thought so."

"I heard the grays were a bunch of murdering motherfuckers."

Kenneth laughs. "C'mon Jake, you know the old story, I'm sure you've heard it hundreds of times. White man breeds into a new area. Demonizes and starts fighting with the indigenous people, steals land, rewrites history, the end."

"Your people were out of control. They wanted to kill everything."

"Oh, of course they did. Even though they had not bothered anyone for centuries. Weren't even known about until suddenly they were in the settler's way, and then they had to go."

"Humans do shitty things, everyone's suffered at some point. But you guys want to kill everything."

"Think about it man. If the Sirobamjal wanted to kill and eat everything like you've been told, what stopped them before? They had tens of thousands of years to do that unhindered. And of course they didn't. Why would they? What would any species do after they ate everything up, other than die?"

So that's what they were called, Jake thinks. The tribe's name doesn't sound nearly as forbidden or sinister as he expected. And as much as he hates to admit, Kenneth is making sense.

"And what about now?"

"What about now? Yeah, they are all screwed up, twisted and broken. But they are locked in their agony. I just want to set them free."

"Set them loose? Let them do to the world what they did to this town?"

Kenneth stops walking and drops his arms to his sides.

"My people were turned into those things, by foreigners, invaders! I'm not going to apologize for what I did to their offspring. Fuck 'em! I won't apologize for my people's anger!"

"They still seem pretty angry to me."

"Because they're still trapped," he tugs the skin under his eye subtly and part of his loose skin shifts. "If I could only set them free, they could move on."

Jake grins, "So, you set them free and they just poof into glowing smoke like the happy ending to some haunted house story?"

Another shot rings out in the far distance and Jake balls his gloved hands into fists.

Smiling Kenneth glances at his hands, "Jake, I've got you. There is nothing you can do. Never was. Just put the little stick down and come with me."

"Where would we be going?"

"Someplace you won't hurt yourself."

"Why me?"

Kenneth chuckles with a cruel delight, "Are you going to start crying? Say it ain't so."

"No, just curious," he says calmly. "I've been thinking about why I'm here, even though I have nothing to do with any of this."

"It's beyond you Jackie boy, don't worry about it anymore."

"You say you've got me, so spill it."

He keeps his predatory stare but takes his time to think. Jake sees Kenneth's smile falter for just a second before his own arrogance wins over intelligence. "When we first met, you mentioned your twin brother . . ."

That *is* the reason! The thought flashes through Jake's mind as he muffles any reaction.

Jake had been worried that somehow he was bringing the taint back to the past with him. That he was the catalyst for letting them out and that Kenneth was ultimately the one controlling his slides through time. But the twin dynamic confirms Kenneth's motives. It also may confirm that Kenneth does not know about the time sliding either. There is still a chance.

"Wait!" Jake interrupts him. "You mean the old wives tale about twins sharing a soul?"

"Old wives tale?" Kenneth's grin melts away.

"He's really isn't my twin, he's my little brother. Half brother, actually. I was just embarrassed by his accomplishments, so I was bullshitting with that cop."

"Fucking liar!" he snaps revealing a glimpse of an inhuman face as he snarls and jabs his finger repeatedly into his forehead, "I can *feel* him, right here! He is the light at the end of this long dark tunnel!"

"That pinhole of light may just be your own delusion, convict."

Kenneth's knuckles pop as he curls his hands into fists.

Jake steps towards him. "After talking to you, I think I may have learned a bit more than you about what's really going on here. How *did* you find out about the things you know anyways?"

Kenneth gnashes his rotten teeth at the air as he keeps pressing closer shaking his head. "I gotta hand it to little sis'. She spent just enough time with you, to make you as much of a pain in the ass as she was."

Jake leans his head back concerned.

"Oh that's right. Sweet Evelyn, feared her own nature, her real heritage. She got me, but good! Would you believe that bitch found a way to mix that red crap in with rock salt?"

Threateningly, he takes another step towards Kenneth.

"Oh? The avenger wants to punish me. If you really were a hero," he leans forward in anticipation of Jake's reaction, "you would have saved her when I strung her up."

Fighting to keep control, Jake tries to think. If that were true then Sam or the other guys surely would have come to her aid.

"Of course the old soldier came trotting in to her aide, but I was confused and upset. I really thought that *you* were going to come and help her. I mean, that's why I made her screams last for so long. Guess I misjudged you." Gleefully Kenneth opens his arms as if to embrace Jake. "I mean, instead of helping her out we find you all the way over here, probably looking for one of those two dead late comers."

Jake pulls his flask out again, hands trembling with anger instead of fear and pours some of its fluid over his stake.

"Come on now. What're you thinking of doing, killing me?" he glares insanely. "You can't."

"I know, but I can still make you scream."

In the blink of an eye Kenneth dashes forward snatching Jake up by his arm and throat. He winces as a few of the stitches in his neck pop.

"You! You think that you're better than me!" Kenneth roars.

Jake spits the extract he was holding in his mouth into Kenneth's eyes.

He turns away with a long angry grunt that continues into a gurgling roar. He cracks his left hand across Jake's mouth sending a long spurt of blood flying from his mouth, then slams him hard into the ground.

Groggy, Jake opens his eyes from the blackness half covered in leaves again and hears Kenneth standing over him, laughing. A heavy boot cracks into his ribs with a thud, sending him tumbling through the leaves again. He is thankful at least they are not on asphalt. The pain is deep and he kicks his feet to push himself away from the lumbering maniac. His back hits something hard and he turns his head back to see the front of the rusted school bus. He pushes himself up against it to stand. Still laughing, Kenneth stops a few feet in front of him.

"We're taking everything! Every human! Every animal and insect, even the fucking plants!"

Jake tries to move but he cannot, his grip is weak on the stake. He feebly swings it at Kenneth who laughingly bats it away.

Kenneth drunkenly steps back, his wicked grin inhumanly stretches wider. He exhales his breath until it become a wheeze and then inhales loudly. He digs his middle finger into the left side of his forehead then slowly tears a jagged line across it. He keeps wheezing loudly until the sound of his inhaling is broken with sickeningly familiar gurgles and cracks. As black filth spills from the tear, he speaks by inhaling and in an otherworldly voice shouts, "We'll devour everything!"

Kenneth slaps his hands into the sides of his head and presses in. Paralyzed, Jake sees his skull snap to the left beneath the skin that is being held in place. The skull slowly twists itself upside down, until Kenneth's shifting elongating teeth show through the tear in his forehead. His fingers lengthen and expand, bursting through the skin to reveal clawed obsidian fingers. Kenneth moves his hands away and slashes two slits into his cheeks, which immediately blink open revealing his whitening eyes. The snapping and breaking sounds of his transformation continue as his neck stretches and his body expands. The three finger claws grab bunches of his clothes and tears them violently away, revealing more of his wrinkling and pulling skin as it dulls to its rotten mottled gray color. His rib bones jaggedly grow from his chest and he throws his head back writhing in pleasure as he sheds and grows. Long sickly black feathers sprout out from the top of Kenneth's upside down head and behind his neck, creating a large wicked headdress.

Worse than the others, he has become over twelve feet tall and is still growing. Not as gangly either, he swells to at least twice Jake's width. A true giant. The powerful odor suffocates Jake, though his heart is racing to the point of giving out. Through will alone, Jake forces his body to turn while still leaning against the bus for support and moves away. Jake staggers to the end and almost falls without the bus holding him up. A deafening roar comes from behind him. It is louder and more terrifying than the other Devourers as well. The ground and bus shakes from the sounds and its remaining windows explode. Jake looks back and sees that Kenneth is no more. Roaring up at the lifeless white skies is the biggest, nastiest and clearly the most powerful of the Devourers, Chief Blackhands.

He turns around the end of the bus and sees that the school building has no doors on this side either. He notices the back door to the school bus is open. The bus will not hold for long, but he wants to make things as difficult as he can. He enters and moves a few seats away from the door, holding his stake at the ready.

The chief takes his first step and the ground shakes. Jake sees its clothes forming, mending and shaping themselves from the flapping remains of Kenneth's skin. Rows of human rib bones run down the front to become a breastplate and trinkets and sacks hang from the abundant overlapping cordage around its neck waist and wrists. It looks to be as much of a witch doctor as it is a chief. The black fluid animates itself across his sweaty hide creating tattoo like patterns and melting and shifting itself into disc shaped jewelry. Mostly dirty bones, leather and wood, the patterns on the clothes and jewelry are hard for Jake to look at, as if his eyes and mind are offended by the designs. More things beyond a human's comprehension.

It crouches down and presses its flipped face against the bus, looking with its mouth directly at Jake. With a loud sucking grunt, the chief presses its black hands back to back and pushes them into the bus. Then with a single loud shriek of metal and glass, opens the side of the bus like it is a curtain.

Jake is tossed up when the bus shakes and the chief slaps his huge hand around his waist, snatching him right out. Not even having a chance to strike, it tosses him through the air and he tumbles away through the leaves again. It catches Jake's leg and drags him underneath it. Jake tries stabbing its leg with his stake but it barely pierces the thick hide. The Devourer tears the stake away from him, almost breaking his wrist and with its one hand, snaps it in two before throwing it out of sight.

It places its large hand over Jake's head and forces it sideways exposing the right of his face. Jake grunts in anger as well as from the pain but he cannot get away. With its other hand it draws a wicked looking bone blade from behind its back and as the one who screams did, the chief runs the blade through its mouth. Its large tongue whips around it, lathering it up with the filthy black slime. From the corner of his eye, he watches it kneel down to him, the venom from the blade dripping onto his temple. The chief inhales creating popping chuckles and he can feel Kenneth's madness hiding, laughing from within it.

Jake does not know if he will become like them immediately or still have time to suffer, before his soul is completely gone. He strains to keep his eyes open to the very end.

Leave it to me to die on a fucking playground, his dying thought flashes.

And then, there is light.

A shattering of glass and a fire flares up from behind the chief. The chief flinches and turns around exposing its burning back to him, only to have another bottle shatter, igniting its front. The Devourer drops its blade and now free, Jake grabs it and scrambles away.

He sees Mike from the first story roof of the school, hurling another bottle at the creature. "Can you run?" he shouts down to him.

"I fucking better!" Jake shouts back, resurrected by the fiery explosion of hope.

"Catch!" he throws him a backpack.

Moderately heavy, he quickly slings it over his shoulders. Mike hops down from the remaining roof of the bus and tumbles onto the ground.

Jake helps him up and they start running to the houses.

"Where to?" Mike looks more terrified than Jake feels.

"A house in the southwest, can you make it?"

"Do I have a choice?"

The chief roars, even at a distance the sound hurts their ears. Jake looks back to see it inhaling all of the air around it, like it is sucking up a fiery tornado. In seconds the flames are extinguished and it thunderously starts stomping towards them.

"Fuck!" Jake calls out.

"Take this, it's the extract!" Mike presses what looks like a syringe into Jake's hand, it is filled with red.

"I'm good man! That's the last of my worries right now!"

Mike throws him a puzzled expression, "It's not for—"

A slap from behind tears Mike away into the air. A second swipe sends Jake skidding into the alley. He rolls up to his knees and throws the chief's blade back at it as hard as he can. The still smoking chief bats it out of the air but jerks as its arm gets cut.

It howls and stomps at the ground shaking every garage nearby.

Jake turns to keep running, but its black hand wraps around his head and pins him once again to the ground. He struggles to look up and winces when he sees the blade rushing down at him. But the Devourer stops itself and enraged only shakes the blade in Jake's face. The giant returns the blade to its mouth again, smacking away at the blade and readying it for the cut. Jake sees on the chief's warped forearm the slash he made with its own weapon and he laughs defiantly for the last time. The dripping blade lowers once again towards him. Jake realizes he is still holding the syringe in his free hand. He worries for a second that the needle would corrode the moment it touches the Devourer then his eyes dart back to the fresh cut on its arm.

He pops the plastic cap in his mouth and pulls it off with his teeth, then jabs it into the behemoth's open wound and pumps the extract in. As if stung by a scorpion it slaps the needle away, but it was too late. It drops its blade again and grabs at its affected arm. It shivers and screams down at Jake who is already getting back to his feet. Jake grabs the blade and takes a swipe at it but it leaps up onto a garage, crushing the top of it and roaring again. It gnaws on its affected hand and bashes it into the roof.

Battered but alive, Mike runs through the alley. Jake waits for him to get closer, then they take off running for their lives together. They are in the back alley behind the downtown stores when they decide to cut south again, trying to avoid the ground shaking footsteps of their smoking pursuer. Jake catches glimpses of the black headdress bobbing from over fences and some of the roofs of the smaller houses. The thing is unbelievably fast for its size. It leaps onto a two story home and spots them, then leaps through the air landing in the back yards.

"Here it comes again!" Jake yells and tries to catch up as Mike speeds ahead of him. Like a runaway train, the chief smashes through the corner of a garage a few feet behind, spraying them with the faster moving projectiles. Mike yells something Jake cannot make out, then cuts right in front of him and disappears. Jake almost trips but sees the narrow gap between two of the stores and ducks in. The chief's claw follows. It smashes away bricks like they are nothing and rakes the back of Jake's thigh, but it is stopped short. Jake looks back to see it bashing down the walls to get at him and he keeps running.

He exits the passage into an open street south of the Forks and sees Mike is already halfway across. A shadow appears over him and he looks up to see the massive Devourer flying through the air. It drops down in front of him but stumbles and crashes into the asphalt and sidewalks like a plow ripping its way through loose soil. It rises, still nursing its arm and in agony.

As Jake runs by, it slaps a car and sends it tumbling through the air nearly clipping Mike. The wind surrounding the large projectile is enough to lay him out. Mike sits up and responds by shooting the giant in the knees a few times.

Seeing that not all of the flammable substance Mike had doused it with had burned away, Jake fumbles out his devil girl lighter and flicks it on.

With a deep guttural roar it bats a loosened chunk of the street in Mike's direction.

Jake uses the distraction to move in close. Still a few feet away, for some reason the lighter flares up and its oil spattered body catches, setting it up again in a blaze.

The heat blasts at him and the creature shrieks again. Jake uses the slimy blade to hack at the back of its left ankle. The heavy weapon cuts again into the juggernaut and it screams more, in anger and pain. Jake swings again but it is too fast and it leaps onto a store. Its inhaling scream, deafening again, Jake can see air thicken into milky gales as it and the fire is sucked into the chief's maw. As with the school bus, its screech is so loud that every intact piece of glass in the area explodes. Chief Blackhands looks down at Jake and with its good hand draws a line from the right corner of its mouth, down to where its eye is, on its warped upside down face.

Jake understands his threat and gives him the finger while scowling back.

Similar howls go off throughout the town and it leaps back onto the ground, cautious now of Jake the creature rushes away to the north.

* * *

Straining to breathe, the men fall to their knees in front of the house with the ornate garden of religious symbols.

"This is the place?" Mike coughs with a strained voice.

"Yeah. Where's Scott?" Jake wheezes back.

Mike shakes his head, the pain in his expression is unmistakable.

"I'm sorry. Those fucking things."

"None of us knew what we were getting into, especially you Jake. At least *we* set out intentionally after a dangerous convict, you were just trying to get to your family."

Sad and angered about the loss, Jake runs his hands through his sweaty hair, his hatred for the Devourers growing deeper.

"What do you think that last call was? A retreat?"

"Let's hope so," Jake stands upright to look at the house. "The bottles haven't moved. Damn! He should have come back by now."

"What do you mean?" Mike dribbles the last of his water from his canteen over his sweaty head.

"We decided to set those bottles up by the door a certain way. To let each other know if we stopped by or were still there."

"The Vet or Evelyn?" Mike asks to Jake's surprise. "Yeah, she came and found me one night, scolded me for being so loud."

"Was she alright?" Jake asks concerned.

259

"It was about a week ago, but yeah. Why not just go inside?" Mike looks around still catching his breath.

"Bear traps and mines in the yard, takes a while to get through safely. I'm guessing that wasn't you firing earlier?"

"Nope, I heard the crawler barking and by the time I circled around to the school, I saw Tanner was trying to corner you. Sorry it took me so long to get up there."

"Don't apologize, you saved my life man."

"The school doesn't have anything useful either, I've been crashing in that church's basement."

With a mildly pained look he flexes his wrist a few times, "Really?"

"Yeah, the building is already trashed. No reason for them to come looking. There is also a sub basement there. Stone, pretty well fortified."

"I'll get you into his house, but I'm heading right over to Evelyn's? They could still be in trouble."

"There's no sense in us splitting up. I wish we could set these heavy bags down. She gave me some things you're gonna want to look at."

Jake looks down the forlorn street hoping to hear a few more shots while he tries to decide on collecting himself in the house or to keep moving.

"I don't know how long those bastards will be gone for, I'm chancing it."

"Then I'm with you Jake."

Mike reloads his pistol with his last remaining bullets and Jake examines the disturbing blade he acquired from Blackhands as they rush through the alleys. It is made from tightly pressed segments of bone, most likely an animal's. Maybe even human's spine. Sharp as hell with pointed teeth growing from the hilt. And made to look like a Devourer's mouth swallowing the base of the blade. A slight disorientation comes over him as his eyes roll over the dirt filled symbols that have been carved up and down the blade. He thanks himself for wearing gloves as he wonders what source the leather material came from that covers the grip. He is sure the urge to gag or vomit would overcome him if his hunger were not so prevalent.

Jake spots the lumbering willow a few houses away, and sees smoke as well.

"That's where it is," he points it out to Mike. "Something's happened!" he accelerates and runs directly at it.

They arrive to a surreal scene of a huge disastrous excavation. The corrugated containers that were once buried beneath the alley are torn open from the top, exposing Evelyn's secret living space to the pale skies. The peeled back metal is shredded and rapidly rusting away before their eyes. Burning bits of the smashed garages have fallen into the huge trench. There is no sign of life.

Almost in a trance, Jake shuffles forward near one of the sunken edges and looks down. Mike is speechless. He is shocked not only by the level of destruction but by the fact that this complex was hidden below the ground. He paces back and forth around the edge trying to take it all in. Jake drops to his knees and places his hands over his head.

After a few moments, Mike's awe of the scene fades and he becomes aware again of their exposed situation. He paces around the edge some and produces a bundle of neon yellow rope. He attaches it to a wood beam from one of the former garages.

"What are you doing?" A disheartened Jake asks without looking up.

Mike stares at Jake, not knowing what he could say to comfort him and continues down into the opened area. With large steps and his gun ready he begins exploring the wreckage listening for calls of help, looking for bodies or anything useful.

Mike calls up, sadness dominating his voice, "Jake."

Jake looks down and sees Mike somberly pointing to where Evelyn's bedroom once was. One of the garages has slid completely into the area and near the bottom, a dusty human form sits motionless. Not knowing how else to react, Jake creeps along the edge by the rope to get down. He removes the heavy backpack and drops the bone weapon to the floor. He stops a few yards away from the sitting shape and calls out, "Sam?"

Sam does not move. Next to him he sees another humanoid shape, smoldering. It's still hot core glows through its cracks. A white ashy head and torso with a large piece of wood from the fallen garage is pinning it to the rusted metal wall. Its legs are concealed beneath more rubble but its arms are exposed, it is a Devourer.

Mike steps close behind Jake, "He killed one?"

Sam's eyes snap open and he raises his rifle at them.

They jump back and Jake holds his hands up calmingly, "Sam, it's us!"

As surprised as they were, Sam sleepily squints up at them, "Jake?"

"You're alive!"

He winces and with a shaking hand, opens part of his olive drab jacket exposing his skinless chest and stomach. Two wicked arrows, which he had broken off, protrude from his chest. "They snatched some of me off," he grunts. "Don't have long."

Jake's shoulders sag, "There's nothing . . ."

Sam shakes his head and pushes his rifle over to Jake.

"Evelyn?" he kneels down next to him.

A tear washes away a path through the dust covering Sam. "So much blood when I got here. An ambush. Didn't see her body."

"Those mother fuckers!" Mike angrily calls up to the skies.

"That's right." Sam says with pained smile. He takes a long shallow breath. "I'm not going alone," he motions with his head to the smoking ash pile next to him."

"The spike?" Jake asks.

"In its head. Dig it out. Popped it right into the fucker's big nasty eye."

"I will."

"Listen Jake, you still cannot kill them with just this. Got lucky, this one couldn't run home. I held its arms so it couldn't take the spike back out."

"But it still—"

"No. You won't get this lucky, that's why we needed everyone. Just you two now?"

"What else can I do?"

Sam's breaths become shallower. He holds his hand up and Jake takes it. Sam grips him powerfully in the handshake.

Jake's eyes tear but Sam stares into his with a piercing intensity.

As his breaths become shorter, Sam starts to nod at him.

"Don't. Fail." Sam releases Jake's hand from his and points his eyes, a military hand sign, then points to the Devourer. He then draws a 'V' in its smoldering chest, "The Forks." then draws a straight line up through the center.

Sam jerks his hand away and closes his eyes. The tears flow as he feels Sam's heart wind down to its last beat.

After a few moments, Mike respectfully leans closer and whispers, "What does it mean?"

Jake stares at the symbol made in the exposed glowing embers where Sam drew the shape. Jake understands. "It means the Forks has a fourth road."

* * *

They scavenge the rest of the wreckage for the next few hours. None of the rooms are close to intact and they find ridiculous amounts blood, black and red but still no sign of Evelyn's body. He did come across a few invaluable things. An apparent cookbook of hers, detailing the many ways in which to use the red death flower. Her horde of gold and other valuables which he forced Mike to take despite his protests. Jake even found the shotgun and special rounds that Kenneth mentioned being shot with. Above all of these things he found the most value in her diaries and the box she kept from his eyes, which is filled with hundreds of photographs of her, her family and friends and Sophie.

With only a few hours before sunset, the men begin to wrap things up.

"What are you gonna do with your friend?" Mike sympathetically asks.

"I haven't decided yet, but I'm not leaving him here."

"Scott wanted me to give him a Viking burial if he died. So I did."

Jake casts him a lightly puzzled but empathetic look as he packs a few more items into a duffle bag and tosses it up out of the hole.

"He didn't want to come back as a vampire, zombie or

anything," Mike explains.

A sad smile happens across Jake's face. "I really would have liked hanging out with you guys."

"Yeah, he used to say the damnedest things."

Both of them laden with heavy backpacks, they carry Sam's body on a makeshift stretcher without complaint. They walk stoically down the middle of the street. No more hiding. Back at the house, Jake shows Mike how to navigate through the animal traps and where the mines are buried. After a short break, they construct a respectable pyre and place Sam's body on top. Jake does not say anything as he folds Sam's hands over his chest he pauses.

He thinks of how he has been getting beat down, drowned in despair, pain and hunger for so long. It is still nothing compared to what Sam and Evelyn had endured over the years, just to be mauled and left to die alone. Jake takes a deep breath and crystallizes his resolve, even becoming a monster himself will not stop him from killing them all.

He empties out one of Mike's black molotovs and with it ignites the pyre. Plumes of the smoke rise as the fire roars and Jake is not afraid. After a while of watching, he and Mike enter the house to begin making new plans.

They have laid out every useful thing they could think of across the top of the construction spool table. Four rifles and three handguns with enough appropriate rounds to make them useful. A pump action shotgun and Evelyn's long barreled twelve, with a couple dozen of her special shotgun rounds. The spike, the bone sword, five molotovs, four treated knives a few flares, medical supplies and enough food for a few weeks.

Jake crosses his arms and sighs. "The one that Sam killed, did you see his bow anywhere?"

Mike shakes his head. "No, but let me get the stuff that Evelyn gave me that night."

He reaches into a smaller bag and lays the bark covered thermos Jake gave him onto the table. Mike points at the thermos and says, "She brought more of that extract and filled this up."

Jake sits down by the table, twists the lid off and begins

guzzling it down.

Mike watches him closely and with disgust as if he himself were tasting the overpowering concoction again. But he says nothing.

He then places a large book, the Lamplighters book onto the table, "And this is what I found in side that floor safe in the jail cell." He places a varnished wooden box similar to a cigar box and a heavy book with a black cover in front of Jake. Both of the objects bear the embossed Lamplighter's symbol.

"That's right! I forgot about that." Jake exclaims and lifts the wooden box's lid.

Inside are seven black identical pieces of metal. They are rectangular with smooth edges and a small dime sized hole going through one end. Each of them is about three inches across and five inches tall. They are solid and an inch thick. All of them marked with a painted red Lamplighter's symbol as well.

Jake holds a few of them in his hands. They are heavier than they look and hot to the touch.

"I showed them to the old lady and asked her about what they could be. She didn't know, but said she would get back to me on it and took one with her. But I think they're ingots."

"Ingots?"

"They do it with precious metals like silver and gold. You know, like a gold bar."

Jake looks at the pieces in his hands and tries clinking two of them together, there is no sound.

For the first time in hours Jake seems lively and surprised he looks up at Mike. "This is! . . ." he holds up the spike. "This is the same stuff as this! Sam called it Parasidium!"

"What? Is it from space?" Mike tries clinking the strange ingots together.

Jake shrugs, "I don't know, it absorbs energy though. Whatever it is, it's fatal to those damned things."

Jake opens the thick black book and thumbs through the pages. The inside looks cleaner and more organized than the red book. It is in English, although a very old form of it, "This must be the founder's book."

"I read from it here and there, lots of weird shit has always been going on here. Look at this page." Mike reaches over and sifts ahead through the book. He stops on a section full of pages that look like chaotic road maps.

Jake's brows furrow as he goes over the diagrams with his fingers.

Mike points out a specific area, "It looks like for a time they were selectively trying to breed out the native blood line after it became intermixed. They marked the natives with an 'S'.

"The 'S' is for Sirobamjal. That's what that tribe was called."

"Cee-row-bom-jal," Mike sounds it out.

"Yeah. I guess there's no worry of someone saying *that* on accident. But what's this?"

"That's the thing," Mike points out underlined areas. "If you follow this backwards, Kenneth's grandparents were never supposed to hook up because they both had the strongest original bloodlines. But they did, and had that piece of shit's mother. Her name changes from Hayfoot to Tanner right here when she marries an outsider."

"Yes. This goes inline with what the founder worried about. That stronger blood ties brings them closer in some ways to the original tribe. Like the knowledge is encoded in their blood."

"But how would Tanner's grandparents have known? Was someone helping them?"

Jake tilts his head back and sighs, "This is all good stuff. But we already have enough to worry about."

Mike sits down on the spool chair. "Speaking of other things to worry about. The extract, Evelyn said you would need it. I mean, there is need and want. The pure form of that stuff tastes like crap. So what did she mean?"

"She didn't tell you?" Jake stands and crosses his hands back over his chest.

"Just lay it on me man, what else could surprise me?"

Jake takes off his gloves and drops them to the table, exposing his obsidian hands to Mike.

"Aw, fuck!" he jumps up from his seat. His eyes dashing from Jake's hands to the suite of guns on the table.

"Don't," Jake calmly gestures to take it easy.

"You're one of them?" he shouts.

"No!" Jake denies. "They're trying though."

Mike stands there, his body tense and confused, bordering on panic. "Over the last couple weeks, when they came right at me, it was right for the kill. That's how they got Scott. With you, it's like they are playing around. Their boss was even chatting you up."

"They're trying to make me like them, so they can get out."

"What?"

"I have a twin brother. They think if I become like them, they can use some link between me and him as a *backdoor* through the barrier."

"Can they?" Mike stands back up and paces back and forth.

"I don't know man! Earlier Kenneth claimed he could sense my brother. But he's a fucking lair. He even told me you and everyone else was dead. And if I can't *feel* my own brother with all this crap going on in me, how can he?"

"What if it's true?"

"I know."

"If they get out–"

"I know!" Jake yells.

Anxiously Mike starts shifting his weight.

"Hey man, I'm me. And hopefully, as long as we kill the chief before I'm completely changed, I can go back to normal. If we pull it off and somehow I'm still like this, I'll gladly push that spike into my own skull!"

Mike calms down a bit.

"This stuff helps me keep it in check." he holds up the wood thermos. "You know what it does to them, right?"

Mike reluctantly nods.

Keeping his eyes on Mike he takes a few more swigs of the extract, "I had some earlier, remember?"

Slowly Mike sits back down, calmer but frustrated. Jake sits down and opens the bag he left at Sam's house before they split up and adds to his notebook. He looks up at Mike trying to smile and lighten the mood and tosses the packages of baseball cards onto the table.

Mike huffs and shakes his head, but manages a relaxed

expression, "So what's the new plan?"

Jake sits and looks over the articles on the table then back to his notebook.

"I'll slide back, but I can't take anything with me that I can't conceal. Are you comfortable using that nasty bone sword?"

"If it gets the job done. I'll use it wearing gloves so something like *that* doesn't happen," he points at Jake's hands.

"You keep the sword, the shotgun, the special shells and the spike."

"What! How are you gonna defend yourself?"

"Well, I'm one of them," Jake smiles.

"That's not funny man!" he says with serious tone.

Still smiling, Jake continues, "I'll take one of the knives and the thermos. Do you have any more syringes?"

"The one you used was the only working one I found, why won't you take the spike? You can hide that."

"When I slide back, young Evelyn ends up telling me where the weapon is. Sam was thinking that because I and it disappear from back then, I bring it here to this time."

"But broken."

"Exactly, so we have to find out how to work this metal. Do you know how to, solder? I was thinking you could get the spike ready to reattach it."

"If I had the equipment. Maybe we can melt one of the ingots and reconnect it the old school way. But I read in the black book, that this metal has to be worked using some sort of vibrations. I'll keep reading up on it."

"Awesome," Jake fills his hip flask with the extract. "I'll take a knife and a handgun just in case I see Kenneth and he's still just a regular scumbag."

"What happened to the .45 I gave you?"

"I gave it to a girl," Jake shrugs.

Mike smiles, "She was that hot, huh?"

"Beyond," He somberly smiles. "Kenneth was targeting people like her, doing who knows what with them."

"There's a few other things we need to do, just in case. I'm gonna check my stitches first though." Jake walks back to the bathroom and slows as he passes by the photo collage in the hallway. He stares at it thinking deeply before turning away.

Jake washes away the lingering traces of the stink then soaks and rings out the bandana. He pours the extract onto it and lets it soak in before hanging it up to dry. He works up enough strength to look in the mirror and when he does he is shocked. Staring at his dark reflection, he thinks of how Mike wasn't looking to good after his own rough times in Prudence. Looking at himself, Jake cannot imagine how Mike could not have assumed that something was not seriously wrong with him. More color has faded from his eyes and they appear even starker against the darker circles under them. He is deathly pale, veins are clearly visible around his temples and neck and they are so dark they do not even appear blue. The cracks in his lips are caked with dried blood and he has lost at least thirty pounds since arriving. He pours some water over his head and notices the tips of his black fingers are even pointier. He taps a finger against the mirror. The tips are hard and sharp. He had assumed they were numb from the constant cold, but the nerves were just dying off or becoming buried beneath the hardening skin. He stretches part of the bandages around his neck away to examine his stitches. Three have popped, but the rest of the wound is still held shut. The meat on the inside is dark and no longer reddish and tiny black vein spread from it. Trying to hold himself together he splashes more water on his face and holds the wood container extract up in the gloomy light. He hates that he has become dependant on it. Having to drink it so often, he imagines how an addict might feel and that he will fall apart without a few hits every hour. He tips it back and takes a few more swigs when something cold and hard slaps against his ankle. He looks down to see a twisted upside down face looking up at him from under the sink. Before he can react, it ducks back and pulls him to the floor.

Jake shouts. The one who crawls had burrowed a hole under the sink and has one of its massive hands clamped painfully tight on him. Violently it starts trying to pull him into the hole.

"Mike!" he cries out.

With one jerk, he is waist deep. He presses his hands against the outside and tries pushing himself out. Mike bursts into the bathroom with a rifle and is stunned. He drops down and fires into the hole, striking the creature. It barks back but does not slow. Frantically Jake kicks at it with his free leg and keeps pushing against the crumbling tiles and wall. Mike drops his gun and tries pulling him back out but only gains a few inches back.

Jake sees the extract spilling out onto the floor. Quickly he sets it upright and is yanked down to his elbows.

"Mike, get the knife. Get the spike!" he cries out.

"Fuck!" he rushes out of the room.

Jake widens his arms trying to anchor himself and sucks some of the extract into his mouth before slamming the container upright on the floor. Struggling he manages a solid kick, knocking it away.

Mike does a sliding leap forward and slides right at him with the spike in hand.

As Jake pulls himself, out it snatches both of his ankles and he feels it bite down hard on his leg. He is torn through the hole to the outside of the house.

It picks him up with both hands and slams him into the ground a few times until he goes limp. Still conscious and having accidentally swallowed some of the extract, Jake jerks forward and bites it in its disgusting rubbery neck. It howls and falls away. With a teeth clenched roar Jake tears a chunk out of it and both the extract the black blood bubbles away in his mouth, giving him a rabid look. It grabs his jacket and Jake spits the froth into its crooked mouth. It slams him hard into the side of the house, winding him. He blacks out for a second and comes to just in time to see its ritual dagger inches away from his eye. Jake thrashes and screams but he cannot get the gibbering creature off.

The dagger pierces his temple and cuts the line down the right side of his face. Time slows. The pain is excruciating like it was before. It feels like his life is a large book and it has been loudly slammed shut in front of his eyes. Unaware if it is out loud or just on the inside, he screams. The one who crawls is no longer aggressive at all towards Jake. It backs away, humbly from him. He turns and looks up at it just as Mike appears behind it with a hammer in one hand and nails the spike into its skull. Time returns to normal as it jerks and falls to the side convulsing. The bit of the spike lodged in the center of its blistering flesh lights up white and a cracking bluish fire flares out blinding Jake. Despite everything sounding like it is underwater, Jake hears it suck in a loud garbled whine but it is short. Its spasms cut to pained quivering. Smoke billows from the wound and the flesh burns away, spreading the cracked white ash from the head throughout its body. He hears muffled yelling and cannot make out the words. Jake looks over to Mike, whose image fades away into the swirl filled glowing outline he had seen before. The light is brighter and welcoming. He stares at the energy's movements entranced. He reaches out to it, his own hand a void and feels the warmth coming from the light.

His hand is batted away by the glowing silhouette but he keeps reaching. The glowing silhouette swings hitting him in his new scar. The pain jolts him as his head is knocked sideways. Jake's vision melts back to normal. He looks back to Mike who is frightened and angry but still sees traces of energy and color around him.

"—at me one more time and you're dead!" Mike's words become clear again.

"M'alright," Jake slurs.

"They got you? Oh man, they fucking got you!"

Jake groans and sits up looking at the devourer's corpse. Other than the heat from the spike, there is no energy coming from it. What has not yet burned away of its hands and feet showed no anti-light, the blackness of being a void. It is like it is not even there.

"What do we do now?" Mike falls defeated against the house.

Jake staggers to his feet and picks the dropped hammer up.

"We stick with the plan," he smashes the ashes away from the spike.

"Can you?"

"I'll deal with it. Its turned black again, pick it up."

"Why don't you? Oh."

He rolls it in his hands a few times, "Yeah, it's cold again."

Jake makes a grabby motion with his wicked looking hand.

"Are you sure?" he asks Jake.

Mike nods and tosses it to him.

He catches it. Although very hot, it is not enough to burn.

"Looks like we're good. Let's get inside and plug this hole."

With plenty of horded junk lying around the house, they quickly find appropriate materials to secure the hole.

"How did it know you were in the bathroom?" Mike hands the extract container to Jake.

"They have a," he becomes dizzy and falls but catches himself on the sink. "They have some type of energy vision." His voice is accompanied by a constant wheezing, and his words are slow and forced.

"You're shitting me!"

"Wish I was. I can see your aura. And see partially through non living things, like an x-ray almost."

"Damn! That explains why hiding from them was always such a bitch. I figured they were sucking in the smells. And you see like that?"

"Maybe it's all connected for them. I'm seeing like that and like normal right now."

Mike looks at him uncomfortably. "Your eyes changed."

Jake drags himself over to the mirror again. The whites of his eyes have become solid black, and his pupils are a lifeless white and seem dilated wide open. The pupils hang there like full moons on a cloudless night. Eerily they seem to flicker at certain angles. He stares at both cuts running down his cheeks and remembers how Kenneth turned his skull upside down under his skin. He pulls at his face and hopes that does not happen to him.

He drinks some of the extract. Hoping it will overcome his urge to attack Mike. It washes down burning hot and he gasps dropping to the floor in pain. Mike rushes over to him.

"Stay away!" he shouts and squirms on the ground.. The extract is nothing but poison to him now. Within minutes, the burning pain in his stomach fades leaving an emptier, more painful hole in his gut. He keeps fighting it, "My notepad."

Mike brings it to him and Jake reverently starts jotting things down, important things. All while trying to combat his own growing thoughts of sinking his teeth into Mike and swallowing pound after pound of his pulsing, warm light.

An hour later their plans are finalized. A patched up Jake zips up his bulging backpack and sets it on the table. While putting his gloves on, Mike returns from the back of the house.

"What are you doing? We still have a couple hours before it is night time."

Jake avoids looking directly at Mike as he had been, "Our plans have been made. You know what to do."

"I know but, are you going to fight them all off until its dark?"

"There's only two of us. By their rules, it is one of them for one of us. So I'm thinking there should only be two of them now. But I don't even know if I count as human anymore."

"Come on man, why risk it? Just wait."

"They got what they wanted from me. Besides if I stay here, you're the one who'd be taking the risk," he picks up one of the black molotovs.

Mike looks around sadly, "If you hang out on the corner, I can cover you from the porch. Watch your back and slow them down with bullets at least."

"Its hard man," Jake looks at Mike then looks away. "Just watch your ass, and try and work with that spike."

Mike crosses his arms and understandingly nods, "Alright, Jake. Kick that fucker's ass."

Jake nods goodbye and exits the house. At the corner he looks back and sees Mike standing there, vigilant with a rifle ready. Jake gives a self reassuring thumbs up in a humorous way. Mike returns it but with a sad expression and Jake disappears from sight.

The new numb sensation creeping over his body is actually beginning to soothe the biting cold he had been dealing with. He debates if there is anything left inside of him to be chilled. As he approaches the Forks, he wonders how much of him will revert to being human, if at all, when he slides back this time. If he can slide back, now that the ritual has been complete.

Boldly standing in the middle of the intersection, he stares at the large square building that caps the north side of the forks. Still as nondescript as it is in the past, designed intentionally to be overlooked despite its size. Mike told him he hid inside it for a few days. That it is a large empty warehouse that seems to serve no purpose. Jake knows now that it does have a purpose and that it fulfilled it well. Concealing the fourth path leading north of the Forks to where the Devourers dwell. Jake walks to its right side to a wide dead end alley and sees its door. Its only door, still open a crack from when Mike breeched it. He steps inside and looks around the dusty gloom. He strains his eyes a bit, trying to somehow put his new vision to work. Nothing happens, as there is nothing living inside of it. He paces around the stale inside for a few minutes until he finds an appropriate amount of wood supports. He snaps open his devil girl lighter half expecting another flare up, as lucky as it was when it happened, but it clicks on smoothly. He admires the shape of the beautiful pin up girl again and rolls his gloved thumb over it a few times, watching the eyes sparkle. He then lights the molotov and smashes the fiery bottle against the supports. After a few minutes he sees signs of the fire from his position outside at the center of the intersection. When he returns to the present, if he returns he thinks to himself, this place should be burned to the ground, providing him a clear path to wherever it is the creatures have been going.

As the smoke rises into the dimming sky, he hears the one who screams howling in the distance. The first sound he heard when he came to Prudence. Across his forehead, the sharp pain returns. Instantly drowning out the tightening agony in his gut from his starvation.

"That's right, I'm coming," he wheezes quietly and looks down at his watch. Before his eyes the beautiful gold watch tarnishes. The hands stop ticking and it crumbles into its separate pieces, cog by rusting cog. In seconds, it falls away from his wrist, like poured sand.

The sky dims out to total darkness and suddenly he hears echoing sounds around him, becoming louder. The lights from the marquee and all of the other stores flash on and in an instant the numbness is gone. His slide back is complete, his hunger and pain only half as bad. He looks around and sees the town is in chaos.

CHAPTER 13

The bright beams of light scream towards him and he jumps out of the way just in time. The car screeches to a halt just long enough for the driver to look back and give him the finger. The car peels out only to be struck by another vehicle. Other cars are rushing around and quickly he gets out of the intersection. People are running around crying and screaming. He can smell fire everywhere but the church is cold and black. He feels coolness in the air and can tell that it is early winter. Smoke plumes are rising, illuminated in the night sky by their fiery sources. He removes a glove and sees that the taint has followed him back, but only slightly. The discoloration of his skin is only as bad as the first time he noticed it. He does not feel either of the cuts running down his face. He tries calling out to a few of the frantic running people but no one stops. Finally he grabs a large man with arms full of groceries and to his surprise stops him in his tracks. The stunned man shakes him off, but not before Jake can ask his question.

"Where are they?" he shouts.

"What? Who the hell do you think you are?"

"What's going on?"

"You just wake up? Earthquakes man! Get the hell off of me!" the man rushes away.

"The seal must be breaking." he looks to the direction of

Sophie's house.

He does not even have a chance to break into a run when he hears a man call out loudly, "Yeah, that's the guy right there!"

He glances across the street, hoping to see someone fingering Kenneth. Instead, he sees Chuck, the general store owner pointing him out to a very shocked and angry looking Deputy Harris.

"He bought the lighter fluid that night, and I saw him running from the burning church!" Chuck continues.

"Shit!" Jake tries running past and sees the deputy has his gun drawn. Jake does not stop until he hears the gunfire, shattering the window from a parked car a foot in front of him.

He stops and raises his arms as he turns to see Harris barreling down on him.

"Deputy listen—"

Harris smashes his gun across Jake's face, knocking him down into the car.

"Motherfucker! You think I don't know what you did!" the deputy kicks him in the ribs, winding him. "You think you can breeze in and outta here, you fucking pyro, drifter piece of shit!"

Jake tries to yell Lamplighter but only a dry winded croak wheezes out of his mouth as he tries to protect his sides with his arms. His wrists are wrenched behind him and he feels the cold metal cuffs sharply bite down.

Krakoom!

The ear shattering boom cracks through the skies and the ground shakes violently sending him and Harris tumbling to the ground. The lights flicker and a fire hydrant explodes sending water gushing into the hazy air.

With the ground still shaking, he struggles to rise and keep his footing. He starts off again but Harris jerks him back to the ground. He stomps him in his same side again then flips him onto his back with another kick. A spurt of blood shoots from his mouth and despite everything Jake is happy to see that it is red. gripping the front of his jacket and hoodie, Harris lifts him off the ground and pushes him backwards into the car again, shattering another window.

He pulls Jake right up to his nose, a look of murder in his eyes.

"You dumb son of a bitch! You came back here!"

Jake tries to speak but he catches a right cross in his jaw and his legs buckle. Dazed he is pulled back up to the deputy's face.

"You cruise in here talking all slick! Fuck my daughter and knock her up!" He punches Jake in the gut but shock of what he just heard supersedes everything.

Sophie is pregnant! The sole thought fills his mind.

The thought is so powerful it leaves no room for anything else.

"Look at me!" the deputy shouts and elbows him in the jaw sending him limply back against the car again.

He thinks only of Sophie as he is sent from the conscious world again.

With a cool surface against his sore throbbing face and the slight smell of piss, he opens his eyes lying on the floor of the jail cell again. A small group of scared, chattering people crowd the hallway by the sheriff's office, occasionally staring at him during their heated discussions. The cuffs still pinching into his wrists, he staggers to the seat and leans forward looking for either of the cops and Sophie. He does not recognize any of the group.

"Harris! Sheriff!" he strains to call out.

One of the crowd turns to him, "They're both out trying to get a handle on things. What are you doing in there at a time like this?"

He tries to think fast, "Aren't there any spare keys in the office?"

"Were not gonna let you out!" an old woman snaps from the group.

"What's going on outside?"

"Quakes keep comin', it's been five so far," another person yells.

"One quake per totem?" he asks himself out loud and realizes he has to get out immediately.

Jake strains against his cuffs and flexes his sore jaw. He is mad about the deputy's unprovoked attack on him but he understands. Sophie is pregnant. He keeps thinking of how hurt she must feel that once again he did not call. She is alone out there, right now while he sits in a cell continuing to be useless. He thinks of what old Evelyn told him happens this night. Horrible images of

Kenneth and the Devourers eating and dragging people off into the shadows bombards his mind.

All of this is Kenneth's fault! Because of his issues with shit from forever ago.

Jake doesn't even care who started what back when. It had nothing to do with him or anyone else alive anymore. Trembling from his bound rage, he looks up at the closed door of the jail cell. Remembering his flash forward from when he was locked in here before. A thought occurs to him and he focuses back to what he saw. And he sees it. His view of the dark ruined cell as it is in his time. The image keeps slipping away, but he focuses his anger and fear of what is about to happen outside to hold it in place. He trembles from the freezing cold then the numbness and hunger. The pain in his head begins again but he keeps thinking of his hunger. Suddenly, there is warmth. He feels a heat coming from his cuffs, he allows his hunger spill into them to taste the warmth.

Crick!

He feels the cuffs snap apart and quickly holds his hands up. They are blackened but they fade back down close to normal looking. He sees the rest of the cuffs corrode and tarnish. With a slight amount of pressure on them, they snap away from his wrists.

"What the hell! Did you see that?"

A woman screams stirring the already nervous crowd into a panic.

"That man just turned into a thing!"

"What do you mean?"

"His eyes turned black and white and his skin!"

"Beth, you've just been drinking again!"

"But look he broke his cuffs!" another man calls out.

"He looks normal now! Did anyone else see what he looked like?"

The crowd is further disrupted when more men burst into the hallway. It is Junior and his bearded friend with the shades.

Jake stands and calls out to him, "Junior! It's me Jake, you gotta get me outta here!"

Junior rushes over to the cell surprised to see him but scowling.

"I know what you did! You just wait until Sophie gets down

here!"

"Sophie! Is she coming down here now? She's in danger," he looks to the crowd, "all of you are in danger, these aren't normal earthquakes!"

A frenzy of questions erupts from the crowd, Junior turns to them trying to calm them. "Don't listen to this guy, he's a liar! A damned drifter with fake ideas and a lot of bullshit. He's the guy who burned down our church!"

"Junior I don't have time for this shit!" Jake yells. "Let me the fuck out!"

"No way. You're staying right there man!"

Jake is furious. He grabs the cell door in both hands and strains to bend them open. On the verge of a breakdown he bangs his head against the bars a few times growling through his teeth. "Let! Me! Out!"

Junior backs away from the cell but his friend just stares, adjusting his dirty orange billed ball cap in disbelief.

Jake's angered breaths become longer and deep to the point where he is filling and emptying his lungs completely. His body shakes and sweat pours from his bruised body as he breathes fully out again. Not breathing in, his heart slows and his view darkens except for the metal bars in his grip. They glow a very pale blue, the warmth is soothing. Jake does not look away but he hears the crowd scream in terror. He inhales deeply sucking up the light from the bars. His vision partially shifts back and he sees the metal rust and flake as he draws the energy in. He flexes and tears the crumbling door off its hinges like it is nothing. He steps out of the cell and turns to the panicked fleeing crowd. He sees Junior has fallen to the floor, frozen and his friend is backing away. Jake feels powerful, as if nothing can stop him and he wants more. A wicked sneer spreads across his scarred deathly visage and he turns his mouth wide open towards the two. While a yellow puddle of piss spreads out from under trembling Junior's ass his friend draws a gun and fires. A searing pain hits Jake's gut and drops him to the floor. Without saying a word, his friend pulls Junior up and half drags him down the hall and out of the police station.

Jake squirms from the pain and he wraps his arms around his

stomach. His vision blurs then normalizes as the energy outlines from the lights and other metal sources fades away.

He looks down to see how much blood he's lost but he sees none. A syringe with a fuzzy orange back sticks out of his stomach. Although glad he was not shot, he is stunned to see it sticking out of his body. He feels weakened but shakes it off as he pulls the empty dart out. Jake vaguely remembers Junior's rat catching friend and is thankful he was there to shoot him and not one of the cops. Back on his feet, he checks the sheriff's office for any spare guns, even handcuff keys just in case he gets nabbed again. He shudders thinking of the sick feeling from using those abilities, mad at himself for loosing control like that. He hears more shouting coming from outside rushes to the front door to try and get out before the deputy returns.

The smoke is thicker outside and the streets are even more chaotic. There is no sign of Junior or his friend but a few of the people who saw him tear out of the cell, notice he is out and flee the scene. He sees his hands are normal again but still puts his gloves back on. Rushing towards Sophie's house from the station, he gulps from his flask. It burns, a lot, but it is more manageable than it last was. He freezes amidst the chaos at the Forks when the painful thought strikes him that he has to get to Evelyn's house instead of Sophie's. He wonders if this was a mistake he made before, when Prudence fell. Fists clenched, Jake is torn between logic and emotion. Before he can choose either path a red cherry light flashes from behind him and a police car almost clips him before colliding in a light pole.

"Get your fucking hands in the air now!" Deputy Harris shouts as he staggers from the vehicle.

With a real gun aimed at him now he complies. The deputy's footsteps a few feet away Jake shouts, "Lamplighters!"

He grabs Jake's arms and spins him around. "What the hell did you just say?"

"I'm here to help, I know about the Lamplighters," he speaks as clear and fast as he can before he is knocked out again. "Kenneth is letting *them* out right now! I'm trying to stop him!"

"What the hell are you talking about you son of a bitch?" he grabs up the front of his Jacket again.

"Harris please listen—"

"Shut your damned mouth!"

"He's going let *them* out! They'll get everyone!"

"How did you? You're working with them aren't you?"

"No! It's why I've been around town, I've been trying to get him!"

"What did Sam tell you in Nam?"

"Nothing! Look around at what's going on! Quakes don't happen around here! The abductions, all descendants from the tribe!" He's trying to take down the barrier!"

"Don't you say another word!"

"The unspoken whatever rule doesn't matter! They're here, they'll get out and they'll kill everyone!"

The deputy unclenches his fists from Jake.

"The founder's weapon! Where is it!"

Shocked at how much the stranger knows about his brotherhood's deepest secrets and with the town shaking apart, Harris feels he has no choice but to listen to him, despite his anger. "I don't know, you took it the night you burned the church!"

Jake remembers what Sam told him and how tightly Evelyn clutched her bag to her chest that night in the church, she had taken more than the book.

"Evelyn! She has it."

"She did this?"

"No! She kept her brother from getting it. We have to get to her, but where's Sophie?"

Harris flashes him a bitter and angry look at the mention of his daughter.

"I just came from there! She's not home, neither is my wife!"

Jake tries to clear his mind, "Evelyn's house then, she might be there!"

"You're going in cuffs!"

"Fuck that!"

"Who the hell let you out just now anyway?"

"Doesn't matter! If you have a knife pull it out!"

"I'm not giving you a knife!"

"Hey! Jake draws his own knife from the sheathe on the back of his belt. "You never frisked me."

"Drop it!"

"I would have pulled it earlier if I wanted to use it! Pull out your damned knife!"

Harris hesitates but complies, and Jake pours the extract from his flask over the blade.

"That's?"

"Yes."

"So this *is* real?"

"Yes! Don't wipe it off."

"Oh my, I never thought," he stutters, "I believed but I never thought!"

"Let's go!" Jake shouts.

KRAKOOM!

Louder than before, the earth violently shudders knocking them off their feet. Followed by the defining noise is a jagged throaty roar, which Jake knows all too well. It goes on for a minute as the men scramble into the squad car. Suddenly every light and utility pole bursts into bright orange sparks then dies.

"I'm too late!" Jake gasps.

Only the lights from a few erratic cars speeding by and the flashing red light from the squad car is lighting up the Forks. Birds take off screaming into the dark skies and blended with their sounds is another noise coming from the North. It sounds a like stampede of screaming lunatics and wild animals has begun storming down towards them. Powerful gales begin kicking up leaves and debris into whistling swirls. The men look at each other to acknowledge and confirm the reality of the growing sound.

"Start the car up," Jake shouts.

Harris wide eyes look fearfully up at the small mountain. "It's them, it is all of them." He slams on the gas and peels away as he turns his sirens on to keep the panicked people from running in front of the car.

"How do we stop them?" Harris starts repeating to himself.

"Snap out of it man! People here need you, we need the weapon."

He slaps himself and swerves to avoid a few panicked looters, "It's not a weapon, it is a tool!"

"Whatever it is! Is there anything you can tell me about it? Do I have to say some magic words or anything?"

He looks over and sees that Jake is dead serious with his questions, as ridiculous as they sound.

"I never saw it. It was always wrapped up. Carried it once even, it was heavier than it seemed, but manageable. Never heard anything about any incantations though. I still can't believe that you know all of this."

"Would you believe I'm from forty years in the future?"

"What?"

"That's how I know."

Deputy Harris shakes his head bracing mentally himself. "You're asking me to believe too much."

"My strange I.D.'s? The dates on them? How you and the sheriff couldn't find any trace of me existing."

The deputy says nothing but Jake sees his mind connecting the dots.

Jake continues trying to drive the ridiculous claim into Harris' mind as quickly as he can. "In that second jail cell there's a small safe in the floor, containing the founder's book and ingots made from that special metal."

"You couldn't have known that!"

"Exactly," Jake nods. "Unless I got into it in the future. Shit! Let's grab those ingots right now!"

"No time. Plus the sheriff had the only key. How did you ever get in?"

"A friend bashed it open."

"From the station? Cops didn't stop him?"

"Cops? Prudence is a ghost town."

"What about all of the people?"

Jake gives him a look that spells impending doom better than he could ever articulate.

"If that's true, and you can zip back here from the future, why didn't you stop Kenneth before?"

"I don't have any control over it. The first time it happened, I passed out and woke up at the Dixon's house. I was there because I was trying to get information from Sam, old Sam."

"If Sam survived then maybe—"

"He survived because he's not here right now."

"Fuck me! Who gets through this?"

"Evelyn and a few others I never met."

"If she's part of this, I'll make sure she doesn't survive shit."

"She has to! She helps me in my time, she's trying to stop it."

"You should have tried harder!" he shouts at Jake.

"Yeah when I was tying to convince myself I wasn't crazy, or when you had me sitting in your jail?"

"How about when you were fucking my daughter?" he jabs at him, but Jake catches his wrist in his powerful cold grip.

Jake lets go and takes the deputy's seething stare.

"I tracked Tanner down to his house and Evelyn answered the door. I didn't even know they were related. I tried to get as much information by hanging around as I could. And Sophie was always there."

Harris huffs through his grimace.

"Harris, when I learned the abductees were all descendants and Evelyn's history with her brother, I stayed close to Sophie so I could protect her."

"You sure did."

Jake slouches back and looks away into the blackness outside of the car, at his own dark reflection in the window. "I love her. And if I had any control over my sliding I would have stayed here."

Harris takes a few deep calming breaths after another near collision, "We'll see."

Suddenly something crashes into the roof of the car and the loud bucket siren goes flying away. Harris swerves again to a stop and a shadowy thing tumbles away skidding across the street in front of them.

"Is that?"

"Yeah, keep going!"

"I'm gonna ram it!"

"No, they drain metal! It'll kill the car engine if it can touch it!"

In the thickening smoke, it crouches in the thick beams from the car. The twitching hindquarters of a large dog sticks out of its mouth. It swallows it in and Harris gags in terror, his body paralyzed when he sees it revealing its upside down face.

"Harris, drive!" Jake sees it is no use and exits the car.

Jake sees the Devourer is smaller than the ones he has come across before, but this confirms that the entire tribe of them is on the loose.

It charges at Jake and he rushes towards it, tackling the Devourer to its surprise. Harris watches Jake fearlessly yelling at it and stabbing it repeatedly in the neck. It makes a blood curdling shriek and skitters away into some bushes.

Jake runs back to the car and retreats his blade with the extract. Harris watches its black blood sizzle away and drop to the floor of his car.

"Harris!"

He looks up to see Jake glaring at him.

Jake's expression mellows when he remembers his same reaction to his first encounter with one of them.

"Harris, we can do this. But we've gotta go."

He starts shaking his head and pulls what he can of himself together. "Not with those things out. My wife and daughter could be back home by now."

Jake cannot disagree. He lies to himself that Evelyn could be at Sophie's house. "Wait, can you call the Sheriff?"

"He's been missing for two days."

"He wasn't a descendant, was he?"

"He was." Harris says calmly, working through his shock. "I don't know what to."

Jake sees the deputy start to falter, as would any man under the circumstances, but he needs him focused.

"I have a plan! Let's get your family outside the barrier. I'm going find that weapon, march down the north forks road, find where they are and shove it is up those fucking creature's asses.

"Outside the barrier? We have to get them to another country."

"No, the barrier holds. Those things just get out of wherever they are locked up. But everyone trapped inside the barrier with them—" Jake sees that he does not need to finish his sentence. He watches people rushing around inside a few of the homes they pass. They are barricading their windows. "How is it that some houses still have power?" Jake asks.

"Blackouts have been a common problem here with the oil drilling operation expanding. So, people keep generators handy."

With a hard fast turn, the car squeals onto Sophie's street. A few houses away a home is already engulfed in flames, which are being whipped around by the powerful winds. He stops the car with the high beams spilling across his home and yells out for his wife and daughter while rushing to the house.

"Wait here!" he turns to Jake while pulling out his gun and a flashlight.

"Put your gun away, use the knife."

Harris hesitates but complies. "Warren!" he shouts to his neighbor's house as he sprints into his own.

Jake stands in the headlights between the house and the car. Knowing how they see, he knows it is pointless to hide in the dark. He looks mainly to the house straining his ears to hear a good sign from within.

Instead, a panting and wild-eyed Harris emerges, "Still gone!"

"I didn't see your neighbor either."

As Harris runs back to the car, Jake notices a figure on the roof of Sophie's house.

"Harris look out!"

The figure dives through the air and crashes into him, sending them tumbling to the ground. Jake charges and swipes at it with his knife, but it jumps away and lands on the hood of the car. Barely a few seconds on the car, sparks shoot from the headlights and die.

"Fucker cut me!" Harris shouts as he gags from its stench and moves over behind Jake.

In the light from the burning house, they see it sitting there staring back. Harris aims his flashlight at it.

Jake has not seen this one before, it's larger than the last but gaunter.

Still gagging Harris covers his nose with his free hand, "Is that a girl?"

Overlooking the horrid face Jake can see its long matted hair.

Even though it is wearing more tattered clothes and trinkets than the others, he can see that, as wrecked as its body looks, the thing is indeed a female. It has curled black talons instead of fingers and layers of nasty black feathers sprouting down from its back and upper arms, like a robe. It inhales making a low growl, like a dying cat and holds one of its hands palm up by its mouth.

"Back away!" Jake shouts as he pulls his bandana up over his mouth.

It blasts a black powder from its hands with enough force to send it through the raging winds without dissipating until it reaches them. Jake holds his breath as he backs away. Harris has no defense other than his arms and chokes on the powder. It sends him coughing violently back to his porch. It screams with delight and leaps at Jake. He swings again but slashes only air. It sways back and forth, ready to strike and Jake fakes with his empty hand. It dodges with its uncanny speed but he manages to crack it in the side of its head with an elbow. It only hits the ground for a split second and is up again. It blurs past him to the easier target that Harris has become.

Jake rushes after it, but is taken down hard from his left. He grabs the creature and hammers it with his knife. It tries to flee but Jake grabs its ankle and stabs it some more.

The creature's guttural shriek bursts out.

Jake lets go, he knows its call was for help. It rapidly crawls on all fours.

He turns around to see Harris on his back, blindly kicking and swinging his flashlight at the female creature. Its deadly talons are working his legs.

"Daddy!"

Enough tears have flushed the stinging noxious powder from his eyes for Harris to see his daughter rushing towards him.

No longer interested, the witch doctor turns its attention quickly away from Harris and sucks in at Sophie to make a warning hiss.

"Sophie!" Jake shouts.

She fires at the thing and the loud cracks from her gun drown out his words. The impacts knock it off her father but he knows it will be right back up. In a fluid motion Jake pops his flask and dowses his blade as he rushes to intercept it from tackling Sophie.

"Sophie jump back!" he shouts.

Sophie knows the voice calling out to her and the surprise causes her to turn to it instead of moving. A screeching blur flies through the air, its claws spread wide open. Jake collides with it sending it safely away from Sophie.

"Jake!" Sophie cries out.

"Get over here!" her father yells.

"Go Sophie!" Jake calls as he struggles with the squealing creature he has pinned down. He manages a few good cuts and stabs before it scratches him up enough to wriggle free and escape leaping over the rooftops.

Sophie helps her father up and takes the flashlight from him. His legs bleed but he stands.

"Dad, they got Mom!" she cries out as the tears stream down her pained expression.

Harris' eyes still red and teary as well from the powder, he is shattered by the news. "Where is she?"

"I don't know," she shakes her head. "They took her away!"

Jake steps to the porch pulling the bandana down. He wants to hold and comfort her but keeps his distance. "Was she alive when they took her?" he asks and Sophie turns her head to him.

"Jake!" She reaches out and touches his cheek.

"What difference would it make?" pained and angry, Harris stares at the exchange between them.

"That thing's reaction to Sophie." Jake explains, "They still seem to be after descendants, there's a chance they need them alive."

"What are you two talking about? What are these things?" confused Sophie looks back and forth between the two. "And where did you go for so long?" she punches Jake in the shoulder.

"I'm so sorry Sophie. We have to keep moving. That shriek earlier was a call for help, more are coming here."

"Have you seen Evelyn?" Harris asks, trying for her to look stronger than he is feeling.

"No." she says

Jake treats his knife again and hands the flask to Harris. "Wait here!" he runs over to the car and tries to start it. "Damn, its dead!" he calls out as he runs back to them.

He hears a whipping sound as something strikes his lower legs and constricts around his ankles. He trips arms first into the lawn. Before he can strain to see what tripped him he hears Sophie firing again, joined by her father. He looks up to see them fighting away two more creatures and he recognizes the one who climbs. He lets his anger flush away his panic and grabs at the slick cordage that has bound him. His treated knife slices though it and he briefly wonders if anything else would have been so effective against it. Free again, he tries to turn back to Sophie as he stands. He is grabbed from behind and torn backwards. He ducks forward to try to stay standing but its long claws dig into his shoulder. He swings an elbow out and clips it, painfully tearing the talons back out of his flesh. It is the female Devourer again. With no time to cover his mouth, it blasts him with the powder. He slashes the knife down and digs deep into it, hacking halfway through its neck. It falls away and he turns his burning and blinded eyes to Sophie and her father.

"No!" Harris cries out.

Jake wipes enough from his eyes to see the one who crawls' withered pincer legs clamped around Sophie's waist. Its massive hands slap the gun from her as she kicks and scratches at its rubbery flesh.

"Sophie!" Jake calls out and it leaps with its arms over the porch banister and takes off down the street. "Get back here you son of a bitch!" he yells as he chases after her.

It drags her screaming through bushes and across lawns. As fast as it is moving, Jake gains on it.

"Jake!" she screams back and reaches out to him.

It glances back at Jake, its large crooked mouth appears to leer and it stops long enough to grab her head and bash it into the sidewalk. Her body goes limp.

Incoherent words of rage bursts from Jake's mouth.

It leaps up onto one of the houses and keeps bounding away with her body.

"No! Sophie!" He runs alongside the houses and is struck from his side again by another creature. With his knife held in a downward grip, he fiercely hammers into the creature's face. It shrieks but will not let go. Jake growls and screams louder as he continues hammering at it. Like before, when he was escaping the jail cell, he feels the emptiness inside again. He unleashes his anger onto it. He sees it with his vision for the void it is. The protective coating from the extract gone, the knife ceases to have an affect on it. The rusted blade snaps away. He pounds at it with both fists. Its grip drops away as the body convulses. Shaking, Jake looks up and stares with his special vision. Panicked people are running, hiding and fighting for their lives throughout the town and inside their homes. There is no sign of Sophie being dragged off. Jake looks down at the creature, its head is nothing more than pulp but it is still alive. He sends it tumbling into the street with a kick. Jake feels his soul fading away and is about to give in to the hunger just to have the power to go after her. Wherever they have taken her.

The tragic sobbing of her father from behind him slowly pulls his mind back from the edge. Harris falls to his knees next to him. His knife in one shaking hand and the flask in the other. They sit there not speaking, both in tears. Jake reaches his black, blood soaked glove over to the flask and takes it from Harris. He tips the flask back and drinks the last of its contents. Jake's white pupils stare at Harris with a sinister look from the corner of his black eyes. He contemplates devouring Harris' light for failing to protect Sophie. The extract pains him and he looks away as the shame of his thoughts roll over him and pushes back the change.

More houses start to burn around them as the residents fight the creatures back with fire. The roaring winds have died down allowing the smoke to thicken and obscure anything more than a few houses away. A half burned man staggers by them in shock, cradling his bleeding stump of an arm.

Soaked with sweat and exhausted Jake stands again.

He places a blood soaked hand on the deputy's shoulder, "Will you keep going?" he quietly asks him.

Harris does not answer or even look up.

"For your family?"

His attention caught, he pulls himself together and starts taking deep breaths. "To Evelyn's house?"

"Yeah." Jake says coldly. "I need to start killing something."

* * *

With their transportation gone they race down the middles of the streets, each with a makeshift torch in hand. Neither of them speaks and there are no further encounters. More houses burn smoking up they air, but providing at least a source of light and available fire.

From behind, they hear feet rapidly slapping against the asphalt towards them. A loud suckling squeal confirms the approach and they break into a run again. From a side street, headlights glow in the smoke. They run towards the car, yelling for it to stop. It breaks then swerves at them. They jump out of its way as the yellow boat of a car bashes into the creature, sending it flying through the air.

Junior sticks his pale head out of the window, "Deputy?" he calls out. "Hop in!"

Harris and Jake hop into the back and Junior speeds away.

"I was coming to get your family and Evelyn!" He calls back without noticing Jake.

"They're gone." Harris says in a pained voice.

"What?"

"They took them," Jake says his voice worn and gravelly, trying to save Harris from having to repeat himself.

Junior looks back, screams and knocks down a light pole in his surprise. "What the hell? Harris, shoot him!"

"What?" Harris looks up, still in his daze.

"Shoot him, he's one of them!" he calls out again, ducking away from imagined hits from Jake.

Jake looks at Harris and tiredly shrugs. In no mood for bullshit, Harris aims his gun at Ralph Junior, "He's alright. Whatever you think, he's with me. Are you sure Evelyn is at her house?"

Sweat streaks down his freshly buzz cut hair and he nervously looks into the rearview mirror to see Jake who is sitting behind him.

"Evelyn! Ralph, is she there?" he pushes the gun closer.

"Ugh, no. I thought she was at your house."

"Go to her house, now!"

Junior turns sharply and changes direction.

"Where's your family, Ralph?" Harris asks him, trying to calm him down.

"Gone," he stutters. "I got them out. One of the guys said they can't go past any of the totem poles."

"Who said that?" Harris barks the question before Jake can.

"Joe said it."

"Joe who?"

"He's the animal control guy for the fields."

"How the hell did he know?" Harris asks, more to Jake than Ralph Junior.

"I asked him that too. He said Mr. Dixon told him. He was right though, they've been stopping right outside of town then running away all pissed!"

"So the Dixon's are out beyond the totems?"

"I don't know. They were not by where we were. I guess any way out of town is good!"

Jake tiredly looks at the burning homes they are passing by. "Harris, when I go north, can I get to where they are on foot?"

"Go to the top, there's a pond. They are buried underneath the seventh totem."

Jake turns to Harris from his last revelation. "Then that's where Kenneth's been hiding this whole time. It also explains the stolen excavator."

The deputy grimaces as he swallows his shame for being ignorant to what he was taught as a Lamplighter. "The seventh totem was not part of our long walks, it was to be avoided. It was too close to believing, too close to them."

"And he counted on that," Jake leans over to Harris and speaks so Junior cannot hear. "Let's keep where I really come from between us. I have a bad feeling that if more people know, it may cause problems later on."

"Can Kenneth travel like you? Is that how he knew

everything?"

"I haven't figured that out yet. He seemed completely unaware that I have been doing it. Right now, I don't even care how he found out. I just want to kill—Up ahead!" Jake shouts.

A pack of seven Devourers fills an intersection, tearing away at an unfortunate truck full of field workers. The men blast scattered and panicked shots into the crowd and it does nothing. Like locusts, the creatures swarm them.

"Cut left here, through the alley!" Harris shouts.

The tires squeal as the massive car makes a hard turn. Another Devourer comes into view outside the alley. At its side, it holds the armless torso of a nude woman by the throat. One of her legs hangs lazily from its mouth as the creature swallows it whole. Unable to stop, Junior screams as his car collides with it. The torso smacks into the windshield and beats the roof like a drum as it tumbles over the car. The beast is pulled and ground up underneath the car. Harris covers his ears as Jake looks back to see it all tumbling away. He hates having to watch just to make sure the thing does not follow. Still panicked, Junior looses control of the car. About to pass Evelyn's house Jake leans over him and yanks the steering wheel to the right. They crash through a privacy fence. Junior more scared of Jake being so close to him than crashing, slams on the breaks. The car stops in the yard and Junior falls out of the driver's seat and scrambles away. They all run to the backdoor. He turns again to see if they were followed and notices the angle of the car. He remembers landing on top of the car sitting exactly where it is now when he makes his escape from the one who screams over forty years later.

Junior tries the back door and it is locked tight.

"A few lights are still on inside. That could be a good sign," Jake tries looking through the boarded up windows.

"Why is that?" Junior sneers at him.

"It means somebody is inside to turn them on and I guess, and the creatures would have eaten the generators," Jake answers.

"I just saw a shadow move up there!" Junior points to the upstairs window.

Jake grabs a plank from the fence that is scattered throughout the backyard and swiftly sends it crashing through window.

They watch a shadow on the ceiling move around then cautiously back away from the window.

A head appears and looks down at them from the window. Hiding from sight against the house, Jake cannot tell who it is until Junior confirms it.

"Evelyn!" Junior calls up in a very loud whisper. "Let us in!"

Seconds later, the grinding sound of heavy objects being slid can be heard from inside. Locks and chains rattle, then the door slowly opens. Evelyn is standing there, frightened but with her long barreled shotgun readied. Blood soaks through her roughly bandaged arm. Junior and the deputy enter while Jake enters last. She sees him and jumps but Jake snatches the shotgun from her strong grip before she can aim it at him. The already skittish Junior tries jumping in but Harris holds him back.

"We're here to help you!" Jake tries to calm her as she tries to wrestle back her gun. Angered, he pins her with it to a wall. "Calm down," he says with a threatening tone. Her body still tense, she stares down at him with her beautiful and deadly black eyes. He sees he has not been convincing and expects her to make a move as soon as he backs off. "I didn't carry your heavy butt out of that fire just to hurt you later."

Finally, she relaxes enough and he pulls the gun away from her.

"What do you want?" she angrily dusts away the front of her green and black velvet dress.

He steps up to her again and looks her in the eyes with a tired serious stare. "I know what Kenneth's done, I know about the Devourers, the descendants and the Lamplighters. I want the weapon the founder made and no more bullshit."

Evelyn bites her bottom lip and glances over to Harris who gives her the same hard look despite being torn up over his family. She looks at Junior who stands there dumfounded and hesitant to break the silence.

She looks at them, pleading, "I, I was trying to stop him."

"I know," he says sternly.

"I don't have the tool."

Jake's shoulders slouch and his head tips back. Wetness builds up in his eyes from sorrow while his jaw begins to quiver from rage. Evelyn sees him and knows he is about to explode. She quickly tries to remedy, "I had to hide it that night at the church. I'll tell you where it is!"

Jake looks back at her and begins to calm down.

"I had to stop Kenneth from getting it and the book so when I found out about them and where they were, I knew I had to get them first. I got them out of the vault, then set the place on fire with the lighter fluid you had with you. I was trying to make Kenneth think they were destroyed in an accident. Then you both showed up. I didn't know what to do. It was heavy so I threw it on top of a roof."

"And you left it there?" Harris shouts.

"I haven't had a chance to get back to it. He's been watching me!"

"What store?" Jake grabs her shoulders.

"Not a store, it's on top of the theater marquee!"

Jake thinks of how many times the weapon was so close to him but his happiness of finally knowing where it is keeps him focused. It sounds too good to be true and he stares at her intently while he fool checks his thoughts.

"Wait a minute," he scowls. "You ran *away* from the marquee."

"I ran back right after you took off after him. I was gonna hide in the theater, but I figured it would be better to ditch it up there and run home."

"How would you get into the theater that late?"

"She works there," Junior proudly adds himself to the conversation.

"And you still couldn't get it?"

She bites her lower lip again, embarrassed. "There was always an extra door upstairs. I thought it led to the top of the marquee but it just went to a storage room."

"I don't care if I have to drop down from the roof to get it! I'm gonna get it, then I'm getting Sophie back!"

Stunned, Evelyn grabs Jake, her long hands drops down between his neck and shoulders. "Back, from where?"

Tears start welling in his tired eyes again.

"Oh no, please tell me they didn't!" she shakes her head in disbelief then turns away covering her mouth with her hands.

"How did you even know about the Lamplighters?" Harris presses bitterly reliving his pain through Evelyn's reaction.

"We can find out later," Jake steps in front of the advancing deputy and stresses. "We get the weapon first!"

Harris backs down, "That theater borrows the fire engine every couple of years to clean the marquee."

Jake leans against a wall and crosses his arms, "Fire truck is probably already roasting inside the library." He looks around and walks to the hallway.

"We should get upstairs," Evelyn quickly regains her composure and cautions them.

Jake can tell she has buried her pain deep and thinks he should follow her example.

Harris looks at her and starts reloading his gun. He notices it is tarnished and rust has spread across it, "Where's your father?"

"He's out of town, business."

"How convenient for you!" he snaps.

"Easy, Harris!" Jake shouts from the front hallway. He looks over the family pictures in the hallway and takes the ones with pictures of Evelyn and the one with picture with Evelyn's mother and Kenneth. He stares at them closely, then smashes them on the ground.

"What are you doing?" she moves over to him.

He tosses back her shotgun and takes the photos from their frames, folds them and stuffs them in his jacket pocket. "I can hear them outside, they're coming for you," he walks by her. "Do you have any of that extract here?"

"Extract of what?"

"The red death camas, the extract you make from it."

"I have the tea, why would I make an extract of it?" she asks, honestly confused.

Jake sighs, then corrects himself, "Sorry. The tea, do you have any made?"

"No."

"Start making some, dump everything you've got into one pot.

We need a new ride too."

"What's wrong with mine?" Junior returns to the back of the house and looks at the yard.

"It's done. That things not moving again."

"How the hell do you know? Weirdo! Evelyn, he's one of them! He broke his cuffs then crumbled the bars away like they were nothing!"

"What?" she shouts.

"Is that that how you got out?" Harris' eyes glare at Jake.

He feels trapped and tries to match Harris' stare, as he is the biggest threat to him out of the three.

"Everyone saw him do it. He's trying to trick us."

Jake gambles blending a lie with the truth, "We don't have time for this! One of them was in the jail and tried to get at me through the cell! You would have seen that if you hadn't have been curled up on the floor pissing yourself!" He points to the still wet stain on Junior's pants, shaming him into silence.

The other two back down and he continues, "There's a pack of those things at the intersection out front. We need a car."

Evelyn frantically packs a bag while running back to the kitchen, "What are you going to do?"

"Help you three get to the barrier, then get the weapon and kill them all."

"You really think its going to be that easy?" Harris shouts.

Jake had never doubted that once he had the weapon, killing them would be easy and his expression shows it.

"You did, didn't you?" the deputy tragically laughs.

"I'm coming, too. Kenneth is my brother and my problem."

"No. I'm getting you out of here."

"I'm the only one here with a working gun."

Junior starts looking around the house, "What else have we got?"

Jake closes his tired eyes and tries to focus. The lure of all three of them has been overpowering and the pain of Sophie's abduction no longer pushes the hunger away. He knows he has to end things soon. "We need knives or anything sharp. We will use the tea and fire. Collect all the booze too."

To Jake's surprise everyone jumps into action. He has never been much of a leader before or a follower, just rebellious. This is a strange sensation to him. He runs downstairs and finds a half empty gas can for the generator, a tin of motor oil and some old rags. Back upstairs, he is met with the thick scent of the flower. He chokes on it briefly but welcomes it. Evelyn has also lit incense made from the flower and a few gallons of the tea has begun to boil. He pushes past her, stirs the pot and sees it is packed with a few dozen bags of the tea. He opens the fridge and starts taking food out and laying it on the counter. She starts helping Junior make the molotov cocktails with the articles they have collected, but both of them watch his strange behavior closely. He fills a large pitcher with some of the concentrated tea then dumps a container of honey and an entire five-pound bag of sugar into the mix and stirs it feverishly. The tight pain in his stomach starts to force him to curl downwards and his special vision is ramping up. He knows his eyes must be changing as well, so he turns his back to them while he downs the super sweet concoction. Nearly drowning himself with it, the sugary hot fluid burns going down. Nevertheless, it helps.

"What the crap!" Junior says under his breath. "I'm telling you, he's one of them."

Evelyn looks at Jake but says nothing. He catches his breath and turns his attention to the food he pulled from the fridge and starts randomly eating it. Feeling better, Jake snaps the ends of a mop and broom off, then sharpens the tips with a French knife. He stands them tip down in the boiling pot of tea and leans the tops against the wall.

Tired with the bizarre show, she asks him, "What's the point of that?"

Jake looks at her nodding while swallowing the food in his stuffed mouth, "This flower is like poison to them! That's why it is planted all over around here."

Her face scrunches, "That's ridiculous!"

"Its true. I've seen it with my own eyes." Harris enters the kitchen. "I found your dad's pistol and hunting rifle, is this all the ammo?"

She nods and finishes making the last molotov. "I saw one of my neighbor's cars still there when I was nailing boards over the upstairs windows. Anyone know how to hotwire one?"

"I can," Harris looks out the front window. "I don't see them down the street anymore either. Let's move!"

Jake fills his flask and douses a few knives with the tea. It is not as concentrated or sticky, but it might help a little. Everyone arms themselves and they place the firebombs in a small crate. With only a sharpened stick and her father's revolver, Harris speedily limps across the street. He makes it to the station wagon and slips in a pool of blood, almost impaling himself with the stick. He sees the passenger's side of the car is spattered and dripping with blood. Harris gets up and notices the window is down enough for him to reach in and unlock it. About to reach in, he sees a headless body sitting in the driver's seat. He crouches and looks around for the assailant, then opens the door and respectfully unbuckles and removes the heavyset corpse from the car. He grimaces when he sits inside the warm blood that pooled in the bottom of the leather seat. Harris sees that the keys are at least in the ignition. He starts the station wagon up and quickly pulls up on Evelyn's front lawn. They spill inside the car, but not before a horrible squeal sounds from the shadows. Just as the car peels away, a Devourer leaps from the roof of Evelyn's house only to crash into the street behind them. Within minutes, they have four more creatures on their tail as they pull onto the south fork road and race north.

Downtown looks like a war zone and the creatures are swarming. The Devourers that followed them become distracted by the easier pray of the unfortunates who are on foot. The savage monsters are dropping down from rooftops and spilling from the small alleys, snatching up adults and children alike. A store to their left explodes blasting a family and their inhuman pursuers away with glass and flames. They bite and claw at each other to get closer to the fleeing people. A lone terrified man armed with an assault rifle is shooting everything moving around him, hitting more people with his gunfire than creatures. Harris aims his gun at him to stop his rampage but something snatches him in a blur from underneath a car.

"We can use that machine gun!" Junior points at the gun the crazed man left behind.

A radial spray of blood spatters out from under the shaking car. "Never mind." Junior leans back.

A string of traffic lights comes crashing down behind them followed by more creatures who take off after some other poor inhabitants. Within the madness, a woman randomly runs out of the bank. Frayed, bloodied blonde hair sticks out chaotically from head bandages that also cover her right eye. She is wearing a dirty business suit and has a large sack over her shoulder. She has a gun in her other hand aimed at Jake and the deputy. "Get out of the car!" she yells at them.

"Are you crazy? There's plenty of room, get in!" Harris shouts.

"Get out of the fucking car Deputy, you *stupid* son of a bitch!" she stomps her foot as she yells then fires the gun through one of the back windows. A shadow tackles her from the side. The impact sends the cash contents of her sack flying through the air. The devourer pins her back to a building across the street. She screams in pain as it frantically starts digging into her stomach. It flings scraps of skin and clothes back towards everyone in the car and plunges its head inside her intestines. It does not stop as it tries to dig its way inside of her like a terrier. Her shrill screams become blood curdling and Harris peels away. Jake looks back just in time to watch the woman blow out her brains. He looks over at Harris and sees the slightest of smiles. Jake assumes that he and the woman must have shared some bad history.

Ahead they see the Forks is thicker with conflict. Up ahead the fire engine screams from the west across the burning intersection. Engulfed in creatures and flames, its sirens still blare as it crashes somewhere they cannot see. The deputy pulls off the south road and back into the side streets.

"We'll never get to it!" Junior cries out.

"Jake?" Harris shouts.

"Cut left, to the oil fields!"

"Why?"

"To create a distraction!"

From the passenger seat, Jake lights up the first bottle. He leans out just long enough to toss it and ignite one of the feeding wretches, and sending it into searing convulsions. Knowing the town lay out so well, Harris cuts left and right down streets and alleys, losing more Devourers than he gained. The car swerves to avoid another jumping attack and they keep speeding until the oil fields come into view.

"We're here, what now?"

Jake looks at him as if Harris should already know, "Into the fields, but not too far."

Out in the open, the creatures start surrounding them. Harris continues to evade them with his skidding circles and battering them with the heavy back end of the station wagon. Jake lights up another bottle and throws it directly at a derrick.

"What are you doing?" Harris shouts.

Jake lights up another bottle and looks at him with a satisfied grin, "I'm setting the town on fire!"

The first burning derrick explodes consuming a group of the squealing creatures. Jake throws a few more bottles and watches more derricks explode into roaring fiery geysers.

A creature lands on the hood of the car and Evelyn promptly blasts it off. Jake and Harris' ears ringing, they keep driving.

Harris recognizes one the Devourers rushing directly towards them and accelerates, "I got you fucker!"

Jake remembers this area as where the barrier cuts through, "Don't do it!" he grabs the wheel but the crazed deputy bats him away.

He hits it head on. Its upper body slams halfway onto the hood of the car.

Before Jake can speak, the car smashes into an invisible wall. The simple law that the Devourer cannot move through the barrier, stops the car in its tracks. Saved by his unnatural strength, Jake managed to brace himself from the cars hard dashboard. He looks up at the smoke rising from beneath the crumpled hood of the car. The creature has been crushed and he sees white flames searing the parts of it pressed against the barrier. Saved by his seatbelt, a wide-eyed Harris stares shocked at what he just experienced. Jake looks back and sees Evelyn and Junior are both stunned but alright. Behind them, he sees a pack of the things catching up.

"Everyone out!"

They pile out of the car and he sees Evelyn's fear.

"We're dead," Junior cries out.

"You guys will be fine!" Jake says reassuring.

He walks Evelyn to the front of the car, "Remember, the barrier is a straight line between the totems. Stay on the outside and you will be fine."

"But what about you?" she turns back to him.

"I know you're a fighter, but this isn't your time. Forget about this place and never come back, please. Don't come back."

Teary eyed, Evelyn looks past him at the approaching disfigured things, then back into his eyes. She leans forward and kisses him on the cheek. The strange time slowing sensation comes over him again and he sees a flicker of rich grassy fields in a setting sun. His view fades back and he sees only her beautiful black eyes. He nudges her gently to make her take a step back through the barrier.

"I'm not going!" Harris barks as he starts shooting at the things.

"Junior, take him through."

"No!" he shouts and keeps shooting.

"Harris! Who is going to keep people from coming back in here? At least get these guys to safety."

The deputy runs out of bullets and stands with trembling fists.

"I'll do everything I can to get your family."

"Why don't you come with us and go back in a different way?" Evelyn pleads.

"I can't," he looks back and smiles. "Besides, this is why I'm here."

Harris steps through the barrier with Junior.

Jake sets the box of undamaged remaining firebombs in front of himself.

He sees seven of them closing in and lights all but one of the molotovs up. He throws them through the air. Evelyn and Junior assist by shooting some of the bottles while in the air, causing the flames to spread out and catch on them. Two of them still advance and Jake catches one in the gut with a stick. It falls back in pain.

The other swings at him and he recognizes that it is the one who screams. It holds a blade in each of its hands and tackles Jake with its arms wide open. Jake falls backwards letting it roll over him, then kicks it upwards and into the barrier. The creature bounces off with a bright flash and its squeal. Jake rolls up and shoves it into the barrier again. It slashes at him and he drives his knife into its shoulder.

A lucky hit? Jake wonders.

Already seeing the blade rust, he twists his hand and snaps it off, leaving it in its body. It drops one if its blades and Jake snatches it out of the air.

A terrible thought crosses Jake's mind of being recognized by it and he pulls his bandana up to cover his face and protect his nose from its stench. The one who screams is out matched and it knows it. It looks pitiful to Jake now and he keeps smiling. He punches it in its head, knocking its head back into the invisible barrier again. He thinks of when it first attacked him. It damaged his mind forever when he saw its insane visage. Then it marked him with a knife, just like this one. It slashes at him, but he grabs its wrist, stronger than it now. With his free hand, Jake snarls at it, then spits on the wicked looking blade. He stabs it in the shoulder again repeatedly, until the shoulder is completely hacked up. Its black blood spurts out in clotted chunks as it dangles then drops away. Jake realizes he was screaming like a madman the entire time. He tosses the sticky blade into a nearby fire.

The others have backed far away from him, beyond the barrier. He looks down at the one who screams and picks its arm up and presses it into the barrier. Still connected somehow to the separated appendage, its guttural mouth inhales shrieks as the arm burns away. Jakes rage winds down and he looks to the others again, to Evelyn and manages a less insane smile before heading off into the swirling black smoke and raging fires.

* * *

Running through the fire and darkness, he encounters none of them. He reties the bandana over his face thinking again that allowing Kenneth or any Devourers to recognize him could change how things happened to him. He could return to the present completely doomed. He feels the hunger returning but does not drink from the flask. With no one human around for him to be temped by, the added abilities of his changed self would help him. His special vision already kicking in, it does not help him find his way through the dark. He looks back to the burning oil fields and they each appear as blazing suns. The warm energy is powerfully inviting and he hopes it will be that way for the other Devourers.

"Other Devourers?" he asks himself out loud. His voice is deep and guttural. He stops running and coughs as if he can dislodge the malevolent tone and wheezing from his throat. He cannot.

"So I think of myself as one of them now," he says aloud in his new foreign voice.

With no need to catch his breath, he breaks back into his run and turns into the cemented alley behind the theater. He hops onto a garbage container then leaps from there onto the roof of a store with ease. Skulking across the tops his bright white pupils float in the darkness. He hears what sounds like a drawn out dry heave mixed with choking. Another similar sound picks up, interrupting the last and overlapping. The sounds make him sick as they continue on, the discord intentional.

A chant? He wonders if it could be coming all the way from the top of the small mountain, the end of the Forks' north road.

Not wanting to risk being seen looking over the edge of the roofs, he continues to the theater. He spots an access ladder bolted into the side of the theater and climbs up its metal rings, hoping they do not disintegrate from his touch. At the top, he looks back to the oil field's blazing life giving energy. Jake finds that it is hard to look away. Whipping streams of gold and silver dance around blazing white spires. From within them, around the millions of rising embers each with its own glow and flicker like crystallized sparks, it rains and radiates outwards. He can feel the lights touching his body, filling it with life.

If only I could only go back to the fields. Just a little closer he thinks, as he stands motionless.

Deep from within, he manages to shake himself from the

trance. Angered that he has stopped just steps away from his goals of freedom, vengeance and salvation. Angered that the corruption inside of him is winning its battle to protect itself, he turns away. Back to the dark and bitter cold. He creeps to the edge of the theater and looks down. Again, his eyes are caught by a spectacle that distracts him from the weapon. In the center of the Forks, he sees Kenneth kneeling as Chief Blackhands kneels over him, cradling him in his arms. Kenneth is on his knees staring up at it, swallowing the filth pouring from the giant's mouth. Surrounding them are five Devourers shuddering on all fours. The one who shoots is there, as is the one who climbs, the female with the razor talons and two other larger ones he has not seen before. Surely, with their own specialized manner of hunting and killing. They are the source of the nauseating sound. Kenneth has the same two cuts running down his cheeks the way Jake was marked, as well as a smear of their foul blood wiped across his head. Kenneth is welcoming it. He is beyond sexually aroused by the revolting act. Jake turns his attention to the top of the marquee. A two-story drop below him, he sees the faintest of glows pushing its way through a dingy cloth cover. As he is now, Jake knows he can drop down and get it without hurting himself, but it would be a loud noise. From the corner of his eye he catches glowing green outlines moving up from the south. Five armed men, are advancing. He strains his eyes into focus and sees their leader is Harris.

Jake figures he must have used Evelyn's idea and just entered the barrier again from a safer location. To his relief, Evelyn is not with them, neither is Junior. A pattering of footsteps draws his attention back to the ritual. The one who screams limps over to them and drops down to join the others in their noise making. Now there are six of them with the chief and Kenneth in the middle.

Jake thinks of the similarity in their numbers to the pillars and knows this is not a coincidence. A chilling premonition comes over him.

Can they really take down the barrier, he asks himself. Of all the terrible things he could not prevent from happening, this may be the one thing he does stop.

Jake knows he will need his unnatural strength to stand a chance against them, but if Harris or the others see him this way, he would be counted as an enemy. Worse, he could lose control and go after them. He looks around the rooftop for anything he can use to either distract the Devourers or get the attention of the five men. There is nothing but leaves and dirt. He has only his lighter, flask and the blade he took from the screamer. He speeds to the other side of the roof, averting his gaze from the hypnotic lights of the burning fields and tears a brick away from the crown of the building. He rushes back and sees the humans are making their move. He throws the brick as hard as he can over the intersection. His aim is true and it smashes its way through a large store window.

Everything starts moving. The one who shoots turns his bow to the store and begins riddling it with arrows while only one of them breaks away to flank. At the same time, the men hurl firebombs into the circle, lighting them up. Jake drops down from the roof. While in mid air, the thought of him crashing through the marquee occurs. Instinctually, he reaches out for the wall, his hard pointed finger tips burst through his gloves and dig in to the concrete. Miraculously slowing him. He still crashes hard into it but does not fall through. As the sounds of gunfire and the men yelling meets with the creatures squealing and roaring, he sits up and pulls the wrapping away.

It is a large three pronged angular piece of the parasidium alloy. Each prong is a different length, with the center one being the longest reaching almost a foot. The prongs do not line up sideways either and bend sharply at their bases coming together into one rounded piece. Its base is particular as well. It has an inset and unwinds at the bottom like a snake's tail winding down and around. Inscriptions have been worked into every surface of the weapon. Seeing it, Jake understands why everyone else referred to it as a tool. It very much resembles an angular pitchfork. Which would be inline with the way the stubborn founder went about doing things. What better shape would there have been in a farmer's mind for an instrument to chase away a devil than a pitchfork. He strains and looks at it with his alternate vision and sees it is also a black void but with a blazing electrified red aura. It is so bright he squints and almost has to look away. He sees and understands the purpose of its three pronged shape. Ambient energy is being drawn in. Rapidly it spins down the prongs, becoming compressed into brighter needles of light. Energy is also being drawn up the coil to the center. All four of its points draw the energy in, feeding it's powerful rapidly cycling field. As the red bolts rush across its surface, they course through the cuneiform. As if the words the symbols stand for are being recited repeatedly, like a recording in a playback loop. Seeing the way it works with his vision, the tool appears more technological than magical.

The base is long enough for it to be gripped by two hands. He wraps his hand around it and the prongs begin to vibrate, like a tuning fork.

In a flash it burns him so bad he nearly screams out loud. Jake realizes that he as become so corrupted, that he cannot even use the thing which he has desperately sought. He looks away and hears the death cry of another man. He downs every last drop of what he had in his flask and lets it burn away at his insides. But his hunger and abilities remain. He balls up the tool's dingy covering in his hand and wraps it around the base. Even with the cloth and his gloves, the same thing happens again but he does not let go. He thinks of Sophie, his brother and everyone that will be afflicted by these creatures if they get out. With clenched teeth, he groans as his hands begin to smoke but he lifts it up. As he expected, it is a lot heavier than it looks and with its vibrating, it feels like it is about to leap from his hands. Thousands of red sparks jump from the tool into his hands, shocking and burning but he still does not let go. He moves over to the edge of the marquee. The Devourers are still protecting Kenneth and the chief, even though half of them have been set on fire. Their guttural screams echo through the streets as they flail on the ground. Harris and just four other men are still alive. A fifth man, out of their reach, is missing the lower half of his leg and bleeding to death. The chief throws his head back and with a deep crackling roar, inhales the surrounding air into thick condensed streams and extinguishes the flames that are burning his creatures.

A lessening of pain draws his attention away from the fiery conflict. He looks back to the pitchfork in his hands and sees its red lightning painfully coursing into the black emptiness of his arms. It is excruciating, but his hunger begins to dissipate. He remembers Sam's theory of the alloy repelling the nature of the Devourers with its own parasitic nature. They are like black holes, consuming energy into nothingness, but the tool is more like a power battery. Needling pains strike his heart and he doubles over. The energy stops advancing into his body and although it is still hot, it ceases to burn his hands. He removes the smoking cloth from the base to get a stronger grip on it. Jake rises. He looks over the edge of the marquee again to see Harris and two other men are the only ones left.

He steps back from the edge and fixes the bandana tightly over his mouth and nose then with a deep breath, runs and leaps from the marquee. As he flies through the air, everyone looks up and he realizes he is yelling out loud. The chief looks up. The skin around its mouth pulls back revealing its long vicious teeth, the black fluid still spilling out from between them. Jake keeps roaring his war cry and the expression on his face is pure joy. He drives the founder's tool, the one weapon against these creatures, right into the giant devourer's neck. The tools begins vibrating powerfully and Jake pours every ounce of his being into keeping his grip on it. He needs no special vision to see the pitchfork light up bright red. White sparks and flames burst from the chief's neck. Its deafening inward scream is so powerful it sucks the air from his lungs. But he holds on. The juggernaut's large body jerks and goes limp. And as it falls, Jake rides it down. He looks to see Kenneth, covered in blood and oily black filth. He reaches out, crying for it and screaming at the sight of the Fork. Still smiling and roaring, Jake looks at him hard. The chief's body crashes into the street and sends an earth shaking shockwave outwards. The remaining men, Kenneth and the Devourers are blasted away. Feebly, the chief reaches up and wraps its massive black hands around Jake. It starts to squeeze and press its claws into Jake's body. Jake feels it weakening and watches the white ash spread from its neck as its flesh is burned away. He responds by leaning forward, using his weight to press it in deeper. Its hands fall away and its body jerks into spasms.

Jake hears someone coming and looks up to see the men running over to him. The other Devourers scramble away in a panic over the buildings and into the shadows.

Screaming closes in from behind him.

He looks back to see Kenneth rushing him, babbling in an incoherent rage. He picks up one of the fallen guns and aims it at Jake.

No longer afraid, Jake smiles back and keeps the vibrating pitchfork buried deep in the smoldering body. As Kenneth pulls the trigger, one of them slams into him. The bullet shoots off course and instead of hitting Jake it strikes the pitchfork. The sudden impact causes a prong to crack and go flying away from the rest of it. The vibrations surge and become erratic. Jake tries to keep his grip on it as the destabilized energy begins to burn his hands again. The man who slammed into Kenneth knocks the gun from his hand and cracks him hard in the mouth. Kenneth buckles to the ground and looks up at Jake with murder in his eyes. He pushes back another surge from the pitchfork and what remains of the chief's body explodes into a blazing white fireball. Blinded, Jake is thrown backwards and slams hard into a building. Dazed and deafened by a loud ringing, his vision clears. He sits up and sees he did not let go of the pitchfork. He staggers to his feet and sees the men crawling up as well. All of them moving towards Kenneth, who kneels there defeated. Jake sees the man who just saved him from being shot. He is covered in black soot from the explosion as he tries running towards a fallen gun.

"Shoot him!" Jake yells but cannot hear his own voice.

The bearded man tears the broken sunglasses away and raises the gun. The one who shoots drops down between them from a building. The ground shakes from the impact and it intercepts the bullet with its body. Harris and the third man rush Kenneth, all firing but the thing protects him. Jake is back on his feet towing the heavy pitchfork with him. The one who shoots looks at him and with a guttural hiss scoops Kenneth up and bounds away over the rooftops. Jake breaks into a limping run and brushes past the man who saved him. He sees Kenneth is gone but he knows where they went. He leans forward to catch his breath then tries to turn and thank Harris and the other man but the long night has become day. He stands alone under the pale skies. He pulls the bandana down and smiles, the pitchfork still in his hands.

CHAPTER 14

As he planned, the plain building that blocked and concealed the path is now a cold and burned away husk. A few charred support columns and piles of blackened rubble are the only remains of the building that hid the town's last secret. On his knees, and clutching his stomach, he can see the long overgrown remnants of a cobblestone road leading up to the forested mountain. His intense shakes draw his attention away from his view. He fumbles his flask from his jacket and dribbles a small amount of the tea onto his leg. It burns like acid. He grunts and looks at the pitchfork in the pale daylight. The runes along its surface are as crude as the markings on the totems. Nonetheless, it is a thing of great power. He thinks of something he had not before, in his panic in the dark. The coiling base would be a good way to secure it to whatever suitable shaft he could find. Incredibly handy for an alloy that could never be reworked, but the shaft would have to be something short to prevent one of the Devourers from snapping it off and throwing it who knows where. Something just long enough for him to use it, because he can no longer hold it.

All of his cuts, scars and bruises have returned and the incessant hunger he has been afflicted with has worsened beyond what he thought was possible. He lingers at the intersection, wanting to march right up there but the pitchfork is incomplete. He slowly takes his jacket off his sore body and manages to wrap it around the pitchfork. Jake turns and walks away, down the cold empty streets. Hoping that Mike is still alive.

Sam's house looks as secure as ever, but when Jake gets closer he sees that the front yard, almost the entire collection of the religious symbols, have been replaced by a blackened crater. He speeds to the house and sees sections of the porch awnings are missing and that there are scorch marks scattered around. The front door is securely closed and the windows have been reinforced with more wood. He stops by where the fence used to be.

"Mike!" He shouts and waits. His deep gravely voice reminds him of how he has reverted back and does not appear to be human.

The door rattles, then opens. A haggard but alive Mike steps wild eyed onto what is left of the porch with the long barreled shotgun. He looks like a castaway who has been lost for some time. The beautiful green light around him and the patterns of light swirling around his center flicker hypnotically.

He stares at Jake intently. "What took you so long?" he says slowly.

Jake stands there, his eyes a stark black and white, his gray skin covered in splattered black blood and wounds. He has become an apparition, a nightmarish reflection of what he once looked like. Jake lazily shrugs the way he does and gestures to the yard. It takes a slight load off Mike's scared mind.

"Are you, *you*?" Mike asks, but Jake struggling internally against his urges does not hear and keeps staring at him.

He aims the gun at Jake, "Please, just go away."

Jake comes to, confused, "What the hell are you doing?"

"Your voice! I thought I was hearing things. You spaced out again!"

"Damn." Jake shakes his head and looks away from Mike, "I'd better stay out here."

"If you're that bad off why did you even come back *here*?"

"Now that I know hell is real, I'm more worried about my soul, because my body has already been taken from me. And we still have a job to do."

"Can you?"

Jake places his jacket on the ground and opens it revealing the pitchfork.

Mike stops himself from rushing over, "Is that it?"

"Yup."

Jake glances at him. Mike has an energized look about him, uncharacteristically overly happy and Jake completely understands.

"Yesss!" Mike closes his eyes and makes a fist, "Finally something is going right!"

"How long was I gone, same as before?" As he speaks he can tell that Mike continues to be unsettled by his bellowing voice. He strains his throat and tries speaking slower and softer.

"Longer. Nearly a month this time. I haven't had any trouble from them, haven't even seen that chief since that day, just the screamer."

"Is that what happened to the yard?"

"Oh yeah. The screamer would watch the house from the street, standing right where you are now. Then one day, I baited the thing. I told it how I killed its buddy with the spike. I don't know if it understood what I was saying, but when it saw the spike it got pissed and charged right at the house," Mike reenacts it, laughing as he continues his story, "it stumbled into all those animal traps and started screaming only to get blown up by the landmine. I laughed for days!"

As happy as he is to see Mike smile, Jake can tell that his friend is starting to crack up.

"That's good man. Any headway on fixing the spike?"

"Ugh, no."

"What?" Jake's voice startles him again. "Sorry," he growls.

"Are you in control?"

Jake turns his back to Mike and stares up and down the street. "For now."

Mike slips back into the house and returns with one of the books.

"Yes this is definitely it," Mike holds up an opened page in the founder's book with a detailed illustration of the pitchfork.

"What about fixing it?"

Mike sighs, "From what I pieced together, this alloy can be liquefied not melted, with some kind of sound wave setup running a particular frequency. The notes are worded funny because they had no concept of frequencies back then. But once it's shaped the alloy, the parasidium solidifies again. And that's how it stays forever."

"That can't be right. How did they put all these inscriptions on it?"

"Somehow, they put a message in the frequency of the sounds. Like the words were recorded onto it, like a record. It's tricky. There is a bunch of pages missing from this book. The Lamplighters had been piecing what may have been on the pages from the other book and from what got passed down between them."

"Fuck! I'm not giving up now!"

"Can you use what you got there do the job?"

"I don't know. This finished the job, but it was the whole thing that started the process. I'm not taking any chances."

"Did you find out how it broke?"

"Kenneth. Piece of shit tried shooting me when I was killing the chief with it. It was all lit up doing its thing. I guess that made it vulnerable enough to be broken."

"I thought Kenneth *was* that damn thing."

"He is now. Back then, I came up on the chief *impregnating* him."

Disgusted, Mike shakes his head and sighs, "These things, man."

"Let me see the spike."

Mike takes it from around his neck and unwinds it from the fresh cordage he wrapped around it. He holds it in is hand and hesitates. "This is all I have to protect myself. From them and you."

"The longer we wait . . ." Jake reminds him and lets his sentence trail off.

It still comes across as a threat. Mike is reluctant but he tosses the spike over to Jake.

Jake catches it but it burns him through his tattered gloves. He pulls his hand away and it falls to the ground.

He nudges it closer with his foot and the spike suddenly slides under its own power and attaches itself exactly where it belonged on the pitchfork. They both jump. A white hot seam glows where they merged, then cools with no sign of ever having been broken at all.

"Fuck yeah!" Jake shouts.

"This is too good! We're getting the hell out of here!"

Jake drops down and examines the completed weapon, using his jacket to turn it over in the light. Touching it through the leather folds of his jacket is still causing him pain, possibly trying to kill him. But he is happy.

"Bring it in the house," Mike motions him in. Jake looks up at him confused but before he can protest Mike continues, "you come in and I'll hang around out back." Then he backs into the house leaving the door open.

Jake gets cleaned up, redresses his wounds and rests for a bit while Mike rigs up a means for him to use the weapon. Mike uses everything from thick leather belts and strong cordage dug up from Evelyn's belongings and other scrap to fasten the pitchfork securely to Jake's left arm without it touching his skin. He also adds a foot long piece of wood inside the coil at Jake's request, so he can stab with it if it comes off his arm.

A few hours later, he slings a decent length of sturdy rope across his chest, his flask, his lucky devil girl lighter, a torch, a newly treated wooden stake and a gun for good measure. Jake checks the arm harness Mike fashioned for the pitchfork. He had even used bits of tire cut cleanly within the treads to provide an extra buffer between him and the pitchfork. It is on him tight, but still remarkably comfortable. Although the weapon is locked in a forward position he will be able to run them completely through and block with it. Jake uses his remaining time to detail the events of his last slide to the past in his notebook. He even draws up crude notes on a map of the town that Mike appropriated and places it, along with the pictures from Evelyn's house, in his bag.

Mike looks over Jake from the backyard to make sure he is not missing anything. "Oh yeah, that nasty bone sword reverted into that black slime a few days after we took it."

"Probably for the best. We don't want any part of these things sticking around."

Jake sees Mike's worried look and he smiles, "I need you down here."

"I know. I just feel like crap leaving it all up to you."

"Just remember, as soon as you see any sign of fire or smoke up there, get everything and run."

"Alright man." Mike tosses him a thick pair of work gloves, "Get your ass up there."

Jake leaves and does not look back this time. He marches north determined win or loose, to put an end to the living nightmares.

* * *

Centuries of growth and neglect has allowed nature to reclaim most of the once cobblestone road. Tall wooden fences line the crumbling path. More like a lost alley now, he sees the back of a junk yard over the fence to his right and tall pale weeds over the fence to the left. Scattered sporadically, he sees small dirty and weathered bits of humanity. Pieces torn away or dropped when the poor people of Prudence were dragged off that terrible night. A shoe here and there, shreds of clothes, glasses. He crouches down and picks up a child's matted doll. Selfishly he only thinks of Sophie. Jake continues until the path is completely gone, but a filthy tell tale trail left from the Devourer's coming and going acts as his guide.

The path he follows stops on a steep rocky incline. He sees the beginnings of a dirt path spiraling up and around, but figures he does not need to waste the time. He crouches then leaps a few meters up, dragging the heavy pitchfork behind him. His sharp fingertips catch on a protruding tree. He continues jumping until he reaches a level part of the small mountain. The windless forest is quiet. He comes to a break in the trees and sees a part of the town down below. Jake follows the disgusting smell to the top of a rocky area and every surface is covered with the black moss. He hears a howling in the distance and knows it is not one of the Devourers. He jumps upwards over the rocks a few times until he reaches the top.

He is looking down a creek filled completely with the oily black fluid the Devourers use as blood flowing from a pond. He crouches at the top of the area watching and waiting. He sees the source of the howling is a crooked opening to a cave, sucking the air in somehow. He adjusts his vision and sees the slightest amount of pale floating particulates, like dust being pulled into the vacuum. The black moss, on the other hand, drains a slight amount of light into itself. Like the energy is being converted into the filth. He takes out his flask and whips some of the fluid forwards, just to see what happens. It sizzles violently when it touches the creek but it is not enough to clear a path. He avoids moving through the sludge as much as he can and jumps from tree to tree until he drops down into the blasting wind being sucked into the entrance. The vacuum is so strong it steals his breath. He stares into the roaring void. Behind him, a shape slithers up then silently rises from the black pond.

Jake thinks of what could be inside other than the Devourers. How far in did Sam go that day and what did he see?

He spins around and pierces the slick creature in its chest with all three prongs. It is the one who screams, caught right before it could inhale to make its ear piercing shriek. It starts to choke and swings its blade at him, but Jake catches it with his free hand. Jake stares into its mouth and as it tries to jerk away, he lifts it up off the ground. The vibrations intensify and he can feel the heat. It lights up bright and burns white sparks and smoke into it. Helplessly impaled, it manages a final but short shriek that echoes into the cave. His element of surprise gone, Jake shakes it in the air causing it further pain. The weapon surges and the one who screams is instantly reduced to ash. It remains hot and the harness starts to smoke. It burns but he uses his hunger to drown it out.

He turns back to the void and lets the rushing winds carry him in. After a steep angled decent, he makes it into a larger area. The whistling and wails of the wind has died down and is replaced by the familiar humming sound coming from the depths. He sees nothing in the dark and the hot glow from the pitchfork has dimmed, so he un-slings his torch and lights it, hoping that the concentrated stench inside is not flammable. Still battered by the weakened gale, the torch flickers wildly, casting a menacing shadow inside the cave. Black moss covers every inch of the inside, the living filth shivers and crawls away from the presence of the weapon. There is only one way down, a narrow slick spiraling path.

The light cast from the torch is dimmed as the walls absorb its touch. The humming becomes louder and slows into a chorus of smaller uninterrupted human moans as he descends so long he feels the pressure change. Jake knows he has actually walked below the surface of where Prudence sits. The spiraling staircase finally ends. In a large domed chamber, giant clumps of the black moss is scattered randomly across the walls and rocky floor. Standing along the walls are six totems. They are the same size as the ones that make the barrier around the town. The moans are coming from the totems. There is a seventh totem in the center of the room. He approaches it and sees it is an inversion of the ones outside. The faces of all of the animals are upside down. He holds the torch as high in the darkness as he can. The top animal is a human, face also upside down. He steps closer trying to listen where the moaning is come from when his leg bumps something. He brings the torch down quickly and inspects the base. Though covered in filth and black moss, he sees an unmistakable human shape. He jumps back and dry heaves at the sight. It is a man, naked facing out and upside down. His legs are wrapped around the pole and he is tied at his ankles. His arms are tied back around the same way. A slender object has been driven through his forehead, nailing it to the pole. Jake reaches his shaking hand out and touches the wrinkled flesh. The man is old and desiccated, but somehow he is still alive. The moaning is coming from him and the other bodies bound the same way to the other totems.

"I see you've met the good sheriff!"

Jake pulls his new stake up defensively but keeps the fork behind himself. Standing a few feet away from him is Kenneth, his voice still echoing throughout the dark chamber. He is naked, covered in sweat and spattered with black moss.

Jake says nothing, but his mind races. The sheriff was the last victim taken and has been alive somehow and trapped like this.

"Confused?" He stalks towards Jake in the roundabout way he did before, trying to get just close enough. "I know, this stuff must be a lot for someone to wrap their head around, especially you." He smiles and looks at his arm, "Speaking of which—" Kenneth stops talking and glares at the pitchfork. "Jackie boy. I'm impressed, I really am. So resourceful—"

"Shut the fuck up, Kenneth!" Jake raises the fork and steps towards him.

Kenneth backs away, and starts trying to walk around him in the other direction.

"And fixed it too. Where did you dig that thing up?"

Jake glances over his shoulder and tries to keep track of where the exit is and if Kenneth came from there or another tunnel.

"That's good Jake, always thinking. I'm so glad you are one of us."

Jake stares at him hard and steps at him.

"Really, you're going to deny it? I know you have started to see things the way they really are. The beauty, the life. Even that feeble torch in your hands looks delicious."

Kenneth is right. Being inside this place, whatever it is, has intensified his hunger. Jake knows he is one stray thought away from loosing himself to it. He rushes Kenneth and feels the pitchfork vibrate faster a few times as it slashes close to him but he manages to slide away. The black moss is abundant and Jake feels it tugging on him to slow him down and worsen his condition.

"What's your problem with me, boy? Look at how badass I've made you!"

"Are you fucking serious?" Jake lunges again and misses.

"If you really wanted to end this, you'd stick that in yourself. That's the only way, don't you think?"

Kenneth sees Jake's reaction and grins. "Wait, you didn't think killing me would fix you?" he breaks into a cackle. "What the hell ever gave you that idea?"

Jake runs through his thoughts. Kenneth is right again, it was always just an assumption. Angry he snarls at him swinging violently but still missing him. He pulls out his gun and unloads the clip into Kenneth's body, but Kenneth just laughs louder. As Jake's anger grows, he feels himself getting stronger, the weapon in turn vibrates and burns his arm.

"Jackie boy, you fool!" he keeps laughing and baiting him.

Jake throws the gun at him, missing. His burning arm reminds him to calm down and think. His condition may be irreversible, but he still has to kill Kenneth. His anger breaks and he looks Kenneth in the eyes. Like the devil he is, Kenneth excitedly creeps closer, baiting him more.

"What? You gonna say something smart? What is it? Come on, lay it one me."

Jake shrugs, "I never really was the smart one. All I can think is if I'm stuck like this, then at least I'll be the king of the freaks."

He laughs at Jake again, "You? Only one leads the Sirobamjal."

"I know," he pulls his filthy gloves off with his teeth. "I might have the same amount of 'ol Chief Blackhands in me as you do."

"You think you can play me at that game?" Kenneth smiles.

"Why not. I mean, which of us would he choose if he had to? Me? The guy with the twin brother, the magical back door out of here, or plain old Crazy Kenny?"

Kenneth sneers, "Crazy Kenny? Really, you're gonna call me names?" He laughs.

"That's what they called you back then, Crazy Kenny right?"

Every time Jake mentions the name, a flash of Kenneth's temper peeks out through the cracks of his weakening confidence.

"My wrinkled little old sister was that pathetic? She had nothing better to talk about than me?"

"No. She never mentioned you two were related, ashamed I guess and who wouldn't be." Jake sees Kenneth is no longer smiling, "I think it was Junior who told me that one night at a party." Jake smiles sincerely and watches for Kenneth's response. He still wants to know how much Kenneth knew about what was going on.

Jake watches him start to breathe heavily as his temper begins to flare up.

"No," he slowly says shaking his head, "no, no," he repeats.

"You?" his lips quiver around his gnarled jagged teeth. "Why not *me*?" he snaps. "First *her* now you?"

Her? The thought smacks Jake in the head, but he hides his reaction.

"No! You shouldn't be allowed!" he clenches his fists, still pacing in an arc towards Jake.

"Ah ha!" he looks up grinning, his anger completely gone he snaps his fingers. "This must be their doing!" he kicks the withered body at the base of the totem.

Jake keeps his smile frozen in place.

"No, I got you! I know a fake smile when I see one! These rat fucks have been trying to change things. There must have been enough, *whatever* left of their minds."

So that's what's been sliding me through time, Jake's mind races. The people that were taken and tortured like this were trying to stop it all before it started.

Jake's shoulders sag knowing that he has failed anyway.

"Isn't this crazy stuff exciting? The rules are always changing!" his eyes bulge open inhumanly wide as does his toothy smile. "How far back did you go?"

Jake feels weaker and he finally understands that although Kenneth was in the dark about him sliding through time, he is stalling, waiting for him to cave. Jake swipes at the slick fluid around his ankles with the fork and sends it bubbling away.

Kenneth sucks in a sickening squeal and lunges at Jake.

Jake punches him with a right cross and sends him flying by into the muck. He rushes after him but Kenneth slips away again and reappears behind him.

Kenneth slicks the black slime off his body and looks up at Jake, slurping it out of his hand. Kenneth laughs, "They obviously didn't send you back far enough!"

Jake pulls his bandana up over his face, "I wouldn't say that."

Kenneth's eyes widen and his jaw drops as his mind sifts backwards through over forty years of imprisoned memories. "You!"

He roars and lunges again, faster than before. Jake ducks down and swings the torch. Kenneth bows around it as Jake planned and he jabs the weapon forward. It punctures him a few inches deep. Kenneth falls back and recovers, pressing his hand against the wound in pain. "If I didn't have to use you as a fucking doormat!"

He springs into the air this time latching on to the side of the central pillar, then in a blur, bounds off it screaming towards Jake again. Jake tries to duck but he is knocked down into the filth. The torch flies from his hand but is not extinguished as it burns away at the black fluid. He hears Kenneth splashing up behind him and grips the treated stake. He spins away hoping to land a hit with either weapon but misses. Kenneth had stopped short. He slings some of the black moss at Jake's eyes. He blocks with the pitchfork and most of it is incinerated immediately. Kenneth grabs the fork and tries to tear it away. Both of them are screaming as it burns them, Kenneth more so. He snarls, yanks Jake towards him, then slams his back against the totem. Still wrenching at it and screaming, Jake stabs him between his neck and his collarbone with the stake. Kenneth finally falls away as he tries wrenching it out of his body. Jake rushes over to the torch and lifts it up. It has created a temporary scum free area for him to stand in.

Kenneth tears the stake out of his body and tosses it, sizzling into the fluid. He leans forward on his knees breathing heavily. Jake steps towards him and leans against the totem catching his breath. The burning pitchfork mounted on his arm continues to get heavier and more unbearable.

Drunkenly, Kenneth stands up straight. "Is killing me really going to make you feel that much better?"

"I think so."

Kenneth sighs and looks around, "You kill me, you kill yourself," he shakes his head. "It won't change anything. Chief Blackhands is forever. He lives in every drop of this deliciousness. "He licks more of the filth from his hand."

"You are full of shit!"

"No, Jake. You were there that night at the Forks. You saw the gift he gave me and then you killed his body. But did he die?"

His eyes become heavy and Jake feels the last strands of his humanity starting to snap, "You are right again, Kenny."

Kenneth snickers, "That's right, Crazy Kenny. I was the kid

whose mother could go back in time. But she would come back with so many secrets."

"Your mother?" Jake wakes up from his groggy trance.

"That's right Jackie boy, just close your eyes. The best thing you could do is slow things down."

Jake heaves his eyelids up one last time to see Kenneth who had been creeping closer as he talked and is now just a foot away. Jake jerks the fork upwards stopping Kenneth's clawed fingers just a few inches away from his eyes. He squeals and Jake shoves him back, twisting the blazing prongs inside of him. A tearing noise and a dark figure flies away. Jake is shocked to see Kenneth's empty skin sizzling on the pitchfork. He flings it off and looks around.

He sees Kenneth, still about the same size but with rotten black and gray skin underneath. Rows of long sharp teeth protrude down from his cheeks and up from his chin and jaw. Chief Blackhands has again revealed himself.

As Jake feebly pulls himself together, Kenneth's last words give him an idea. Though still tired, he staggers grinning stupidly. Jake aims the spike down at the body bound to the pillar.

"What are you doing?" Blackhands stands up, his voice changed to the same grinding mess that Jake's voice had been.

"Slowing things down," he smiles.

He breaks into a wild cackle, "Look around you Jake! Use those eyes I gave you!"

Not knowing why. Jake obeys. He sees nothing but darkness and the wild patterns from the pitchfork and the torch. The totems glow a pale white color. Faint and twisted spirals float inside the bodies of the abductees.

Jake looks at him with an irritated, confused look.

"Closer." he says slowly. Already doubled in size, his living headdress sprouts from the back of his head.

Jake looks past him and strains. In the large clumps of the moss he noticed before, he sees faint green outlines of people, all connected and being fed light somehow by the moss.

Chief Blackhand's gaping inhuman mouth sucks up the air to grind in the words, "That's right."

Jake's look of surprise sets the creature back this time. Jake feels alive again, with hope. He wraps an arm around the totem, then jabs the pitchfork deep into the body. The entire cave quakes, just like before when they were breaking the seal. The chief is knocked off his feet. Jake pulls it out and the body continues burning away to ash.

He tries hacking at the totem itself but it only clears the moss away. He stabs the totem with it and nothing happens. Jake assumes that as evil as its purpose is, it is still only made from wood and not a conductor. He lays the torch down at the base hoping it will burn. The sounds of bones snapping and skin tearing gets his attention. Jake takes off stunned to see how fast the chief is changing this time. He is on all fours sucking in large amounts of the black moss. Jake leaps into the air and rams it into his spine. He roars and thrashes. Its growth halts but it catches him with a sharp elbow. Jake grabs the wooded grip just as the arm mount snaps. His left hand free he wraps it around the base of the pitchfork, searing his own hand. The chief's spine blazes into ash and his legs go out. Its powerful arm knocks Jake away, but he takes the weapon with him. He starts sucking up more moss, mending himself and Jake rushes back stabbing him in the neck this time. He gets slapped off again but charges back, the chief rapidly crawls away. Jake follows him, stabbing then ducking away. He realizes Blackhands is too powerful inside this place to be killed. The black moss just keeps feeding it. It starts to shrink back down to Kenneth's size as it wails and roars. A hybrid form of Kenneth and Blackhands looks back at Jake and curses in its lost language then submerges itself completely into the black moss.

"No!" Jake roars and slams the fork down into the ground. A wave of white flames explodes around him, burning and splashing to the far corners of the room. The blazing fork lights up the room far better than the torch. He sees a large mass of the moss slithering and he chases it. It wriggles its way into a small crack, escaping.

"Fucking coward!"

Jake looks around for another way down and finds a second path winding down. He turns around and sees that between the torch and the blazing hot ashes from the body, the base of the seventh totem has burned through. He picks up the torch and runs to another totem.

He stands over the body, "I'm sorry." He plunges the weapon into it. It lights up and another quake goes off. He places the torch down by the base. The black moss slithers away from the fire.

A bellowing roar echoes from the deeper passage, and is followed by a cacophony of dozens more.

He stares around the room, looking desperately. He strains his eyes harder as the screams get louder. He sees the green outlines trapped and unmoving, but he cannot make out any particular shapes. He thinks of killing the rest of the poor souls bound to the totems, but fears Kenneth would only replace them with another victim trapped in the moss. Another of the descendants from his allegedly beloved people.

Enraged, he runs into the center totem and tries to knock it down. It cracks but does not fall. He hacks at the base and runs into it again, cursing. Finally, it gives and falls over, causing another quake. Using his anger he lifts an end of it up and runs it to the even louder passage. He throws it down its winding path, hoping it will slow them. He rushes back to the other burning pillar and leaps to its top. He wedges behind it as best as he can, with his back against the cave wall and pushes with his legs. It cracks and topples over. He falls through the air as the earthquake goes off. He leaves the burning pillar there and looks around one last time. He clenches his fists and yells as he heads for the exit. Just before he steps into the tunnel, a sensation comes over him and he stops and turns around.

He stares again seeing all of the outlines. One of them is brighter than the others. He runs back to where he tore down the second pillar. The moss is still trying to reclaim the burning area. He kneels down and sees an outline with a smaller outline inside it. A small delicate hand protrudes from the black mass. He pushes the pitchfork in sideways and it screams as it is burned away. He sees a red bandana tied around the wrist and he pushes it further. It is Sophie.

He trembles as he drops the pitchfork and rips her sleeping body out of the clamoring filth. Black vine like tendrils run down her mouth and nose. He tears the elastic cables out of her body in long pulls. As the last chuck of black moss spills out, she gags and vomits. Barely conscious, she looks around. She has not aged a day since he saw her. Miraculous or bizarre, he questions nothing. He grabs the fork and lifts her into his arms. The light coming from her is more beautiful than anything he has seen with his cursed eyes. His hunger tears at his mind. Suddenly, Jake realizes, his brain is just an organ like any other. It can fail like any other organ and control what he sees or thinks, but it does not house his soul. He holds her tightly against him and speeds towards the tunnel he came in through. He can hear the slapping sounds of more footsteps than he can count behind him. He does not care, he just runs.

He gains some distance from them in the narrow winding tunnel and finally, he was never so happy to see the pale gray skies. His eyes stinging, he looks down at Sophie. She is still barely conscious. He still cannot believe she is real. He rushes out through the sunken pond and speeds into the forest. He stops briefly but with no torch clicks open his lighter. It flares up as it did before, quickly catching the abundant leaves on fire. He continues racing down the small mountain, pressing his unnatural body to its limits. He makes it to the bottom and the Devourers are close behind him. He glances back wondering, that if they could have all come out the entire time, why they did not?

His greatest worry is getting Sophie to the barrier and he hopes the damage he caused the pillars undid the trap barrier Kenneth had created. He dashes across the Forks and looks back. The top is burning true. He keeps racing south, back to where he entered Prudence. Over thirty of the disfigured creatures are racing not far behind him.

Sophie comes to and screams. Gagging on their stench, she starts beating at him.

"Sophie!" he calls but his voice terrifies her even more. "Sophie please." He strains to make his voice more human, "It's me."

She is still terrified with a look of fear that even makes him feel scared.

"It's me Sophie." Jake says as calming as he can.

Pale and trembling, she shakes her head and looks as though she is going to faint.

Still running fast, Jake looks back and sees they are seconds behind and gaining when he makes it to the rows of willows. Sophie, terrified of him, hears the Devourers roaring behind them. She looks over his shoulder and jumps.

"I'm getting you out of here," he breathlessly pants.

She sees the bandana around his neck that she gave him, then looks at him confused but less frightened, "Jake?" she croaks out.

"He looks down at her and smiles, "It's me."

"What's—" she tries to speak but coughs up a last bit of filth.

"I found you."

He looks up ahead and sees Mike. He is out of breath with a large duffle bag strapped to his back and he is exactly where he is supposed to be, past the totem on the other side of the barrier. Jake makes it to the totem and gently sets Sophie down. He struggles with himself to let her go, having found her again across the spans of time and the impossible.

"Who is this?" Mike starts firing the shotgun at the creatures.

"Mike, have her drink the extract! Get her out of here!"

"Where did she even come from?" he fires again.

"Jake?" she feebly tries to stand.

Mike boldly rushes past the barrier and pulls her back across.

Confused she looks at Mike then Jake, "What's going on?"

"Sophie, I love you!"

"Jake!"

"He'll explain everything to you!"

"Come with me!" she pleads,

Jake looks at her, so much of their short fragmented relationship was unfair to her.

He looks at her and presses his hand against the barrier, knowing he should not. A spark goes off stinging him. The pain is all consuming but also sobering. He turns to impale one of the creatures and knocks it back into a few of the others. Mike continues shooting, dropping them with the painful special rounds. Sophie tries to crawl across the barrier to get to Jake.

Jake turns and sees her, "Don't let her see this!"

"I've got more shots!" Mike yells and fires again, skinning a creatures face that was about to stab Jake in the back.

"It is too late for me. Get her out of here!"

Mike wraps an arm around Sophie and pulls her away from the barrier.

Jake is embroiled in battle, stabbing and getting stabbed. A few arrows fly into his back. He bats a few more of them into the barrier and sends them running back screaming. Jake is still not overwhelmed.

He takes off, away from Sophie and does not look back.

"Jake! I love you!" she screams.

Jake hears her cry out over the guttural squeals of the Devourers and he smiles.

EPILOGUE

Morning daylight streams in through the windows giving the drab blue and white diner a fresh warm hue. A beautiful dark haired waitress brings him more coffee and he looks up to thank her and pay his tab. He turns his bright eyes with their hazel centers away as he continues pouring over the pictures and the handwritten books laid out across the table. He scratches at his thick curly beard.

Eight months ago, his brother vanished without a trace. Then one day a gaunt man shows up at his apartment with a confused and exotic young pregnant woman. The man tells him one of the wildest stories he has ever heard. And right before he slapped his cuffs on him, he drops an opened notebook in front of him. Written by no one else than his missing twin brother. There is personal information about him inside the book that only Jake could have known. The fingerprints on it matched as well. The downward spiraling nightmare of Jake's story written inside is impossible and terrifying if it is real.

His brother is in trouble. In a living hell and needs help bad, so he is pulling out every stop to save him. And apparently to save the world. He closes the books and puts everything else into his briefcase. If manipulating time really is plausible as well, having both of them in Prudence would be a delicate situation. Despite how crazy the story is, he has no choice but to believe it. He stands and stretches, squinting in the sunny morning light. He is fearful of the things he might still have to confront. Worst are the parts of the story he does not know about. He puts on some oversized aviators then slaps on an orange brimmed baseball cap to complete his disguise. James leaves the diner and continues on his drive east, to the town where the black moss grows.

ABOUT THE AUTHOR

Alexander Fisher has worked in the entertainment industry for over eight years as a hands on creative developer and problem solver. Focusing on his own ideas he has started to compile his real life experiences and blend them with his strange thoughts and day dreams. He has begun using what free time he can find to compose the ideas that haunt him into book form. Currently he has two more books in the works.

The Devourers

Made in the USA
Las Vegas, NV
04 January 2023